FEAR YOU

Broken Love Series

BOOK TWO

B.B. REID

TABLE OF CONTENTS

DEDICATION

This book is dedicated to every heart out there that believed in this book, this series, and in me.

DEAR DIARY . . .

It's been a long time now and I miss my parents. I wish they would change their mind and not leave me behind. Every day I go to my new school and every day he makes me cry. I think I'm supposed to hate him, but all I want to do is help him.

CHAPTER ONE

KEIRAN

THREE WEEKS AGO

THE FIRST FORTY-EIGHT hours were spent in an interrogation room trying to persuade the moronic detectives I hadn't tried to kill my own brother.

They were convinced if I didn't put the bullets in him myself, then I was somehow responsible for what happened to him.

I told them all to get fucked.

The last forty-eight hours were spent looking for Mitch. My fucking father.

I slipped from the black leather seat of my car, and before I could even close the door, I was swarmed.

Endless condolences and questions.

Pats on the back.

Sympathy.

Pity.

It was all unwanted.

The exposure was even more annoying.

My desperation for a distraction overshadowed my better judgment, and before I could rethink it, my attention turned to the nearest hopeful notch.

She batted her eyelashes for the hundredth time, officially going into overkill. She was perfect for what I had in mind.

One flash of a smile and she was instantly on me. Her breasts pressed against my chest when I caught her. My hands instantly sought out her ass, and when I felt the soft globes under my hand, disappointment flared.

Nothing.

Not even a twitch.

This chick made my dick want to deflate and die.

I was thinking of ways to change my mind without embarrassing her because I wasn't a complete dick... at least not to people who didn't affect me. It was backward, and it would only make sense to someone who walked in my shoes.

It was a good thing I had lifted my hands when I did, or I would have lost them when the blonde was snatched away and thrown on the ground.

My eyes refused to believe what was taking place before me, but when her fist reeled back, I snapped into action, saving the face of the wide-eyed girl who wasn't expecting to get her face pummeled for being groped by me.

"What are you doing, Lake?" I managed to keep my tone level while holding onto her wrist for dear life. The rage in her eyes was not to be mistaken. If I hadn't been so surprised, I would have been turned on.

"What am I doing? What are you doing?" She snatched her arm away and shot me a look meant to maim. My dick jumped in my jeans.

Ah, there it is.

"You disappear for days, and the first time I see you, I find you with your hands all over the nearest skank?"

"It's not that big of a deal."

It was a lie. I knew what I was doing when I grabbed the girl who had already run off, clutching her head in pain. Who knew little Lake was a scrapper?

"The hell it isn't, asshole."

Now that pissed me off. My nostrils flared and the beginnings of a headache stirred. I just needed to do what I came to do and leave. That was the plan. Not feeling up random chicks in the school parking lot and fighting with Lake in the open for everyone to see.

"Let's go."

I walked away without looking back, knowing she would follow, and didn't stop until I reached one of the empty classrooms that served more as an oversized storage closet. I can remember over the years wanting to pull Lake in one of those very rooms and committing forbidden and uncensored acts against her body.

"Where have you been?" she asked as soon as we were inside. I willed my hard-on away and released a breath for patience before responding.

"Look, I'm sorry I disappeared. How are you?"

"Pissed and I don't know... maybe hurt? Where were you?"

"I had to figure shit out." I didn't want to tell her about the two-day interrogation and then my endless search for Mitch because worry was the last thing I wanted to see in her eyes. She had managed to make me care despite my best defenses.

The look she gave me was full of disappointment. "But how could you just leave Keenan alone like that?"

"He isn't safe as long as my father is out there and he has John."

"But he needs you too, you're his bro—"

"Don't. Don't say that." I've known since the beginning Keenan was my brother, but it didn't make others knowing any easier. Especially now. I may have been cold and cruel, but I never wanted Keenan to find out the way he did. Now I was forced to wait while my brother died in some fucking hospital to see how much damage I'd caused or if he would forgive me.

"Did you know all this time?"

"Yes." I could tell it shocked her.

"How?"

"I saw her picture on Keenan's nightstand the day John brought me home. He said she was his mother."

My heart started pounding just as it had the day I discovered my mother had another child. One she loved enough to keep. At least that's what I felt then. I don't know what to feel now except confusion. I sure as hell didn't like the vulnerability it created.

"What did they make you do?" The drastic change in subject didn't go unnoticed. Parents were a sore spot for her though she cared enough to hide her pain.

Just like her parents were a taboo topic for her, talking about my days of enslavement was or should have been forbidden. After spending time in my father's company, I felt like I owed her at least a condensed explanation. I would never be able to bare myself enough to reveal everything. Besides, after today, I was letting her go.

"I guess it doesn't matter anymore, anyway." I ignored the increasing pain in my chest. No amount of mental preparation could make what I had to do any easier. "I made my first kill for them when I was six."

"How? You were so young."

She stared at me in disbelief. I wasn't surprised by her reaction. No one was willing to believe in anything other than the perfect image of innocence that children projected, but with the right conditioning... anything was possible. After all, ignorance is a person's greatest enemy. It makes you weak and vulnerable, but it's better received than knowing because no one wants to allow the darkness of the world to enter their lives. So, instead, they choose to ignore what's happening right in front of them.

"It's amazing what you're willing to do when you're starving and don't know a way out. They used anything they could in order to control us. Before long, I stopped noticing the hunger pains or thirst, and the scars healed before I knew they were even there."

The way I grew up those first eight years put a new meaning to the idea of a privileged lifestyle. Compared to what I endured, kids on the streets near our homes were considered privileged.

I could see the questions in her eyes along with the pity, but thankfully, she didn't interrupt. "They started me off small. First, it was other kids they wanted me to punish until I made my way up to adults. After two years of training to be a murderer, I became one of their best students. I was a fucking eight-year-old kid. I stopped thinking, and I stopped feeling. It kept me alive."

"That isn't living," she argued.

"How would you know?"

My defenses went up at the look in her eyes and the way she spoke those words. She was judging my choice to live rather than die. Sometimes I wondered why I didn't give up. Was it hope for a life that I'd never known, but only heard of from the others that kept me going?

"I'm sorry," she whispered.

I could only nod and continue. Looking at her

standing there, I could picture Lily. Always Lily. Lake was her ghost and as hard as I tried, I couldn't disconnect them.

"She came in the middle of the night like a bad fucking dream." I stared at her, imprinting her to memory as I recounted the night my fate was sealed. "Just like you, except you were much more real. I spent weeks ignoring her while they beat her endlessly. She was so small and so innocent. I thought she was weak when she wouldn't do what she needed to survive. One day, I guess the hunger overrode her fear. One of the runners caught her digging through the trash for food and he beat her. He beat her so badly that day, I finally did something I shouldn't have."

"What did you do?"

"I stopped him from caving her head in with the heel of his boot as if she was nothing." I shook my head to escape from being trapped in the too real memory. "Two years of work went down the drain because of one wrong move. I still didn't regret it, at least not at first. She clung to me after that and looked to me as her protector. Every day I took her beatings and mine and often, I was too weak to make any kills so they became crueler. I began to hate her after a while. I blamed her for making me weak again even though all she wanted me to do was care about her. I didn't want to care so I don't know why I helped her. I just did."

I was sitting down at a desk before I realized I had even moved. I dug my fingers in my fist for the pain—to remind myself that I was alive.

"What happened to her?"

"One day after a run, they told me I had a job to do, one that would cost me my life if I didn't do it. What they didn't know was I didn't care if I lived or died, but I accepted anyway. They took me to a room I'd never

B.B. REID

seen before. Lily was there, waiting. She was naked and crying, and I saw the bruises and gashes all over her body."

"Why was she naked?"

"They wanted me to—we had—they wanted me to fuck her for some sick fantasy a lot of sick, old fucks were paying a shit load of money to get on camera."

"Oh, God, Keiran..."

I didn't let her finish. I rushed through so I wouldn't have to hear her words of pity. I didn't need another reminder of what I almost became wasn't supposed to happen. "She looked so broken, and I could tell she had nothing left. I couldn't do it. Out of all the jobs and people I'd hurt, this was something I couldn't do. That's why I was relieved when she asked me to do it."

"Do what?"

"To save her."

"But you were in danger, too."

I finally met her eyes. "I didn't care what happened to me."

"How could you have saved her?"

"The only way that mattered." The horrified look in her eyes told me I wouldn't have to explain.

"I took away her pain, and I took away her fear. I went to her, and I laid her down and closed her eyes. In that space of time, I tried to find another way, but in the end, I kept coming back to the same answer."

"You were only a child."

"I was never a child, Lake. For ten years, my decision has haunted me. When I saw you for the first time, I thought you were Lily, and then I thought I was hallucinating. You looked just like her. But when I finally realized it wasn't her, I knew I was being punished. You reminded me so much of her." I couldn't stop myself from asking my next question. It didn't matter how much it exposed me. "Are you here to punish me?"

"I never wanted to punish you, Keiran." I didn't miss the look of surprise that flashed over her features.

"I think I was punishing myself and looking for someone to blame." That was only partly true, but how did I tell her I had punished her because of a ghost?

"Did you love her?"

What the hell?

"No."

It took everything in me not to scream my denial. What I felt for Lily was the need to protect the small light I had in my dark, dark world. What I felt for Lake was... indescribable but I knew without having to define it that it was dangerous.

"Because you don't believe in love?"

Wrong. It was because someone like me would never be capable of love, but still I asked, "Would you?"

"How did your father get you back?" she asked in-stead. "Wouldn't they have killed you when you ruined their plans?"

"I wasn't killed for disobeying them by a stroke of luck named Mario. It seems his only vice was child prostitution and pornography. He saved me from being killed and severed his business ties with his partner shortly after. However, not before leaving me a way to contact him if I ever needed anything or, more so, if I ever wanted to work for him. I didn't fool myself to think he cared."

"And your father?"

"A couple of weeks after Lily died, I was snuck from the compound by one of the runners my father had in his pocket." It just went to show anyone could be bought for even the smallest of prices. If my father was broke, then I knew what he paid the runner was next to nothing.

"I was with Mitch for a week before Sophia showed up, though. I didn't know who she was—not at first. He told me who he was right away. I didn't know who she was until after she died."

"Did you really kill her?"

"Yes." I watched the hope die in her eyes and gritted my teeth. She wasn't supposed to have any expectations of me. I am still the monster hiding under her bed.

"Why?"

"Why not?"

"Because she was innocent."

"Was she?" Lake spent hours with Mitch, and in that time, I knew he talked. At this very moment, I probably knew less about my mother than she did, but it didn't mean she knew her enough to proclaim her innocence. It didn't matter. I wasn't interested.

"But—"

I cut her off, causing her to jump at my harsh tone. "There is no such thing as *innocence*. How many mothers do you know who would let their child be taken without even trying?"

"So you killed her because of it?" she snarled.

"I didn't know she was my mother when I put the fucking bullet through her fucking skull."

She shook her head and looked away. "Are you even sorry for it?"

"I don't regret what I can't fix. She's dead." I felt my breathing quicken and my palms grow steady. I needed out and fast. "You don't come back from that."

I stood up and rushed for the door. She quickly caught on to my intention to leave and attempted to stop me.

"Where are you going?"

"I'm done talking."

"But what about Mitch? He knows where you are

now. He knows where all of us are."

"I know." My hand was on the door, ready to escape, but I couldn't resist looking at her one more time. "You were almost killed because of me. I do regret that, which means I can fix it."

"How are you going to fix it?" I could hear the suspicion in her tone.

I opened the door and finally forced out the words that before had been caught in my chest where a heart was supposed to be. "I'm letting you go."

I quickly closed the door causing it to slam. I wouldn't be able to look into her eyes and follow through. My fist gripped the doorknob once and finally let go. It was done. I could walk away now.

I should have known she wouldn't let me.

I was barely five feet from the door before I heard her voice full of pain shout at me.

"So that's it then?" Those in the hallway, along with time, stopped to watch us unfold.

I reluctantly turned back. It was a mistake I would regret for the rest of my life. When I looked into her eyes, I saw something I hoped never to see—even when I hated her.

"That's all I'm willing to give you."

I felt her indrawn breath even from a few feet away. She hardened her jaw but still, the tears glistened, ready to spill over and mark me forever.

"You torment me for ten years, fuck me silly for the past two months, and make me fall in love with you. Then, if that's not enough, you almost get me killed because of your asshat dad, and you think you can just walk away because you think it's the right thing to do?"

"I don't give a fuck about what's right." At least that was true. If I cared about what was right, I wouldn't be having thoughts of running away with her and stealing her future forever. "It's safer this way."

"Says who?"

"Says my brother who is lying in the hospital fighting for his life because of me!"

Fuck. I didn't mean to yell at her. I didn't care that I had just revealed my real relation to Keenan.

I wanted the blow to be as soft as possible. I did enough damage to her.

A part of me knew it wouldn't be easy, but my mind told me she would only be happy if I were out of her life permanently.

"So you're going to walk away from him, too?"

No, just you, baby.

Keenan's blood tied him to me and to the danger that followed me. There was no reversing it.

"If that's what it takes," I lied. "He's still out there."

"Because you chose to save your brother's life!"

How did she know?

It was dark. Dust was everywhere. Those moments when I couldn't find her in the dark were the scariest of my life.

No, she couldn't know.

"You love your brother, Keiran..." She moved closer, making me feel like cornered prey. "...and you love me or else you wouldn't care."

Love? Did I love Lake Monroe?

Oh, fuck no.

I couldn't.

It wasn't possible.

I shook my head in denial and turned to go.

My back erupted in pain as something hard and round hit and bounced off it. Before I could determine the source, she was on me, pushing with desperate hands. Tears clouded her vision before trailing down her face. I wanted to kiss every single one away. I wanted them gone. I wished I'd *never* made her cry.

"You don't just get to walk away."

She beat on my chest, and though her hits weren't strong enough to do physical damage, I felt every single one and fuck if it didn't hurt.

"You don't get to leave." All I could do was move back from the onslaught of Lake at her weakest and most vulnerable.

"You can't," she whispered out of breath. Her body trembled uncontrollably. I needed to stop her before she hurt herself.

I lowered my lips until they were centered right above hers. I would miss kissing those lips.

"I... don't... want... you."

I went too far.

I pushed her away.

Literally.

I had to watch her fall and know I couldn't do anything to break her fall. The laughter that sounded around us brought forth a murderous rage. I had to leave before I made things worse.

As I turned to go, I spotted Quentin standing nearby, watching silently. I locked eyes with him and silently sent him an order.

Help her.

CHAPTER TWO

KEIRAN

NOVEMBER

I'M GOING TO wring her fucking neck.

Of course, it probably wasn't the poor fuck's fault whose neck I currently had my hands wrapped around. He just happened to be in my line of fire when I grew sick of smelling her, feeling her, and seeing her stupid fucking eyes taunting me in my head when I couldn't have her.

Fuck.

I squeezed harder.

"Inmate 960, let go of the other inmate, now!" I heard the command loud and clear behind me, but couldn't care less. They were all scared to come in here so they talked shit behind the safety of the bars. *Pussies.*

"Come on, young blood, you don't want to give them a reason to keep you in here. Keep it together," the gruff voice of a well-respected, older inmate said.

Right, I was locked up again.

Only this time, I wasn't in juvie.

I was heading to the real deal if this shit stuck.

Prison.

I wouldn't see the light of day for a very long time, and she could escape me forever.

Funny how that last one made me want to let go. Only I was a second too late as I felt the electric volts pass through my body just as I let go of my cellmate's neck. My muscles locked up, and all I could do was grunt as I hit the floor, counting the seconds until it was over. It lasted ten seconds but felt more like ten life-times. I guess I deserved that. I looked over at the form of my still gasping cellmate as he tried to catch his breath.

My calves where they hit me burned, and I felt a lit-tle weak in the knees when I tried to stand. I let out a laugh when I remembered a promise a certain someone made me when I entered here for the first time.

I guess she kept her promise in a roundabout way, and I wondered what made me hard more—thinking about the feeling of her pussy or the fact that she finally fought back.

Dash said my obsession with her was unhealthy. He might be right, but it didn't mean I had to give a shit. She was mine. But when I saw her face again, I wondered who really owned who. I willed my erection away by thinking of any and everything other than her.

"Somebody get him out of there," one of the guards ordered. I prepared myself for a fight because the one thing I hated was someone thinking I could be handled. When the guard cautiously bypassed me and grabbed onto Billy, my unfortunate cellmate, I relaxed.

I probably shouldn't have attacked him for simply admiring a picture but three minutes ago, you couldn't have told me it wasn't justified. It was who he was admiring in the picture that set me off. It was the picture of her I swiped the morning after our date.

I don't know what made me take the picture of her. I just knew I had to have it. I carried it everywhere, always, and didn't even realize when I'd stopped clinging to Lily's necklace. She looked happy in the photo, and my gut told me it was taken while I was gone. My throat burned, and my fingers dug into my fists thinking about her being happy. I don't want her happy... I want her to pay.

Truth is, as much as I really wanted her to pay for making me feel, when the time had come, I couldn't bring myself to be as ruthless as I was taught. I know some people would think what I'd done was more than evil, but I could and should have done much worse. It was a mistake I made, and I won't be making it again. This time I wasn't going to hold back.

Monroe was going to feel me—all the pain, hatred, and anger I was going to give to her, one way or another.

Fuck, I'm hard again.

***

"WHAT'S HAPPENING TO you, young blood? I thought you had better sense than these knuckleheads in here," Rufus, the older inmate from this morning, gruffly scolded as he sat down with his tray next to me.

It had been a few hours since the incident this morning, and surprisingly, I escaped it unscathed minus the tazing. Now I was enduring lunch chow, which was food I wouldn't even insult my dog with if I had a dog.

"Your faith in me is misplaced and unwanted," I responded. No matter how much I was a dick to the guy, he always came back for more. It reminded me a lot of how Dash and I became friends. I didn't want friends, but he was intent on showing me he wasn't afraid of me, which was kind of fucking funny.

The older inmate chuckled, forcing my attention back to him. He rubbed his fingers across his lips, and I took in the markings above his knuckles. I couldn't really make out whatever the hell it was supposed to mean, but I knew instantly he was a member of a gang. I had run across plenty of them and was even made to kill a few in training. It seemed like a whole lifetime ago. I also knew this guy wasn't from around here so he must have gotten caught up.

"I'm not your enemy, and I'm not trying to be, but I imagine you had someone on the outside who kept you levelheaded."

"Yeah, he had a problem getting lost, too."

"Well, consider me your guardian angel."

"Why?" I asked. My suspicion and ire rose simultaneously.

"Because you need one, and I hate to see kids fall because they're too stupid to know when they need to stand down."

"Is that why you're in here?" I asked sarcastically.

"You can say that. But I'm not a kid anymore either. It's too late for me, but not for you." I turned back to my tray of untouched food and dug in. "Why are you in here," he asked after a few moments of silent eating.

"Suspicion of murder."

"So if you made it past the holding cell, I imagine they have some kind of evidence on you."

"A witness," I answered, and immediately wondered why I was confiding in him.

"That can be eradicated." He shrugged.

"Not this one," I said, hearing the dangerous tone

of my own voice. The thought of someone hurting Monroe brought out a protective instinct in me that I hadn't been able to feel since Lily. The irony of it did not escape me.

"Family?" he asked with raised brows.

"No, she's—" I hesitated because it wasn't easy describing Monroe and what she was to me. "I go to school with her," I finished.

"Girl, huh? She important to you?"

"No." I reached for my water and chugged it down. I knew what a lie tasted like. I washed the bitter taste down and then shoved a fork full of... *I don't even know what it is.*

"Son, you mean to tell me you're willing to go to prison for a girl you *don't* care for?"

"It's complicated," I barked, taking a bite of my food to keep from saying more.

"Love always is, young blood." Reflex, or whatever the fuck you call it, made me swallow down my food a little too quickly, causing me to choke. Rufus's heavy hand slammed down on my back repeatedly until I was no longer being assaulted by my own fucking food. "So I guess that means it is serious?" he laughed outrageously.

I clutched my tray and considered hitting him across the face with it. I let go after a few deep breaths because it wasn't exactly wise to insult what could be my only ally until I got out of here. *If I get out here.*

It wasn't that I wasn't able to trust people—I wasn't willing. Why let anyone in when the majority of the people I met I would be likely to kill just because it suited me?

Maybe Monroe was right and I was sick. I could tell she wanted to fix me. I could see it in her eyes. She looked at me with hope and... something else. I didn't bother to tell her my sickness couldn't be fixed. There wasn't a cure other than death, and I don't plan to die anytime soon.

One thing was certain though—I do not love Lake Monroe.

"So what's your story, kid?"

"Why do you want to know?"

"Because you never know what can come of telling someone your story. Could be good. It could be bad. It all comes around anyway."

"I'm not interested."

"Try me, anyway."

***

TWELVE YEARS AGO

"YOU," THE BURLY man with an enormous amount of facial hair pointed at me with a chubby finger, "get dressed. Your training starts today."

"Training?" I asked while trying to hide the fear I felt. I saw what happened to the others who showed fear. They were beaten, starved, or just disappeared.

"It's your lucky day. You get to start earning your keep and maybe we'll even feed you more." He laughed hard causing his belly to shake.

"Wha—what do I have to do?" The man's eyes narrowed as he peered down at me cowering on my hard, stained cot. It wouldn't be so bad if they let us have sheets or a blanket, but they said we didn't deserve it yet.

"Are you scared, little boy?" he snarled.

"No, sir," I quickly answered and jumped to my feet.

"Good." He grinned. "Because today you get to

learn how precious life is and how fun it is to take it."

* * *

PRESENT DAY

I JERKED AWAKE, covered in sweat and filled with anger. The blanket and sheets were balled up at the foot of the bed as usual. I rarely felt the need to cover myself when I slept. I snatched the corner of the cover up to my face and wiped off the perspiration, fighting to relax my aching jaw muscles. I must have clenched them in my sleep again.

I shook off the remnants of sleep and what was left of my memories of Frank. He was an evil son-of-a-bitch, and now he was a dead son-of-a-bitch. He was the only person I'd ever killed willingly. As usual, I waited for the feeling of guilt or remorse I should have felt but never did.

I felt the onslaught of the familiar yet intense need for Monroe, and when I get her, I will do one of two things—kill her or fuck her.

CHAPTER THREE

LAKE

"I DON'T THINK this is such a good idea." My gaze passed over everything in sight in frantic repetition, looking for the source of my anxiety even though I knew he wouldn't be there.

"Come on, Lake," Willow huffed. "I thought you said you weren't afraid of him anymore, starting today."

"When did I say that?" I shot my best friend of ten years an accusing look.

"Five minutes ago," Sheldon teased.

That's three words.

Keenan's condition had only worsened, and he was quickly becoming critical. Two weeks ago, when Sheldon called me in near hysterics, she told me Keenan's only working lung was beginning to fail. To make matters worse, after the doctor's questioned the probability of both John and Sophia being Keenan's parents due to their blood combination, a paternity test was advised.

Just who is Sophia Blackwood anyway?

She is the only mystery remaining in this tangled

web I've been repeatedly fucked in.

With Keiran arrested, I wasn't able to breathe as easily as I thought. In fact, I was more worried than ever. When Keiran came back into my life a few months ago, he came with a vengeance. As it turns out, his vengeance was misplaced, but this time I earned it.

I turned Keiran in.

I fought back.

And somehow, I knew it wasn't over. He would be back.

"Yeah, so come on. It will be fine because we'll make it fine," Willow ordered. Willow wasn't taking any prisoners. She and Sheldon spent the last two weeks campaigning for me to stay. I think there was even a threat or two thrown in there.

In the end, I relented because what else could I do? I loved them too damn much. Now here I was, about to walk the halls of Bainbridge for the first time in three weeks. Thank God I was caught up on my work or else I wouldn't be graduating this year, and that just wouldn't do.

"Besides," Sheldon added, "he can't get to you now. You're safe."

"But what about tomorrow? What happens when he gets out?"

"He burned two people alive. He won't get off."

But did he really do it? The question burned my throat, and I almost blurted it out but resisted. It didn't occur to me until it was too late that I had no real proof of Keiran's guilt. Sure, he was the last person to see them alive but—

The shrill of Sheldon's phone broke through my thoughts and she immediately answered. The look of relief mixed with pain on her face held my attention as she spoke into the phone. Her side of the conversation consisted of terse, clipped answers as she looked down at her feet, sometimes only nodding. If the sunlight hadn't picked that moment to break through the clouds, I might not have ever caught the lone tear that trailed down her throat.

"I can't, Dash. I just can't. I'm sorry. No. Yes. Oh, God," she sobbed and hung up the phone. Willow and I were on her instantly as her knees buckled.

"What? What is it?" I asked fearfully. We fought to hold her up but eventually, let her crumble to the ground as we followed her.

"The doctors were able to patch the part of his lung that was failing, but it's only a temporary fix. He'll need a lung transplant or he won't live a full life."

"Oh, no," Willow whispered with a sheen of tears in her own eyes.

"Oh God. He's—" She brought her knees to her chest and began rocking back and forth. We were oblivious to the fact we were in the parking lot of the school. Most of the other students were inside, but there were a few who watched us while talking behind their hands.

"He what?" I urged.

"He's awake," she forced out through trembling lips.

"Well, that's good news... isn't it?" Willow asked

"Yes but—" She shook her head furiously. "Dash said he's barely able to talk, but he did ask for one thing."

"What did he ask for?" I asked while fighting back my own tears. Her eyes were filled with sorrow and complete desolation as she looked at me.

"Me."

* * *

"How was your first day back at school?" Aunt Carissa asked as soon as I was through the door after school.

"Uneventful."

If you don't count Sheldon's emotional breakdown in the school parking lot. I attempted to make a clean getaway to my room, but my aunt's next words stopped me in my tracks.

"A Detective Daniels came by here today."

A lie immediately spilled from my lips. "Oh, really? I wonder what he could have—"

"So help me, if you are seriously thinking to lie to me..." she growled and stood up from her seat on the couch, planting her fists on her hips.

"No more than you lied to me, you mean?" I swallowed down the sting of bitterness

"Lake..."

"No, Aunt Carissa. I can't hear this right now."

"You have to hear it sometime," she argued.

"I know, just... not right now." She nodded her understanding, but instantly, anger reappeared in her eyes, and I knew our fight was only just beginning.

"Why is a detective coming by here for you?"

Good question since he would know I had school. But I knew what game he was playing. I turned Keiran in, and they made an arrest, but they didn't have a case against him unless I testified. After the shock of turning Keiran in, and Keenan's condition wore off, I began to have second thoughts. I even tried once to go back and retract my statement to which they didn't react kindly.

Keiran was denied bail given his record and his history with Trevor Reynolds, one of the two victims who were burned alive. The other being Anya Risdell, Keiran's ex... something.

After I sat down to think on the possibility of Keiran's innocence, I realized my reluctance to go through with it was more because I didn't want him to be guilty. Keiran was the last person to see Anya and Trevor alive. After the fair, Trevor attempted to kidnap and hand deliver me to Mitch, Keiran's father, who wanted to use me as a pawn to kill his own son for money.

The things that can occur on Monday nights...

"Lake?" my aunt prompted with a raised brow after I took too long to respond.

Shit, shit, double shit. "I, uh... forgot to tell you... the house was broken into a month ago. I'm so sorry, Aunt Carissa," I rushed out at the perturbed look on her face.

"What? Were you hurt?" She rushed to me and immediately began checking me over.

"No, I was able to lock myself inside my room until the cops came."

"Why didn't you tell me sooner?" she screeched. I wasn't prepared for her strong reaction, and I realized it was the calm before the storm.

"I didn't want you to worry. I *thought* you were on your book tour," I quipped.

"Lake, you have to know I had the best intentions. I didn't want to get your hopes up in case I came back empty handed."

"It's too late. My hopes died a long time ago."

"Oh, honey, don't say that. Your hopes aren't dead. You just need to find them again."

"I'm sorry I didn't tell you sooner about the burglary," I said, changing the subject.

"As long as you're okay, but don't ever think about pulling that stunt again. I don't care what you think is best for me. I am the adult, and you don't make those decisions. I decide what's best for us, got me?"

It was safe to say I was feeling a little bit more than uneasy when she was done. My aunt's tongue was as sharp as a whip and could bring grown men to heel, but one would never know just by looking at her.

"I got it." We hugged before I finally managed to escape upstairs. I released an audible breath once I was safely inside my bedroom.

One day down and six months to go. I'd be free.

Only... would I really be free?

Keiran once told me, no matter how far I ran, he would never let me go. It seemed my sole chance at a new start would come only if Keiran remained behind bars.

Even so, Mitch was still out there... somewhere. Waiting and lurking for his chance to kill his sons.

Wow. Just a couple of months ago, Keiran and Keenan Masters were cousins, and now they are brothers. Once the truth was out, it suddenly all made sense. Of course, they were brothers. The two were more alike than anyone could see with the naked eye. Keiran carried a dark aura everyone could feel, but Keenan's was more of a shadow.

I crossed the room to my bed and flung myself on the mattress wanting the comfort of sleep, but as soon as I felt the soft material engulf me, memories burst forward. Suddenly, I could smell him. His scent still lingered in the fabric.

When I decided to return to Six Forks, I did everything I could to wash him away, starting with my bed sheets. I didn't want the memories. I didn't want to remember how it felt to let him push me to my limits and beg for more. But he was there, even today. When I tried to be strong, he was always there, and I fought to hide it.

I couldn't hide it anymore.

I didn't feel my hand move until they were already pushing into my jeans. I screamed at myself to stop while burrowing my hand deeper.

With a groan full of need, I flipped over onto my back and ripped the button of my jeans loose and shoved them down my hips much like he did the first time he touched me.

Fuck yes.

My fingers finally reached where I needed them most and slipped through the slickness his memory created. Only I needed more than a memory. I needed his touch. I closed my eyes and imagined that it were his fingers teasing my clit, drawing out more evidence of his effect on me.

It wasn't me. It was him.

"Keiran," I whispered, letting the lust I felt for him fill my voice.

In my head, I heard his voice ask, *"You want more, baby?"* just like he often would over the weeks we were together.

"Yes, more," I moaned as if he were right here. Before I could think twice, my fingers were stroking the inside of my pussy, and I was writhing and gasping in tandem to the rhythm of my fingers. It was amazing how well Keiran could fuck me without actually fucking me.

When my clit began screaming for attention once more, I searched it out with my other hand and began rubbing furiously. That was when my phone decided to ring. I was too far gone to bother to answer, but when it rang for the second time, I felt for my jeans with one hand while touching myself with the other. I wasn't in the mood for anything that wasn't an emergency, so whoever was on the line was getting hung up on.

"Hello," I growled while trying to conceal a moan of frustration. My orgasm was evading me for some reason. Sometime later, I would be embarrassed at my audacity to touch myself while on the phone, but not now.

"This is Bainbridge County Jail," the automated voice greeted me.

My fingers caressed my pussy faster before I could fully understand what was happening.

"You have a collect call from..."

My legs spread wider of their own accord as far as my jeans would allow as the slow build-up suddenly burst forward at light speed, and then I heard his rough voice growl...

"Keiran."

I came.

Hard.

The sense of urgency and frustration and need all exploded on a silent scream.

"Do you accept?"

"Yes!" I screamed in ecstasy from the well-needed release. I didn't hear the silence on the other line. All I could hear was the ringing of my ears as the image of him faded away, and the imagined feeling of him touching me left with it.

After a minute of lying there, catching my breath, I realized I dropped the phone next to my head. Mortified, I picked it up, my finger hovering over the end button, but something told me not to. The very last time I heard his voice, it sounded very real and very close. But that had to be my imagination. He was in jail. He was...

This is Bainbridge County Jail...

...on the phone.

Oh, God.

"H—Hello," I spoke hesitantly. *Please don't be him. Please don't be him.*

"Were you touching yourself?" His cold voice was like a blast of frigid air, yet my body heated up as if it were set on fire.

FEAR YOU

I struggled to talk from the shock and mortification.

"Were you?"

His mocking tone and the cocky grin I knew he would be wearing replaced my embarrassment with anger.

"No," I laughed mockingly. "I had help." I pulled my mouth away from the phone and said to the empty room, "Thanks, baby. You were great."

The low growl was music to my ears.

"It's good for you that I have a sense of humor, or I might be inclined to break out of here," he threatened.

"Is there a reason for your call?"

"I didn't want you to forget me."

"Too late. I'm past you and your sick sense of humor." A knowing blush spread over my skin as I straightened up my pants.

"Is that why you were just touching yourself?"

"I—I was—wasn't."

"You forget... I've made you come, and I've heard you lie. I know both sounds very well. Were you thinking about me?'

"What?" I shrieked and almost dropped the phone.

"Were. You. Thinking. About. Me. When you touched your pussy?"

I scoffed and rolled my eyes. He couldn't see me, but he could hear me. "You do have a sense of humor."

"My, my, aren't we brave?"

"I'm getting the feeling this conversation is over so I'm hanging up now. Nice talking to you."

"It was my voice that made you come, wasn't it? As hard as you tried and as much as you gave, you just couldn't find that push..."

"Don't—"

"Flatter myself? I wouldn't dare, but you flatter me.

Do you know what it does to me to know you were touching yourself because of me? It makes me hot, Lake, and it makes me hard."

"Well, you aren't bad looking so I'm pretty sure there are plenty of men in there who are willing to keep you company," I snapped. In truth, I wanted to hide the nervous lust in my voice from thinking about him hot and hard.

The line was silent for a heartbeat before he asked, "So, you're back?"

I knew what he meant without having to ask. "I shouldn't be."

"So what changed?"

"Because you're going to prison?"

His dry laugh washed over me as if there wasn't a phone and a jail separating us. "I'm not going to prison, baby."

"I'm not your baby," I argued petulantly.

"You were the last time I had my cock inside you."

"You're going to prison," I repeated.

"Why are you so sure about that?"

"Because you killed them, Keiran." I stood up to pace the room, trying to get my bearings. *You aren't afraid of him. You aren't afraid of him.* "You're sick."

"That may be, but I didn't kill them."

"I don't believe you."

"I don't care."

"Why did you do it?"

"Why do you care? They wouldn't have batted an eyelash if it had been you who were burned alive."

"I don't think I should be talking to you," I said instead. He was right, and I hated it, but it didn't make it okay that they were tortured and killed.

"Why is that?"

"Because I turned you in?" I laughed humorlessly.

"Because I'm testifying against you?"

"No you're not."

"Oh?" My pacing abruptly ended as I came to a halt in the middle of my bedroom.

"You won't," he smugly repeated, and I could hear the smirk in his voice.

"Why are you so sure?"

"How else would you feel me between your thighs again if I'm locked away?"

"That's not going to happen," I snapped.

"Yes, it will, and do you want to know why?"

Don't ask why. Don't ask why. "Why?" I asked, ignoring my gut for the millionth time.

"Because I'm coming for you, Lake." His voice lowered, and I could hear the smile in his voice. "Are you ready for me?"

No. I wasn't even close to being ready for him. I knew what he would come for when he got out. Keiran was a vengeful person and didn't like losing control. I took that away from him by turning him in. I swallowed down the familiar stirrings of fear and told myself if he came after me again, this time would be different.

I was different.

"Hey, Keiran?"

"Yes?"

"Don't drop the soap."

CHAPTER FOUR

KEIRAN

"Don't drop the soap." The click of the line told me she had hung up, but all I heard was, *"Get fucked,"* which was exactly what I knew she meant.

My only question was when did she grow a pair of balls? Part of me was turned on, and part of me was mad as fuck. I was losing control.

That wasn't allowed to happen.

But I knew, once I got out of here, I would scare her back into submission. I just had to figure out how I would get out of here. Between my uncle and Dash's parents, I had the best lawyers working my case. The fuckers wearing the big wigs denied my bail so I was stuck here until trial...

Yeah, that's not gonna happen. I needed to get out of here. I needed to feed my addiction. At times like these, I wondered who controlled who and that was usually when I turned especially sadistic and went full force at her. In the past, she would always get this look in her eyes that begged for me to tell her what she had done wrong.

How did I tell her it was because of who she was and not what she had done? I had wanted to tell her many times, but what was the point? Making her wonder and worry was part of the thrill. I smiled when I thought about the day it all began...

* * *

TEN YEARS AGO

I LIKED TO SWEAT.

No one ever really wanted to sweat because it made you messy and it made you smell. I liked to sweat because it was raw and because I couldn't cry. Sweating was as good as I could give. It's how I shed my anger and my feelings. Years later, I would learn it was pent-up aggression that I needed to release, and pushing past my limits was the way to do it, so I started with basketball. I discovered it a year ago when I stumbled upon some of the runners watching a game, and I was instantly drawn to it. Of course, I wasn't ever given the chance to play. Not until much time had passed and my already messed up world spun on its axis, toppling me over in the process.

Who would have thought, not even the turn of events that brought me here would top the day the world really fucked me over.

It was the song.

That damn song.

And the voice that followed.

Today was the day I would meet my obsession.

No amount of training could have prepared me for this. I was so very fucked. Of course, I was only eight, so I wasn't supposed to know the meaning of that word, but I did because I wasn't a normal eight-year-old.

I am a slave.

Was a slave, I corrected. The jobs were gone, the men were gone, and she was gone. And I was here. Watching the little blonde bundle of happiness burst from the small yellow car, and frantically, dancing around without a care in the world or notice of anyone watching, including me.

Lily.

Wait... No. Lily is dead. I killed her.

I peered closer and realized it wasn't Lily, but I wasn't completely convinced. It had to be Lily.

How did she get here? And most importantly... why is she here?

Just then, she turned around, giving me a brief glimpse of her face before spinning around again, this time throwing her hands in the air.

Not Lily.

Then who?

The song cut off abruptly when an older lady, who didn't look all that old, shut off the engine and stepped out of the car. She took the girl by her hand and led her toward the burger joint. I saw the glimpse of sadness flood the girl's face as she was being led inside. Not long after, I would learn the name of the song and how it fit her so perfectly.

When the door closed behind them, I got the un-controllable urge to jump from my bike and follow. I didn't understand the need to see more of her, but I needed to meet the girl who looked so much like Lily.

Who is she? I swung my leg over my bike and stepped forward to follow.

"Hey, Keiran, wait up!"

I released an audible groan at the annoying kid

who wouldn't stop following me around. It just so happened to be we lived together too, and we were cousins.

He raced forward with a smile, but when he saw the look on my face, he came to a dead halt in his tracks, his smile dropping and replaced with a worried look. I started to smile as I watched him shift his feet and look away. Instead of coming closer, he then looked as if he would bolt in the other direction. Served him right. I needed to see the girl, but now I had to deal with him.

"What?" I yelled when he continued to stare.

"Nothing. I—I wanted to come play with you. I saw you take off with your ball. Do you think you can teach me how to play?"

"Why?" He shrugged his trembling shoulders, and I almost took pity on him. Almost. "Go away then. I don't want to play with you. Why don't you go draw or something?" He was always drawing and coloring, and when he wasn't doing that, he was asking me to play with him. I don't play.

"P—please?" His eyes lowered to the ground, but I could still see the tear escape and watched it fall onto his shirt. "My dad told me to go find you. He never wants me around. No one wants me around anymore. I think that's why my mom ran away."

He looked back up at me with hope in his eyes and his chest moving up and down rapidly. "I'll be good and I'll be fun, I promise! You won't ever get tired of me."

"I'm tired of you now, kid. Go away before I hurt you." I turned away to pick up my bike but watched him out of my peripheral.

"Everyone is an enemy, kid. Everyone!"

I shook Frank's voice out of my head in time to see

Keenan's eyes harden and narrow into slits, and out of the corner of my eye, I could see his fists ball. Interesting.

"You're a kid, too. I'm not afraid of you."

I laughed because I couldn't help it, and I never laugh. "Yes, you are, and I'm not a kid."

"You're only a year older than me and—"

"Your mom's dumb, and so is your dad. Maybe it's better she's dead. I could—"

I never got the chance to finish the rest before Keenan's fist connected with my nose, knocking me down. My bike nearly fell on top of me.

"Don't you call my mom and dad stupid!" he screamed. "She isn't dead! Why did you say that?" He stood over me as I brought the back of my hand up to my face and then peered down at the crimson smear on my skin.

Blood.

Instead of the anger a normal person would feel, I smiled.

The little shit made me bleed.

I let the smile drop from my face before I looked back up at him. I quickly jumped to my feet causing him to take a step back warily.

"One on one?"

"Wha—huh?"

"Would you like to play one on one?"

"I... don't you want to hit me back?"

I huffed and let my annoyance show on my face. I was just a little taller than he was so I could easily intimidate him if I wanted, but after what he had just shown me, I no longer had the desire to. I hated weak people, but this kid isn't weak. He's angry... and doing a damn good job of hiding it.

"Tell you what... if you can score a basket, I'll nev-

FEAR YOU

er tell you why I said she's dead. Deal?" I held out my
hand for him to shake and waited.

He frowned and eyed me strangely before taking
my hand. "Deal."

* * *

PRESENT DAY

"ONE HUNDRED AND twelve. One hundred and thirteen. One hundred and fourteen."

Sweat. Anger. Lake.

Up and down my arms went. I fought the images of her fucking face and her smell and her voice. I needed out of here.

On my last push, I jumped to my feet and called for the guard. It was time to execute the next part in my plan. When the burly looking guard finally showed his face, I fingered the picture in my pocket with a slow smile spreading across my face.

Soon, baby.

"What, inmate?"

"I need to make another phone call."

I went through the usual procedure of being shackled before being led to the phones. I dialed the number from memory and waited for him to pick up. I was allowed three rings to mull over my decision, and by the time he picked up, I was sure of the course I needed to take.

"Quentin, I have a job for you."

"Yeah?"

"I need you to find Jesse Fitzgerald."

"On it."

* * *

"WHAT THE FUCK, Masters?"

Two days after I gave Q the order to find Jesse, they came for a visit. Judging by the look on Jesse's face, it wasn't exactly voluntary.

I almost laughed at his attempt to intimidate me. Fitzgerald had earned my respect when he stood up to me to protect Monroe, but it didn't mean I had to like him. After all, he *did* try to keep me from what's mine. He's lucky I didn't kill him.

I ended up laughing anyway when Quentin shoved him in the seat directly in front of me as Jesse shot him a dirty look.

By some miracle, my visitation rights weren't taken away, which made this little meeting possible. "Did you have any trouble?" I directed the question to Quentin though my eyes never left Fitzgerald.

"Tons. The fucker never shuts up."

"What is this about? Why am I here?"

"See?" Quentin gritted his teeth. "He *never* shuts the fuck up." My gaze passed slowly between the two of them. Suspicion clawed its way out as I studied them.

"Did something happen between you two?" I'd never seen Q's feathers ruffled before. He was about as emotionally challenged as I was. Anger wasn't a common occurrence for him.

"No." They answered simultaneously and then shot each other a look I didn't understand.

"Do you two know each other?" The sharpness in my voice had both of their heads whipping back to face me. Jesse wore a wary expression while Quentin looked contrite.

"No," Quentin sighed and took a seat next to Jesse. He shot me a look to drop it, and after I held his gaze long enough, I finally decided to do just that. For now, anyway.

"As to why you are here," I started without missing a beat. "You came highly recommended as someone who could find things that aren't meant to be found." I waited for the sign of recognition and waited a beat for his response.

"So what? You need help with your history homework or something? I'm sure you can find someone willing to tutor you. You seem to be really talented at getting people to do your bidding."

"Well then, I won't have to convince you."

"Convince me of what?" he gritted.

I had chosen my words carefully before I spoke. "That I will do anything I can to make you do my bidding."

"Stay away from her," he warned.

It was all I could do to keep my fists from his clothing and yanking him across the table where I could pummel him. Instead, I let amusement show rather than anger. Quentin tensed on the other side of the table, ready to break up the fight he sensed coming.

"She isn't yours to protect."

"She's my friend."

"And *she is JUST mine*."

"You have a lot of nerve staking a claim that you have no right to. You do nothing but hurt and torment her."

"What do you think you know about it?"

He leaned back in his chair with a smirk that held too much confidence. "Whose shoulder do you think she cried on when you were just another statistic?"

I shot up from my chair, intent on breaking his face when Quentin stopped me with a heavy hand on my shoulder and a hard look.

"Keiran, chill." He shot a pointed look at the guards

standing around the large room against the blank, depressing walls. All of their attention was now focused on our table.

"960, you got a problem?" The closest guard called out. Without acknowledging the guard, I sat back down and in my peripheral, I could see their shoulders relax and their nervous looks fade. They may have been the ones with the handcuffs and the weapons, but I was the one with the power. Just for kicks, I blew the guard who challenged me a kiss and smirked when his face and neck reddened. *Nutless fuck.*

"Are you done?" Quentin asked annoyed. I ignored him and focused back on Fitzgerald.

"I need you to find someone."

"Why would I help you?"

"You know why. Are you really going to make me say it?"

"Do you really think your reach is that far?"

"I know my reach is that far, but are you willing to test it? Besides," I continued before he could respond, "you're already here. There is no time like the present."

His jaw muscles clenched and unclenched, and I could read the indecision in his eyes and the moment he made it. "Who do you need to find?"

"Quentin will give you the information you need to know. He'll also make sure you don't try anything. I'm sure I don't have to tell you—"

"You don't," he interrupted, "but you should know I'm only helping you because of her. I'm not afraid of dying."

"I wouldn't be too sure until you've looked death in the eyes." I leaned forward to get my point across. "Because it won't be swift, it won't be painless, and it won't be reversible."

"Are we done?"

I leaned back and watched him rise from the chair followed by Quentin, who remained silent throughout the exchange. "For now."

He started to walk away, but my next question stopped him.

"Do you want her?" The question came out blunt and laced with my irritation with Monroe for sharing a part of us with this douche—even if it was the ugly part.

"No," he answered just as bluntly. "It's never been like that with us—"

"There is no us." The growl erupted from my chest and was a shock to everyone around the table including me.

Jesse's face was stuck in astonishment before he stated accusingly, "You like her."

There wasn't much that caught me off guard, but his accusation caused my tongue to feel like it shriveled and died in my mouth. "What?"

His eyes narrowed as they pinned me to my seat. "Admit it."

"No." A grin spread his face as he stared at me. "Please share the joke." My patience had just about hit its peak.

"The joke is you so obviously care for her and it's making you miserable. Tell me... how does it feel to be on the receiving end?"

I stood up to... *what?* Fight? To leave? I didn't care for the way his questions left me feeling exposed. The vulnerability was worse than a kick in my nuts. "Fitz-gerald."

"Yeah?" The smirk on his face pissed me off even more.

"If you say anything to her and if you cross me, I'll murder your entire family. Including the pet goldfish."

His smirk was finally gone.

* * *

I PLACED THE phone call a week later after Quentin delivered a slip of paper containing the ten digits to my freedom. The only hiccup was it wasn't the direct line to my target, so I pissed off a lot of people including the man himself.

"Whoever this is better have a damn good reason for calling this number."

"Arthur, it's been a while."

I smiled into the receiver. It wasn't joy that brought the smile to my face. Jesse had delivered. It was a wonder what a few well-placed threats could get you. The fact it only took him a week was impressive in itself.

"Who the fuck is this?"

The generally calm and authoritative man had become unhinged. It wasn't every day someone was brave enough or stupid enough to call making threats until he could speak with the man in charge.

"Keiran Masters." I gave my name even though I knew he wouldn't know who I was.

"Who?'

"That's right. You never cared about names, did you? Well, let me refresh your memory. Ten years ago, you had a trainer named Frank. He liked to play with little girls and boys, but he liked the little boys the most. He was your favorite puppet and bodyguard. Ten years ago, there was a little boy who lodged a hunting knife in his throat, and well... no more, Frank. Does that jog your memory?"

"Son of a bitch. Say it ain't so. Is it really you?"

"That depends."

"On?"

"Whether or not you can help me?"

"And why would I want to do that? I haven't seen you in ten years. I assumed you died a long time ago."

"Because I can hand-deliver your mole and the person who helped me escape."

CHAPTER FIVE

LAKE

"WE SHOULD GO catch the rerun of *Breaking Dawn*. It's showing in the old theater tonight."

"Why the hell would I do that?" Sheldon stopped in her tracks to snarl at Willow, who rolled her eyes. Sheldon hated any and everything to do with a chick flick. Give her the guns, explosions and raging muscles. She said she tolerated them because Keenan secretly liked them, but he would put on a front when around the guys.

"Because vampires are cool?"

"Not cool enough to make me watch that movie."

"Oh, come on. I went to see the freaking *Expendables* with you last week!"

Wait... what?

"Um, excuse me?" I interrupted their bickering for what seemed like the hundredth time today. Willow and Sheldon often fought like a couple who had been married for fifty years. When they each turned wide eyes on

me, I popped my hand on my hip, unleashing my attitude on them. "You guys went to see a movie without
me?"

"Huh?"

"Uh..."

"Was there any particular reason why you guys
went without me?"

"Well, you were kind of..."

"Kind of *what?*" My voice rose on the last word as I
stared them down and watched them squirm.

"Pouting," Willow finished and Sheldon nodded
her agreement. Just as I was about to argue, I heard my
name being called. I turned to find Detective Daniels
and his partner, Detective Wilson, approaching with
solemn looks on their faces.

"Good afternoon, Detectives," I greeted while re-
garding them curiously. Sheldon and Willow wore deep
frowns as they looked from the detectives to me. I guess
not telling them I had turned Keiran in would make this
encounter awkward.

"We need to talk," Detective Daniels ordered without greeting. His grim expression immediately raised
flags. Whatever it was couldn't be good.

"Lake, what's going on," Sheldon asked absently
while looking the detectives up and down.

"Could you give us a minute?" Sheldon turned
sharp eyes on me when I ignored her question. I looked
to Willow for help. She hesitated before tugging on
Sheldon's arm.

When they were out of earshot, I rounded on the
detectives and started in on them. "What are you doing
showing up at my school?" I stressed in an angry whisper.

"We have a problem," Detective Wilson spoke up.

"What could it possibly be?" Across the parking lot,

I noticed Sheldon and Willow staring at us unwaveringly. "You could have called me or—"

"He was released."

Time standing still. Thick, heavy, air. Reeling mind. World crashing. I couldn't figure out which was harder to deal with.

"...I'm coming for you, Lake... Are you ready for me?"

Had it really only been a week since I spoke with him?

I swallowed hard to find my voice. "What do you mean he was released? How could he have been released? We didn't even go to trial!"

Breathe, Lake. Breathe.

"Miss Monroe, we are as baffled as you are. I assure you this wasn't our call."

"Then there has to be some kind of mistake. Can't you just arrest him again? What am I supposed to do?" I rambled, and screamed and fussed, never letting the detectives get a word into the conversation. Frankly, they'd said enough. "He knows I turned him in. Do you understand that?" I pulled my jacket closer to me to fight the frigid November air and looked around.

"Yes, that's our biggest concern at this point. Apparently, from your reaction, he hasn't tried to make contact with you."

"No, I—" I stopped when the detectives cast nervous looks at each other. "When was he released?"

"Three days ago."

"Three days ago!" I spoke with him four days ago. "Why am I just finding out? You said if I testified, I would be safe. My aunt doesn't know anything about this. She's in just as much danger." My fingers clutched at the strands of my hair and dug in, but I never felt any of it. "I never should have—oh, God."

"We can have you and your aunt placed under witness protection. You will be under surveillance. He isn't allowed to approach you under any circumstances..."

The detective's words drowned out as I felt a chill run down my back. It could have been the wind, but I knew better. I discreetly looked around, feigning anger, which wasn't hard to do. I didn't see anything suspicious, but I knew he was there...

"It's too late," I whispered, feeling the impending doom of his arrival wash over me.

I just fucking know it.

"We can still keep you safe."

"But not forever. So this isn't going to trial?"

"He was only released on bail, but he will still be tried."

"That isn't enough!" I shrieked. "He kidnapped two people and murdered them!"

"Lake, this was above our pay grade, but I want you to know we aren't letting this go. The son of a bitch isn't going to walk away."

"I—I need to talk to my aunt. Excuse me." I started to walk away when Detective Daniels called my name. I almost didn't hear him because my mind was racing, and the prickling feeling of being watched wouldn't go away. *Where are you?* I discreetly looked around again but didn't see any sign of Keiran. "Yes?"

"We know you and Masters had some sort of relationship." I sucked in a breath and stared blankly at the detective. "We don't want you to make a grave mistake."

"What mistake could that be?"

"Trusting him. Letting him get close. Guys like him know exactly how to entrap a girl like you. You weren't made for someone like Masters to corrupt and beguile. Don't let that happen."

"If he comes near you or threatens you in any way,

call us," Detective Wilson said. "Immediately. Your life may very well depend on it." They headed back in the direction they came.

* * *

"SPILL," SHELDON ORDERED as soon as we were through the door of her house. This was my first time here, and I couldn't help but admire the grandeur of the monstrosity of a house they lived in. I didn't have a clue as to how much money Sheldon and Dash's parents had, but it was apparent they were wealthy when you took in the decor.

"Geez, Sheldon. Your parents are loaded," Willow interrupted with wide eyes. She spun around in a circle and peered at herself in the polished, wooden floors. "I bet you guys have a tennis court and a movie theater," she laughed.

"Don't be a dick, Willow. Of course not. We have a basketball court and a movie theater," Sheldon answered with a hint of embarrassment in her voice.

"Fucking rich people," she muttered while looking around longingly. I knew Willow wasn't upset because of the twins' wealthy upbringing, but seeing all of the extravagance was probably a reminder of all the things she didn't have. Willow's parents were poor, and while they got by, there were a lot of things they had to go without. I looked at Willow, and when she saw my expression, she sent me a reassuring smile. She was okay.

"Anyway, I'm hungry. You guys want something?" Sheldon headed to what I assumed would be the kitchen.

"I'm fine." My stomach had other ideas, and it wouldn't welcome food.

Their kitchen was every chef's dream with state of

the art everything. Half of the appliances I didn't recognize. Everything was sleek, polished, and oversized, but there was warmth too. The refrigerator doors were covered with crafts and pictures clearly made by a young child. There were family portraits on almost every surface and inch of the house. I stopped to admire the picture of an older, attractive couple, who I knew were their parents. I sort of met their dad the morning after my house was broken into, and Keiran had been mistaken for the culprit.

"Where are your parents?"

"It's date night for them." Sheldon pulled out sandwich makings and dumped them on the counter. "They usually go into the city and spend time alone being gross."

"Hmm..." Willow looked around nervously. Being here must have made her uneasy. She confirmed that when she asked, "And your brother?"

Sheldon tossed her hair over her shoulder and huffed. "Why do you care? You don't want him, remember?"

"That's not the point, Sheldon. You know he hates me. We can't even be in the same room without getting into an argument."

"So fuck him instead," she retorted.

"Why do you want me with your brother so bad?"

"Because he deserves someone like you."

Willow's eyes lowered, and I thought to cut in when I heard the purr and rumble of multiple engines pull up followed by car doors slamming.

"Shit!" Sheldon exclaimed. "He promised!"

She ran over to the window to look outside and whatever she saw made her curse and dash out of the kitchen screaming obscenities. Willow and I looked at each other and shrugged before simultaneously rushing to the window to see what had Sheldon so worked up.

"What the hell do you think you're doing?" she yelled and shoved Dash sending him backward, allowing me to see the person standing behind him.

An eternity seemed to pass before I was able to breathe again.

He's here.

He watched Sheldon push and scream at Dash with a bored expression, and when she turned her anger on him, he barely blinked. Dash looked on with an amused expression, which only made her angrier.

As hard as I fought, my gaze wandered to Keiran repeatedly. I looked him over carefully, but he was still the same. Had it really been almost a month since I last saw him? Not a hair out of place or even the slightest bit different, but I could tell by his stance he was getting impatient. He wanted near me. Considering the last time we were face to face, all I wanted to do was scratch his eyes out, dick-punch him and jump his bones all at once.

"Shit, I knew this was a bad idea," Willow whined. "Should we go out there?"

There were a million valid reasons why I shouldn't, but I reminded myself I wasn't afraid of him any longer. When he turned his steely gaze on me, clearly seeing me through the window, I met his stare dead on. He was challenging me, but this time, I challenged him back. His mouth lifted in a smirk, and he nodded his head once in assent, accepting our silent standoff.

Never again, I vowed. So much had changed inside me in a matter of months. I felt like an entirely different person. Sure, I felt my moments of skepticism. No one really changed overnight, but I had the last ten years to build up immunity to him and it was just only starting to kick in.

The sound of the door slamming broke me out of the trance he had me caught in, and all I could hear was the sound of running footsteps traveling throughout the house.

What the?

When Sheldon reappeared, she looked out of sorts with a worried look in her eye. "Guys, I swear I didn't know they would be here. Dash promised he would stay away, and he promised to keep Keiran away."

"Wait... you knew Keiran was out?" I asked incredulously.

Sheldon bit her lip worriedly and nodded. "I didn't know how to tell you. You were just starting to relax, and it's crazy because he hasn't said a word about you." She lifted her eyebrows and cocked her head to the side.

"Well, are they still outside?"

"I think so." She stalked over to the window and peeked outside. "Damn."

"You think so?" My teeth were grinding against each other as I prayed for patience.

"I locked them out and told them to go away."

"But doesn't Dash have a key?"

"Yes. I did it to piss them off so it won't be much help. I wonder what's keeping them?"

"Maybe their male egos finally fried their brain and they forgot how to use a key?"

"One can hope."

"We should just go." Willow released a deep breath, and I suddenly heard her voice call out for me. "Lake?"

"Yes?" I answered absently, barely paying attention. I hadn't realized I had turned back to the window. Keiran was sitting on the hood of his car now with a foot perched on the bumper, watching me with his eyebrow raised and his arms casually resting on his legs.

Fuck you. I stuck up my middle finger to piss him

off, but he only blew a kiss before turning back to Dash, dismissing me.

"Should we go?"

"Yes, I think that would be best." I took a deep breath and released it slowly before turning to face their curious expressions. "I have to tell you something." I beat down the onslaught of panic and regret and forced the words from my chest. "I was the one to turn Keiran in."

"What?"

"Come again?"

"Yeah, I uh—didn't think I had a choice."

"But... how do you know he killed them?" Sheldon asked.

"You guys know what happened at the fair. You were there. He was the last one with them."

"Yes, but so were Dash and Keenan, but you didn't turn them in."

"Because they didn't have anything to do with Trevor and Anya's actual deaths. I overheard them talking the night we went out to play laser tag.

"It doesn't make sense." Sheldon shook her head. "Why would he kill them? He was bringing them back." She looked at me in disbelief. "Lake, I think you were mistaken. He didn't kill them."

"What do you mean he was going back to get them?"

"Right before Keenan and I had our fight, he got a call from Keiran. I could only hear Keenan's side, but he asked Keiran why he was going to help them. I didn't know until he ended the call that Keiran was going to bring Trevor and Anya back. I just never found out why. Keenan was pretty tight lipped."

"If Keiran didn't kill them, then who did?" I challenged.

FEAR YOU

"I don't know. Keiran was turned around before he could reach them. I guess that's when he got the phone call from you."

"He could have gone back to do it," Willow argued.

"With his brother fighting for his life in the hospital? Keiran can be a cold bastard, but he isn't that unattached to human emotion."

"So where was he for the week he was gone?"

"I don't know, but something tells me he didn't do it. It just doesn't make sense."

"It doesn't matter. Keiran is responsible for their deaths whether or not he lit the match."

"Well, what are you going to do? He can't find out you turned him in."

"He already knows," I admitted slowly. To them, things just went from bad to worse.

"How could he know?"

"I told him." I shrugged noncommittally when I was anything but. I was a wreck, but no one had to know that but me. My battle with Keiran was mine alone. He'd already shown he wasn't above using the people I loved and cared about against me. This time I wouldn't make it so easy for him.

"Why did you tell him?" Sheldon gritted. Willow looked as if she wanted to strangle me as she pinched the bridge of her nose.

"I don't know. He called a few days ago. I got really upset and it just came out. I know it was a dumb move, but I needed to show him I wasn't afraid anymore."

"So you do and say the one thing that would put you in deeper shit with him than you already are?"

"I don't know what you want me to say," I snapped defensively. Sheldon released a curse and began pacing the tiled kitchen floor while shaking her head.

"Do you think he's here for you?" Willow asked.

"I know he is," I said, glancing back out the window, but this time, not catching sight of Keiran or Dash.

"How are you going to handle this?" Sheldon demanded. "I hope you have a plan of action because no way is Keiran letting this go. This is the second time Keiran landed in jail for what he thinks was your doing, only this time, it really is."

"I don't care. He murdered two people."

"Let me know how explaining that to him will work out for you."

"Where are the guys?' Willow asked.

"I don't know. They are awfully quiet."

Too quiet. I peeked back out the window but didn't see them.

"Maybe I can get Dash to talk to him. If Keiran knows you turned him in, then Dash knows, too."

"Do you know why he was released?" Willow looked back and forth between the two of us.

"No clue," Sheldon answered before looking to me for answers.

"Detective Daniels and Detective Wilson said it came from over their heads."

"Well, my dad didn't get involved this time and neither did John. In fact, John reacted very little to Keiran being arrested. He's barely been to the hospital to see his son." Sheldon's voice choked over her tears on the last part. I could tell Keenan's condition bothered her, especially on the wake of their breakup.

"Did they ever take a paternity test?"

"No. John said he didn't want to."

The day I turned Keiran in, and Sheldon called to tell me Keenan's only lung was failing, I'd thought a paternity test had been given. I later found that much hadn't been done to determine paternity at all. Keenan was able to sustain a patch to his lung to buy him more time, but he wasn't out of the woods. I made a mental note to visit him when the coast was clear. Being shot and finding out your father wasn't your father and your cousin was your brother, and then losing his girlfriend, who he loves, had to be taking a toll on him.

"Did anyone else get the impression Keiran wasn't too surprised that they are brothers?" Willow asked.

Sheldon cocked her head to the side before nodding slowly. "Yeah, I got that, too. Do you think—"

The sound of the front door opening drowned out whatever Sheldon had been about to ask. I could hear heavy footsteps heading toward the kitchen, but the blood rushing to my head made it impossible to hear clearly. *Was it one or two sets of footsteps?*

We all stopped and waited for them to appear through the door, and when it finally opened, I felt my knees weaken.

No, don't do this. You aren't that girl anymore, Lake.

I willed my legs to straighten and plastered what I hoped was a brave look on my face.

Dash appeared through the door first as he took a quick glance around, and I could tell he was fighting not to laugh. I kept my eyes glued to the door waiting for him to walk through next, but he never came.

"Damn, you chicks are all drama. Relax, princess," he snapped, drawing my attention. "The big, bad wolf isn't here to eat you up." Dash rolled his eyes and snagged a bottle of water from the refrigerator and left, but not before sending Willow a nasty look that made her retreat a step.

I looked back out the window once Dash was gone and saw Keiran's car gone. I blinked a few times and questioned if I imagined it. *What game is he playing?*

CHAPTER SIX

KEIRAN

TEN YEARS AGO

I WAS BLINDFOLDED and told to keep quiet before I was driven away from the compound. When we arrived, they finally removed the smelly rag from my face, and as my eyes adjusted, they slowly took in the scary building ahead.

The big empty room they led me to was dark and had puddles of water everywhere. The smell of the building was horrendous. It was something I'd never smelt before. There was only one door leading in and out and no windows.

The screams of the man tied to the chair, drenched in the water the men were pouring on him, were terrifying. Some of the men they called 'trainers' were standing around with mixed expressions of awe, amusement, and anger.

I just wanted to run and hide.

After Frank had told me I would start training to-

day, I didn't know what to expect. I was confused and scared, but I knew better than to show it. They would beat me again if I did.

"Come on, you. Today you become a man."

"Wha—what do I have to do?"

Frank pulled out a cigarette and lit it with a match. The smoke he blew in my face made me choke, and I almost didn't notice when he handed me the match.

I eyed the burning sliver of wood he had stuck in my hand before he shoved me toward the hurt man. The sudden movement caused the flame to flicker, and my eyes widened out of fear that I would lose the flame. When it continued to burn, I relaxed a little and looked up at Frank.

"I want you to throw it on that piece of shit."

They wanted me to throw it on him, but why? What would happen if I did? What would happen if I didn't do it?

"I don't want to do it. Please don't make me." Tears blurred my vision as I began to do the one thing that would mean pain.

"Do you want to be next, you little shit?" Frank spit at the ground next to me and pushed me down, causing the flame to burn out. "Stop your fucking whining and crying before I kill you right here." He kicked my side so hard I flipped over on my stomach. I got a heavy boot on my back for the trouble. "I asked you a question! Do you want me to kill you?"

"N—no."

"Then get on with it. I told you it's time to earn your keep." I heard the sound of another match being lit, and then I was snatched off the ground by the rags covering my upper body and placed on my feet.

"What's going to happen to him? Will he be hurt?"

"He's going to die. Now kill him."

* * *

PRESENT DAY

I BATTLED WITH myself over whether to leave or just snatch her out of the house and take her with me. The decision was made for me when Dash's busy ass twin tore out of the house to curse us both out. I didn't pretend to care about anything she had to say until she threatened to call the cops on us both, and unknowingly reminded me of the order to stay away from her.

Like that's going to happen.

I found it amusing how anyone would think they could keep me from what's mine with a sheet of paper they called protection. What the fuck was she supposed to do with it anyway? Play rock, paper, scissors when I got her alone?

Because I will get her alone.

As I drove, my eyes zoomed in on the exit up ahead leading me to my brother—I mean, Keenan. I didn't know when I got onto the highway. I just hopped into my car and drove. Speaking of which, I had to get rid of it. I wasn't too attached, so I shrugged it off. I wasn't attached to too much at all. Everything was dispensable. Everything.

The last time I saw my—Keenan, he was fighting for his life and riddled with bullet holes. Now, he was still fighting for his life, but he carried much deeper scars. Scars I put there, and for the first time, I felt something I didn't want to feel. I felt regret. So now that I finally felt it, what was I supposed to do with it?

The vibration of my phone saved me from the long dark road I didn't want to travel. I quickly checked the screen before chucking it into the passenger seat. I didn't have time for my uncle's bullshit. If he were where he should be, he could dish out his shit soon enough.

When I pulled into the hospital parking lot, I admit, I actually felt nervous. This would be the first time I had seen Keenan conscious since he was nearly killed by my fuck of a sperm donor. I couldn't forget the look in his eyes...

The sterile smell and cool air of the hospital greeted me as the automatic doors opened, and I strode through with purpose. By the time I had reached his room, the muscles and veins in my hands and arms were straining from my too tight fists. I stood at the door, listening for what felt like hours, but mere seconds had passed.

Quit being a fucking coward.

I steeled my jaw, pushed through the door, and stopped short at the sight of him sleeping. I gritted my teeth at the sight of his frailty. He looked so still and lifeless and every bit like the hell he'd just been through. It made me want to rip out the useless lump Mitch called a heart. But then... who was I to talk, right? I stood there awkwardly, not knowing what to do. There wasn't any sign of John, but I wasn't too surprised. The man was barely a father so it was just as well he wasn't there.

I crossed the room to sit in one of the ugly burgundy chairs and got comfortable. The least I could do was to wait for him to wake. As I sat there, my mind drifted back to Monroe. It was never hard to do because she was always there on the surface. I was supposed to stay away from her yet somehow, I knew I never would. She's different. Different in a way I didn't expect, but she was still my Monroe. Beautifully submissive although a little too weak. A smile spread on my lips when

I thought of the ways her weakness benefitted me in the past. Those six weeks being my favorite. Whatever I had expected to gain out of taking her body, her passion wasn't one of them. Never did I miss the way her eyes would light up when I issued a command, or the way her pussy gripped and flooded my dick when I took her hard.

She hated that she wanted me.

At least we have that in common.

Sometimes I believed I was as much her sexual prisoner as she was mine. Those would be the times I took her the hardest and unleashed my cruelty on her. It would excite her, no matter how much she cried and bitched about it. But it also confused her.

The occasional soft touch and whispered word and random acts of kindness. It was when I was the most sadistic, and she didn't even know it. I manipulated her and bent her to my will without having to lift a finger.

If I were capable of feeling any type of remorse, I might have felt bad about it, but then it became necessary when she and that fucktard, Fitzgerald, started to dig into my past.

She actually admitted to wanting to use my past against me as revenge. It was the moment I started to actually respect her and isn't that screwed up or what? Respect or not, she was playing a game I would never let her win.

When I started out, I had one purpose in mind and it was to break her, but at some point, my mission became fuddled and I didn't know what I was after anymore. I just knew I wanted her, and when I started to want to keep her, I knew I was fucked.

I started to hatch ideas on how to distance myself away from my obsession when the door opened. I reached for the gun at my waist immediately before remembering I was in a fucking hospital.

Get a grip, man.

I wasn't in the habit of carrying it around until Mitch showed up, and Anya and Trevor were murdered. Of course, everyone thinks I killed them. Even Dash thinks so, but I can tell he tries to hide it.

My uncle walked in, and his eyes immediately landed on me. He stood there while we stared each other down, neither one giving in. My uncle and I never saw eye to eye. I hated him from the start and he avoided me. I guess I would avoid the son of the mother you convinced to leave behind. The beginnings of a smirk pulled at my lips when guilt started to show in his eyes right before he looked away and cleared his throat. I didn't even know why he bothered anymore.

"Has he woke up?" he asked without taking his eyes off the floor.

"No."

He released a heavy breath and shut the door before moving toward the other chair. Silence filled the room, creating a stiff atmosphere. I stared at the wall ahead, but my attention was fully focused on my uncle as he stared at his son lying in the hospital bed.

"You know I, uh—" He cleared his throat and leaned forward in his chair. I could see him staring at me now through my peripheral. "I never got the chance to thank you."

"For what?" I asked a little harsher than necessary.

"For saving my kid's life. I... I know what the doctors might say about him being my son—"

"He's your son," I affirmed. "He doesn't deserve to have someone like Mitch being his father."

"I haven't been the best father either. To either of you."

"I'm not your son."

"Yes, you are, Keiran. In the only way that counts."

"Is that why you made Sophia forget I existed?"

"It's not that simple. At the time, I thought it was the best thing to do to protect the family I still had. I screwed up. Bad. It's something I live with everyday, and I'm reminded of it every time I look into your eyes because I know what you could have become and what you almost became."

"You're wrong. There's no *almost* about it. I did become, and it's staring you right in your face. You're fucked if you don't see it."

"I'm sure you survived something far worse than I would wish on my worst enemy, but you are not beyond saving. You are your own worst enemy now, but I love you despite it."

"I've seen what your love does. No thanks."

"But you have it anyway. You have it from me, your brother... because he is your brother," he emphasized when I made an attempt to interrupt him. "You have it from Dash and that girl... the one with the weird eyes."

"What the fuck do you think you know about her?" My body tightened in defense mode, and I had to tell myself to pipe down. I wasn't supposed to care.

"Not much. But I see what you refuse to, and I know you will find some way to screw that up because you think it would be better for her. You don't do that if you don't care."

"So maybe I keep her." I felt my lip curl and eyes burn as I glared at him. "That would suit me best, and I could fuck her over along the way. At least then I could keep my personality."

"I won't let you hurt that girl anymore. Sheldon told me what happened, and what you did. I know she was there the night Keenan was shot. What were you thinking?"

"I was thinking I could get my revenge and my rocks off at the same time. I mean... why not, right?"

He looked away from me to stare out the window.

"I guess I can't blame you. Part of this is my fault."

"You think?"

I half expected him to lash or demand respect or whatever it is that parents do, but he didn't. He sat back with a shake of his head and rubbed his chin thoughtfully. I fixed my gaze on Keenan. My cousin, brother, best friend, and the first person who actually gave a fuck about me. I know it may look as if I was the one to give him a chance ten years ago, but it was he who gave me a chance, and I corrupted him.

John spun a tale of how Sophia ran off because she couldn't handle the pressure of having a kid, and I helped him. It was a seriously fucked thing to do, but at the time, there weren't two people who hated her more. John, for his reasons and me, for mine. I think he even regrets loving her.

"You did the right thing, you know."

"What's that?" I asked without taking my eyes off Keenan. *Wake up, man.*

"Not telling him the truth about your mother and my part in your disappearance. Thank you."

"You know the corny line people always hear in movies? I never thought I would use it, but... yeah. I didn't do it for you."

"Nonetheless—"

"Do you think we made it any better? Telling him his mother was a selfish whore who couldn't keep her legs closed and didn't have the maternal instincts of a goat?"

"Watch your mouth," he barked.

"Oh, that's right. We don't tell the truth in this family. We throw money around to cover up our bullshit and step on anyone who gets in the way. You did a fine job of raising us. No wonder our family is dying out. Who would want to be born into a scumbag family like this?"

"Keiran, I'm warning you..."

"At least, I know early on. I guess you can say marriage is out. I sure as fuck ain't giving some unlucky bitch my seed so she can sprout more evil spawns just like me. I'm cruel, but I'm not that cruel. I guess that's more than I can say for you and my pussy ass father."

John was out of his seat with my shirt in his hands before I could fully release 'father' from my lips. His eyes were nearly black with rage as he stared down at me, almost lifting my feet off the ground.

"Watch your fucking mouth."

"Truth hurts like a dick in the ass, doesn't it?" I grinned at him, and I guess that might have been a mistake because the next thing you know, I was flying across the room, crashing into the door behind me. I watched John's face redden, and the muscles and veins in his neck pop but instead of charging as I expected, he stood in place.

I let out a laugh that was misplaced.

What can I say? His anger amused me.

My hoarse laugh started to die from the beginning sound of a groan as Keenan woke from his drug-induced slumber. I was completely silent as soon as his eyes popped open and immediately landed on me. Even though he was doped up with drugs and painkillers, his eyes became clearer as they took me in.

We stared at each other for what seemed like an eternity as I began to understand what he was telling me with his eyes. I nodded once before turning to leave and shutting the door. I didn't feel the massive slump of shoulders or the rhythmic beat of my heart as it slowed or the fucking emotion foreign to me but quickly becoming familiar—Regret.

My cousin. My brother. Hated me.

* * *

I DROVE AROUND aimlessly until Mario called saying he wanted to meet. I wasn't in the mood for his shit. He had been after me to work for him for a long time, and the answer was always the same.
I wouldn't work for anyone.

It wasn't until I found myself in deeper shit that I started to consider his proposition. It had been years since I had been on that side of the law, and even then, I was just a kid.

I pulled into the hotel where he pretended to be holed up and parked. I didn't immediately get out. Instead, I checked my surroundings, looking for any unfriendly or unwanted faces. My slime of a father managed to evade my eyes and ears, and there were even a few out there watching and listening for me. Eventually, I would have to stop playing hide and seek with my past. It wouldn't wait forever.

Once inside the hotel, I surveyed the lobby and surrounding areas again before moving toward the elevator. I made my way down the hallway when the elevator stopped on his floor.

The door opened before I could knock, and he ushered me in.

The room was barren and empty of luggage or anything indicating the space was inhabited. Mario was extremely cautious and distrusting, so he wouldn't let anyone, including me, know where he laid his head.

"What was so important?"

"There is something you need to see."

When he pulled out his phone, I quickly became annoyed.

"And it wasn't something you could have sent to me by email? Text? Fucking Facebook?"

I knew my anger was unnecessary, but I was in a shitty spot. Everyone was a target.

I needed Lake.

I had to remind myself I wasn't using her that way anymore. She became something more precious than my personal punching bag over the last few months and fuck me if I knew how.

"Trust me. This isn't something you want to be caught with."

He tossed the phone to me and I caught it in mid-air. I looked down at the phone and saw what looked like a video before raising my eyes to meet his and hold them.

After moments of silent communication, I tapped the triangle symbol and the video began to play. The quality of it was good so I could see everything clearly. A bed with red satin sheets came on the screen, and a young girl, who looked around nine or ten, appeared, blindfolded with her hands restrained.

A lump began to form in my throat as I gripped the phone in my hand. I wanted to break it.

I knew what this was, what he was trying to show me. It was déjà vu all over again, except this time, it wasn't Lily and me. It was some unknown victim and a grown ass man on the screen.

Before Mario could react, his phone flew through the room at the nearest wall and shattered to pieces before falling, much like the girl in the video might have done after being—

Fuck.

I could form only one complete thought.

Somebody needed to die.

Mario remained silent against his perch on the wall as if the phone hadn't just crashed just two inches from his head.

"Why did you show me that?" I barked, finally finding my voice.

"So you could wake the fuck up, man."

"You don't think I'm awake?"

The base of my voice rose to a deafening roar. So many emotions and none of them wanted. The same emotions many thought were nonexistence. I was to blame for it. The last thing the world needed was someone like me being led by feelings.

"Not if you can continue to sit by and let this happen to hundreds, no, thousands more kids. How many do you think it's been since you, huh? You think it stopped when you left? It sure as hell didn't stop after you had to kill the little girl."

"You motherfucker…"

His throat was in my hands as I pinned him to the wall before I could think twice about it.

I needed to hurt someone. To lash out.

I needed Lake.

I needed to make her feel my sick obsession with her. Mario had at least forty pounds on my hundred-ninety, but at the moment, I was far beyond reason. It took some elaborate moves on his part to dislodge from my grip.

"You can stop this, Keiran," he urged through labored breaths.

"I intend to." I spoke calmly as if I hadn't just tried to murder a former undercover FBI agent who'd gone rogue when the bureau determined he was corrupt and unfit for duty.

"What do you mean you intend to?"

"I am going to bring that motherfucker down. But on my terms."

* * *

I spent the next few hours hashing out a strategy with Mario until it was well after dark. John never bothered to call after I had left the hospital, so I knew he was still at hospital letting his guilt turn him into a wannabe decent father. Imagine that.

After reaching Six Forks, I drove down endless streets to avoid going home or the one place that would land me back in jail. I wrestled with all the different hands I was playing—Mario, Lake, Keenan, John, Mitch, and Arthur.

I took a risk when I called my former owner because he now knew where I lived and where my family lived. He could have me killed at any time, and it was likely I would never see it coming. I did have a small advantage. It was why my heart was still beating. He wasn't as untouchable and well hidden as he thought he was—not to someone who had been there. I may have been young, but I wasn't blind, and the conditions I grew up in made me comprehend faster than any kid my age should have.

Over the years, his illegal slave ring had become too big and ultimately, so had his visibility. There were many moles on his payroll who were willing to talk for extra cash. But while his operation was a little less of a secret, it didn't make him any easier to catch. Like me, kids had managed to escape here and there, but Arthur kept his own hands clean. Legally, his wife runs a home for runaway or homeless children. To keep up pretenses, they often toss some of them back into the streets or turn them into authorities, but the kids they keep are

FEAR YOU

never seen again.

They never took kids over twelve. The younger they are, the easier they are to lure and control. The infants they acquire are always sold by their parents, just as I was, but are in less demand.

The thought of being sold made me relive almost every hell I had gone through in order to survive.

"Is that what you want to hear? That I am afraid of you? That I am still afraid of you? Yes, I am afraid, but it's all I will ever feel for you. It is the need to survive. You can't control me beyond that..."

Monroe's word rang loud in my ears and I felt as my hand gripped the steering wheel tighter and anger rolled over me in hard, unyielding waves. For ten years, she let her fear override her better judgment and called it surviving. She was weak... and maybe just a little bit of a masochist. So what did that make me?

She could have stopped me a long time ago, but instead, she chose to give in. She wanted to preserve her precious innocence. I know she thought I was talking about sex. That was just the bonus.

What I wanted to steal from her ran far below the surface. I wanted to see her selfish side. I wanted to see her save herself. I wanted to corrupt her. Why? Because I fucking hate heroes.

The rest of the world would have fought back and damned their family, friends, and whoever else I could use against them. They would have done it out of pride because their ego wouldn't allow them to admit defeat.

The truth was, not many people had the strength to do what she did. Chances were, I would have killed her aunt and broke her little friend. She was smart enough to see that. Over the years, I would push and take just to see how far I could go before she would bend. I wanted to knock her off her pedestal and dirty her up, but she fought me. All this time she thought she was losing be-cause she didn't see what the real fight was. In the end, she didn't break, and I became less concerned with her morals and more interested in owning her.

When I was finally prepared to let her go, she fucked herself and me by turning me in. Her defiance was unprecedented. While I wanted to corrupt her, I still demanded the control. She needed to realize she would always be mine.

By the time I stopped the car, I was in dark place, and in an even blacker mood. I realized I wasn't home but it was too late. I needed to satisfy an urge and I wasn't about to deny myself.

CHAPTER SEVEN

LAKE

WHEN AUNT CARISSA called to tell me she would be driving up to visit Grandma Lane for the entire weekend, I was relieved. It would be hard to answer her questions when he showed up because I knew he *would* come. It was just a matter of when. His pending arrival kept me on edge for the rest of the afternoon.

Willow begged me to come stay with her, but what good would that do? I couldn't hide forever, and he knew as much. I couldn't hide, but I could do the next best thing.

After an impromptu stop, I finally made my way home just before dark. Stashing my purchase somewhere safe, I made my rounds through the house to make sure every door and the window were locked. I threw myself into homework and college applications for the rest of the night, ignoring my racing mind and tense body.

I wasn't waiting for him. Satisfied I might still have a future, even after the less than ideal school year, I decided a long soak was in order to relieve my anxiety and strained muscles.

Seeing Keiran today set me back a few milestones. He certainly didn't look and act like a guy prepared to leave someone alone. He's been out for three days, and I wondered if he even went to see Keenan in the hospital. *How was he able to get out on bail?*

I thought about what Sheldon had told me earlier this afternoon. Was he really going back to get them because I called his soul ugly?

The doorbell rang as I was searching for bath salts. A quick look at my phone perched on the vanity told me I hadn't had any missed calls and it was well after midnight.

It didn't take an elaborate or scientific guess to figure out who it was. I raced downstairs but paused near the entryway with my hand near the knob.

One day, I would question why I opened the door. One day, I would question if it was the smarter choice, but today, I had something to prove. He needed to know the girl who would cower before him was gone.

I finally gripped the doorknob, but a combination of nervousness and sweat made my hand slip, so I slid my palms roughly down my jeans and tried again.

Racing heart? Check.

Fast breathing? Check.

I willed my emotions under control before snatching open the door. A snarky remark was on the tip of my tongue, but when I realized it was Willow standing on my doorstep, and not my tormentor, I bit back the remark and ignored the disappointment.

"Willow? What are you doing here?"

I forced my eyes to remain on her to keep from searching the night for him. Out of fear? Hope? Why did I want him on my doorstep so much?

"I'm sorry," she apologized as she brushed past me. "I just had to check on you. I know you're going through this new phase where you're not afraid of Keiran anymore, but I couldn't stop worrying. He fucking burnt two people alive."

The door closed a little harder than I had intended. "You don't know that."

"Now you're defending him?"

"No. I just—" I stopped to consider my words. Keiran nearly broke our friendship before. I wasn't about to let him have a second go at it. "I don't want an innocent man to go to prison. What if Sheldon is right?"

"You were there the night of the fair. How wouldn't he be guilty?"

"Yes, but so were Dash and Keenan. They actually kidnapped them. Do you think they killed them, too?"

I was harsher than I had to be. Her face tightened with anger and then uncertainty. I realized that I sounded like Keiran when he played mind games. I didn't want to be him. Least of all to Willow. I needed to save my aggression for the person who deserved it.

"Willow, I'm sorry..." She stared down at the floor and took a deep breath.

"No, you're right. If Keiran is guilty, then so are they." Her eyes shined with the sheen of tears as she backed toward the door.

"Willow, wait, please," I pleaded, but it fell on deaf ears as the front door opened and closed with her departure. "Shit!" My fingers gripped my hair in frustration.

I thought to go after her and apologize but knew she needed time. Willow wasn't someone you pushed when she was hurt and angry. I knew how much she loved Dash despite her claims and wrongfully convincing her that he was guilty of a brutal murder wasn't something a best friend would do.

The sound of running water could be heard from upstairs. I remembered the running bath water. I was no longer in the mood for it but now needed more than ever.

I ran up the stairs, silently hoping the tub hadn't overflowed. When I made it to the bathroom, I dashed for the knob to shut off the running water only a few inches from spilling over and then let some of the water drain from the tub before plugging it again.

I stood up and began lifting the hem of my shirt when the sound of the doorbell ringing for the second time tonight stopped me. My feet swiftly carried me out of the bathroom and into the hall.

I was living one bad cliché after the other. Just when would this hellish nightmare end? For the second time tonight, I was standing in front of my front door with sweaty palms.

This was it. I could do this. He was just one guy.

But he wasn't just a guy. He was someone who was unafraid to draw out a person's weaknesses and to use them against them. He was a guy who could make me feel things I never knew anyone could feel. He wasn't just a guy... but I wasn't just a girl, either.

I turned the knob and opened the door to the past ten years. It was waiting for me on the other side with hooded eyes and an imperceptible expression, just as I knew he would be. We stood there gazing at each other, completely lost.

"I would say I'm surprised to see you, but you're a lot more predictable than you think," I said, breaking the ice that started to form from his cold gaze alone.

"So you were waiting for me?" His eyes trailed me leisurely as a small smile teased the corner of his lips. "I got to say, you're a little overdressed for the occasion."

FEAR YOU

"Actually, I wasn't thinking about it. I was just about to bathe. What are you doing here, Masters," I asked, taking a page out of his book and calling him by his last name. "You aren't supposed to come near me."

"Did you really expect me to stay away after you turned me in and accused me of murder?"

I took a deep breath and gripped the door tighter for support. "In case you missed it—that was your only warning."

His eyes darkened as an indescribable expression clouded his features. I didn't see his hand move. My grip on the door loosened as he pried my fingers from the hardwood one by one. "It requires a little bite with your bark to get your point across. You don't confront the monster hiding in the shadows or under your bed without first getting rid of the fear in your eyes. Wasn't it you who said you preferred a person's eyes over their words because they told the real truth?" His mocking grin, as he quoted something from my journal, spiked my temperature, creating a heated flush over my skin.

"Give me back my journal. You had no right to read it and no right to take it." I hadn't realized until after I turned Keiran in and had gone home to cry my heart into the pages, it was missing. I knew there could only be one culprit. It was then I realized a photo of me was also missing from the desk, but why would he take them?

He walked into my home as if he owned the place and closed the door, locking us both in. Without invitation, he moved further into the house and disappeared into the living room. I stomped after him like a two-year-old and saw he had made himself comfortable on the couch.

"So what could you have possibly said to send your *best friend* away crying? Your track record is amazing.

Page | 76

Some might say you're a terrible friend."

"Go to hell."

"Is this the part when I say, *'I've been there'*?"

"This is the part when you get the hell out of my house."

"And miss the chance to watch you bathe? Matter of fact, I think I'll join you."

Say what?

The chance at a witty comeback or scathing remark passed me by when he crossed his arms and lifted his shirt over his head. I was stuck in a state of drooling and muscle clenching as my pussy salivated over the exposed muscles of his abdomen and chest and those arms...

Keiran's body was fit for a man, not a teenage boy. It was seriously unfair. "What do you think you're doing?"

"The idea of bathing in a bowl full of bubbles never appealed to me before now."

I turned on my heel and headed for the stairs. "I'm calling the police," I warned without looking back. Detective Wilson's warning was still fresh in my mind. What if my life really did depend on it? Keiran could really hurt me this time.

Before my feet could touch the first step, I was lifted in the air and staring down at the floor from an up-ended angle as I was being carted up the stairs. "You can call Detective Daniels and Detective Wilson later. I'll help you dial."

"You son of a bitch, put me down!" I screamed and beat on his back during the short trek to the bathroom where he set me on my feet and began to undress me. My hands slapped at his as he unbuttoned my jeans with an amused expression. That was until I sunk my teeth into his shoulder. He grunted in pain and then gripped me tighter, pulling me in close to him.

"Is that how you want to play it, baby?" he growled against my lips. The next thing I knew, I was submerged in water, still dressed in my panties and shirt. He actually *dumped* me in the tub while I was still partially dressed.

"Why are you here?" I sputtered around the water.

"I needed to see you, but you aren't exactly making this visit pleasant for me." When I growled at him, he grinned back.

"You saw me, now get out," I ordered while feeling and looking like a wet dog. "It doesn't require you taking your clothes off."

"Oh, but it might. That depends solely on you."

"You're out of your mind." He didn't bother to answer and instead, shed the rest of his clothing. I gritted my teeth in anger even as I ogled him. The way he shed his jeans as he stared into my eyes, called to my baser instincts, and I clutched my thighs together to will the arousal away.

"It's not polite to stare," he cracked. I sent him a glare before turning my face away. I knew the exact moment that he was naked. My nipples hardened and my pussy began the aching pulse I hated but loved so much when he was inside me. "Scoot forward."

I did so without hesitation and ground my jaw harder after I had done so. *You're not supposed to obey him,* I told myself, but my body had different plans.

He stepped into the tub and sat behind me. Before I could scramble to the other side, he wrapped his arm around my waist and pulled me between his legs. His cock was already hard and pressed against my lower spine. I shivered involuntarily. I wanted to shed my wet clothes from my body and feel his skin against mine, but I wouldn't give him the satisfaction.

"Relax," he ordered.

"No."

"Should I make you?"

I knew what he meant. There was only one thing that made me weak and it was his touch. I couldn't take his touch and not want to give in, so I leaned back against his chest. My head was cradled on his shoulder, and I tried not to think about how good it felt. As we watched each other silently, his thumb brushed my lip briefly before sliding down to grip my neck. I knew it was a warning when his other hand rose out of the water and began to tease the edge of my panties and the skin of my lower stomach. "Take them off."

"Why?" The single word trembled on my lips as my hands itched to obey.

"Don't worry," he sneered and gripped my neck tighter, threatening my air supply. "The water will hide how wet you really are for me."

I elbowed him in the stomach, and other than a grunt of pain, he stayed perfectly still, watching me and waiting for me to obey.

"Fine."

I hooked my fingers in my panties and pulled them down slowly to aggravate him. The deep chuckle near my ear told me he had noticed, but it didn't hit its mark. I expected him to issue out some scathing remark or to punish me with his high-handedness, but instead, he lifted my sponge from its hook and squirted body wash on it.

"What are you doing?" I snapped. It came out a little harsher than necessary, but I was a little on edge. It was becoming a natural state for me. His hand had paused above my breast for a small space of time before he began bathing me.

"Are you trying to piss me off?"

FEAR YOU

"Is it working?"

"You can say that, however, the end result might not be what you had hoped."

"You know nothing about my hopes."

"Maybe not," he whispered low in my ear as he skimmed a finger across my puckered nipple, "but I know you."

"It would be kind of hard not to since you made me who I used to be."

"Used to be?"

"I'm not afraid of you anymore, Keiran." I didn't miss the brief way his hand froze from rubbing small, soapy circles over my stomach.

"Oh?"

"Are you surprised?" I stretched my neck to see his face, not wanting to miss his reaction, but his expression was as closed off as normal. I knew he cared or else he wouldn't be here. He once told me he needed the control he had over me and would do anything in his power to keep it. So what was I doing?

"I can't say I am too surprised considering the reason I've been locked up the past two and a half weeks."

"I hope you didn't come for an apology."

"I came for much more than that."

"I'm not going to sleep with you."

"You will if I want you to, and I do want you to, Monroe. So how do I get you to say yes?"

"I've never said yes."

"But you have. When I seduced you, when I was inside of you, when I asked you if you needed more..."

"Semantics."

He laughed again, and I couldn't help but smile at the rare sound. "You're really adorable when you get like this."

"Adorable isn't—" A shocked gasp escaped my lips

P a g e | **80**

when he dipped the sponge beneath the water and skimmed it between my thighs.

"This reckless behavior of yours is only going to be a major disappointment on your part. You see, I have no intention of letting you go again. I tried, Monroe, and do you know what you did?" He continued to use the rough material of the sponge to stimulate my clit as he growled his words in my ear. I began writhing against him, seeking more and at the same time, wishing I could end the feelings he was stirring within me. "You sucked me back in. Was it on purpose? Did you turn me in because I let you go? Were you getting your revenge?"

"I turned you in because—" My screech of pain when he wrapped his hand around my throat and squeezed cut off my remark. He never ceased caressing me with my sponge.

"You know how I feel about your lies, so fucking tell me it was for those two scumbags. I dare you." He let go of my neck but continued to torture me. "You did it because I hurt you. I hurt you worse than I ever have when I let you go. If I wasn't so angry, I would say I was impressed."

"Keiran, you killed—"

"Let's play a game of don't talk until I tell you to."

"Bite me," I spat. I didn't intend for him to take me so literally.

His teeth sunk down on my cheek and wouldn't let go no matter how much I begged and cried. The pulsing between my legs increased as he continued to use the sponge against me.

"Keiran, please. You're hurting me."

"I want to fucking hurt you," he said when he released my cheek. "I want to hurt you and make you scream."

"Oh, God."

"Just let go."

"I can't," I whimpered.

"You will. Come for me."

"Keiran, please don't do this to me." I pressed against his hand, creating waves in the water around us.

"Should I give you my dick instead?"

Yes, please.

When he started to lift his hand, I panicked and grabbed onto him, keeping him there. Together, we stroked me to a volcanic release that had to be the most intense orgasm I'd ever experienced though, with him, it was always intense.

As I caught my breath, he kissed the spot where his teeth had undoubtedly left marks, and I wondered how I could possibly explain it to my aunt when she returned.

"Now that you've stroked your ego, you can go," I stated in a dismissive tone. "If that's all you had to say, you wasted your time."

I was up and out of the tub before he could respond and made a dash for the door. I needed to get to my bedroom. Locking him out would do no good, but I had something better.

Two can play this game.

I completely forgot about my naked state and ignored the chill bumps that covered my skin by the time I entered my bedroom. Wasting no time, I whipped open the top drawer of my desk, pulled out my purchase from earlier, and waited for him to come after me.

I didn't have to wait long.

CHAPTER EIGHT

KEIRAN

I WAS STARTING to believe cat and mouse was Monroe's favorite game. She never missed an opportunity to run from me even though I would always catch her. When she ran from the bathroom like a bat out of hell, I fought the urge to laugh. She did exactly as I expected her to and was pleased to find she didn't disappoint. I ignored the urge to chase after her.

Instead, I picked up the sponge I had just used to make her come and took a quick bath. I wasn't one to take leisurely baths in garden tubs with bubbles and shit, but I did it to mess with her head. It was also an excuse to get close to her and touch her as I had been itching to do since the last time. It seemed too fucking long ago.

I gave Monroe enough time to find her hiding spot before stepping out of the tub. After a quick towel dry, I stalked out of the bathroom in search of my prey. I didn't have to search hard. The noise coming from her bedroom let me know where she had disappeared to and that she wasn't hiding. Her bedroom door was open, and when I stepped in the doorway, my heart actually skipped a beat.

Son of a bitch.

Legs spread, feet planted, arms extended, and with a determined look in her eye, Monroe held a gun that was pointed straight at my heart.

"What is this," I asked, attempting casualness. I wasn't afraid. In fact, I felt quite the opposite. My dick had never been harder.

"I want you to leave and never come back."

"Or you'll shoot me?" I took a step inside the room and closed the door behind me. Confusion appeared on her face when I moved closer. It wasn't the reaction she expected.

"That would be why I have a gun pointed at you." The hard edge in her voice faltered, but only for a moment.

"Why a gun? Why not call the cops?"

"So you can get out of it and come after someone else I love? Forgive me, but I don't have much faith in our justice system anymore. The penal system sucks."

"So why not just kill me?"

"Are you seriously going to tempt the person with the gun?"

"I'm thinking I should call your bluff."

"That would be stupid. Leave and don't come back. Whether I put you away or kill you, I will not let you hurt me again."

"Why the change of heart?"

It was the picture of a dam breaking as large tears rolled down her face and her hand began to tremble. "Because," she sobbed. "Because I'm done surviving you. That girl is gone," she screamed.

"So who is standing in front of me?"

"The girl who will fight you even if it takes her last breath."

"Then why are you crying, baby?" I took another step toward her, but she didn't seem to notice.

"Don't... don't call me that, Keiran. Please don't call me that. You're just trying to mind fuck me."

She wasn't completely wrong, but she wasn't entirely right either.

"You'll always be mine, Lake." I took another step. "You can use a gun..." Another step. "You can use a knife..." *Just a little closer.* "You can fucking kill me, but you'll always be mine."

By the end of my little speech, my chest was pressed against the gun, and I felt her fear. I lifted my hand slowly and flipped the safety off. Her small gasp of breath blew across my neck, and I felt my dick stiffen.

"So shoot me."

Her arm whipped out faster than I've ever seen her move. The butt of the gun slapped brutally across my lip, and I could instantly recognize the metallic taste of blood.

She hit me.

She fucking hit me.

The expression on her face told me she was just as surprised as I was, but she recovered quickly and tipped her righteous chin at me in a challenge.

Fuck. Me.

"You're going to regret that."

"Somehow I doubt that. What I can't seem to figure out is why you're still here."

"You fucking hit me." I thumbed at the moist spot on my lip and peered down to see a bright speck of red coating the tip of my thumb.

"Are you going to cry about it?"

"Monroe," I started but stopped and took a few

deep breaths. I was having a hard time controlling whatever the hell was pushing against the surface for a taste of her. Whatever I was feeling, she must have seen when her expression became fearful, and she took a step back. "Have I ever hit you?"

"N—no."

I snatched her by her shirt and brought her chest to mesh with mine.

"Then you don't hit me."

I felt my teeth grind against each other and practically felt the grit in my voice as I spoke to her. I could tell myself I was mad because she hit me. That maybe I was even mad because she shed my blood. But no, I knew why I was really upset. Doesn't she know who I am and what I am capable of doing? What if I had been someone else? Someone wouldn't hesitate to hurt her.

She held the gun in her hands, and she mistakenly believed it made her strong when it only made her much more vulnerable. She wasn't ready to use the gun, and I didn't mean on a physical level. Mentally, she was still too protected by her innocence. Someone more depraved than me would have killed her with her own gun by now.

"It's just a little bloodshed," she mocked. Her body betrayed her as I felt her quake and listened to the uneven rhythm of her breathing.

"Are you nervous?" I fought the smile tugging at the corner of my lip.

"In your dreams."

"You have no idea what I dream about."

"Dead little girls and the other people you murdered?"

Her back had hit the wall with a violent crash, and I was on her before I could waste time to regret my next move.

I was going to own this girl.

I braced the back of my arms against the wall and leaned down, bringing our faces close together. It was the closest I was willing to allow myself. I didn't dare touch her again. Not now. My demon was raging a war against my will power and was calling me to hurt her, to give her the bite of pain she reserved to like only during sex.

The gun in her hand hung almost limp as if she'd forgotten that it was even there but the fight was still in her eyes.

Everyone, including me, was still waiting around for her to change, but instead of wanting to build her up, I wanted to tear her down, to bare the deepest part of her soul, and to taint it.

"You have no idea of the things I've done. What I told you was filler, nothing more. My secrets are far more sinister than you can handle, Monroe. I can drag you into that world. I can make you a person who never has to worry about fear again."

"There's more?"

"There's always more."

"Just get away from me," she bit out.

I grinned down at her but didn't budge. If she thinks I would leave without my goodbye kiss, she has another thing coming.

"No."

"If you're going to kill me for putting you away, then do it. All this nauseating foreplay is boring me."

"Nauseating, huh? Boring?"

Before she could respond, I stole her lips with mine in a hard kiss as I shared my leftover blood with her and did my best to bruise her.

"You have no fucking clue what you do to me, do you?" I asked when I finally allowed her air to breathe.

Her lips were stained in crimson red, and there were little bite marks from where I had bit her. Nice. I couldn't explain the unspoken need to mark her, but it felt right.

She was breathing hard as if she'd just run a race. I think the sappy love stories would say 'I stole her breath away.'

"I told you not to touch me," she panted.

"And yet here I am."

She hadn't realized I had taken the gun from her, flipped the safety on, and stuck it in my jeans. My hands itched to touch her, but I braced them against the wall again and watched her squirm under my gaze.

"I hate you."

"You don't hate me." I lowered my lips to her neck and licked the spot where her pulse was beating faster than usual. "You hate that you can't."

"I should say the same to you." I heard the angry bite in her voice and smiled.

"You're right. I don't hate you, Monroe. Not any-more. I'm obsessed with you," I admitted.

"Why do I get the feeling that is much worse?" she whispered woefully. I lifted my head to meet her eyes, and I could see the question and the fear. "Why are you here, Keiran?"

"I told you I needed to see..."

"Me?" she whimpered.

"Yes."

"You needed to see if I was still afraid?"

She now had a faraway look in her eyes, and I experienced the unfamiliar, yet intense need to hold her and protect her from the world, but most of all from me.

I remember the first time I felt a similar need.

I had just come back from a summer at basketball camp. Instead of fun, it had been grueling and a waste. I got into countless fights, many of which I started and stayed pissed practically the entire time. It was the first time I'd been away from Monroe for so long. The school year began, and I saw her walking down the hall the first day of school. She looked so beautiful. She was different now, too. I couldn't put my finger on it, but there was a more womanly quality about her. I had reached out to caress her face as if it were the most natural thing to do. It was her flinch that brought reality crashing down on my shoulders, and I quickly recovered by slapping her books out of her hand. I had to force my feet to keep moving and fight the urge to look back.

It wasn't until I had her for the first time that I realized the petty shit I had done to her gave me only a false sense of satisfaction. Making her fear me was only half the battle. I needed to make her want me, too.

"Yes," I lied. I didn't give a damn about her fear anymore, but I would lie if I said I didn't still want to control her.

"Well, then I'm sorry to disappoint you."

"You didn't." I shrugged and moved away to sit on her bed. I needed the space just as much as she did. At this point, it wouldn't take much for me to fuck her right there against the wall. It would be hard and unapologetic. I would make her want it, and then I would make her cry before leaving her like always.

"I'm not afraid of you anymore."

"So you said." The murderous glint in her eye, and then the way she stared down at her hand in shock as she finally realized her gun was gone, told me what she was thinking. "I took it from you while I kissed you, silly."

"Give it back."

"Why did you get a gun?" I didn't try to hide my smugness. I wanted her to know I was aware of my effect on her.

"Do you really have to ask? Between you and your sick, crazy father, I felt it was more than necessary. When I think about what he did to Keenan, I—" She snapped her mouth closed and regarded me with a worried expression. "Have you gone to see him yet?" she whispered.

The change in subject took me by surprise but I hid it well. I even found myself nodding. "He's awake now," I volunteered.

"I know. Sheldon told me a few days ago. How is he?"

"He isn't the same." We stared at each other for long moments as she tried to interpret my meaning. The deep frown marring her forehead only deepened before suddenly clearing.

"Keiran, I have to know..." She closed her eyes and took a deep breath. "Why did you kill her? Before you said you didn't believe she was innocent but there has to be more."

"Why would you think there was more?"

"Because I don't believe you kill for the hell of it."

"You don't know me beyond my cock, Monroe. Don't pretend otherwise."

"Even a closed book can tell a story."

"Yeah, well, mine is no fairytale."

"And your mother? What about her story?"

She's still on that? Her persistence in learning more about Sophia's death was something I could use to my advantage. "What are you willing to do for the answer?"

"Come again?"

"You can have your answer if you give me something I want."

"Such as?"

"You. Tonight. Right here and now."

"Not happening."

"Not even if I promise to fuck you hard and long?" I almost grinned at the way she squirmed and the way her mouth dropped open. Her body had already said yes, but her mind had yet to catch up.

"You make such a compelling argument," she quipped.

"You're the one standing here as naked as the day you were born. You know how much I appreciate easy access."

"Screw you. I don't want the answers that bad." She stomped over to her dresser and with angry, jerky movements, pulled out a pair of sweats and a shirt.

"Should I take that as a no?"

"You bet your ass," she snapped.

I rose from the bed to stalk toward her, wearing what I knew was an intimidating expression. While a part of me liked her new defiance, the other half wasn't willing to give up control. The last thing I needed was for her to think she was free from me. I backed her up until the back of her thighs touched the dresser and then lifted her to sit on the polished top and held her there.

"Your desperate attempt to be someone you're not is only giving me the ammunition I need to have you at my feet begging for my mercy."

I took her chin gently in my hand and lifted her face, forcing her to witness the cold manipulation calculating in my eyes.

"You remember what that's like, don't you?" A whisper, and then a soft kiss was unexpectedly pressed against her lips. "Only this time, I won't need to coerce you, force you, or threaten you. You'll do it for me, baby. Just like you always have."

* * *

I NEVER THOUGHT I'd walk these halls again. Sometimes I thought even I could be a bit dramatic, but the way my already fucked up existence had been spinning on its axis, I was deserving of a few dramatic moments.

The weekend was the longest of my life. It took everything in me to stay away from Monroe. I spent my days dodging Arthur, Mario, and John, while sneaking in and out of the hospital to see Keenan while he was asleep. Not to mention, my unsuccessful search for Mitch in between. For a greedy fuck, he was great at hiding. I guess years of borrowing money from dangerous sources, and failing to pay back what's due, afforded you particular skills.

"How's it hanging, man?" Dash greeted as he walked through the front entrance where I was hanging. It was a little early, but I wanted to beat Monroe at her own game. I wanted to know the exact moment when she walked through these doors.

"A little lower and a little to the right..." I stopped short when I realized what I was saying. That was usually Keenan's line and a standing joke between the two of them. I scowled at Dash, who only smirked at me, unfazed by my anger.

"I miss him, too," Dash offered.

"What the fuck are you doing, Dash?"

"Not pretending he's already dead," he barked.

"Fuck off. I'm not in the mood for your shit."

"You need to talk to him. You sneak in and out of his hospital room trying to protect him, and yet you haven't spoken one word to him."

"How about I put one in your mother's head and see if you would be ready to engage me in conversation."

I never saw the blow to my face coming. Hell, I could barely see after his fist impacted with my face, snapping my neck to the right. "Too fucking far," Dash gritted.

I didn't apologize. I wouldn't. He knew that, so I let him have his pound of flesh without retaliating.

"I don't know what went on in your fucking past, but at some point, you are going to have to man the fuck up and leave it in the past. It's getting old, man. It's getting real old. Whoever they made you to be doesn't have to survive."

Usually, I didn't give a shit what someone thought or the invaluable shit they had to say, but he always knew where to strike.

I straightened from the wall and met his eyes, matching his stance. It wasn't about who the bigger man was. I just needed to see the truth in his eyes.

"How many people have you been forced to kill including your own fucking mother? How many days have you starved? How many nightmares have you had? How many people have you been forced to fuck as a child?"

"None," he answered in a hard tone. Dash was a hard person to shake. It was one of the reasons why I respected him the most even though I had a shitty way of showing it.

"So, if you ever have to do even *one* of those things, *then* you can let me know when it gets old."

"That was ten years ago, Keiran. If you want to continue to live your life as if you are still someone's fucking slave, then do so. You're capable of making your own choices. I'm only allowed to care about you, but at some point, you have to stop inflicting your own personal form of punishment on the people close to you."

He stalked off and disappeared down the hall.

Dash never usually called me out on my shit, but when he did, it only served to make me angrier. Self-righteous asses like him were what made me hold on tighter to who I was. I gave up on trying to be good a long time ago. It was a hopeless pursuit for people who weren't born with it. Arthur was the one to teach me that the first time I met him...

I felt like I had bathed in blood. My face, hair, and hands were covered in it, but it didn't belong to me. The bound, nameless man, whose throat I just cut open, stared up at me with lifeless eyes. Each time I took someone's life, I would start to feel guilt, and each time, I beat it down. It had been a year now since I made my first kill. I was still considered in 'training', as they called it, because of my age and size. Frank said I wouldn't be ready to be on my own until I was far older, and this was just a mere introduction.

It already felt so very real.

The beginning had been rocky, and I suffered countless beatings. I could never understand what they wanted me to do. Sometimes, even now, it was a little hard to understand. I would do what they ordered me to do when they ordered me to do it.

I didn't dare tell them about the nightmares. They would see it as a weakness and beat me for it.

I was learning, they called it. I was progressing. I saw kids far away who lived a different life. Sometimes I wondered what that life was like. I would learn about it when they brought in new kids. They would often talk about their parents, siblings, and home. It made me wonder about this life. Was there something better? Didn't everyone live like this?

"Good job, son. You show much promise."

An unknown man stepped out of the shadows

dressed in a shiny suit. I took in his clean appearance, and the way everyone seemed to snap to attention when he made his presence known and figured he must have been the boss Frank spoke about often.

"Sir?"

"You see that?" he pointed to the dead man who was bleeding out on the floor. "Good people have no place in this world so we must eradicate them. Only the strongest survive, and to be strong, you have to be ruthless and prey on the weak. Do you understand?"

I nodded that I did even though I didn't. I would ask one of the older kids later.

"You did a good thing here. This man was a rat. He was a disease that had to be cut off before it could spread, and you did that. What is your name, little one?"

"He doesn't have one," Frank spoke up. "We just call him slave."

"Even better," the man grinned, evilly. "I've heard quite a bit about you. You're smarter than the rest and willing to work, is what they tell me. Tell me... how do you like our line of business?"

* * *

"MR. MASTERS, YOU'RE late. I expected you thirty minutes ago," Mrs. Gilmore admonished when I stepped foot inside her office. I'd waited for Monroe well past the first bell for class, but she never showed. I sent a quick text to her and told myself I wasn't worried. I was annoyed that she denied me my morning fix by not showing up.

"Well, I'm here now so say what you have to say and let's get this shit over with," I snapped.

I normally wasn't rude to the school staff, but my

patience was long gone. Monroe's absence was just the thing to send me over the edge.

"All right. You won't have a future at the rate you're going this year. When college is no longer an option so is basketball. Lucky for you, you've been a somewhat of an outstanding student these past three years... academically. You've been jailed twice already, and you are looking to fail another year if you don't button up. So far, your future is promising if you are looking to pursue a career in the penitentiary. If that is what you want, then a high school diploma isn't what you need and you are wasting my time. I realize you have a lot going on considering the tragic accident with your cousin—"

"My brother," I snarled.

"Excuse me?" She stared at me with shock etched on her face.

"He's my fucking brother. If you are going to talk about my family as if you have a fucking clue, then speak correctly. He's my brother."

"Well, I—"

"Never mind all that. Continue. You were telling me how I'm a waste without a future."

It took her a few moments to pick her face up before she spoke. "Yes, well, not in exactly *those* words, Mr. Masters. What I am trying to say is you are a smart young man and a leader. Whether you know it or not, there are people who look to you. Is this the kind of example you want to set for your peers?"

What the hell was up with people telling me what I needed to do today? "Well, then, I'd say they have a bad judge of character, and it should be them you need to speak to."

"Nevertheless, you are on your last strike. There are no more chances, Mr. Masters. I suggest you heed this warning. You may go."

I didn't waste any time leaving her office. After her condescending speech, I had half a mind to skip, but that would just be petty. My phone vibrated in my jeans, and I quickly fished it out.

As I recall, my whereabouts are NONE OF YOUR BUSINESS. Kindly fuck off.

I smiled and pocketed my phone without replying. Monroe continued to dig her hole and I let her. When she finally realizes she's dug too deep, she'll be too far in to escape. It didn't stop me from going after her though. I still needed to feed my addiction. It was time to change classes, and so it took me a little longer than I liked as I tried to dodge the unwanted attention and ignore the wary looks from some of the other students. I wasn't surprised most of them had heard by now how I was suspected of Trevor and Anya's murder. I was almost sorry I wasn't the one to do it.

Trevor and his father were planning to lock Monroe away in their basement like a fucking dog and use her in ways she would never survive. Thinking about it had me wanting to bring that motherfucker to life so I could kill him myself. I almost didn't believe the shit they were planning to do. Not until I did a quick inspection of their house while they were gone which showed me everything I needed to know. They had a mattress pushed in the corner and a chain mounted to the wall to imprison her. Trevor never had any intentions of delivering her to my father. His father wanted revenge against me for convincing his wife to leave his abusive ass. Turns out, his mother wanted to leave years ago but couldn't escape. She'd been beaten and raped by both father and son for years.

I don't know what made me help her. To be honest,

FEAR YOU

I couldn't stand Trevor. I never could. Maybe I did it to hurt him. His mother was able to leave with my assistance and never looked back, not even when he was murdered. I hadn't heard a peep out of his father since he lost his job. He was still on my to-do list because no way was that sick fuck walking away. I wouldn't even give him the option to waste himself away by drowning in booze. For Monroe, he will answer to the grim reaper.

I finally caught up to Monroe just before she disappeared in the gym. She must have sensed me because she whipped around and her eyes immediately landed on me.

She rolled her eyes and crossed her arms over her chest, unknowingly pushing her breasts up. "You just don't know when to quit, do you?"

I didn't bother to respond as I walked up on her, grabbed her by her delectable throat, and backed her into the gym doors. "I realize you haven't been owned by me for a while. Believe me, baby. I know it's been a while—too fucking long, but this shit right here," I bit her lip and looked deep into her eyes, "will get you into a lot of fucking trouble. Quit acting up."

"What am I? Your two-year-old?"

"You sure as fuck are acting like it, but I don't fuck children, so if you keep it up, you'll never get back into my pants."

She rolled her eyes. "Woe is me."

"There's that mouth again."

"So what are you going to do ab—"

My lips slamming down on hers cut off the smart remark that would surely get her fucked right against these doors for all to see. There was no way I would let anyone see, though. The hounds were always lurking and ready to sniff around my girl. It was a full-time job

beating them away for the last few years and making sure she was none the wiser. The need to possess was even worse now because I had her, and there was *no one* who fucked like Monroe. No one.

"I don't hear you." I kissed and bit down on her bottom lip. She still sported some of the bruising from Friday. I almost grinned when I thought of how she might have explained it to her dear aunt. "Let me hear you say something smart."

"Something smart," she whispered and met my eyes challengingly.

Such a fucking handful. Little bitch.

I flipped her around to face the wall and smacked her ass drawing out a shocked squeal from her. The button of her jeans flicked open with my fingers and I worked my leg in between hers, pushing her legs apart. "One might think you want me to fuck you... Is that it? Are you purposely trying to piss me off?"

"Keiran, we're in a hallway in our school!"

"And yet you keep pushing your ass on my dick." My hand slid down her pants and cupped her through her panties. Her heat was scorching. I could barely concentrate on what I had come to do. Generally, when I would seek her out for my fix, I would try to humiliate or scare her, but we were playing a different game now. One that affected me just as much as her. *Go fucking figure.*

"So you think I'm going to just let you fuck me right here?"

"I don't think that's an answer you really want. Besides, I can feel how wet you are. I wouldn't need to persuade you."

"My body's betrayal doesn't change the fact that I despise you."

My finger slipped inside her panties and entered

her heat causing her to lose her breath and grab the wall as an anchor for support. "You feel that?" I asked and added another finger. "The fact that you despise me doesn't change the way your body betrays you. I could fuck you right here, and you would take it because you want it, and you would love it."

"What makes you so sure I would love it?" The rhythm of my fingers increased their tempo, making her whimper and beg. *Music to my ears.*

"Tell me yes, and I will show you."

"Not here."

"Fuck." I was already searching my head for places to drag her off too when we were interrupted.

"Mr. Masters, the bell has already sounded for class... What on Earth are you doing?"

"Oh, my God," Monroe squeaked. She frantically ripped my hands away, and I cursed the loss of her body. I waited until she fixed her clothing before moving away.

"Miss Monroe," Principal Lawrence acknowledged disapprovingly. "Don't you have class?"

"Yes, um, sorry." She shot me a murderous glare before disappearing inside the gym.

"As I recall, you were ordered not to approach Lake Monroe. Is there any particular reason why you are violating that agreement?"

"None of it concerns you."

I walked off leaving her baffled. I was pissed that once again, Monroe managed to slip through my fingers.

CHAPTER NINE

LAKE

"CAN YOU BELIEVE that prick?" For most of gym, and after in the locker room, I ranted and raved over Keiran's latest stunt. To be honest, I wasn't sure how to react when he approached me in the hallway. In the past, whenever we were in the same vicinity together, as briefly as it may last, I would try to make myself as invisible as possible. But when I saw the unmistakable heat in his eyes, I was frozen to the spot. All I could do was to hope I could survive another encounter unscathed. .

"It sounds to me like you were enjoying yourself just as much as he was."

I turned on Willow and planted my fists on my hips. "Whose side are you on?"

"I'm on yours. I'll always be on your side, but you have to decide whether you are going to hate him or fuck him. Apparently, the two don't mix well together."

Oh, how wrong she was. "This isn't just some run of the mill romance or school rivalry. He threatened to kill my aunt and to leave my best friend," I indicated her for emphasis, "heartbroken."

"And yet, despite all that, you still want him. Look," she took a deep breath and released. "I've gotten over it."

"No, you just blame Dash. You're still angry too, Willow."

"Are we here to talk about you, or are we here to talk about me?" she snapped, defensively. That was my cue to bow out, but instead, I continued to stand with her, holding her stare. It seemed neither of us would back down until she sighed and asked, "Do you realize we almost never argued before them?"

There wasn't a time I could remember ever arguing with Willow. The biggest disagreement we'd ever had was choosing a movie or pepperoni over sausage, and even then, we'd compromise. We'd spend all night at the movies to please each other and order a specialty pizza because neither of us was willing to see the other unhappy.

But I couldn't deny how something had changed for us these past few months. I only hoped our friendship would survive it.

"Forget about it. Let's just go to lunch and hope they have something half decent or edible." We finished dressing in silence and met Sheldon outside of the cafeteria. I could immediately tell something was wrong from her sunken expression.

"Sheldon, are you okay?" I asked as I took in her wrinkled clothing and unkempt hair. She looked as if she'd rolled out of bed and gotten into a fight with a bull.

"I received a message from Keenan this morning." She opened her mouth to say more, but it all seemed to disappear as she silently choked with tears. I placed a soothing hand on her back, which seemed to calm her. "I've never heard him speak to me like that. He sounded so cold and distant."

"What did he say?"

"Not much. He basically called me a cold, heartless bitch and let me know, in no uncertain terms, he hated my guts."

So much like his brother. It was a wonder no one picked up on the similarities before.

"So I take it you still haven't gone to see him?" Willow questioned. She wore a sympathetic expression, but I knew she didn't approve. She believed just as much as I did that Sheldon should have gone to visit him once more if only to soften the blow. Likewise, I could understand how the emotional turmoil seeing him in his state combined with the broken heart he left her with could make her keep her distance.

"I know what you guys are thinking, but I don't know if I can do this." Her broken whimper pierced my heart, and I glared at Willow, who shrugged her apology. "My heart is crying out for him, but I know I can't go back and now he—he..." She choked on her words again and began to cry. "He hates me," she whispered.

"Sheldon, you can't blame yourself for his mistakes, and it certainly isn't your fault his family is screwed up."

Namely Mitch.

"I know I didn't do anything wrong. I just remember how much he hurt me over the years with his constant cheating and reckless behavior, and I remember all too vividly the pain. I never wanted to hurt him as much as he hurt me, and it just kills me knowing he's all alone."

"But he has his father," Willow pointed out. "Surely, he would be here for him after everything."

"His father is just as screwed up over his mother's

death as Keenan is. Can you imagine believing all your life the one person who is supposed to love you walked out on you just to find out later they've been dead this entire time?"

I knew Sheldon wasn't directing her question at either of us in particular, but it nearly wrecked me just the same.

"Mom, how do I just tell her that her parents didn't abandon her? They didn't just die. They were murdered."

Thankfully, Sheldon continued to speak, keeping me from falling further into the black abyss that was my parents.

"He told me once that he could never understand a mother's ability to leave her own child. We were watching one of those television dramas on Lifetime, but I knew his mother was the reason he felt so strongly about it. It doesn't help that his dad is barely in his life and hasn't been for a long time."

"Do you think he has abandonment issues?" I asked.

"I don't know. Maybe. Whatever his issues, I know it's because of his parents."

"Don't you girls ever get tired of gossiping?" Buddy interrupted as he approached with his arm thrown around a blonde girl, who I was pretty sure was in my English class. I often caught her sending Keiran sultry looks, all of which he always ignored. "Doors are for walking through not blocking."

"Buddy, you are the biggest gossip queen there is," Willow scolded.

"Hey, hey, hey. I like to gossip just as much as the next man, but I'm no queen."

I laughed when I took in his grave expression. He looked as if we seriously offended him, which only proved that Buddy really could be a drama queen.

"Come on guys, we should go to lunch." I pushed open one of the doors letting Buddy and his latest lay in, followed by Willow, but when Sheldon continued to stand and stare off into the distance, I let the door close.

Even from her profile, I could see the darkening circles around her eyes and the weight she had lost.

Has she not been eating or sleeping?

Sheldon was never someone to skip a meal, so if that was the case, I knew this was more than a simple case of the high school breakup blues. I made a mental note to talk to Dash. If anyone could get through to her, it would be him. They were more than brother and sister. They were best friends.

"Sheldon?"

The sound of her name snapped her out of her trance, and when her eyes met mine, she seemed to look straight through me. My throat tightened painfully. I couldn't stand to see her as a ghost of the girl she was. Five months ago, I never thought I would come to care so much for her or anyone else.

"I think I'm going to go."

"Go? Go where, Sheldon? Please come inside. You need to eat."

Her amber colored eyes hardened and pinned me to the spot. "Sometimes it's not that easy. Eating won't change the fact I left him alone to die."

She was gone before I could take my foot out of my mouth.

* * *

Thank God for tests.

Tests weren't what people made them to be. Tests were a means of escape.

At least it was supposed to be.

If I didn't already, I definitely hated fifth period now. Every shift, shuffle, and cough in the silent room had me ready to bolt.

As a result of my recent adventures, I needed to ace every assignment for the rest of the year to avoid having to endure summer school in order to graduate. My attention should have been on graduation and the test in front of me, but professional development and the importance of social responsibility were the least of my concerns.

Every hair on my body was raised and goose bumps traveled every inch of my too warm skin.

I had been stuck on question three for the last fifteen minutes with only sixty minutes to go, and while I should have known the answer, I couldn't concentrate long enough to comprehend the question. An hour would have been more than enough time if my focus weren't on the mercurial boy at the back of the class. At this rate, I would never finish in time.

Which of the following statements are true?

A. CSR stands for Corporate Social Responsibility

B. Keiran is going to hurt you.

C. CSR applies to large and small businesses.

D. All of the above.

I circled the last and moved on, but instead of reading the question, I abruptly turned and sought out Keiran at the back of the class. I couldn't take it anymore. The temptation was too great.

My gaze zeroed in on his dark head bent in perfect concentration. I watched his large hand grip the thin yellow pencil as he scribbled his answers.

The weight on my chest lifted, but my heart constricted now that I knew he wasn't watching me.

As if sensing I was watching him, I was suddenly

met with stormy gray eyes that shifted and changed as they assessed me. A sly smile slowly appeared, and I realized too late that his lips were moving.

"Mr. Lawson, could you explain this question to me?"

Keiran was fully grinning by the time I realized he'd led me into a trap. It was too late to pretend nothing had happened. I was caught.

"Miss Monroe. Eyes on your own test. I will not tolerate cheating," Mr. Lawson scolded while making his way to the back of the classroom.

Subtle snickers echoed around me, fueling my embarrassment.

I swiftly turned in my chair, swaying slightly and feeling my cheeks heat. I forced myself to work through the test I had spent all night studying for, and by the time the bell rang, I was putting the finishing touches on the last question. I hadn't noticed Willow and Sheldon had left with the rest of the crowd, and when I finally looked up, Keiran was in front of my seat with his back turned to me.

"Piece of cake, Mr. Lawson." I narrowed my eyes at his back. "Shame about those cheaters." He turned suddenly and winked at me before leaving.

I was tempted to hurl my entire sack of books at his head when an idea occurred to me.

Cheaters, huh?

The day Trevor and Anya were announced dead, I made a vow to see Keiran in prison once and for all. Until I was able to make good on my promise, I could resort to petty revenge to hold me over.

I grabbed my test and backpack and practically jumped across the table to reach Mr. Lawson's desk. He shot me a disapproving look as he took my test.

"You know, Ms. Monroe, I'm surprised by you."

"What do you mean?" My face immediately fell and my plans for sabotage faded into the background.

"You were always considered a model student and well respected among the staff. Your potential to do well in the world has always been measured highly. However, over the last few weeks, it has severely plummeted."

"I, I—"

"Senior year is hardly the time to lose focus, young lady, no matter the motivation."

"But, sir, I—"

"There is no excuse. If kids like Keiran Masters can turn themselves around, there is no reason you can't continue to uphold yourself in a way that is beneficial to your future."

Keiran? Turn himself around? Did Mr. Lawson and everyone else forget he was the very person on trial for a double murder? I wanted to scream at the man and remind him I wasn't the one who torched two people alive. I wasn't the monster, but yet Keiran was still being viewed as the golden boy?

"Mr. Lawson, speaking of Keiran Masters, I overheard him mention his intention to use a cheat sheet for the test. I think, as a *model student and a person who takes social responsibility seriously,* I should let you know."

I managed to hide the bitterness I felt from his unwanted judgment with a sugary sweet tone matched with an expression that screamed concerned student. His words actually stung but only because they were true.

"What? Are your absolutely sure about this?"

I ignored the suspicious look he cast me and nodded my confirmation. I wanted to break out into a hysterical fit and unleash on the world the same cruelty it wreaked on me.

"Thank you, Miss Monroe. I'll look into it." He bent his head to study the test papers in front of him, dismissively.

I took my cue and left. As far as I was concerned, my job was done.

CHAPTER TEN

KEIRAN

I STRUGGLED WITH the decision to wait around for Monroe, but when she didn't leave class immediately after me, I figured she was hiding. My feet reluctantly carried me away from the classroom after I reminded myself there were too many prying eyes, and I was still barred access from her.

When I reached the doors, I braced myself for the frigid air that would greet me and pushed through them. As much as I didn't like the cold, I embraced it. It kept me rooted in the past so I didn't waste time hoping for a future that wasn't meant for people like me.

"And to let him back in the school, no less. It's preposterous! What about the other students? Why isn't he deemed a danger to them?"

"Ma'am. Keiran Masters is out on bail and has not been convicted of a crime. Therefore, he cannot be kept from schooling."

I heard the hushed murmurs of what I assumed to be bystanders, and when I cleared the corner leading to the parking lot, my suspicions were confirmed.

Silence fell over the parking lot as soon as I was spotted. Realizing the attention of her audience had been diverted, the socialite turned her angry gaze on me. I didn't react when she charged forward and I stood in place to watch her approach.

"You son of a bitch!"

"Mrs. Ridell, you must calm down or else we will have to restrain you," the officer admonished with a bored tone while desperately attempting to hold back the enraged woman. I wondered if he was trying to protect the woman or me. I would have laughed if there hadn't been such a large audience. The last thing I needed was people thinking I thought Anya and Trevor's death was funny. Not that I gave a shit what people thought, but it wouldn't exactly help my case to be seen openly mocking their murders. It also didn't help that it made national fucking news, and I was front and center. Word had gotten out about Keenan's injuries, and so the newspapers were desperately attempting to connect the two incidents.

"Restrain *me*?" She fought against the officer's grip. "Who let this *monster* out of jail? I want him put back or so help me—"

I tamped down the fury I felt boiling up inside and bit the inside of my cheek. I refused to show emotion. It wasn't the first time I was called a monster, but the familiarity didn't soften the blow any.

"How could they let him free? He burned my daughter alive. What sort of animal does that?" Spit flew from her mouth as she glared at me with a murderous rage that could rival my own.

The officer shot me with a silent order to leave, and I took the opportunity without hesitation. There was nothing I could do to help the situation. No amount of pleading my case would amount to anything. The truth was I didn't really care to. I wasn't sorry they were dead. I was very aware of the fact I could still go to prison very soon.

"I have proof he killed my daughter! They all did! I want them jailed!"

I stopped in my tracks against my will and felt the first crack in my mask while struggling to keep my breathing even. On the outside, I was a perfect model of indifference, but inside, I was crumbling.

"You will burn in hell for what you all did to my daughter, and you will finally feel what she felt when you burned her body alive!"

The sound of her shrieking, deranged voice followed me and bounced off my back, which I kept ramrod straight as I walked away. I felt her words like a sword cutting me into tiny pieces.

I wasn't afraid of hell.

Didn't she know hell was where I crawled out from? She had to know. She had to see when she looked at me. They all should. Monroe always did. It was why she let me control her all these years. She wasn't as naive as people believed she was. She had a keen sense of judgment that many people lacked because they couldn't look past the attractive appearance, money, status, and popularity to see the real person lurking inside. The monster.

They all saw now. Unknown, overeager girls no longer brazenly pushed their breasts against my arms. Random handshakes and pats on the back were a thing of the past when I walked the hallways of Bainbridge and even the town. I was now an outcast. A murderer. A monster.

And through all the looks, the whispers, and the knowing glances, could I bring myself to care? I didn't miss it. I couldn't miss what I never really had. These people weren't my friends or my family. They cared about status. They wanted only what I could offer them.

My car loomed ahead, eager to help me escape, and when I finally reached it, I tugged on the door handle, opening the door.

All I needed to do was drive away.

So why did I look up to search through the crowd?

The answer didn't seem to matter when I spotted her immediately, leaning against the only tree near the parking lot.

I knew immediately she was a witness to what just took place, but just how much. I studied her face for an answer, but for once, it was set in an unreadable mask. Her emotions and thoughts were carefully tucked away.

The time we spent staring at each other was immeasurable. I could still faintly hear Mrs. Risdell's shrill voice raising hell as she was being escorted away.

When it seemed none of us would back down, I decided to amp up the intensity. How quickly she forgot... I knew every button to push and when to push them.

I braced my forearms on the car, feeling my murderous instincts take over and letting the tormentor she grew up with manifest before her eyes. I waited for the recognition, the apprehension—the fear. I wanted a fucking reaction, and she didn't keep me waiting long.

The bitch smirked.

* * *

I LEFT SCHOOL and went straight home to pack an overnight bag. Tonight would be another night spent at the hospital. I'd barely slept in my own my bed since returning home. It was a small sacrifice to pay for my brother almost losing his life because of me. I would travel from school and back until any and everything that was a threat was dead.

The house was quiet when I stepped inside, but I knew my uncle was home. His truck was parked outside, so I figured he'd locked himself in his office, using work as an excuse to avoid us as usual whenever he was home.

I didn't bother to announce my presence and made my way up to my room two steps at a time. I wanted this to be a quick in and out.

When I pushed open my bedroom door, I almost lost my shit.

"What are you doing?"

He continued to look through my shit unfazed. "Looking for reasons why my son is lying in a hospital bed dying."

"You mean other than the fact your parenting skills suck?"

I tossed my book bag on the floor, crossed the room to my closet, and forced my jaw to relax. I wasn't worried about his snooping. After Monroe found the locket and gun, I made sure to move everything to a more secure place.

"Are you heading to the hospital?" he asked.

I pulled down my duffle and began filling it with clothing. "Yeah."

Socks, jeans, shirts, and boxers filled the bag by the handful.

"I just left myself. He's worn out so he'll be asleep for the rest of the night."

"I know." I left the closet and moved around the room packing whatever I thought I would need. I managed to avoid eye contact though I felt his eyes track me around the room, appearing too comfortable for someone who had just been caught trespassing.

When everything I needed was packed, I picked up my bag and looked at my uncle expectantly. He took the hint and stood up from his seat at my desk.

"We need to talk before you go."

"I'm sure it can wait for another time."

"No, son. It can't. I want you in my office in less than five minutes," he ordered before leaving my bedroom.

I waited a beat before making my way downstairs. I had every intention of walking through the front doors but found myself making a hard left instead.

I might as well get this over with.

When I reached his office, I didn't bother knocking and pushed the door open. I found him sitting behind his desk, waiting.

His expression changed from curious to expectant as he watched and waited for me to say something first.

With a single lift of my brow, he sighed and gave in.

"I think it's time for us to have a talk about your mother."

I couldn't help it. My mask slipped and my face fell.

"I'm not interested."

"Don't feed me that bullshit, boy. You're going to want to know this, and I need to say it, so sit."

I looked around the immaculate room, taking in the dark browns and burgundies. Leather and wood encased almost every inch of the office, and thanks to the housekeeper he hired once a week, it was kept clean, fresh, and dust free despite his lengthy absences.

When my gaze finally met his once again, I took in the darkening irises and suppressed a smile.

Fine. I'll humor you.

I took a seat in front of the desk, and he relaxed back against the large leather chair.

I watched him struggle with the words to say and

fought the temptation to roll my eyes. Despite my open indifference, I was actually a lot more curious than I was willing to let on.

"Sophia was a gentle soul. She was kind, soft spoken, but incredibly gullible. I didn't meet your mother until two months after you were born."

The sound of my mother's name heightened the urge to walk through the front doors and never come back. It was a thought I'd been having for years, but my obsession held me back.

"After my brother managed to disappear for nearly a year, I did some digging and tracked him down to an apartment he was able to purchase somehow under an alias. To this day, I still have no clue how he managed to do so. Mitch is extremely resourceful among many things. Growing up, he always managed to find himself in trouble and just as quickly would find a way out of it. It was one of the reasons we never got along. We were never brothers the way brothers should be. We shared the same blood, but we might as well have been strangers. We used to drive our parents crazy to the point they had to separate us. Since the age of fifteen, we grew up in separate homes. I stayed with our parents while Mitch moved in with our grandparents. They died three years later after Mitch had gone to college. It was a robbery gone wrong, though sometimes, I wonder if your father had anything to do with it..."

John's hard gaze was fixed on the desk. His jaw was set in silent concentration.

"Anyway, your father's disappearance began to affect our parent's health so even though I thought it was better he was gone, I tracked him down. For them. I'd written him off long before since we never really possessed a brotherly connection."

At least you had the chance. It was on the tip of my

tongue but decided it wasn't worth the argument.

"After Mitch was forced to move in with our grand-parents, his relationship with our parents was ruined. He accused them of favoring me. I never argued his claim and neither did our parents. I thought they preferred me too, and I think my parents knew it, too." He moved to sit behind his desk, pouring a drink, and choosing to stare at it rather than drink it.

"I'll never forget the day I stumbled upon your mother. She was the most beautifully broken thing I'd ever seen. When she saw me, she immediately asked me to save her. She didn't even know who I was. She was so desperate. Her gown was torn and she wore fresh bruises, and instead of being afraid of the man who'd just broken into her home, she looked at me as the man who'd just broken open her cage. I fought not to care and won. After I confirmed the place did indeed belong to my brother, I turned to leave, having obtained the information I needed to mend my parent's broken heart. I could tell them their youngest son was alive."

"So why did you do it?"

He looked up and uttered one word.

"You."

When I didn't respond, he ran his fingers through his hair and tossed back his drink.

"I heard your cry. I turned around to question her, but she was already gone so I followed. I followed the sound of your cry, and it led me to her. It led me to you. I stood there watching the both of you. I watched her rock and soothe you back to sleep. I watched her tears fall on your face. I watched her hold you tight. I heard her prayer. I heard her ask how she could save you. It fucking broke me. I went against my instincts. Damn what was right or wrong and damn the consequences. I took you both to my home. When Mitch decided to resurface and pay an unexpected visit less than a week later, we knew it wasn't safe for you to stay. I tucked you both away in a neighboring town, packed up, and moved here to Six Forks, never telling anyone where or why I had moved. I also never told anyone about you two. Not even our parents. We couldn't risk Mitch learning of her whereabouts. She was terrified of him. Your father held her prisoner in that house for her entire pregnancy after she tried to break things off with him once he told her about his plans to use the two of you to collect on his inheritance. She had a home birth using an unregistered midwife that he must have paid a lot of money to keep quiet. That's why there wasn't any record that you were even born. Sophia moved here shortly before she became pregnant with you. Her father died while she was being held prisoner. It didn't matter because she never got the chance to tell anyone she was pregnant."

A natural silence fell between after he finished, each lost in our own thoughts. No matter how many times I rehashed it, I kept coming back to the same question.

"How did you do it?"

His surprised gaze met my unwavering one. "Do what?"

"How did you manage to convince a mother who prayed over her child and was willing to ask a complete stranger for salvation to abandon her child?"

I watched him shift and swallow repeatedly, and I wondered if he was using the time to form a lie.

"Keenan," he finally answered.

"Come again?"

"I convinced her that it was safer to keep quiet about your disappearance because she was still hiding from Mitch and had another child to protect from him."

"Why didn't you turn Mitch in for what he did to her?

"Our parents would never have let the charges stick. They would have chosen him over her despite what he'd done. Sophia came from a working class family. She had no one to stand behind her."

"She would have had you... or would she?"

"It was too risky. My family's resources far out-reached mine."

"You're pathetic," I barked.

"I did what I thought I had to do."

"Because you thought Keenan was your son and I wasn't?"

"That's not—"

"That's exactly what it was. You had a choice and you made it. You're no better than your fucking parents."

"Making tough decisions in the heat of the moment is not always as simple you think. Choices have to be made, and often it is the wrong decisions that take precedence."

"So how did my brother convince her to leave me behind?"

He cleared his throat and shifted in his seat. "I promised her that I would find you. I hired some of the best men, but you were fucking gone. Just like that. It was like you never existed. There wasn't a trace of you left. Weeks passed and your mother became more and more frantic. She stopped eating and she barely held or took care of Keenan anymore. Her suffering meant his and she started to threaten to involve the police. I couldn't allow that."

"What did you do?" I growled.

"I threatened to take Keenan from her if she didn't forget you."

"You son-of-a-bitch." I took a step forward threateningly but quickly reminded myself that I didn't care. "Why?"

"To protect the one son I had left. I loved you, Keiran, and I didn't protect you. I wouldn't make that same mistake twice."

"Did you ever suspect Mitch?"

"He was the first person I suspected. I had him watched for months, but he was never seen with you. He must have—" John sucked in a ragged breath before continuing. "He must have sold you quickly."

"So how soon was it before you gave up?"

"I never gave up, Keiran. I never stopped looking. I'm not perfect. There were many times I can recall wanting to give up. There were days when it was hopeless. Your mother stopped talking to me altogether. We lived in the same house, but we were strangers. She never forgave me."

"Why did you get involved with her?" It was a struggle to keep my voice neutral when all I felt was anger. I fucking hated heroes.

"It's complicated. I didn't think I loved your mother. I didn't think I could ever love her, and then one day, I did."

"So what changed?" I growled impatiently.

"She told me she needed me. She told me she needed to forget. She needed to erase him. I—I wanted to be her hero."

"Haven't you ever heard the phrase 'chivalry is dead'?"

"If that girl ever looked at you and asked you to save her, would you do it?"

"How is screwing my mother saving her?" I asked rather than answer his question. The only person Monroe would ever need to be saved from was me.

"Despite what you boys may think of her, your mother was a good woman who was corrupted by men who didn't deserve her. We ruined her. We ruined you."

"Trust me. It takes more than bad parenting to cause my type of ruin."

"Nevertheless, if we hadn't," he paused to take a deep breath, "if I hadn't let you go, you would be okay."

"You don't think I'm okay?" My lips curled in a humorless grin as I watched him from the other side of the desk.

"Cut the shit," he said in a hard tone. "Don't hide behind sarcasm. It isn't cute. I don't care what those little girls think."

"I'm sensing this conversation is over. Good talk." I turned to leave, but when my hand gripped the door handle, another hand gripped my shoulder. I didn't even hear him cross the room.

"You need to hear this."

"No, I don't. It's done. This is what I am, and I don't plan to change."

"That makes for a pretty bleak future, son. Do you plan to drag that girl of yours into it?"

"And if I am?"

"I won't let you hurt her anymore."

"How do you plan to stop me?"

Why did he care anyway? From the tale he had just spun, he pretty much just confirmed that he was a selfish bastard. Now he was determined to protect a total stranger. He didn't need to know I had no intentions of hurting Monroe unless she gave me no choice. My desires have long since morphed into a different kind of need. The need to own.

"Let's just hope it doesn't come to that." He continued to stare at me with a curious expression, and I could tell he wanted to say more. "Why her?"

"Why not?" I countered without missing a beat.

"She doesn't seem like your type."

She's exactly my type. "You don't know what my type is."

"But you do have a type?"

"Fuck." My patience was nonexistent. "Is this conversation going somewhere? I have somewhere to be."

"Look," he released a harsh breath. "Before you go... there's something I meant to give you." He walked back over to his desk, unlocked one of his desk drawers and pulled out a small stack of aged envelopes. He pushed them across his desk and nodded for me to take them.

"What is that?"

"Letters your mother wrote. None of them are addressed. I think it was how she kept a journal."

"Keep it."

"They aren't meant for me. Take them," he urged. "Get to know your mother, son."

"I've been without her for eighteen years. I don't need to know her."

"Will you ever let go?"

I gritted my teeth to keep from spewing the hateful words I felt from my gut and the black hole some called a heart. "No. Keeping my hatred reminds me of what you've done. That's something I never want to forget."

* * *

SHE'S CRYING AGAIN. *She was always crying.*

If she didn't stop, they would punish her, and when they grew tired of punishing her, they would make me kill her. That was the way it had been for the last two years. I was in charge of killing the prospects as they called us. It was my 'reward' for doing such a

P a g e | **122**

great job.

I hated my reward.

I hated killing.

But I could never let them see what it did to me. The hardest part of doing everything they told me was pretending to like it. Every day was colder than the last. At least that's the way I felt inside.

I swung my legs over my dirty, hard cot, and when my feet hit the concrete, I used my toes to grip the cold ground for balance. It was late, and I was barely fed because the trainers decided to leave a little less for us to eat that night. Even though I was treated better than many of the other underperforming prospects, sometimes I still starved like the rest.

I made my way over to her cot. As my eyes adjusted to the dark, I could see her cradling her arm to her chest.

I knew something bad happened to her. She'd only been here less than a week and had more beatings than I've had for the last eight years.

"You need to stop crying... now," I ordered harshly when she continued to vocally shed her pain.

She flinched at the sound of my voice and scrambled up from her prone position to face me. Her cries only increased in volume as I approached, so I stopped and watched her watch me. She stared at me with fear apparent in her eyes, and even though I felt the same, I couldn't share her feelings.

"P—please don't hurt me."

"If I wanted to hurt you, I would have waited and put the pillow over your head in your sleep." Her eyes widened at my threat. "I will still hurt you though if you don't stop crying."

"I'm sorry. It just h—hurts so bad."

I peered down at the dirty and bruised arm she

held that was swollen and red. "What happened to your arm?"

"The big man with the red hair yanked it, and now I think I broke it."

"Well, you've got to stop crying anyway."

"I can't. It hurts."

"They'll do much worse to you," I whispered harshly. I knew why I was angry, but I didn't know why I cared.

"Why are you so mean?" She pouted.

"Because I have to be."

"Why?"

"If I don't, I'll die. I can't be weak. I'll never let them see. Never."

She chewed on her lip as she watched me with a curious expression. "You don't act right. Not like me."

I didn't bother to argue because she was right. I was one of the few whose life began here and even some of the others didn't survive long. I picked up words and actions from the trainers and workers in the compound. Anything else, like toys and video games, I learned about from kids who brought them here from their homes. It was how I learned not all the parents were giving away their kids. Some of them were stolen.

Like her.

"My mommy says all kids are angels."

"Your mother is wrong. I'm no angel."

"Did your mommy and daddy lose you, too?"

"No... they left me here." Frank always made it a point to remind us that our parents never wanted us so they left us here.

"Were you being bad?"

"You ask too many questions." I looked over her arm even though I didn't really know what I was looking for. I've seen plenty enough broken limbs to be able to tell that hers wasn't broken. It was bruised and swollen, but that was it. She finally quieted down enough, and when the silence between us stretched too long, I turned on my heel and started back for my cot, but her next question stopped me.

"What's your name?" she called out.

I made the mistake of turning back around. "I don't have a name."

"Everyone has a name."

"I don't. I don't need one."

"I could give you a name," she offered, seemingly unfazed by my short answers.

"Why would you do that?"

"What else would I call you, silly?"

"Slave."

She frowned her little face and stared at me hard. "I don't like that name... Oh! I know! I'll call you Keiran!"

"What?"

"Keiran is my brother's name. I'm sure he won't mind since you don't have one."

"Keiran," I tested the name on my tongue.

She looked at me expectantly, and I figured she was waiting for me to ask hers. I didn't.

"Don't you want to know my name?"

"No." I really didn't want to know her name. Making friends would be a mistake. I knew just by looking at her she wouldn't last. At least... that's what Frank would say about the kids they often brought in. I was the only one who held any promise he would say. I wasn't too sure if it was necessarily a good thing, but it kept me fed and from being beaten.

"It's Lily."

Pretty. Nice. Light.

Those were the words that came to my head.
It had to go.
"No, it's not. It's slave."

* * *

THE CONVERSATION WITH my uncle was safely tucked away for me to dissect later. The plethora of information my uncle was suddenly inclined to divulge couldn't have come at a worst time. At this stage, I was prepared to eradicate the past. How my past came to be was inconsequential. It was done, and I managed to live through it.

It was all that was supposed to matter.

Living and making sure I never became a slave to anyone or anything ever again.

That included the idea of love.

"You love your brother, Keiran... and you love me or else you wouldn't care."

No one will ever know it—least of all her, but she destroyed me that day in the hallway. Pushing her away was the hardest thing I ever had to do next to killing Lily and my mother.

When she left Six Forks... when she left me, I started to slowly crumble back into the black abyss I had crawled out from. I finally cracked and followed her aunt to a town about an hour away. When she arrived at this picture perfect house with a white picket fence, carrying a suitcase as she went inside, I knew it was where Monroe was without ever seeing her.

4756 Perish Lane, Columbus City, Nevada was where she went when she finally ran from me.

Where she finally sought the chance to be happy.

It was how she found a way to save herself.

If I didn't mean it before, the decision to let her go

for good was made then.

Less than a week later, I was being arrested for murder.

The heavy bass of Slipknot's psychotic tone filtered through the speakers as I drove down the darkening streets. I turned up the volume to an ear-splitting roar to drown out the past and one blue-eyed temptress. I needed to focus.

I had an impromptu stop to make before I could make my way to the hospital. One phone call to Quentin let me know he was in place at the hospital.

My destination wasn't too far away so I was in place within minutes.

The community wasn't as lavish as the estate Dash's parents owned, but one my uncle could have easily afforded, but chose not to live in.

I'm not sure if I would ever feel the need to surround myself with wealth. It was money that led me to be the person I was today.

One man's greed is another man's tragedy.

Though my uncle, Keenan, nor I ever displayed or flaunted it, the status of our family's old wealth was well known. We were estranged from whatever was left of our family.

I parked in a copse of trees near the community and jogged swift and quietly up the good doctor's driveway. He was likely lying in his latest mistress's bed paid for by him. There were too many drunken nights I had to hear about it with the hopes I would care.

I never thought her endless ramblings or mindless chatter would ever come in handy.

I was almost sad I wouldn't get to spend the time needed to search for a soft spot.

Almost.

Dressed in all black, I moved carefully through the

night. Being the community it was, no one would hesitate to call the police if I were spotted. I needed to avoid run-ins with them for as long as possible. Each time I even looked at Monroe, I felt the noose tighten.

The tree near one of the second-floor bedroom windows was my point of entry, and thanks to Anya, I knew it was the only way I was getting in without triggering the alarm system. She disabled it a long time ago thinking she could persuade me into sneaking up to her room. At the time, it was something I would never be caught doing just to get my rocks off.

Monroe, once again proved that theory wrong.

Scaling the tree and prying her window open was easy work. I was stepping into Anya's bedroom in no time. I felt a little weird being in her bedroom, but I didn't know if it was because it was a foreign place or because she was dead.

The mystery of who killed her and Trevor was still at large. As I took in Anya's typical teenage girl's bedroom, I realized I hadn't spent nearly as much time needed to clear my name. Killing wasn't something I was new to, but it didn't mean I was willing to spend possibly a lifetime in jail for one I wasn't responsible for.

As far as I was concerned, I paid my dues when I went to juvie.

Various clothing and heels were scattered on the bed and floor. Makeup littered the dresser. Band posters adorned the walls.

It was all a blur as I passed through and entered the long, dark hallway. I didn't know the layout so I checked every room in search of my target.

I was the big bad wolf come to blow the squealing pig's house down. Anya's mother claimed to have evidence proving I murdered Trevor and Anya, and while I didn't actually kill them, I was there to find out what she knew.

After every room was searched, I confirmed she wasn't home, and no one else was lurking. I proceeded to search the house from top to bottom. When nothing was uncovered, I sent out a quick text to Quentin to stay guard, and I bunkered down to wait.

CHAPTER ELEVEN

KEIRAN

"Do you see these gloves?" I pulled the black and gray leather material from my back pockets and waved them tauntingly for her to see.

They were still new and unused. I bought them the day I decided revenge was served best in its purest form.

"If you ever see these gloves again, it will mean the end for you. It won't be swift, and it won't be painless, but I can guarantee that it will be really messy."

It wasn't until after midnight that Mrs. Risdell finally made an appearance. The solitude afforded a lot of time to plot without the influence of Mario or the distraction of... everyone else.

"I'll have you arrested!" she screeched.

"So you've said."

"You're a murderer."

"Yes, I am... but I did not kill your daughter. You won't believe me, and frankly, I don't care, but earlier today, you mentioned evidence."

"Why would you care what evidence I have if you didn't kill her?"

"Because I'm not entirely innocent. Your daughter wasn't either, but burning her alive was not my work." I've never felt the need to explain myself before. I wasn't all that sure that was what I was doing now. "But it doesn't really matter," I added, regaining myself. "Tell me what you know."

"I don't know anything. I said it to scare you."

Is she fucking serious? I leaned down and braced my hands on the kitchen chair she was currently tied to. "Do I look like I want to play the 'Whose Dumber Than Who' game?"

"It's true. I don't know anything, and even if I did, I wouldn't tell you."

I slowly and calmly reached behind my back and pulled out the long hunting knife I kept from my past life, and a rag I'd found in the garage. "Well, that wouldn't be very smart of you." I yanked her head back, stuffed the gag in her mouth, and brought the knife down swiftly. Her muffled screams carried on long after the blade was lodged in the wood between her legs.

"The next one goes in your knee cap. I'll dismember every part of your body and will keep you from ever walking, talking, hearing, touching, or tasting." I removed the gag from her mouth. "Are you listening now?"

Her breathing shuddered as her body shook, and she looked up at me with fear. "Who are you?"

"I'm someone that not even your worst nightmare wants to fuck with."

"But you're just a boy."

"Well, then I guess that makes me a unique breed. Tell me what I want to know. The clock is ticking."

"I told you, I—"

The knife was against her face drawing a thin, red line against the painted and powered skin of her cheek. Her shaking became uncontrollable and continued even when I withdrew the knife. "Oh, God. Please don't."

"Are you going to make me have to kill you?"

"No." She shook her head vehemently.

"Then give me what I came for."

I knew the exact moment the fight left her. The threat of death was enough to persuade most, but the thought of living life physically impaired was the most persuasive.

"In my purse," she directed. I continued to stare at her until she nodded her insistence. "In the inside pocket is an envelope marked with my name."

I left her side to retrieve the medium sized, designer bag that was strewn on the floor. When she had come home, I took her by surprise and managed to restrain her with little fight, but not before she had tossed her purse at me.

To be honest, I hated it. It was hard being victimized in your own home, but it was just as hard to be the aggressor when you didn't want to be. I wasn't by any stretch of the imagination a psychopath. I didn't enjoy stalking and terrorizing but I did what any person would do when threatened. I retaliated.

I grabbed the envelope from her purse, and instead of ripping into it immediately, I eyed her up and down. There was something I needed to say before I saw whatever it was in there that had her convinced I had killed her daughter.

"I'm sorry you lost your daughter."

It was the most I was willing to give her. Saying that I regretted her daughter was dead would be a lie. Anya chose to be a part of a very sinister plan against Monroe and she lost.

Mrs. Risdell's face was masked in confusion before she seemed to catch on. She didn't nod or acknowledge what I had said as she continued to stare. It didn't matter. I wasn't here to make amends. I needed to save my ass.

I opened the envelope and ripped out the only thing inside.

A card.

A fucking sympathy card that read '*Sorry For Your Loss*' on the front in colorful cursive print. I flipped open the card and almost swallowed my tongue.

A picture—with enough evidence to put more than just me away for a long time—was inside. The edges of the card crumbled under my tight grip when thick bold writing on the inside caught my eye:

You're welcome.

* * *

I'D LEFT HER house as silently as I had come. Twenty minutes later, I was sitting in the hospital parking lot, unsuccessfully beating down panic and the feeling of failure.

A game plan was needed fast. Dash was on speed dial, so in less than ten seconds, I had him on the line. "Dash, we need to meet."

His voice was full of sleep when he growled, "What? Right now?"

"What do you think man?"

"Where?"

"The hospital. I'm already here."

I hung up the phone and peered down at the photo again, studying it, and hoping it might change and that I hadn't royally screwed up. I had the good sense to know when I was fucked, but now I'd made the mistake of bringing my friends down with me.

I waited outside for Dash to arrive, and less than twenty minutes later, he pulled up wearing a grim expression and with bed mussed hair. Lately, his attitude had been worse than a bear with a thorn in his paw and a certain voluptuous redhead had everything to do with it.

"What was so important I needed to be out here at one in the morning?"

"She still isn't talking to you?"

"I don't want to talk about her. She's nothing to me."

"You don't act like it."

"Look, I did what you asked, and now I moved on from it. You got whatever the hell it was you needed out of Monroe and cleared your name. It's over and done with."

"Except you caught feelings."

His expression contorted with barely concealed rage before he expertly recovered. "I didn't catch feelings. She was an amazing fuck."

For some reason, hearing him speak about Willow like that, and knowing Monroe wouldn't like it, pissed me off.

And then, the realization that I wanted to defend her best friend to make her happy pissed me off. I wasn't her savior, and I wasn't her friend. I tried that route, and she stabbed me in the back the first chance she got for trying to protect her.

I had no right to be pissed with Dash. I put him in the situation to mess up a chance with the only girl he'd ever been crazy about despite his firm denial. I knew it was only his ego talking. The girl was definitely giving him a run for his money when any other girl just wanted to run with his money.

It was the reason why I decided to break my own rule.

"Dash... I know it won't help but... if I could go back..."

His grim expression was quickly replaced with astonishment. I wouldn't bother to say more because apologies weren't something I ever did. In fact, this may have been the only time I ever had. There were many times I'd come close to giving in to the torment in Monroe's eyes but never did.

I never would either.

Because she was also the only person who could destroy me.

She just didn't know it.

His eyes widened and then narrowed. "Are you actually apologizing?" I'd caught him off guard, so naturally, he would be wary being the person he is. He may have grown up with a silver spoon, but it didn't mean he wasn't street savvy. He trusted as little as I did.

I shrugged and watched his shrewd eyes assess me. When he found whatever he was looking for, he nodded and turned to the building. "Let's get this over with."

We headed to Keenan's room in silence. Quentin was still standing guard when we arrived, but someone else was in the room, which explained the nervousness I noticed when I entered.

I groaned in frustration before asking, "What are you doing here? I told you I had it tonight."

"Where have you been?" my uncle barked and stood up in my space. He towered over me by a good three or four inches, but I refused to feel small next to him.

"I had something to take care of."

"It's almost two in the morning! What could require you to be missing for over eight hours?" he shouted.

"I wasn't missing. I was busy."

"You told me you would be at the hospital. I expected you here."

"Are you actually trying to be a parent?" I smirked despite the fact I was a hundred miles past pissed off.

"Keiran, you are trying my patience—"

"Then leave," I interrupted. It's what you're best at, isn't it? You run and you hide. You aren't a parent, and you never will be. Keenan and I take care of each other."

"Is that why he's lying in a hospital bed? Because you took care of him? You protected him?"

"No," I growled, feeling my blood run cold. "He's lying in a hospital bed because you didn't protect *me*."

Fuck.

That wasn't supposed to happen.

I wasn't supposed to care.

John had gone still along with everyone else in the room. I felt a pull that couldn't be mistaken, and when I looked at him, I met darkened eyes much like mine.

Keenan was awake.

The last time I saw him awake, there was hatred, but with hatred came anger and pain. Pain that I had caused.

It wasn't new to me, but I'd never done to anyone I cared about.

I blamed him.

He was the one who made me care when I told him repeatedly it was a mistake. A mistake that I knew he now regretted.

"What are you doing here?"

His voice was raspy from sleep or from not being used. Knowing Keenan, he'd already befriended all of the hospital staff and made them love him.

He was always best at that.

I had been a coward before today, not wanting to face him or relive the very look he was giving me now.

I guessed I deserved it. It was the same look I used to torment Monroe for ten years.

"We need to talk." I silently communicated to him that it was bad, and it was necessary. He wouldn't talk to me otherwise.

"Sheldon?"

I shook my head, but then remembered what else happened that night. "I'm not sure yet." I made sure to make eye contact with Dash as well.

"What have you done?" John spoke up. I'd forgotten he was in the room when Keenan woke up. "What are you up to?"

"I'm cleaning up the mess you and my mother started. Someone has to do it since you've been a coward the last ten years. Your decisions have come back to bite you in the ass. It's coming for your son next, so if you want to be a father for once, you'll stay out of my way."

"Keiran, I could help you. I want to help, but you can't keep shutting me out. I know what I did, and I know nothing can change the past, but I can do something about tomorrow. My brother may be greedy, but he isn't stupid and right now, I am the only person you have who knows him."

It never occurred to me before John would be exactly what I needed to draw Mitch out. The fact of the matter was I didn't know my father. I was only with him for little more than a week, and in that time, he barely spoke to me. Food was shoved in my face, and I was kept isolated in a barren room of a small shack that was likely loaned to my father by an acquaintance.

"He's right," Quentin said.

He was right, and I knew it.

FEAR YOU

"I don't trust him."

I stared into my uncle's eyes as I spoke so I didn't miss the glint of pain before it disappeared.

"I'm sorry to hear that, son, but as the adult I have to step in. I can no longer overlook your indiscretions."

Disbelief and anger flared inside me. My feet brought me closer to my uncle until my chest brushed his. I was ready to threaten my own uncle if need be, and Keenan must have known because his voice cut through the thickening tension.

"You should leave."

John's head, along with mine, snapped to face Keenan. He was struggling to sit up so Dash rushed over to help him. Keenan begrudgingly accepted his help, but I could tell his pride wanted to push him away.

I wondered who he was speaking to until his hard gaze landed on John.

John noticed as well and started to protest. "Son—"

"I think that's a little misleading, don't you think?"

"What are you talking about? You are still my son."

"But you've never been a father."

"Keenan—"

"Leave."

After a few moments of glaring, John finally stormed for the door. He opened the door to leave but stopped to direct his threatening glare on me. "I want you home straight from school tomorrow. We need to talk."

He left without an answer, which was just as well because I wasn't about to give him one. After a beat, I nodded to Q to make sure he was gone. My uncle wouldn't give in to anyone so I knew there was a reason he did now.

"All right, what the hell is going on? I've never seen you afraid before."

"I'm not afraid. I'm worried."

"So what's up?"

"This." I threw the now crumpled photo on the table near Keenan's bedside. Dash grabbed for it first and cursed before passing it to Q, who clenched his jaw and finally handed it to Keenan.

"Son of a bitch." He finally looked up at me after staring down long and hard at the picture. "Who?"

"Who else? It had to be Mitch. It seems to be his M.O. He left Monroe the same thing on her birthday—a card with a picture."

"Have you heard from him since it all went down?"

"Not a peep." I thought of what John said about Mitch being as smart as he is greedy. "He's laying low."

"How did you get this?"

"It's the proof Mrs. Risdell had."

"Again..." Dash said, eyeing me warily. "How did you get this?"

"I paid her a nighttime visit."

"Jeez, Keiran! What are you thinking? What if she calls the police?"

"She won't and if she does, I'm prepared for it."

"Do I want to know what that means?" I shrugged my answer and looked at Keenan, who had been sitting silently since he heard Mitch's name.

The slick fucker had taken a picture of Keenan placing Trevor and then Anya in Dash's car the night of the fair. The other picture was of them driving off.

It was all that was in the envelope, but I knew there had to be more. The girls were there that night so there would be pictures of them, also. Mitch would be saving them for a better advantage, which meant I needed to get to him before he had the chance.

"So what's the plan?" Keenan asked and tossed the pictures down. "We have to protect them."

Them being Monroe, Sheldon, and Willow. Five months ago, I never thought I would be in a place where I would fight to protect her from anything. I had mixed feelings because of what had gone down two weeks ago. I was still mad as fuck for a number of reasons, and they all involved her.

"We wait for him to make a mistake."

"That could take months," Dash argued.

"He doesn't have months. He needs money, and if he used the amount of resources he needed to get this far, then I'm sure he'll need it fast."

"We could lure him out," Quentin suggested.

"But if he took that picture, it means he's watching and closely. He'll know if we try anything. He will react."

"So let him try something," Keenan growled.

"And if he runs?" I couldn't keep the exasperation out of my tone. "What if he exposes the rest of those pictures? If he has these, then he has pictures of Sheldon, Willow, and Lake. We can't risk them."

"But we have to do something, or we will risk them."

"Keenan, we need to do this with a level head." The tension in the room kicked up a notch or two, and I knew that he was pissed.

His eyes narrowed into slits, turning darker by the second as his lips curled into a sneer. "A level head? Please share your idea of a level head? Did you have one when you killed our mother?"

"This. Is. Not. The. Time."

"Let's get something clear. The only reason I didn't kick you out along with my *father* is that I needed to know how much you screwed up. We aren't cousins, we aren't friends, and we definitely aren't brothers."

"Are you done?" He only glared back at me. "You

may hate me, but I'll always protect you. I fucked up, but I told you, Keenan. I fucking warned you all those years ago... I'm not a good person."

"At least we know you can tell the truth."

"I've never lied to you."

"But you sure left a lot of important shit out. Kind of convenient, don't you think?"

"I didn't know she was our mother."

"It doesn't matter. She could have been someone's mother, but that didn't matter to you. You killed her anyway."

"You don't know what the hell you're talking about."

"I know enough."

"You don't know anything but what Mitch told you."

"You didn't bother to say otherwise either."

I didn't realize we were shouting until a nurse came in and ordered us to leave. Visiting hours were over.

"They are going. I'm staying," I told the nurse.

"I don't want you here."

"Don't be a brat."

"Fine. Then I don't *need* you here."

"Tough. You aren't staying here by yourself."

Before I could argue, he called out to the nurse waiting by the door. "I want him gone and removed from my list of authorized guests."

"You got it, sweetie," the nurse gushed. When she turned her attention to me, her eyes widened in that familiar look of lust. She moved as if to usher me out, but one look at my face had her stopping in her tracks.

"Keiran, leave," Dash offered, his voice gruff with aggravation. "Just go. I'll stay with him."

* * *

"STAB HIM." THE knife pierced flesh.

"Again."

The sound of tearing flesh and running blood as it seeped from the man's body mingled with the emotionless commands from Frank.

"Pierce him deep, boy. That's it," he encouraged when I obeyed.

A profound and unsettling feeling continued to build in my stomach as I mindlessly drove the knife into the bound man. Arms, legs, and even his knees. The sickening crunch of bone was worst of all.

His screams were muffled by the gag, but his eyes watched and pleaded with me as he held on to what little life he had left. Even now, I could see the life draining from his eyes while I used him for practice.

Think of them as your canvas, Frank would tell me.

They would never let me outright kill them. I had to torture them first with pain that would maim but not kill.

I was no longer sure this was what other human beings were meant to do. Lily said it was wrong when I finally confided in her. I don't know why I told her about the things they took me to do. After a month of not being able to shake her, she became someone to talk to, and when she still wouldn't give in, and do what they wanted, she became someone to protect.

Lily.

I let my mind wander to her and all the good she was teaching me. She told me about home, she told me about her parents, her dog, and even her older brother, Keiran. I wished secretly that one day I could be Keiran. Someone with a family, home, and even a school to go to.

Finally, the man died with what might have been a gut-wrenching scream. His gag saved me from having to endure the sound of his life fading away, but somehow, the effect was just the same.

I stopped driving the knife into his lifeless body and desperately swallowed back the need to empty my stomach.

He was the fourth man I killed today, and when I looked around the room to see the other bodies, I knew he wouldn't be the last.

CHAPTER TWELVE

LAKE

THE TAPPING AT my window started off as a figment of my dreams. A dream I didn't want to wake up from so imagine my irritation when the tapping continued followed by the melodious chiming and buzz of my cell phone. Fantasy and sleep faded away to the less appealing reality of being woken in the dead of the night.

If it carried on much longer, my aunt would wake up, and then I would have to spend the rest of my night explaining to her why there was a teenage boy throwing rocks at my window.

I knew without answering the call that it was Keiran. He was the only one who dared to go against his own rule to pursue me.

"This is getting really old, you know. You can't just pop up and worm your way inside my house whenever you feel like it," I grumbled to myself, knowing he couldn't hear me.

I stomped to the window, my bare toes gripping the plush carpet, muffling the sound of my anger. Frost covered the window from the cold night air, and when my fingers gripped the window to pull it open, it was a little more forceful than necessary.

"You're kidding me, right?" His face and body were partially obscured by the night shadows. Even so, I could make out the dark hoodie he wore, the hood pulled over his head with the shiny locks of his dark hair peeking out.

"Did I wake you?"

"It's three in the morning, Keiran. Care to take a guess?"

A boyish grin tugged at the corner of his lips. "I never took you for a cranky sleeper."

"What are you doing here?"

He shrugged carelessly and looked away before meeting my eyes once again. "I wish I knew," he finally answered and scratched at the stubble on his chin. I loved the light spattering of facial hair on him. It was a glimpse of the man he would one day become. A shiver worked its way through my body at the thought of an even more powerful Keiran.

"You obviously came for something or else you're just a creeper."

He snapped back his hood and narrowed his eyes, anger gleaming from his stormy gray orbs.

"Are you going to let me in?" he asked impatiently.

"I wasn't planning to," I answered back sweetly and twirled my hair around my finger for further insult.

He nodded once, and when a smirk appeared, my hand dropped apprehensively. "Baby, I'm getting in there one way or another. So you can either let me walk through the front door like a good girl, or I can make a lot of noise climbing through the window. Then I'll watch you explain to Auntie dearest why I'm in your bedroom at three in the morning... especially if you were caught in a rather *compromising* position." The smile that lit up his face was charming and playful, but the message in his eyes was anything but.

"I could call the cops."

"And what will you do when I'm out again and standing on your front doorstep? Are you prepared to pay the consequences?"

"Stop trying to mind fuck me," I spat.

"It's not your mind I'm interested in fucking."

"At last... the real reason you decided to look like an idiot in the middle of the night. Goodnight, Keiran." I gripped and slammed the window shut before he could say anything more. Already, I felt myself caving under the powerful spell of his possession.

I slipped back inside my covers, closed my eyes, and pretended the complicated, emotionally wrecked boy standing outside in the dark didn't occupy all my attention. We both knew what would happen if I let him inside. It was likely the same potent pull that always tugged at my heartstrings that led him here.

The sound of my phone chiming broke the silence. I knew it was him without having to look. Unfortunately, curiosity won the brutal fight over my resolve, and I checked the message:

Remember it was your choice.

Just as I read the last word, a hard noise sounded from outside my window. I was out of bed and down the stairs in no time, all the while praying my aunt didn't wake up. A feeling akin to rage bubbled up inside me and took over my train of thought.

He was trying to get in.

What if he changed his mind and wanted to retaliate?

To hurt my aunt.

I foolishly believed in the justice system, thinking

that finally Keiran would finally be the one caught in a corner with no way out.

The door opened wide under the force of my anger, and I was met with the smug face of Keiran on the doorstep before I could step outside.

"I—you were—"

"I told you I would get you to let me in."

"Keiran, you have to leave. My aunt is asleep upstairs and if you think I will let you anywhere near her after what you tried to do..."

"Do you really believe if I actually wanted to kill your aunt that she wouldn't be dead?" He forced his way past me without waiting for an answer and shut the door.

"What do you think you're doing?" I whispered loudly, trying not to wake my aunt. He ignored me and snuck upstairs, leaving me with no choice but to follow after him. My heart was pounding a hard staccato as I prayed my aunt wouldn't wake. I was more nervous about her catching me with Keiran than the danger to her safety. A part of me honestly believed when he said he was no longer interested in using my aunt to hurt me, though I would never admit it out loud. I needed to hold on to that part of him as a safety net. If I became too comfortable... if I gave into him again... if I *trusted* him, I would lose much more than he threatened.

When we reached my room, I hurried past him and grabbed my phone from the bed where I had tossed it after reading his text. The screen lit up under my command, and I immediately began dialing Detective Daniels. I had his number committed to memory, though I'd hoped I would never have to use it.

Just as the phone began to ring, a deep laugh erupted from Keiran's chest before he snatched the phone and pocketed without taking his eyes from me.

"Who were you calling?" he questioned. Amusement teased his lips. "No. Let me guess... Detective Daniels?"

"No one ever accused you of being stupid."

"If you're going to try to scare me, you're going to have to do better than that."

"Well, I tried to kill you, but it seems only one of us can kill innocent people." I immediately regretted my words when he flinched and look of pain crossed his features.

"I—I'm sorry."

"Why?" he looked at me curiously. "You meant it, didn't you? Besides... I'm not innocent."

No, you never were.

"Regardless, it's not as easy for me to kill someone as it is for you."

"I never said it was easy."

"But you're willing to do it," I countered.

He shrugged as if it wasn't a big deal. "If it means never losing control, then yes... I am willing to do it. I'm even willing to kill you."

I sucked in a breath and narrowed my eyes. "Then why don't I believe you?"

"Because sometimes, I really do wish I could kill you," he whispered.

Sometimes, I wish you could love me.

Somehow, it was an unspoken rule that my breakdown in the hallway a month ago when I had admitted I had fallen in love with him wasn't to be mentioned. It didn't matter in the end because admitting I loved him didn't make him stay, and it didn't keep him from killing Trevor and Anya.

"Why do you think death is always the answer?"

"Because it's the only answer you can't change—no matter how much you wish you could." His voice trailed off at the last, and when his gaze became clouded, I wondered if he was thinking about Lily and if he regretted killing her.

"Has she said anything yet?" His gaze was now trained on me, and I stared back in confusion.

"Who?"

"Your aunt. I saw the paper today. Everyone did."

"Is that why you're here?"

"Did she tell you to stay away from me?" he asked, ignoring my question.

"And if she had? What would you do?"

A half smile curled his lips as he said, "I would be tempted to steal you away."

"First blackmail and now kidnapping. If you keep this up, you could become boy scout of the year."

"You didn't answer my question."

"No, Keiran. My aunt has no idea that the same boy who showed up on our doorstep for Monday morning pancakes—"

"Wednesday."

"What?"

"It was Wednesday morning pancakes."

"Fine. Whatever. Wednesday. Why does that matter?"

"Because the next day I tasted you for the first time, Monroe." His eyes darkened and drew me into the memory of his lips between my thighs, owning me. "And I'll never forget how good it was."

My mouth dried, and I found it difficult to speak, but somehow, I managed. "Good. I suggest you hold on to the memory because it will never happen again."

"Don't make promises you don't intend to keep. It will just make your fall from grace much more difficult than it has to be."

We were treading into dangerous territory, and I

needed to change the subject. Fast. "You had my aunt followed for six weeks..."

He shot me a knowing look before asking, "And?"

"Did you know she wasn't on her book tour the entire time?"

"Yes," he answered without hesitation.

"Why didn't you tell me?" He raised an eyebrow, and I realized my mistake. It was hard to remember sometimes that just a few weeks ago, he had blackmailed me for sex by threatening to kill my aunt. Giving me information on her whereabouts was the last thing he would have cared to do.

"I was curious," he answered anyway.

"You were curious?"

"I wanted to know why the aunt of someone who was willing to endure so much for her would lie to her, so I continued to have her followed."

"Where did she go?"

"Ten years ago, where were your parents vacationing?" I frowned when I realized Keiran knew more about my parents disappearance than I thought. I wasn't from here so no one knew my parents, and I didn't exactly make it public information.

"They said they wanted to see the world but always talked about seeing Niagara Falls. It was the last known place they went when we had contact."

"Your aunt never left Canada, Monroe. For the first week, she went to a few events I imagine had to do with her books, and then after that, she met up with some guy."

"She met a guy?"

"A private investigator. An excellent one, too."

"She was looking for my parents."

"I know." He watched me carefully, but his eyes held no warmth or sympathy in them for someone who

B.B. REID

had just found out about their dead parents. "Why don't you want to know?"

"Because my parents have been dead in my mind for a long time now, but I always thought maybe I was wrong. Hearing it will just make it irreversible."

"We'll just have to help you forget."

I didn't miss the sexual shift that took place. If having sex with my enemy meant forgetting about my parents for a little while, then I would give in... just this once.

His hands removed my sparse clothing and dropped them carelessly to the floor. I wanted to undress him too, but there was no way in hell I would give him the satisfaction of appearing overly eager.

I was naked and feeling even more vulnerable in no time. He started to undress, first removing his shirt, and I nearly salivated at the sight of his chest once it was bare. Did all eighteen year old's look like that? His body was unreal. It also made me embarrassingly self-conscious of my own.

Was I too thin? Was my chest too flat? Was my ass too flabby? Oh, God... What if my ankles were ashy?

I discreetly did a quick check of my ankles. *All seems to be properly moisturized.*

Frustrated, I ran my hand through hair and stared down at the floor. I was acting like a complete nitwit. This wasn't our first time together. Not even close.

With a light push of his hand, I was flat on my back, looking up at his smirking face. The sound of his belt unbuckling and his zipper lowering made my core clench with need. His gray eyes were glowing with a possession, and from the predatory look on his face, I knew he was going to eat me alive... and I wouldn't have the good sense to stop him.

"Wait."

His eyebrow rose at my hesitation. "Do you think you're really able to tell me no?" he asked as he crawled over my body that had already gone lax in submission.

"I thought you didn't ask questions you already know the answer to?" His hands ran up my thighs while he sat on his haunches above me causing me to lose the rest of my words, but I still managed to hold his gaze.

"You've become a hard person to read these days," he admitted and looked none too pleased about it.

"I don't want to want you. Is that clear enough for you?" We glared at each other in our typical fashion of foreplay, and I would be damned if it didn't get me hotter than the dirtiest words or the softest touches.

"Spread your legs for me," he ordered, breaking the silence. "You can still hate me now and pretend again in the morning."

"What would I be pretending?"

"That you aren't mine." He lifted my leg around his waist and slid inside me in a single, smooth motion that drew out a gasp of pleasure and pain. I'd forgotten how big he was...

"Quiet now," he mocked to cover up his low groan. "You wouldn't want your dear aunt to hear."

I pressed my hand against his chest to stop him, and even though I wasn't strong enough to actually stop him, he paused and waited anyway. "Before this goes any further, I want you to agree to two things."

"My cock is already inside you, Monroe," he rolled his eyes, appearing annoyed. "This is hardly the time to make demands."

"You either hear them and agree or get off me, get out, and never speak to me again. I will only agree to one night. Take it or leave it."

"Is that one of your demands?"

"Call it a prelude."

"Go on," he answered warily.

"First, I want you to stay away from my aunt and stay away from Willow. You don't use them against me, at all."

"What—"

"It's non-negotiable."

"Fine. Agreed. You drive a hard bargain." His voice oozed sarcasm.

"I'm not finished."

"What is your heart's desire?" he sneered.

I lifted my upper body enough to bite into his chin and whispered as seductively as I could manage, "I want you to make love to me."

That was a mistake.

He reared back as if I'd slapped him and stared down at me with an unreadable expression. "Come again?"

A little of my confidence dissolved at the sudden chilly vibe I was getting from him. His body had gone rigid, and his jaw clenched and unclenched as the silence stretched between us.

"For once, I want to have sex and not be treated as an object."

Some unnamed emotion changed his features, and then he was gone. My body mourned the loss of his, as I suddenly felt cold and just a little foolish. I closed my eyes and reminded myself that this is what I wanted.

"An object? You think I treat you like an object?"

"I don't think, Keiran. When this all began, you used me as some sick pawn for your misplaced anger and need for revenge. Where do we stand now?"

"It's sex, Monroe," he answered as he pulled on his jeans. "We fuck. That's what we do. Don't romanticize it."

"You don't mean it," I said even as tears welled up

in my eyes.

"You don't know me well enough to tell me what I mean. I may not hate you anymore, but nothing has changed."

"Everything has changed. Why can't you see that?" He ignored me as he pulled on his shirt. Suddenly, I was very aware of the fact that I was naked and quickly used as much of the bed sheets that were accessible to cover up.

"I see everything. It's why I'm telling you this," he motioned between the two of us, "is a mistake. What you're trying to create will never happen."

"What gives you the right to choose the boundaries of our relationship? You think you can control what happens between us by being a dick, but I know you care about me. Sooner or later, your feelings are going to catch you."

"There's nothing to catch. I'm only trying to right a wrong."

"Screw right or wrong. You don't give a damn about doing the right thing. You never did."

"Well, I like to think I'm an advocate of new beginnings," he replied sarcastically.

"I agree. I think maybe it's time I start dating." When his eyes cut to me, and a look darker than I've ever seen clouded his features, I knew I had him. A small smile tugged at my lips, but I concealed it with a frown. I didn't stop to think of the consequences of baiting him. "You know... the more I think about it, the better the idea sounds... I'm sure there are plenty of guys who wouldn't mind fucking me... nice and slow... over and over. Oh, the possibilities! We could—"

I was face down and nearly suffocated by the bed sheets. I barely noticed my hips being yanked into the air. However, the slap to my bum made me painfully conscious of that very fact. The sound of his belt loosening, and then first one and then the other of my hands were yanked behind me. The familiar leather of the belt was smooth on my skin as he wrapped it around my wrists. I was bound and bare before I could gather my wits or catch my breath. "Keiran, what are you doing?" I gasped.

"I want you to repeat what you just said to me."

Shit. "Huh?"

Another hard slap to my ass was my answer. "Repeat."

"This is ridiculous," I spat while trying to control the trembles of my body. "Untie me and get out."

"You don't want me to leave, Monroe."

"And how do you know that? Believe it or not, your company isn't all that pleasant."

"Because you would have kept your mouth shut. Now repeat what you said to me."

"I can't remember," I pouted petulantly even though he couldn't see.

"You can't remember, huh?" His hands ran up the length of my back slowly until he came to grip my ponytail. "Should I remind you then?"

I peeked over my shoulder in time to see his hand lower his zipper. I lost my breath to the anticipation. I felt him inside me already tonight, but I needed to feel him own me. I wouldn't deny myself a second time.

I waited with barely concealed excitement for him to bare himself to me, but he moved his hand away to strip off his shirt, leaving his jeans open. "Wait here," he ordered unnecessarily. *Where would I go?*

His footsteps retreated the short distance to my dresser and pulled open the third drawer. Oh, no... he couldn't know, could he? I watched him lift my clothing to unveil the shiny black and yellow vibrator neatly lying at the bottom. I bought it on a whim a week after he was sent back to jail, but never used it. How did he know it was there?

"Imagine my surprise when I found you have a kinky side. How many times have you used this to touch yourself?"

"Wouldn't you like to know."

"Did you think of me when you pleasured yourself?"

"I didn't think of you at all because I didn't use it. It was a stupid impulse buy."

A wicked smile spread across his lips as he picked up the small bottle of lube Sheldon and Willow insisted I get. "Not anymore."

"What?" Without answering, he moved toward the bed and grabbed my hair, pulling my head back. His sudden assault on my lips was hard and combustible as he devoured me.

"I'm going to make you come so hard," he whispered harshly against my lips after he finally came up for air. "Is that what you want?"

"Yes," I panted softly.

He tugged on my hair, deepening the arch in my back and forcing me to look into his eyes. "Louder."

Did he expect me to beg and scream my need knowing my aunt was only a couple of doors away?

"Yes." My voice was louder that time and filled with desperation, but it didn't satisfy his urge to humiliate.

"Yes, what?" he taunted. "Let me hear you say it."

"Please make me come... hard."

He nodded his head, and the buzz of the vibrator sounded throughout the room immediately. He moved out of sight but kept his hand on my hips as he knelt behind me still dressed in his jeans.

I thought he would touch me, but I should have

known better. The instant the vibrator touched my lower back I jerked in surprise and let out a nervous laugh. "I don't think that's where it goes." With my hands tied behind my back, I was more vulnerable and out of sorts. I guess I should have been thankful I wasn't blindfolded.

"And where should it go?" he asked quietly, but there was a hard edge, too. The vibrator slipped around my side to my lower stomach, making butterflies erupt. I turned my head to see his face. "Eyes forward..." The sharp command had me snapping back obediently to my annoyance. "...or I'll have to blindfold you."

"Yes, sir," I mocked. I would have saluted if my hands weren't bound.

The vibrator left my skin when his hand lifted. I stared down at in shock when it appeared leveled with my lips.

"Natural lubrication to the artificial kind? No contest. Suck it."

When he pressed the vibrating length against my lips, I obeyed without a second thought. I felt the vibration against my tongue as I licked and sucked around the head of it.

"All of it," he ordered.

My mouth opened wider to slide lower and closed my eyes pretending it was him.

Just as I had the vision of him bare for me as I pleasured him with my mouth, he pulled away.

"Monroe, I'm waiting."

"I, uh..."

"Suddenly at a loss for words?"

You have no idea. "Kciran... don't tease. Touch me."

"Where?"

"Where you own me," I coyly answered.

FEAR YOU

"Fuck. You don't play fair, do you?"

"No more than you."

The tip of the vibrator teased my entrance causing me to jerk forward and then arch my back. It was a shock to my senses and completely caught me off guard.

"With you, Monroe, I'll never be fair."

He slid the vibrator slowly along my slit. Teasing and taunting. Pushing and pulling. My moans were becoming uninhibited, so he pushed my head into the pillow and ordered me to bite. Muffled, I let my need take over as I moaned and wailed into the pillow. "There was something you were saying to me. Repeat yourself, baby."

"Wha—huh?" How could he expect me to speak much less form a coherent thought when he teased me so?

"I believe you said you wanted to date?" The vibration reached my clit, and I bit into the pillow harder as trembles instantly wracked my body and wreaked havoc with my senses. The sound of a condom wrapper tearing was in the distance as I tried to catch my breath. My orgasm had been swift, but I knew this was far from over. Keiran had a point to prove, and I was eager to see it through.

"Tsk. Tsk. Consider that the last one you get without permission."

CHAPTER THIRTEEN

KEIRAN

WHO THE HELL does she think she is? I was smart enough to know she baited me into a trap, but I didn't have enough control to resist. Jokes on her anyway. Didn't she know what the thought of seeing her with someone else would do to me?

A visual of someone else with his hands and lips on her, touching and tasting her, invaded my mind, pushing and tugging at the black hole where my heart should have been. There was no way as long as I was breathing someone would ever get their hands on her. I would mark her, fill her up, and ruin her so no one would ever stand the chance of having her.

I snapped.

I waited only the second it took to check her readiness before pulling out my cock and slipping on a condom. Her ass was still raised for my access. I gave it a hard slap, satisfied at the handprint left behind and plunged into her.

I didn't stop taking.

I didn't give her time to adjust.

I drove into her pliant body over and over, racing to slate my lust and anger.

If only she didn't feel so damn good, I could punish her without letting my desire take over my intentions. This wasn't for pleasure. This was to own. I needed to make her feel my ownership.

"Tell me," I urged again. "Tell me again how you plan to let another guy fuck you."

"Keiran," she stuttered and gasped. She tried to turn and face me, but I quickly wrapped a restraining hand around the back of her neck to keep her in place while I continued to take her pussy.

"You are going to lose this war you're trying to wage against me, Monroe. One orgasm at a time."

"Keiran, please." Her moans were full of pain and the need to come. She wanted the permission. She wanted me to ease her and make her come, but she knew better than that. First, I needed to have my way. I needed to make her beg for it.

"Please, what?" I leaned over to rest my chest against her back. "Fuck you?" I shoved my cock into her harder. Her squeal of painful pleasure was music to my ears. "Nice and slow was it?"

"It was just... Oh, God... a joke."

I kissed down her back slowly without letting up on my possession of her. "So who's joking now?" I whispered hot against her skin.

She shook her head and moaned, "I didn't mean it."

"Shame... because I mean this." I shoved her body flat on the mattress and proceeded to pound into her without interruption. I clamped a hand over her mouth to muffle her screams. It was good her aunt's room was at the other end of the hall.

On my fifth or six thrust, her pussy clenched

around my cock, locking me inside her, and I stilled to enjoy the sensation of her coming on my cock... even if it was without permission. When it became too much to hold back, I gripped her hips and tried to bury my cock as deep into her as possible while at the same time, burying the feelings she was intent on drawing out of me. My release was violent in its intensity. At any moment, I expected to combust into flames as her greedy pussy sucked at my cock, milking my release. I bit my lip to keep from moaning like a bitch. The last thing I needed was for her to realize the effect she had on me. Her body alone was to die for.

I stayed on top of her longer than necessary but taking care not to crush her. I guess you could say my plan to own her backfired. Even though I was the one doing the fucking, in the end, I was the one who felt well and truly fucked—and not just in the physical sense. What is she doing to me?

After I caught my breath, I stood up from the bed and pulled on my jeans and shirt. Once decent, I stared down at her. She seemed to be out of it because she didn't stir once. I knew she could feel when I watched her. It was another connection I had yet to understand. I quickly looked her over before determining she was just exhausted and then slipped from the room. I was mindful of the creaky spots in the floorboards as I made my way down the hall. Unfortunately, the bathroom was closer to her aunt's bedroom so I had to be careful not to make unnecessary noise.

Once inside, I quickly ran a cloth under warm water and then headed back to Monroe. I felt like a lovesick puppy not wanting to be away from her for too long. I decided it was okay for me to admit whatever it was I felt for her, but it was something I would never let her know. It was too dangerous, and she didn't deserve to be stuck with someone like me who was incapable of love.

Her breathing was still even when I returned and I smiled. I wouldn't deny my male ego was through the roof. My smile dropped, however, when I moved closer and saw the bruising of her skin on her hips where I had gripped her. Shit. Did I go too far? Was she seriously hurt?

When I fucked her, I didn't care if I hurt her or how much I pushed her—my only concern was to make her feel me the only way I needed her to feel me. But after, it never failed to make me feel like shit, and so I would immediately leave her so she wouldn't see the turmoil within me.

With light touches so not to disturb her, I quickly checked her over and determined I hadn't caused any damage, though I wouldn't know for sure until she woke. Gently spreading her legs, I took the warm cloth and cleaned her up. It didn't escape me that this was the first time I ever took the time to care for her after. With her being asleep, it was easier for me. Otherwise, Monroe would see right through me, and I couldn't let that happen.

A low moan passed through her sweet lips as I finished cleaning her. I couldn't resist slipping a finger inside her while leaning down to kiss her lips. When she finally opened her eyes, I was the first thing she saw and fuck if that didn't make me hard. It was something I could easily get used to until I craved it.

Words were meaningless and unnecessary. My clothes were shed and I was sliding back inside her heat. This time, instead of the normal pounding, I moved inside her slowly, testing the waters. I couldn't resist slipping deeper inside, causing her to moan from my possession.

"Keiran—"

"If you ever let another man touch you, I will kill you on the spot. Are we clear?"

"Your crazy has no limits," she groaned.

"Only when it's you." I felt her body soften while I bit back a curse. Why hadn't I known I would say that?

"Are..." She hesitated. Uncertainty plagued her eyes as she stared up at me with too trusting eyes, her body moving with me. "Are we making love now?"

Shit.

The self-satisfied smirk plastered on her face was beautiful. Instead of recoiling, I found myself wanting to capture this moment. The look in her eyes. The smell and feel of her skin. The sound of her soft moans.

She was everything.

I needed to stop this shit. If I weren't careful, the little bitch would have her way. I moved to separate our bodies, already mourning the expected loss, but she must have sensed it because her legs locked around my waist.

"Don't," she demanded. "Don't do it. Don't run."

"What makes you think I'm the one who needs to run?"

"Because I'm not afraid anymore and that scares you. I'm—" My finger slipping inside her mouth shut her up.

"Suck me," I ordered harsher than I had intended.

Her eyes closed as she obeyed. Her lips closed around my finger, taking it deep and my dick hardened even more inside her. Together, we rocked each other to completion.

* * *

TEN YEARS AGO

I WAS BEING led somewhere. *They were always taking me to places where they made me do bad things. Each time I wanted to say no but knew if I ever did, they would hurt me and not let me eat for a long time.*

As I followed behind them with my hands tied, I wondered who they would make me do bad stuff to today. For two years, this had been my routine. I go where they take me and do what they tell me to do.

It was always the same.

So why did this time feel different?

They didn't blindfold me like normal, and when we stopped outside a room, I knew why. We weren't leaving the compound.

The door opened to a room I'd never seen before, and the first thing I noticed were all the bright lights. And the cameras. There were at least three, which was strange for a normal sized room.

What is happening?"

I looked around the room curiously, forgetting my training. We were never allowed to speak or to look anywhere but straight ahead when training. The room was empty except for the lights, cameras, and in the center of the room was large bed, and it was then I noticed the tiny form lying in the center of it.

I squinted through the bright lights, and as my eyes adjusted, recognition followed.

Lily.

What is she doing here, and where are her clothes? She was completely naked without even a blanket to cover her. I didn't understand why, but I knew it was wrong. She shouldn't be here. These men shouldn't be here.

A scary thought wormed its way into my mind. Was I here to kill her? Sometimes, when they wanted to punish the other kids, they made me do it. It was much easier to kill the children than the adults. They called it extra practice. With the other kids, it was different, and each time, I was hurt because they made us fight. They wanted me to prove myself, and so I didn't just have to kill them, but I had to fight them to the death.

"It's just another way to toughen you up, slave,"
Frank would say.

All the cruel things they did were always for the same purpose. Didn't they know I didn't want to be tough? I wanted to have the fun I would hear about in the other kid's stories. Lily was always telling me about her life with her parents and her older brother. She'd told me they even had a dog that played with her. I hadn't seen many dogs, but the dogs I had seen were mean and scary.

"All right. Let's get this show on the road. The clients are getting impatient. They want to see what our fresh talent can do. Get the boy's clothes off and get him on the bed."

Hands were on my rags grabbing and tugging. I didn't want them to take my clothes, but I knew better than to fight them. "Today, you become a man." Snickers and hoots sounded around the room, but I didn't understand the joke.

As my clothes were discarded, my eyes connected with a man who stood out from the rest. His clothes were neat, and he wasn't heavily armored like the rest of the men. He watched on with an air of authority.

When I was finally naked, they shoved me toward the bed. Toward Lily. She visibly shook, and her eyes pleaded with me to help her. I didn't know how. I had no weapon, and I was just as scared as she must have been. I was just much better at hiding it.

As I got closer, I noticed the fresh bruises covering her body. They must have beaten her. They were always beating her, and she would always take it but never do what they told her. I didn't understand her. I didn't know how she could be such a coward. All she had to do was give in and the beating would stop. She wouldn't have to cry or feel hungry anymore.

I finally reached the bed, and when I did, she sat up to reach for me. "Keiran—"

My finger quickly brushed against her lips to shush her. We were never allowed to talk. Didn't she know that? I pushed her down until she was lying on the bed once again and ran my fingers down her face, starting at her forehead.

"Keiran, help me," she whispered with her eyes still closed.

Did she know what she was asking? There was only one way to stop this. Only one way to save the both of us. A quick glance around the room showed me each man was armed.

I leaned down until my lips rested near her ear. "I want you to count to five, and then start screaming as loud and as long as you can. Whatever you do, don't stop. Do you understand?"

She nodded slowly and thankfully, didn't open her eyes.

Five seconds.

It was all I could give myself.

To think of another way out.

To say goodbye.

Five seconds was all it would take.

Because if I wait a second longer, I won't be able to do it.

I wouldn't be able to say goodbye.

"Are you ready?" I asked her shakily. She nodded

again and started counting softly.

"One."

I looked at the men. Most were talking while others fiddled with the camera and lights. My eyes connected with the man again to find him watching me. If he knew what I was up to, he didn't show it. He couldn't know anyway.

"Two."

I looked over her naked body. The sight of her bruises made my throat close.

"Three."

If I did this...

"Four."

She would never have to feel pain again.

"Five."

Lily's piercing scream ripped through the air. I didn't think any more of what I had to do. I waited patiently for the guards to react.

"What the hell?" The man fiddling with the camera looked up with a fierce expression. "Someone shut her up!" he bellowed when everyone continued to stare.

When the first man came forward, I sucked in a breath and held it. My eyes never left his and Lily continued to scream. Some of the men cursed and yelled while others laughed with ugly leers plastered on their faces. I hated them all.

"Shut up, girl, or you'll get more of today right now." When he reached the bed, and Lily continued to scream, he spit out a harsh curse and leaned over the bed to grab her. It was the opportunity I needed.

It was now or never.

"I said shut up!"

He was dumb enough to carry his gun in the front of his jeans with his shirt tucked behind it. It provided easy access for me. With his eyes focused on Lily, I was

*able to snatch the gun and flick the safety just as they'd
shown me many times before. I willed my arms to be
strong enough to hold the gun steady in my hands and
aimed at the man's head before he could react.*

*He jerked back a second too late, and when he fi-
nally registered his gun in my hand, his eyes widened
in surprise a split second before a sneer marred his
features.*

*Lily continued to scream, but I could feel her eyes
watching me as well as the eyes of the unknown man
across the room. I didn't dare take my eyes or aim off
the worker. He could take this gun from me without
much effort if I looked away for even a second.*

"What are you going to do with that, boy?"

*"What you taught me to do." I re-aimed the gun,
and without hesitation, I squeezed the trigger.*

*The room was now silent, and my beating heart
slowed to an ethereal cadence.*

* * *

PRESENT DAY

"KEIRAN, I NEED a favor."

These impromptu meetings with Mario would have
to end. The school's parking lot in the middle of the day
was hardly the place to plan mass murders or acts of
conspiracy.

"And by favor you mean something I'm likely going
to regret agreeing to?" Mario was constantly involved in
numerous dealings that required more than a few favors. Many times, he hinted at recruiting me into his
business, but the idea of organized crime bored me.

"Call it an act of good faith," he grinned jovially.

"Spit it out." The answer was already no, but whatever it was, I needed to hear. I didn't trust Mario. He wore too many faces.

"It's my daughter."

"You have a kid?"

I didn't bother to conceal my surprise. As long as I've known Mario, he's never once mentioned a daughter. What else was he hiding? It occurred to me that I hadn't been doing my homework thoroughly. If all this were going to work in my favor, I would need to ensure all the cards were on the table.

"Yes. She's a little older than you are, but not by much. With Arthur out for blood, I can't keep as good of an eye on her."

"Where is her mother?"

"She's never met her. Her mother was a crack whore and not a very good one because she's dead."

"What does this have to do with me?"

"I need you to keep an eye on her until the heat dies down."

"No."

"Keiran—"

"I'm not running a babysitting service. I have my own shit to deal with."

"And how much do you expect to accomplish if I'm weighed down? Remember, you need me just as much as I need you. This can and will work out for all of us," he stated harshly.

Did he just threaten me?

I stared at him long and hard, weighing my options. There wasn't a chance in hell that Mario scared me, but that didn't mean I couldn't pretend.

"Where is she?"

Could I really be entertaining the thought of babysitting his daughter? She may have been older, but her life was essentially in my hands. Mario wouldn't take that lightly.

"She's on standby. Somewhere safe for now where my men are watching her."

"Like the men who watched Trevor and Anya?"

"Look, I still have guys on that to find out what happened. I'm just as shocked as you are. No one is talking, but I promise you on the life of my daughter that I did not order the hit. It was a freak accident at best."

"Someone poured gasoline on two of my classmates and set them on fire and you're calling it a freak accident?" He still had yet to explain how Trevor and Anya were killed under his watch. Not only were they killed, but they also managed to make it fifty miles away from where they were being held and burned alive just outside of town.

"I know how it sounds, but what would you like me to say? The men on guard were taken care of."

It was always the same response, and eventually, I would start to do my own digging. If I found out he was responsible, it would tip things in another direction. I didn't care at all about what had happened to them, but my freedom was on the line.

"How long?"

"Come again?"

"How long do I need to be your daughter's bodyguard?"

"Until we can find her a safer hideaway or until this is all over."

"Fine. Let me talk to my uncle. Is she ready?"

"My men have her on standby. She should arrive in a couple of weeks."

"Fine."

I turned on my heel and left him standing alone in the parking lot. Lunch had just ended when I entered the building, and I knew Monroe would be looking for me soon. She never admitted it out loud, but she was always on the lookout for me. I wondered if it was only fear that still drove her to search me out. Whatever it was, something told me she wasn't running anymore.

* * *

I MISSED MONROE after lunch. Two classes later, I trudged into last period after class had already begun. Mr. Lawson looked down his too long nose at me as I entered the classroom.

"Mr. Masters, it's great to have you back, but please try to be on time. Tardiness will not be tolerated."

Bite me.

A smile spread my lips when I repeated Monroe's favorite expression. She was already rubbing off on me in ways I never would have imagined. I nodded in his direction and took my usual seat.

Monroe was back to sitting in the front again with Willow and Sheldon flanking her. Her back stiffened at the sound of my name, but she didn't turn around. She wouldn't dare.

I wanted nothing more than to grab her up and keep her close, but I wasn't allowed to approach her. I wasn't keen on obeying some piece of paper they called an order of protection, but I wasn't stupid either. I also had to admit it pleased me she had someone to look out for her. Five months ago, and even long before that, I would have tried to do anything in my power to take away her security and protection. I wanted to keep her isolated because then I could better control her. Now I was more than grateful that she was never alone. As much as I hated it, I couldn't always be around. There was no way in hell I would ever let her know everything

FEAR YOU

I did now was to protect her. She already wanted more and had no problem demanding it. I smiled again even though my blood boiled when I thought about her little so-called threat. Jealously apparently was a trait none of us could escape. I really did mean it when I said I would kill her before I let anyone else have her. It was the very reason why I was no good for her. The days of my bullying her were long gone, but I was still the same person who pushed her off those monkey bars, and even more tragically, I was still the same person they trained me to be. It wasn't until her I realized how fucked I really was and how my life before was so much worse than I could have imagined. People like her had it good. They never suffered or did a bad thing.

I felt some of the familiar anger from before rear its ugly head. The teacher's lecture faded into the background until I could no longer hear him at all. I developed tunnel vision. Blood rushed to my head. All I could see was her. She could still make me feel that black part of me. The self-loathing, the violence, the hatred... *the pain.*

I didn't even begin to fucking understand.

All I knew was that I blamed her.

Her innocence was the key.

Lily was the catalyst.

My mission for the past ten years, and especially these last five months, had been to break her. Make her tick. To see how long before she became just like the rest of the world.

I wanted to see her save herself. Damn her aunt and best friend just so she could be free from me.

It's what I had to do. I had to sell my soul for a warm blanket and maybe even more than scraps to eat. And if I performed really well, I could even forego my daily whipping.

"It keeps you tough," Frank would always say. To him, a beating would make my skin tougher so I could kill easier. The night I took Monroe's virginity, she told me she'd grown a thick skin because of my torments. I don't know why it made me so angry. If she hadn't have said so, I might have stopped. I might have checked my anger in time to merely scare her and leave.

Monroe was right. I am sick.

The realization didn't make me want to stop or quell the need to control her. It never would.

I did, however, realize this couldn't go on forever. My fingertips dug into the table. In just a few months, we would be graduating and she would be gone forever.

The gut-wrenching part of it all was I had no way in hell of stopping her.

By the end of the period, I was in a foul mood and everyone was a target. I had to get away fast. When the final bell rung, signaling the end of the school day, I was out of there. There were only two things that could bring me down from the black cloud my mind now floated in, but one of them was no longer an option.

I headed out to my car where I stored my gym bag. The parking lot filled fast with my overly eager peers. Sometimes I envied their normal lives and normal teenage problems. How many of them could say they were in the process of taking down a slave ring?

Maybe that was why I was so worked up.

Yeah...

It had absolutely nothing to do with never seeing Monroe again.

I made it to the empty gym without delay and headed to the locker rooms. The team had already left school early to play another team tonight. Dash took over the team in my absence and given my recent jail time, I was no longer on the team. The decision of whether or not I would be allowed back on was still up in the air. With everything I had going on, I was a little relieved to have one less responsibility on my plate. For now. Basketball was something I relied on to keep me from reverting back to the person Arthur and his trainers tried to make of me.

After I had changed, I ran drills and made shots until my arms were sore. I kept going despite the ache in my limbs and the fatigue that slowly started to set in. I needed to work off all the pent up aggression I was feeling. It was working until I heard her.

"Can I play?" The softly worded questioned stopped me mid-dribble.

"What are you doing here?" I asked, taking the shot without looking back.

"I came to find you."

"Are you in danger?"

"Not at the moment."

"Do you need to be fucked?"

"Keiran—"

"I'll take that as a no, which means there is no reason for you to be here."

"Why are you so pissy today? It's perfectly okay for you to invade my space, but I'm not allowed?"

"Damn it, Monroe. I'm not doing this today." I dropped the ball and let it bounce away while I headed to the bleachers where I kept my gym bag and bottles of water.

"You're a walking, talking contradiction, and just a little bit of a tease, do you know that?"

I could hear the smile in her voice. She approached me cautiously as if I were a ticking time bomb. I guess she was more perceptive than what I gave her credit. Monroe could be incredibly naive at times.

"What do you need?"

"You seemed upset when you left class."

I blinked twice and mulled her statement over in my head. "Are you actually asking if I'm okay?" I didn't bother to hide the disbelief from my voice.

"Yes, I guess so..." She looked as confused as I felt, and surprisingly, I felt myself relax but not much.

"I'm fine, okay?"

She cocked her head to the side and studied me. Despite the way I was treating her, she didn't appear angry, merely curious. "Why don't I believe you?"

I exhaled a harsh breath and felt my fists clench. "What do you want from me?"

"Answers."

I turned away because I didn't want to look into her eyes. It was my turn to feel like a cornered animal.

"I think we need to talk, don't you?"

"Why are you chasing me?"

"Why are you running?" she countered. This time there was a little snap in her voice.

"You think I need to run from you?" I spun on my heel and stalked up to her until my chest was pressed against hers. I clenched my fists to keep from touching her. If I got my hands on her, I wouldn't stop until I fully consumed her.

"I think you're running from something."

"What's your deal?" My lip curled as my ire grew. I could feel myself transitioning back into Keiran the tormentor. The one who hid in the shadows waiting to pounce and attack just to see her cry. "Less than a month ago, you turned me into the police for murder, and now you're standing in front of me wanting to *figure me out*?"

"Somebody has to, don't you think? You're dead inside, Keiran, and if you don't—"

"Stay the fuck away from me..." I cut her off mid-sentence. "...or the nice couple you ran to before you ratted me out will pay the consequences of your actions."

Shock and disbelief registered on her face. "How did you know?"

"I always knew where you were. It wasn't hard to figure out. There is nowhere you can go that's too far, and no one who can protect you from me."

"I wouldn't be so sure about that." Her voice hardened with each syllable that passed through her lips, and her eyes narrowed to slits. "You may have been able to escape the law thus far. However, I promise you, if you go anywhere near them or harm them in any way, there will be nowhere you can run or no one you can call who will protect you from me."

Careful not to show my true reaction to her threat, even though she mentally knocked me on my ass, I smirked down at her and leaned closer to whisper in her ear.

"Then you'd better be ready to pay the consequences. You don't want me the way you think you do, and you definitely don't want me as an enemy. This isn't going to end with love, baby. This is just another tragedy waiting to happen."

"Like Lily?" she asked. "Was that really her tragedy or yours, and whose will it be this time? Yours? Or mine?"

"It will be both of ours."

CHAPTER FOURTEEN

KEIRAN

TEN YEARS AGO

"I HAVE A job for you, son." I looked up from drawing in the collecting dust on the wooden floor.

He left hours ago saying he would be back soon. Night had since fallen, and I was relieved that he had come back. I hadn't eaten since last night and my stomach had begun to protest—not to mention being in the old house alone scared me.

Nothing much had happened since he rescued me from the compound. He barely looked at or spoke to me. He would provide food and tell me everything would be right soon.

"A job?" I recognized the word and tensed at the meaning of it and the look on his face. He was smiling, but it was a smile meant only for devils who knew an evil secret.

"Yes. I have heard so much about all that you have learned from your training, and now I would like to

see. Can you do that for me, boy?"

He knew my master? Did that mean he knew Frank, too?

But, if he knew where I was all this time, why hadn't he come before? What took him so long?

He waited for me to say or do something, but I continued to sit and watch him, feeling confused. Lily said daddies were nice and protected you. They weren't supposed to do bad things and they would be upset if we did bad things.

His face had changed to anger before he smoothed it over again. "Don't you want to make your father proud?"

So maybe killing wasn't a bad thing. He said it would make him proud. If I make him proud, then maybe he will keep me. If I go back, then they will think I ran away and kill me.

I nodded though it was a lie. Whatever he wanted me to do, I knew it wasn't good. I thought my father rescued me... Why did he want me to do bad stuff?

I followed him out to the main room, and immediately, I noticed a strange woman balled in the corner. She looked as if she'd been beaten or worse. I didn't know what could be worse than being beaten since she wasn't dead, but whatever it was, it was there in her eyes. She made a sound when she saw me that sounded like she was in pain, but it was weak.

"No," she moaned. Her eyes widened and tears streamed down her face, running over her trembling lips. She reached out her hand to me, but it was a sluggish attempt. She managed to lift it only for it to slump back to her side.

She tried to speak, but she couldn't seem to manage more than a mumble. "I think something is wrong with the lady."

I moved forward to help her, but his hand on my shoulder stopped me. In his hand was a gun. "She's fine, son. For now. I want you to kill her."

"Wh–what?"

"If you simply kill her, you'll be free."

"But, Dad, I don't want to hurt the lady." It was the first time I had called him dad, and strangely, it didn't feel right. He didn't feel like a father. He didn't feel like my father.

He pressed the gun in my hand and lifted it with my hand to aim. "You've already done this many times. What's one more?"

The gun felt much too large for the hand I held it in. I'd only begun to practice with them before the life I knew changed drastically. It was loud, and my arm would always be sore after they made me shoot it. Each time I held one didn't do anything to diminish the foreign and uncomfortable feelings.

The last time I used one was still fresh in my memories. It was the first time I'd ever used one on my own, and, unfortunately, I remembered my training too well.

Lily was gone.

I blinked away the tears, afraid my father would mistake them for something else. I managed to keep it steadily trained on the woman who knelt in the corner. She was much too pretty for the tears streaming down her face.

Her eyes were much too bright for the sadness it held. I knew she must have been afraid to die, but why didn't she beg and plead for her life like everyone else?

"Gabriel, my sweet boy," she whispered soothingly, finally finding her voice. Her voice held an unnatural quality to it, and her eyes, wide when I entered, drooped. Her whole appearance just seemed to fade.

"It's okay, my little boy. Do it."

Why was she telling me it would be okay? She was the one who would die. She must have thought I was someone else. Maybe she was looking for her son.

Suddenly, I wished she were my mom.

A strange, beautiful woman who I'd never met before but felt a connection to.

"Why are you calling me Gabriel?" I lowered the gun to study her. I couldn't shake the familiar feelings, and the feeling that hurting this woman would be a mistake.

I looked to my father for guidance. "Dad?"

"It doesn't matter what the bitch calls you. Do you want your freedom, boy?"

"Yes."

"Then kill her," he sneered. He took my hand and lifted the gun again, pressing my finger into the trigger. All I had to do was squeeze a little more, but for some reason, I didn't want her to die.

I shouldn't do this. I couldn't do this.

"It's okay, Gabriel." She nodded her head weakly. The tears were endless as they fell from her eyes.

You're not Gabriel. Just kill her. You'll be free.

"I will always love you."

What?

The gun went off.

The blast was loud, but I didn't feel the pain in my arm. It reached far beyond the physical.

I didn't remember squeezing the trigger.

I didn't remember killing her, but there was one thing I would always remember hearing...

"Good job, son." My father's evil chuckled echoed behind me. "You just killed your mother."

CHAPTER FIFTEEN

LAKE

PRESENT DAY

THERE WAS NO possibility of redemption. What was I thinking? Threatening Keiran like that was like committing suicide. The rush of it all, mingled with fear and hate, clawed at my emotions. When I went in search of Keiran after class, I merely wanted to see if he was okay. The look on his face as he left class was one I'd never seen before. It was a mixture of pain and anger, and with Keiran, who knew how deadly a combination that could be?

I only meant to peek in on him when I saw him rush off to the gym, but when I saw him playing basketball alone something compelled me to call out to him. I had known before it happened that it was a mistake, but sadly I was never one to listen to my instincts.

How could he have known about my Aunt Karen and Uncle Ben, much less where they lived? Surprisingly, I recovered quicker than I would have in the past.

Keiran was much more effective in tearing me apart to near destruction in the past.

My anger was unprecedented, but the threat that followed was even more surprising. More than that, it was the realization I had meant it. I was done letting Keiran use my family against me. I was done letting him use me period.

Before today, I hoped deep down that Keiran could be redeemed but now it seemed nearly impossible. I had to figure out a way to beat him at his own game.

Keiran was guided by his ruthlessness, but I was guided by my love for my family. It was no contest on which was more powerful.

He wasn't the only one who watched and waited. I knew he was up to something, and I knew whatever it was had to do with Mitch. It wasn't surprising to me how closed mouth he was about his plans. So much so, prying Sheldon for information would be fruitless. For all I knew, Mitch had already been taken care.

Mitch wouldn't go too far. His first attempt to kill his sons and brother for money may have failed, but he would try again. The only question remaining was which one would Mitch come after first this time? He used me as a pawn the first time. Would he do so again? He knew where I lived, and it could very well be my aunt who steps through the door next time.

With Keiran gone I had a chance to keep everyone safe. I was going to put him away once and for all.

I just needed to find the chink in his armor.

* * *

INSTEAD OF GOING home after school, I decided to pay Keenan a visit. The last time I was there, he was still very much close to death, and with Sheldon still being an emotional wreck, I figured I could step in. He had become a friend, too.

"Hi, handsome."

Keenan startled at the sound of my knock followed by my voice.

"Lake," he questioned. What are you doing here?"

I paused in the doorway and rethought my decision to come. His voice wasn't cold or angry, but it wasn't exactly welcoming. He sounded sad most of all.

"I wanted to visit a friend, and I'm sorry, but you agreed to be my friend, so I'm afraid you're stuck with me." I walked in and took the chair next to his bedside. He eyed me and then looked at the object I held in my hand. I had almost forgotten about the flowers I held. I thrust them awkwardly in his face, and he took them reluctantly, though I could tell he was fighting back a smile.

"I hear roses are your favorite."

"Actually, I prefer daisies and walks in the park, but this will do for now. Besides, how can I say no to someone so beautiful?" he flirted.

Normally, I would scold him, but I could only feel hope all of Keenan wasn't lost. Going through as much as he had could really change a person. Sometimes for better, but often, it was something much worse. I could only hope that, for Keenan, it was the former.

After a couple of hours watching the stale television shows the hospital provided, and then completing several crossword puzzles, I finally decided to ask the question at the back of my mind.

"So when are they letting you out of here?"

He piped up a little at the mention of leaving the hospital. As energetic as he always was, I knew being cooped up in a hospital had to be driving him crazy.

"It's not prison, pretty girl. I actually spoke with the

doctor today. They want to run more tests, but I should be released by the end of the week. I've been ordered to bed rest so it looks like I'll only be getting a change of scenery. The doctors warned I'm not out of the woods yet. The patch on my lung won't hold forever."

The air in the room was stifling at the reminder of Keenan's death sentence. Keenan made his mistakes—daily in fact, but he didn't deserve to die. He still had so much to live for—even though he wouldn't agree now, but something told me he wasn't ready to die either. Judging by the hard look on his face, I knew it to be true no matter what he said.

I doubted Keiran would let his brother die anyway. No, he would find a way.

"So, are you back now?" Keenan broke the silence.

"Yes. I figured with your brother going to jail, I had the all clear, but imagine my surprise when he didn't go to jail after all." As soon as I said the words, I realized my attempt at humor was poorly chosen. I watched the change of emotion cross Keenan's features. I thought he would defend him or express his anger over me turning his brother in, but his response was unexpected.

"My brother," he repeated harshly. "He's not my brother. He's not my cousin. He's not my anything. He's a fucking mother murderer."

"Keenan—"

"So it was you who ratted him out, huh?" There wasn't anger or accusation in his tone. He sounded proud, and his eyes held respect in them as he gazed at me.

"Yes, but—"

"Good. Don't let him make you weak again. Don't let *yourself* be weak again. My brother—" He paused and ground his teeth. "Keiran is dangerous. I don't doubt that, but he also has a thing for you. I saw it years ago. Everyone did but you. That *thing* might not be so good for you. It could get you killed. By him or his enemies."

"It's hard to believe he's only eighteen, right?" I laughed dryly.

"He's turning nineteen in a couple of months if that helps."

"And you, you're turning eighteen," I teased. "I guess that makes me the only adult in the room."

"Why aren't you already in college?"

"I was held back in the second grade because of my dyslexia. It was before I was diagnosed, though. My parents were devastated at the thought of me being learning impaired." How I wish they could see me now...

"It's almost like it was fate..."

"What do you mean?"

"You being held back, your parents disappearing... Maybe it was fate."

"You think fate would be this cruel?"

"I just found out my father isn't my father, my real father wants me dead, and my brother who I thought was my cousin, killed our mother. Yes, I think fate is beyond cruel. It's fucking evil."

Wow... Point taken. I didn't know the extent of Keenan's anger before, but now it was very much apparent as I watched the play of emotions on his face.

It hit me.

How could I have missed it? It was something I should have seen before.

All the jokes, the whoring, and the troublemaking were all cover-ups. Keenan was just as affected by his past as Keiran was—he was just better at hiding it.

Keenan was tormented.

"Keenan, I'm sorry about what happened to you.

I—"

His dry laugh was humorless as it filled the air, cutting me off. "That's your problem, you know that? It's what has made you a target all these years. Stop apologizing and stop cowering. My fucked up past has nothing to do with you. You didn't cause my mother to leave, and you didn't cause my fucked up brother to kill her. She's his mother too, you know. Where the fuck does he get off?" A tear slid down his cheek, and he angrily wiped it away.

Seeing him so broken and pained weighed heavy on me and I couldn't bring myself to stay any longer.

* * *

I WALKED INTO my home after visiting Keenan to find a strange man in my house for the second time—not counting when Mitch broke into my house to leave a creepy birthday card.

I was either prone to the idea of being caught unaware or the fact he was relaxing on the couch, holding a coffee cup that read 'I love Jax Teller' on the front.

"Um, who are you?"

Before he could answer, my aunt came down the stairs. "Oh... Hi, honey. Where have you been?" she questioned.

She was flustered, and I then got the feeling I had walked in on something. Their attempt to look innocent was overdone.

"I was visiting a friend. Did I interrupt?" I couldn't conceal the surprise I felt even if I tried.

"Of course not. Uh, Lake, this is Jackson. Jackson, this is my niece I told you about." He stood up to shake my hand. He was tall with medium brown hair and a muscular build, and I couldn't help but admire how gorgeous he was even with the jagged scar on his right cheek. It only boosted his appearance making him look dangerous and rugged. I wondered what type of work he did that might have led to that scar. Maybe he was ex-military. He definitely fit the profile.

"It's nice to finally meet you." I looked at my aunt.

"Finally?" I asked and then turned back to Jackson. "I'm sorry, she never mentioned you."

"Jackson was the private investigator I hired to help me find your parents while I was gone."

"How did you have time?"

"My book tour was actually only a week long." I couldn't conceal the hurt I felt finding out that she told another lie. "Oh, honey, I'm so sorry I lied to you. I didn't want to say anything until I had some information."

I felt the familiar ache that came whenever my parents were brought up, but this time, it wasn't followed by anger. "That's okay, Aunt Carissa. I know you meant well." I turned and shook Jackson's hand again. "Thank you for taking care of my aunt and for finding out what happened to my parents. I can't thank you enough."

"No thanks necessary, Lake. It's a pleasure to finally meet you."

"So what's going on?" It was the only way I could ask what he was doing here if she'd already found the answers to my parent's disappearance without coming across as completely rude.

"Our investigation is still ongoing."

"But you said my parents were murdered."

"Yes," Jackson spoke up. "But we still have to find the person who murdered them."

"If you don't know who murdered them, then how do you know they were murdered?"

"Are you ready to hear—"

FEAR YOU

"No." I cut her off while taking a step back. "I don't want to know."

I needed to retreat fast, but Jackson's sharp eyes held me captive. He looked like Keiran did when he was assessing me and calculating what to do next minus the heat.

"Okay, honey. Whenever you're ready. Jackson will be staying in town for a while at a hotel, so he'll be around a lot." I nodded silently and turned to go.

"Lake," he called before I could escape.

"Yes?" He pulled out a card and handed it to me. His full name and number was engraved in bold writing on the front.

Jackson Reed: Special Investigations.

"If you ever need anything, please, don't hesitate to call."

"Why would I need to call?" It was genuine question meant to gauge just how much he saw when he studied me moments ago. Having him here could be bad, but not because he could be dangerous. More because I had the feeling he really was good at uncovering secrets.

"I'm not sure, Lake, but I'm hoping you'll tell us before it's too late."

CHAPTER SIXTEEN

LAKE

THE POLICE STATION was fast becoming a familiar place to me. The next morning, before school began, I walked into the station with new determination and a goal in mind.

Some of the people moved about in a chaotic manner while others were stagnant, pouring over files, or dealing with frantic citizens and arrestees. I quickly signed in and made my way to the detectives' desks where they talked amongst themselves. They were so engrossed in their conversations that they had failed to notice me until I was standing practically on top of them.

"Lake," Detective Wilson greeted, noticing me first. "How's it going, Lake?"

I took in the detective's face and noticed the haggard lines of fatigue and sleepless eyes as they stared back at me. Something told me they weren't getting very far in the case that now made national news. It would only be a matter of time before Aunt Carissa caught

wind. She normally stayed away from the news, prefer-
ring fantasy to facts. In fact, the only television she
could be caught dead watching was the sci-fi channel
and the Sons of Anarchy.

It also didn't help that Keiran was the golden boy of
Six Forks. Not many people were willing to believe he
was involved in the grisly murder of Anya and Trevor
though many still kept a wary eye. The nature of the act
committed made even his most loyal fans cautious. Anya had always made it a point to tell everyone she was
his girlfriend, and when Keiran barely blinked or
showed remorse over her murder, it raised eyebrows.
The history between Keiran and Trevor, once it came
out, didn't help either.

If Trevor hadn't made bail, he might have been
alive today. Would the same happen for Keiran?

It was still a mystery as to how he made bail after
being initially denied.

Could it have been his family? It was a testament to
how far his money and family connections went; the
same family that no one has seen or heard of outside of
John.

What happened to the good ole days when money
bought you a car instead of getting you off from a double murder and a string of other crimes committed?

"I know you aren't getting very far in the case... I
think I can help."

"How could you help?"

"Besides his two friends and his brother, I am the
only one who can get close to him. I can get evidence."
The detectives were shaking their heads before I could
finish. I thought they would jump at the opportunity.

"We can't risk it. You're testifying when this case
goes to trial. That's enough."

"And if it isn't? What if he's never tried? He managed to get out on bail."

The detectives said nothing as they studied me silently. I showed all the signs of distress but was too desperate to scare. I'd managed to give in to him once... twice already... and now he was back to threatening my family again.

"Has he threatened you? Approached you?" Detective Daniels questions. "We can place you under witness protection..." He was already reaching for the phone.

I panicked and did the worst thing I could do—I lied. "No." I regretted it as soon as the word was spoken. "He hasn't threatened me."

Two sets of eyebrows lifted at my hesitation. I knew I hadn't sounded believable, but what else could I do?

If I were placed under witness protection, I would never get the answers I needed. I would be carted off to some undisclosed location, far away. Keiran would think of a way out of being tried, and where would that leave me? Besides, he threatened my godparents. I couldn't leave them unprotected, and I couldn't tell the detectives he threatened them either. They would place me under protection for sure.

"What if I can get you the information you need without setting him up or getting close to him?"

"Naturally, we are inclined to use any information we can get so long as it's done legally."

"How are you planning to get this information?" Detective Daniels questioned. I could see the suspicion in his eyes.

"By using my wits."

* * *

As soon as I had left the station, I headed for school and phoned the one person who could help me get the information I needed. "Jesse, we need to talk. Can you meet me?"

"Sure, but what is it about?" He sounded hesitant and nervous, but I shrugged it off thinking he may have been distracted or busy.

"I need your help digging up more information on Keiran." An extended silence fell over the line so I checked the connection. "Jesse?"

"I don't know..."

"What do you mean?" Just a few weeks ago he was insisting on helping me and now he was hesitating? Something was up.

"The guy is under investigation for a double murder. Do you really think this is the best time to piss him off by playing detective?"

"Just a few short weeks ago you were insisting I do something about him."

"That was before he murdered two people, Lake. It's obvious he is something much more than your average bully. I just don't want you getting hurt."

"If I don't stop him, he will hurt more than just me. Please, Jesse. I don't know who else to ask."

I could hear him take a deep breath and release it. "Lake, I have something to tell you. It's about Keiran."

"Yeah?" My heart was already racing but from what? Anticipation? Fear?

"I saw him while he was in jail."

Whatever I had expected him to say, it wasn't that. *Why would Jesse visit him in jail?*

"W—wh—why?" I stammered. Not only was my heart racing now, but my mind was racing at a catastrophic speed, as well.

"He *asked* me to."

"And you went?" The hitch in my voice was a testament to the turmoil I was currently feeling.

"I didn't exactly have a choice. His henchman paid a visit to my home. I'm just glad my family wasn't here."

"Who?" *Oh, God, did he send Mario?*

"Keiran called him Q."

Quentin! I never would have thought Quentin would be involved in something like that. He was the silent and brooding type, but he didn't give me the impression of a criminal. The realization of how far Keiran was willing to go had me reeling. It wasn't until Jesse's next revelation that I lost it.

"Why didn't you tell me sooner?"

"He threatened my family if I told you. I hadn't realized how dangerous he really is, Lake. I'm sorry for pushing you before. I had no clue what you were really up against."

I swallowed down the guilt that rose up. Jesse's apology reminded me of what I was asking him to do. His reluctance now made sense, but it also strengthened my resolve and my need to fight back.

Keiran was done collecting victims.

"Jesse... We need to do this. He'll hurt our families if we don't."

"What can we do? This guy is like a cat. He always lands on his feet, and it's like he has nine lives or something."

"He's not invincible, Jesse. His lives will run out sometime, and he has weaknesses, too. It's about time we found them."

When he released a reluctant breath, I knew I had him. "All right. Give me a week or two."

* * *

I WAS ON edge all day, and it had everything to do with Keiran never taking his eyes from me. Even during the periods when we didn't share a class, he always seemed to be around before and after each class. I knew him well enough by now to know he was making his presence known.

He may not be able to approach me, but this was still his kingdom. He had eyes and ears everywhere so I constantly found myself in the vicinity of a henchman or two. Yesterday, we each issued threats, and it seemed as if we were both intent on keeping them. Other than watching me during class, and each time we passed in the hall, he proceeded to ignore me while I failed to reciprocate.

By lunch, I was too freaked out to be able to endure sitting through lunch in the cafeteria surrounded by him and all his faithful followers. It seemed as most people were slowly but surely getting over his involvement in Trevor and Anya's death. The cafeteria might have been bearable if Sheldon wasn't skipping to hide God knows where and Willow hadn't disappeared to argue her way into a better grade. This might have been the third time this week. I think she was also looking for reasons to skip lunch and avoid Dash.

I ventured outside, prepared to eat my lunch in the frigid air that I didn't exactly care for, but I figured anything had to be better than risking my sanity or dignity. The night before last was still very much fresh in my memories. Even now, I could feel my body tingle from the remembered sensations of all I allowed him to do to me.

I was a total lost cause when it came to having the common sense needed to ignore my body's demands. It helped that the sun was out, which might have helped to make the cold bearable. Normally, I would run to the library whenever I needed to hide from Keiran, but my secret hiding place wasn't much of a secret any longer.

I looked around for a place to sit. The ground was my only option after the school administration decided to have the benches removed when students made it apparent they would rather hang around and sit on the benches than at desks in the classrooms during class.

I eyed the only tree on school grounds and made my way over to it. It wasn't until I reached the tree that I had noticed it was currently occupied.

"Hi, Collin."

A head full of red curls snapped up, and when his bright blue eyes landed on mine, his eyes widened in surprise as if he couldn't believe someone would actually speak to him. He looked ready to bolt. I'd never before talked to him. Unlike me, he was better at blending in with the shadows despite his overly bright features. He was known as the bug boy because of his fascination with bugs.

"H—hi."

"Can I sit?"

I tried to appear as non-threatening as possible. He was perched under the only tree on school grounds with a thin book in his lap. It didn't look like our standard textbooks so I figured it must have been something he checked out from the library.

"Sure. Um... if you want."

I smiled and sat down with my lunch tray. The ground was softer than I had thought, and when I leaned against the tree, I found myself relaxing. After Keiran and my latest fallout, I was officially dubbing this my new place to eat. I could effectively avoid the cafeteria and ignore the demands of my clueless vagina.

"What are you reading?"

"*The History of the Ctenocephalides canis.*"

I didn't have the slightest clue what that meant. "What's that?"

"Fleas."

"Oh... is it any good?" I was surprised when he actually blushed and wondered why my question made him react that way.

"It's okay." He ducked his head back into the book and I decided to leave him alone. For the rest of lunch, I picked at my food until the bell rang. Collin didn't waste any time dropping in for his books and hurrying away without a word or backward glance.

"Lake! You are one hard person to find." Willow flounced up to the tree, and when she was close enough I held up my hand for a boost.

"Sorry. I forgot to text you." I brushed the seat of my pants off before grabbing my bag.

"So did you manage to avoid detection?"

"For today."

"You can't hide forever, Lake."

"I know. That's exactly why I'm planning to do something about it."

* * *

DECEMBER

IT HAD BEEN two weeks since Keiran, once again, pulled us in a direction of no return. We haven't spoken since our argument in the gym. The days had been filled with long hours of school and tension each time I passed him in the hallways, met his eyes across the expanse of the cafeteria, or felt his presence in class.

Each time I'd see him, he looked tense and distracted. The weirdness kicked in when I realized that sometimes he wouldn't notice I was even around. The anxiety I felt whenever he overlooked me frustrated me the most. When would I ever kick the spell he had over me?

"Lake? Lake!" My aunt's raised voice snapped me out of my thoughts.

"Huh?" *Oh, right...* My aunt had been talking to me for the past five minutes.

"I asked if you submitted your applications for early admission? The deadline was a few weeks ago, wasn't it?"

Aunt Carissa made it a mission to remind me of college every day. She also made sure to review every application I filled out and pushed me to fill out as many as possible. She was also pushing for me to stay close to home.

I had the feeling my aunt was going to have a harder time letting go than I was. How could I tell her it was my plan and every wish to get as far away from Six Forks as possible?

This place had taken ten years from me, and I wasn't about to let it have more. Deep down, I knew it wasn't the city I grew up in, but rather who the city kept within that I needed to run far and fast from.

"Oh... Yes, I submitted them all before the deadline."

"Well, where did you go just now? You looked distracted. Is there anything you need to talk to me about?"

Damn. She was fishing.

Ever since she introduced me to Jackson, she's watched my every move with a critical eye. I knew it wasn't out of mistrust because, though I haven't been honest these last few months, I hadn't given her a reason not to trust me. She was worried.

"Aunt Carissa, I'm fine. School is fine," I offered, beating her to the punch before she could ask.

"If you're sure..."

"I'm sure, Aunt Carissa. How's the investigation going?" I asked to distract her.

Her face fell, but she quickly recovered. "It's going, Lake. Jackson is actually coming over tonight while you're gone. He thinks he's found something."

I didn't want to fall into the emotional trap that was my parents, so I kissed her cheek, grabbed my bag, and rushed out the door. I had a dinner date with Jesse that I had been anticipating for two weeks. It was the first time he could get away, and I needed answers.

My parents would still be dead after Keiran was behind bars...

When did I become so cold?

* * *

THE RESTAURANT WHERE we had agreed to meet was just outside of town to avoid detection. It wasn't until I made it just outside of Six Forks that I realized my gas light was on. I had no clue how long I'd driven with it on so I decided to stop. Being stranded on the side of the road was not my idea of a good time.

I filled up the tank and went inside for a pack of gum. I immediately regretted it as soon as I emerged from the store with my pack of winter fresh in hand. Two men were standing next to my car, which would have seemed normal except it was the way the men stood around my car as if they owned it. Instinct told me they were waiting for me.

A well-dressed man in his early to mid-fifties in a dark gray suit and a man dressed in all black typical of a bodyguard screamed trouble, and trouble found me.

"Hello," the suit greeted when I reached my car. His dark brown hair was expertly styled. He wasn't much taller than I was with his average build. He shouldn't have been a threatening presence, and on a normal day in a normal life, he wouldn't have been.

I took in the expensive looking watch while I nodded my head in greeting and waited for him to move. He didn't. He was blocking the driver's door, and though he attempted to appear casual, I knew he was purposely blocking me.

"Can I help you?"

"Might I say you are much more beautiful up close."

Say what?

"Um... I think I should go." I took a cautious step back but stopped retreating when I remembered I was moving in the opposite direction of my car. I was trapped without actually being trapped.

"Why? We've only just started talking. I've been looking forward to meeting you for some time now." His malicious grin spread wider with each word he spoke. "I've heard a lot about you."

"Oh, yeah?" I managed to speak over the nervous flutter in my stomach. "From who?"

"Let's just say I like to keep an eye on my interests. Some are more valuable than others."

There was only one person who could be the cause of this meeting.

"Keiran," I guessed while hoping it would somehow summon him magically. Funny how my once tormentor became my unforeseen knight in all black armor. The man's eyes twinkled at the mention of his name.

"Yes, Keiran. I'm very fond of his... potential, if you will."

My mind furiously attempted to connect the dots, but I couldn't figure out who was standing before me. "I'm sorry. I didn't catch your name?"

"I'm Arthur Phalan."

"Arthur Phalan?" I repeated.

"In the flesh." He spread his arms wide in a magnanimous gesture, but when I continued to watch him silently, his arms fell. "I see he hasn't been any more forthcoming with you than he has been with me."

"I don't know who you are so why are you here?"

"I believe you bumped into me, young lady. It is a mere coincidence we met here today."

"Somehow I doubt that. I meant, why are you here in Six Forks?"

"Ah, well. I came here to collect. I paid a very fine price to get your little boyfriend out of a sticky situation."

"What do you mean?"

"It was you who was going to testify against him for the murders of your little classmates, was it not?"

"You got him out jail?"

"That is correct."

"Why? How?" I stumbled over my questions and each word came out harsher than I intended but I was stumped. *Why would he help Keiran?*

"Which answer would you like first?" He chuckled.

"Any," I snapped. I didn't miss the brief flicker of anger in his eyes or the way his jaw had clenched before he settled himself.

"I got him out because he promised me a valuable service. It was easy, although costly, to do considering I had to lace a lot more pockets than I cared to and call in a few favors. The thing about government and the law is it is very easy to corrupt."

"What was his promise?"

"His servitude, Miss Monroe. And his undying loyalty... well, until he dies. The work can be a little... tricky... at times. There are a lot of risks and—"

"He's going to kill for you," I whispered. "Again."

I'd already pieced together exactly who this man was and what he represented.

"Yes, and I have the feeling he'll be very good at it. He showed much promise as a child. I remember him most of all."

"And Lily? What about her?"

"Who?" His brow rose in question at the mention of the little girl who suffered gravely.

"Lily. The little girl you were planning to turn into a whore before she even had the chance to learn what love was."

"I've turned many little girls into whores, young lady. Their names don't always resonate in my mind or matter."

"You're a sick fuck," I spat.

"I'm a very rich fuck. Speaking of which... I am so glad I ran into you. Saves me the trouble of having to do this the hard way." He signaled for someone in the distance and a burly man with a grim expression came forward.

"What—what are you doing?"

"Your little boyfriend has yet to deliver himself to me. I am tired of waiting so I'll just have to find payment another way." His leer as he stared at me and licked his lips was sickening. "You, my dear, can also provide a valuable service."

The bodyguard gripped my arm, and I immediately began to struggle. The scream that was building up from my lungs was cut short by the deep voice and unmistakable sound of a round entering the chamber of a gun.

"Take your fucking hands off her, and I'll let you live another day."

Keiran? I said a silent prayer of thanks that my tormentor/ex-lover had a tendency to stalk me.

"Why, Keiran—"

"I'm not interested in small talk. Tell your dog to obey or this bullet goes in your head." I followed the sight of the barrel down an extended arm encased in black until I was finally able to see Keiran's formidable expression. *He's here.*

"You are trespassing on dangerous grounds, son."

"I'm sure I can make it up to you," he retorted sarcastically.

"I hope she's worth it then because this will cost you dearly."

"Her worth is none of your business. His hands. Now." Arthur nodded to the henchman and my arms were released. I wanted to rub them in comfort but didn't want my hands where his had just been.

"Lake, get in the car," he ordered without taking his eyes off the two men. I hesitated because I was more than reluctant to leave him alone, but when Keiran turned his head slowly and met my eyes, I moved to obey as a chilled shiver ran down my spine.

CHAPTER SEVENTEEN

KEIRAN

"THAT WAS A bold move, son. Risky and stupid. It's exactly why I need you working for me."

I watched Monroe close the car door to make sure she was safe before I stuck my gun back into my waist. I was one wrong word away from blowing his head off his shoulders.

"Don't ever touch her again. I don't care how far your reach goes. I will kill you for her even if I have to die in the process. Are we clear?"

"I was prepared to take her as compensation. I haven't heard from you since your release. The release I orchestrated. Why is that?"

"I'm busy with school."

"Is that so?"

"I have to finish."

"I'm not interested in your education. What I have in mind for you doesn't require a degree or diploma. I don't want your brains. I want your soul."

"And you don't think anyone will question if I disappear? You got me out on bail, but you didn't make the charges go away. I still have a noose hanging around my neck and can't leave the state or even the county. Do you really want to chance being brought down for aiding and abetting? And then there's my uncle."

"He can be taken care of." It was meant as a threat, but what he didn't know was I didn't harbor any familial feelings for my uncle.

He chuckled after a while and turned to regard his bulldog. "Are you seeing this kid? No emotion. Nothing." He turned back to face me with a curious expression. "You don't have much give, do you, boy?"

"I don't have time for this." I spun on my heel and started for my car. I needed to make sure she was okay. I was kicking myself for letting her out of my sight. I told her about the organization, but what she didn't know was I had only scratched the surface. She had no idea of the shit she was almost dragged into. If he had succeeded and taken her...

"Keiran." My name caused me to stop in my tracks. His tone was no longer charming and easygoing. I had crossed the line but was beyond caring.

"Yes?"

"My fondness for you, and most dangerously, my patience, is wearing thin. I had to pull a lot of strings to get you out, and in return, you promised me an important package. However, my sources have reported to me you may not be able to deliver... or maybe that you had no intention to do so."

Shit.

I managed to keep a straight face but felt my muscles bunch and strain. I've been too distracted with this mini war with Monroe to cover my tracks. He had me caught in a corner, but I wasn't about to give anything away until I knew how much he knew. "Well, then, I guess you should recheck your resources."

"Are you saying you aren't collaborating with Mario to infiltrate my organization? Because if you are, I have to say..." he waggled his finger, "it wouldn't make me the happiest man. I may be forced to do something *irreversible.*"

"There is nothing you can do to me I haven't prepared for my entire life."

A conspiratorial grin bared his white teeth. "I hear you have a brother. Is he still checked in at that hospital? Let's see... what was it called..."

"Don't fucking think about it."

"I'll do more than think about it. The question is— are you going to make me have to prove a point?"

"I said I'll give you Mario and I will—"

"Not soon enough. I could just kill you and the girl right here and now, but that idea doesn't appeal to me as much, so how about I sweeten the deal?"

"You don't have anything I want."

"No, but your brother does." He made me wait a beat before he clarified. "He needs a lung, does he not?"

"How do you know that?" I gritted. I was going to have Mario increase security at the hospital as soon as this was over.

"Connections and money, dear boy. It is the very reason you are standing here now. It is also how I will be able to procure your brother a lung."

"Come again?"

"To guarantee you will work for me and you will bring me Mario, I'll procure a lung for your brother. I can have one ready as soon as you deliver."

My eyes narrowed as I regarded him suspiciously. "And how do you intend to do that?"

"That's for me to worry about, but you can call it an act of good faith. Do we have a deal?"

"I don't have a choice, do I?"

He smiled, but it didn't reach his eyes. "Maybe I should use your brains after all."

"Look, if you want your mole, then we do this on my terms for now. I have a lot of eyes on my back. I haven't forgotten what you did, and I remember what you can do if I don't deliver. However, right now, I need you to back off. I need to be as unassuming as possible."

Arthur studied me for several long moments, gauging my sincerity and also, letting me see the threat in his own.

"You have until you graduate and not a day later. I'll be watching you, Masters. I want my mole, and I want you under my command. Nothing less is acceptable. Anything less and I start picking off your loved ones... even the one you hide in plain sight." His gaze traveled over to my car and back, a clear indication.

"Understood." I turned on my heel without saying goodbye and headed for my ride where Monroe sat safely inside.

Too close.

She came way too close.

And someone was going to die for it.

* * *

"WHAT WAS THAT about?"

"What was what about?" I asked absently. My only concern was getting her away as quickly as possible. If Arthur decided to change his mind and kill us both, I wasn't so sure I would be able to save us.

Just as I peeled out on the main road, I winced slightly at the unexpected jab in my arm. I realized it was a stupid question and blatant attempt to avoid the question.

"Don't do that. You know exactly what I mean. Why is he here? What's going on?"

"Which question would you like me to answer first?"

"The first one!" she growled.

"He's here for me, Monroe, and until today, he knew nothing about you."

"He sure as hell didn't act like it."

My head whipped around to watch her seething in the passenger seat. "What do you mean he didn't act like it?"

She shrugged as if it was inconsequential, but I could see the nervous twitch she always got in her eyes. It used to be reserved only for me. I can't say I miss her fear, but I sure as hell didn't enjoy seeing it because of someone else. It made me want to hurt someone. "He said he heard a lot about me and had been waiting to meet me.

"Son of a bitch. Anything else?" She flinched at the hard edge in my voice, but I was too pissed to care.

"Just that he always kept eyes on his interests. Keiran, you have to tell me what is going on. Why is he here for you? How did he find you?"

"My bail was denied, and with Mitch on the loose and Keenan in the hospital, I had to find a way out of jail. There was no way in hell I was sitting by until trial. And then there was you."

"What about me?"

"When I realized you turned me in, my resolve to stay away from you once and for all, vanished. I would have done anything to get to you. I wanted to hurt you, Monroe."

"So what changed?"

"What makes you think anything's changed?"

"Because all you've done so far is to give me severe

whiplash."

"What were you doing out here?" I asked, changing the subject.

"I, uh… I was meeting Jesse for dinner," she answered nervously and began to fidget in her seat. I slammed on the brakes and jerked the car onto the side of road haphazardly.

"Come again? And before you answer, I want you to think real hard about the words you are about to let come out of your mouth."

"What's your problem? I don't answer to you."

My fist was in her hair, and the other followed suit, snapping open her seatbelt and yanking her by the waist of her jeans across the console. I ignored her yelp of pain and anchored her in my lap. Here I could get a good look in her eyes.

"Hear me now, Monroe. You will always answer to me." I quickly kissed her lips and then bit down on her cheek to stifle the smart remark that was sure to come out of her mouth. God, I needed to keep her mouth shut. It did things to my dick that not even the world's best blowjob could do.

"What world are you living in, Masters? I'm my own woman now. Your intimidation tactics don't work anymore. It's… old… news." She smirked as if she'd won some great argument.

"No? Well, maybe I can just fuck you harder than I've ever taken you right here until you see things my way." I returned her smirk when the pulse at her neck quickened.

"I would have to let you touch me, and we both know that isn't about to happen again."

"But you want it to."

"Don't be so sure about that. Your ego needs to take a nosedive."

I let out a deep yet ironic laugh and tossed her into the passenger seat none too gently. If I didn't take my hands off her fast, I would show her just how much she wanted me right against the steering wheel. "I kind of missed the fuck out of you, you know that?"

"It's only been two weeks," she snapped. Her eyes widened the exact moment she realized her slip. She had been counting. I could have taken it as an opportunity to humiliate her, but decided to show a little mercy.

Once she was settled back into her seat, I dialed Mario and headed back to Six Forks. "I need you to double security," I said by way of greeting. He didn't miss a beat or bother with the nuisance of conversational courtesy bullshit.

"What's up?"

"I just saw Arthur. He touched my girl." I heard the intake of breath from the passenger seat but chose to ignore my slip-up. I was still reeling from the reality that I'd just come face to face with the man who thought he could own me.

"Shit. Is she all right?"

"Yes. I want to know how he could possibly know about her?"

"What do you expect, man? You haven't exactly been laying low when it comes to the girl." I gripped the steering wheel tighter, realizing he was right. Monroe drew me like a moth to a flame, and even when we were practically enemies, I still found reasons to be near her.

"He was going to grab her as payment for not delivering you. We need to move faster."

"We can't move faster. I don't have everything in place."

"You don't have what in place?" I barked. I could see Monroe jump from the corner of my eye. She turned her wide eyes on me while her hand fluttered near her chest where her heart lay. I wondered what she saw when she looked at me.

"I need to make sure I have concrete evidence in place to put him away forever. I've already lost my career to this motherfucker. I want him to get a *lethal dose* of what it's like to fuck with me."

"If you want him dead, you should have just said so. I can end this now." I was tempted to turn the car around and do just that. I had to protect Monroe. She was part of the stakes now.

What about your brother?

I forced myself to shake off the thoughts. Arthur had successfully planted a seed in my head that was spreading faster than a deadly disease. I had no reason to betray the man who'd given me a shot at life. It was Mario who had brought me home, and it was Mario who was there when I was released from juvie, ready to do anything I needed to exact my revenge against the bright-haired, blue-eyed drug sitting next to me.

There was no way I could double cross him.

But there was no way I could let my brother die when there was a way to save him.

"No," he rushed out. Suspicion naturally perked up at his rejection, but I shook it off. "We don't kill him."

For some reason, I heard the unspoken 'yet' in his statement.

"Why not?"

"Because if we kill him then another will take his place. It won't bring down his organization. We need to do this carefully. We need evidence, and we need Arthur vulnerable. If we flush out everyone, we can take his organization."

"I don't want to *take* anything. I want him dead or rotting in a jail cell. Either way, he suffers."

"You know that's not what I meant," he laughed.

"Just fix it, Mario." I hung up the phone and texted Q and Dash to meet me at my place. First, I needed to get her home.

"How did you find me?" Her small voice infiltrated my attempt to block her out.

"Would you believe me if I told you I was passing by?"

"No."

"It's true. I passed you on the way into town. I wasn't going to follow you, but that lasted only a few miles. I had no clue where you were going, but—"

Hell, I had no clue what I was doing. I was prepared to track her all night if need be. This had to be the first time when my obsession with her came in handy.

"But what?" she pressed.

"But nothing. I'm just glad I did."

"So if he knew how to find me, why did he come after me and not you? He said he wanted to take me as an alternative payment."

I felt my blood boil and my knuckles whiten further as I gripped the steering wheel tighter. I was surprised it didn't bend under the pressure.

"He was likely going to use you as leverage rather than payment. He still wants Mario, and as long as I can deliver him, he won't do anything drastic."

"You don't call public kidnapping in broad daylight drastic?"

"He could have killed you." I couldn't resist meeting her gaze if only for a moment.

"I am done getting caught in the middle of your shit storm, Keiran."

"I tried doing the right thing and letting you go. You are just as much to blame." When she turned me in, she broke any resolve I managed to build to stay away from her, and now my biggest enemy knew about her. Of course, I had no idea who was feeding him information, so it was likely she would have been a target whether I stayed away or not. It all began when I decided I had to have her and used revenge as an excuse.

"You killed Trevor and Anya!" she shouted.

"You're beginning to sound like a broken record."

"What are we going to do about my car?" It only just occurred to me that it was left behind. I wasn't even sure what station it was we had just left. From the corner of my eye, I watched her pull out her phone as she sent a text message.

"What were you going to dinner with Jesse for?" I asked instead of answering her question.

"I don't know. What do people usually go to dinner for?"

"Have I ever told you that I find your sarcastic nature sexy?"

"Don't make this about sex, Keiran."

"It's always about sex."

"Yeah, well... I'm not your sex toy anymore so you'll have to get reacquainted with your hand."

"I'd rather get reacquainted with your pussy."

I enjoyed the answering, lustful growl disguised as anger that passed through her lips.

CHAPTER EIGHTEEN

KEIRAN

TEN YEARS AGO

WE TRAVELED FOR a long time, and in that time, I got to see a world outside of the compound. I'd only ever been in the compound, and any time they took me out to train, I was blindfolded. Mario wouldn't tell me where he was taking me or why. He would only say it was for my own good.

After a long flight, we landed and then drove for what seemed like hours. This was the first time I'd been in a car without blindfolds, yet I couldn't find any excitement over the scenery. Mario had never done anything to hurt me, but it didn't mean he wouldn't. After my father made me kill the lady he said was my mother, he had left. Alone and hungry, it was days before I found the courage to leave the house. I took the gun for protection just in case they came looking for me. Two days later, Mario found me on the street digging through garbage. The number he had left me to call him was tucked in my pocket, but without a way to call him, it was useless.

We pulled into a lot surrounded by partially built buildings and lots of dirt. There was a large truck already waiting and a man standing beside it. He was tall with dark hair like mine. My nervousness picked up when the car slowed to a stop in front of the man. Mario didn't waste time exiting the car. He motioned for me to stay put and then approached the man. I waited for the customary handshake I was used to seeing men make when they met, but there was none between Mario and the strange man.

The man wore a deep frown on his face as he listened to whatever Mario was telling him. He looked toward the car suddenly, and I met his stare. It looked as if Mario was still speaking when the man stepped away and headed for the car. Mario made no move to stop him, though he wore a frown on his face. I was too guarded to keep my hand away from the knife inside my jacket.

Wearing a jacket was also a first. It felt constricting around me, but the good thing was it kept me warm from the harsh winter air.

The man's hand reached for the door handle, and I quickly scrambled to the other side. Mario must have come to his senses because he moved toward the car and stopped the man. I could hear them arguing outside the car while I watched on.

Was I here to kill this man? I figured this had to be a test, and suddenly, I felt unwanted fear snake its way in.

When they finally stopped arguing the man stepped back, and Mario turned to open the door. He leaned down to peer inside. When he noticed the way my hand clutched the knife inside my jacket, he chuck-

led.

"It's okay. No one is going to hurt you, and this isn't a test," he said, reading my mind.

After a few moments spent looking between him and the stranger waiting for me to exit the car, I finally got out. He stepped forward immediately, and I showed my teeth the way I often saw the guard dogs in the compound do when they felt threatened.

"Gabriel?" His shock was obvious. "Is that you?"

I watched the shell-shocked man approach me, hesitantly this time. I had no clue who he was, and he must have mistaken me for someone else.

I gripped the knife under my jacket again, ready to defend myself if need be. He must have noticed because he stopped and looked me over carefully before looking back up at Mario.

"Be cool, little man. This is the uncle I told you about."

The strange man glared at Mario before his eyes lowered to meet mine. His gazed softened as he said, "It's okay, Gabriel. I'm not going to hurt you. My name is John. I'm your uncle."

My eyes narrowed. His attempt to console me only strengthened my distrust. "Yeah, but I could hurt you," I countered.

"Gabriel—"

"My name is Keiran."

I was only ever called two things in my life. Slave and Keiran. Gabriel was someone I never got to be— and someone I never would be.

Keiran was here to stay.

I don't know exactly when I accepted the name Lily gifted to me, but I suspected it was the moment I freed her.

"What?"

"You say you're my uncle, but you call me the wrong name. My name isn't Gabriel."

He looked at Mario in confusion before turning back to me. "I'm sorry... Keiran. It's just that your mother named you Gabriel, but if you prefer Keiran, then that's what we'll call you."

"My mother? You knew her?"

Pain filled his eyes when I mentioned her. It was deep and unmistakable. I didn't know much about her, and even for the short time that I knew her, it wasn't until the end of her life I discovered who she was.

"Yes, I did, son. Your mother and I were very close. She would have wanted nothing more than to be here to meet you."

Do I tell him that I've met her? That I was the reason she wasn't here now? I thought about the man who said he was my father and what he made me do. I should have been able to trust him, but he was the exact opposite of what I thought he would be. All those kids who would cry for their parents night after night made me think parents were good people.

"Who is we?" I asked since my mother is dead and he stood alone.

"Yes, you have a cousin who is only a year younger than you. His name is Keenan and he's my son."

Instead of acknowledging his mention of more family, I looked up at Mario who watched on silently.

"Why am I here?" After meeting my father, and after what he made me do, I was afraid.

Mario stared at me for what seemed like forever before he met the gaze of my uncle and held it for long moments.

My uncle finally took the hint and spoke up. "Because you belong here."

My gaze passed between the two men, and when I

realized it was for real, I didn't say more. Maybe this time it would be a good thing.

John seemed to sense my acceptance and reached out to grab my hand. I stared at it for a few moments before taking it. He led me to the car, but then Mario called out to him.

"Wait. There's something else."

"What are you talking about?" A frown now covered my new uncle's face.

"I need you to do something for me."

"Excuse me?"

Mario walked back to the car and opened the door. That's when I realized I almost left without saying goodbye.

"Who is that?" John asked.

I decided to answer him because I knew Mario didn't know his name.

"His name is Quentin."

* * *

PRESENT DAY

"KEIRAN. YOU KNOW I choose not to say much about anything you do, but now isn't one of those times. What the hell are you doing, man?" Quentin had been waiting outside my place by the time we pulled up. I ignored the numerous protests from Monroe when I dragged her to my house. She was even more pissed when I ordered her upstairs.

"Whatever it takes."

"When is *it* going to be enough?"

"It may never be. What's your point?"

"You trying to ruin that girl?"

Five months ago, it was exactly my plan. But now, I

didn't know what I wanted from her. I just knew she was someone I needed. Period. I shrugged, feigning nonchalance, but he knew better. The look he gave me said so.

"She's different now, you know."

"What's it to you?"

Since when did Quentin nag? That's what I had Dash for. Quentin usually gave less of a fuck than I did. It was why I called on him for all the illegal tasks. Dash dubbed himself my moral compass, and I'd only ever wanted to protect Keenan.

"She's not going to make it easy for you. Whatever you decide. She will fight you."

"She won't win."

"You might let her."

"Q... Fuck off."

"Look," he said, getting in my face. "She's yours. I don't give a shit what you do to her, but these games you're playing with Arthur is going to get you killed."

"Maybe so, but he'll be taking his last breath with me."

Quentin gritted his teeth and shook his head, looking away for a beat before turning back to me with angry eyes. I knew my stubbornness was pissing him off, but I didn't know how much until now.

"I remember, okay? I remember how it was. I remember all the fucked up things they made us do. It would have only worsened."

"Mario saved you," I reminded.

"He saved you, too."

"Mario didn't save me. He helped me out of guilt." Everyone knew Q and I were close friends, but no one knew besides Dash and Keenan that we were more than friends. We had history. Quentin was owned by the same people who enslaved me, and that was how we met. He took a lot of beatings on a daily basis and was often called retarded by the other trainers because he would never talk. It wasn't until discussions of putting him down circulated that he mysteriously disappeared.

"Look," he huffed. "I got your back. Just don't be so fucking stupid. If you die, then who will help those kids?"

"You will."

He shook his head with a solemn expression. "I'm not you, man. I can't—" He stopped to watch me carefully.

"Kill?" I finished what he couldn't say and watched him squirm.

"Yeah."

"Then don't. I'm not asking you to."

"I know. I just wish we could leave it behind for good." Before I could respond, his phone began to ring, and after briefly talking to the caller, he hung up and announced he had to go home.

"Foster parents?"

"Yeah. Stephanie is having nightmares again, so they want me home more often."

"She still won't tell you what is causing her nightmares?"

"No, and she gets so scared when I ask her. It pisses me off because I don't know how to help her."

"What about the parents. They straight?"

He rolled his eyes before answering, "Not all parents are bad, Keiran."

"That doesn't answer my question."

He took a deep breath before releasing it slowly. "They're okay, but I've been keeping an eye on them. Maybe I should ask about her real parents and find out where she came from."

He left after we formed a new plan to deal with the

threat of Arthur close by. Dash was running late so I would have to run it by him and get his opinion once he arrived.

As soon as the door was closed, Monroe attempted to casually walk around the corner. I sent her a knowing look, and she blushed. I loved the sight of her skin reddening in embarrassment, but this time, I was too distracted by the sorrow present in her eyes.

"He was there?" she asked so softly, I almost didn't hear her.

"You weren't supposed to hear that." I lowered my voice to a low level that usually made her squirm. I could practically see the goose bumps on her skin now. The perverse part of me still got off on her fear.

"I—" She swallowed back what was probably an apology, lifted her chin, and demanded, "Tell me what happened to him."

"He was sold like I was." I shrugged as if I was discussing a bag of apples rather than a human being.

"How did he get here?"

"It's not my story to tell."

"Come on, Keiran. You have to give me something. You once said you wanted me to trust you. How can I trust you if you continue to keep secrets?"

"Why is it so important for you to know? You think you can fix me? Is that it?"

"Sometimes I don't believe there is any hope for you." She lowered her eyes as if she felt guilty for admitting to the truth. I fought the smile tugging at my lips.

"Smart girl." I meant it sarcastically but knew it was the truth.

"Your past doesn't have to define who you are today. It doesn't have to define who you can be."

"I don't need a therapist." I brushed past her to leave the room, hoping she'd take the hint and drop it, but I should have known better.

"At least tell me if you hate heroes so much why, did you save me?" she shouted.

"Because you're the fucking exception, Monroe. Does that make you feel special?" I continued my retreat for the stairs.

"I swear if you don't finish this, I will leave here somehow and you will never touch me again."

I was prepared to ignore her, but her last threat stopped me in my tracks. "Come again?"

"You heard me."

I quickly descended the steps once again and didn't stop until I had her face pressed up against the wall and her back arched so that her ass pressed into my front the way I liked her.

"You want to play this game with me?"

"Just tell me what I want to know. Tell me the truth."

"You don't want to hear the truth. You want the fairytale. I want to ruin you." I whispered the words against her ear and felt her body tremble against mine.

"So here's your chance. Ruin me, if you think that's what it will do. What are you afraid of?"

"We had this conversation before. I'm not interested in repeating myself."

"Then tell me a bedtime story."

"Fuck, girl," I barked against her hair and released her. "You're a pain in my ass." She turned around with a self-satisfied smirk. *That's new.* "You know I can't let you leave me."

"Then give me what I want."

"Do you really want it?"

"Is that a trick question?"

I crowded her against the wall and grabbed her face between my hands. "I told you about that sarcastic

FEAR YOU

mouth." It was the only warning she would get that she had fucked up. My lips slammed down on hers, taking ownership of her every thought until she was only thinking of kissing me.

She was climbing up my chest by the time I made my point.

"Again... do you really want it?" When I kissed her, it was only meant to teach her a lesson, but I guess it backfired on the both of us because the next moment, I was ripping into her jeans while I bit down on her neck. I needed to mark her so when she left here, it would be with the reminder of who she belonged to.

"Keiran..." The moan that fell from her lips went straight to my dick.

"Two weeks. It's been two fucking weeks since I felt you, and I'm not about to wait a second longer."

"Keiran, we can't."

"Tell me yes," I urged and shed her jeans. As she stepped out of them, I took my knife from my back pocket and sliced her panties in half.

She pulled my shirt up and dug her nails in my stomach as I unbuckled my jeans. I donned a condom and lifted her, wrapping her long as fuck legs around my waist.

"I fucking hate you," she growled.

"Good. Then I expect you to fuck me as hard as you hate me."

Her arms wrapped around my neck as she slowly impaled herself on my cock. Her throaty moan mixing with my groan nearly finished me. I gave her only a moment to adjust before I was gripping her hips and driving into her. I wouldn't stop until I was tattooed on every inch of her.

When I felt I was ready to explode, I slammed her back against the wall and rammed into her almost brutally.

"I own you, Monroe."

Once... twice... three times.

"And you still... don't... fucking... get it!" I punctuated each point with a hard thrust of my hips, driving my dick inside her with an unrestrained ferocity. I was not to be tamed.

She clutched my ass in her hands and tried to hold on as she came around my dick, milking my own orgasm from me. I gripped her shoulder between my teeth, and her answering cry of pain was music to my ears.

We stood clinging to each other as we fought to catch our breath, and when we managed to regain ourselves, I finally let her go. She avoided eye contact with me as she dressed. I already knew without having her speak that she regretted it, and for some reason, it pissed me off.

When I took her home, I left her on her doorstep to face her aunt alone without a word or backward glance.

I'd officially become the evil bastard she knew me to be.

CHAPTER NINETEEN

KEIRAN

"KEIRAN, THIS IS my daughter. Diana, this is Keiran. He'll be looking after you for a few weeks."

A girl, donning a skintight dress that was entirely too revealing for casual wear, and sunglasses too large for her face, stepped forward. A lascivious smile spread across her lips as she looked me up and down.

Last night, when Dash had finally come over, Mario called to tell me that he would be bringing his daughter by in the morning, reminding me of the favor I had promised him a couple of weeks ago. Dash didn't think it was a good idea, and I couldn't agree more, but what could I do? Staying on Mario's good side would get me what I wanted.

"Well, well, well, this little criminal getaway might not be so bad after all."

"Diana, behave yourself. That is not why you are here," Mario scolded.

He turned his hard gaze to me, and I could see the clear warning in his eyes that said *'Don't touch my daughter.'*

I snorted. After Anya, there was no way in hell I would ever touch another broad like her. Besides... Monroe already ruined me for all girls that weren't her.

"Relax, dear ole dad. I won't do anything he doesn't beg me for." She winked at me and licked her lips.

I did snort that time, and I even rolled my eyes. Big hair and too much makeup didn't do it for me. She was pretty, but in an obvious way that said she tried too hard and cared too much about her appearance.

"Are we done here?" I was growing impatient and needed to be in place for Keenan's transport back home. With all eyes on me, I needed to make sure he was guarded at all times. Speaking of which... I typed out a quick text to Quentin letting him know to be ready. No matter what happened to me, Keenan would be protected at all costs.

"Sure. Diana, give us a moment to talk, will you?"

With one last lustful look, she strutted away to stand by my ride. I shook off the warnings telling me this was a bad idea. I'd already agreed, and I figured this would be a sure way to keep Mario close.

"Another one of mine on the inside was found out. He's running things tighter, and his trust is waning. We need to move faster."

"No, we need to move smarter. The people you got on him are stupid and weak. He's been in this business for a long time. He knows all the tricks."

"He also knows I'm gunning for him just as much as he's gunning for me, so he's even more cautious."

"Yeah, well, he's expecting me to deliver you to him soon. I have to figure out a way to stall him a little longer. I've got too many eyes on me with the investigation and my uncle being in town long term now."

"How is your brother holding up?"

"He's surviving," I answered simply. I wasn't about to disclose any information about my brother to Mario. We may be working together toward a common cause, but it didn't mean I trusted him.

"If he's anything like you, then I'm sure he'll pull through."

"You don't know me well enough to say that."

He regarded me with a serious look. "I've seen enough."

I didn't have a response, and so I shook hands with him and parted ways. Diana was standing by, chattering on her phone. I walked up to her and snatched her phone away. The last thing I needed was her leading a bunch of unknowns to my place. I didn't know her, and I didn't trust her. I considered trashing the phone but thought better of it. Maybe there was something useful in it. There were still a lot of unanswered questions, and Mario was the culprit.

"Hey! Excuse you!"

"You're fucking excused. Before you get any ideas of how this is going to go, let's get something clear. I don't care about you. You aren't my priority. I'm doing this as a favor, and while I'm at it, I'm going to pump you for information. You do what I say, or I kick you out, and I won't look back. Is that clear enough for you? I won't repeat myself again."

She peered up at me, and rather than appearing afraid, she looked curious if not amused. "Are you sure you're eighteen?"

"My age is none of your business, but what I can and will do to you *is*. Are. We. Clear?" I held her gaze while counting down the seconds in my head before I risked it all and left her standing on the pavement alone.

"Understood." She nodded once and then grinned

up at me while extending her hand. I ignored it and made my way to my side of the car, sliding in without acknowledging her further. She finally took the hint and hopped in the car when I was less than a second away from pulling off.

"So who is she?"

"She?"

I pulled out onto the main road and headed in the direction of my house. She had arrived sooner than expected, so I still hadn't run it by my uncle yet. I decided to cross that bridge when I got there.

"Yes. The 'she' who has you overly guarded around me. Is *she* your girlfriend?"

"I don't do girlfriends," I answered without sparing her a glance even though I could feel her eyes boring into me.

"So there is a she?"

"Even if there was, I wouldn't fuck you, so I guess it doesn't matter if there's a she, does it?"

"Who says I'm looking to get fucked? Maybe I want to do the fucking."

"You don't know me from Adam, girl."

"Oh, but I know your type. You like to be in control when you take her, don't you? You like to handle her, test her limits... maybe even make her beg a little?"

I gripped the steering wheel tighter out of aggravation. Even if what she said was true, I didn't like to be read. Especially by a stranger. "No."

"No?" I could hear the disbelief in her tone.

"I like to do much more than make her beg." I briefly glanced at her in the passenger seat and caught her leaning forward with anticipation. "I like to make her cry so I can lick her fucking tears. I like to make her hurt so I can hear her scream. And most importantly, I like to make her want more."

The lust building in Diana's eyes was unmistakable.

"Something tells me she's inside your head just as much as you are in hers. I'd like to meet this girl."

"She's not in my head and that's not going to happen."

"Yes, it most certainly is. Before you started speaking about her, there wasn't as much as a flicker…" she used her fingers to emphasize… "of life in your eyes. I think I might be jealous."

"Brunettes aren't my type anymore."

"It's quite all right. Maybe I'll dye my hair and figure out another way to get in your head as well. This could be fun."

"You wouldn't do well as a blonde."

"Oh, so she's blonde?"

I spit out a curse and scowled at her. "You're annoying me, Diana."

"It's just Di, so call me that. I hate Diana." The conviction in her voice made me pause.

"Your father calls you Diana."

"My father doesn't listen to much if it doesn't have to do with money."

My attention zeroed in the comment about her father, but I didn't let on that I was interested. "Why would you say that?"

"Sorry, super spy. That conversation is more suited for a fifth date, and I just met you."

"Yet you were salivating over my dick moments ago."

"So what do you say we trade? A fuck for an answer?"

"What makes you think I'm that interested?"

"Oh, you are. Something tells me you and my father didn't meet over coffee. So are you in business with him? You're kind of young."

"How old are you?" I asked, dodging her question.

"I'll be twenty-one in a few months."

"Where is your mother?"

"Strung out somewhere… I haven't seen her since I was eleven."

"So what really happened to make your father feel the need to relocate you?"

"What makes you think something happened? My father has always been cautious."

I pulled into my driveway and put the car in park before turning my full attention on her.

"Don't insult my fucking intelligence. What. Happened?"

"Are you this bossy with everyone?"

"I'm less than three seconds from sending your head through the windshield."

She studied me for a few moments, gauging my sincerity before releasing a long breath and running her fingers through her hair. "One of my father's men tried to kill me. I don't know why, but he almost succeeded."

"What did your father do?"

"What do you think he did? He killed him."

"And you're okay with that?" I lifted my brow at the nonchalant way she admitted her father had committed murder. How close did he raise her to his business?

"He tried to kill me. I'm not exactly expected to cry over his casket. It's just crazy, you know? He's worked for my father for years. It doesn't make sense, but I'm guessing it was over money."

"That would be the easy explanation." I sent her a look to let her know I wasn't buying. I already figured her father warned her to watch what she said. Mario trusted me as little as I trusted him.

"It's a valid explanation. The men who work for my father are always harping about more money. He pays them less than the price of shit."

"How would you know that?"

"I'm under close guard every day of my life. The men talk." I let my hard gaze bore into hers until she shifted and looked around. Her gaze focused on my house and she said, "You have a nice home."

"It's a house, not a home."

"People do say there's a difference, don't they?"

I shrugged and exited the car. She silently followed after me to the house, but when we reached the door, I stopped and turned to face her. "I'm sure I don't have to tell you that if you try anything, I will not hesitate to cut your throat open." She didn't as much as blink at my threat, and again, I wondered how close her father kept her to his business. I still had yet to figure out what it was about her.

"Wow. Are all teenage boys as intimidating and violent as you?"

"I'm not a boy, and there is no one like me."

"Cocky much?"

I didn't try to stop the smirk that appeared on my face. "It comes with the territory."

"I'd like to tread in that territory." She slid her hands slowly up my chest as she leaned into me with a secretive grin and a gleam in her eye meant to seduce. I placed my hands firmly on her hips and flashed a panty-dropping smile. I would have liked nothing more than to see her on her back in the bushes than in my bed. My chance to humor myself was lost when an irritated growl interrupted.

"Oh, for fuck sake. It's Anya reincarnated."

Our heads snapped simultaneously to Sheldon and Dash standing in my driveway with astonished expressions... well... Sheldon looked more pissed as she glared at Diana.

"Trust me, sweetheart—that's one line you don't want to cross for numerous reasons. And those reasons are way too fucked up to talk about even over a bottle of whiskey." She switched her glare to me and bared her teeth. "Isn't that right, Keiran?"

I didn't bother to answer her question or acknowledge Dash's inquisitive stare. *What is he doing bringing her over here anyway?* I didn't give a shit about being caught in a compromising position. I had no intention of ever touching Diana and even less intention of explaining myself. I unlocked the door and entered, leaving the door open because what else would they all do but follow?

Ever since Sheldon became friends with Monroe, she had watched me like a hawk, critical of every move I made. It made my previous tolerance of her almost unbearable. She didn't think I was good enough for Monroe... well, that was one thing we agree on at least.

"Who is she?" Sheldon demanded, crossing her arms over her chest. I didn't miss the eye roll she directed her gaze toward Diana.

"Why is that your business?" I asked casually. Truth is, I was really curious to know why she cared so much.

Sheldon's eyes narrowed and her lips set to deliver a scathing reply, but Dash interjected before she could. "Actually, I would like to know myself."

His hard gaze met mine, and he silently communicated that he wasn't about to let it go. I sighed and relented because I trusted Dash and much more than that, I respected him. "She's Mario's—"

He eyed Diana with a look of disgust while Diana checked him out with a lascivious look. "She's a little young..."

"Eww. I'm his daughter."

"Oh, she speaks," Sheldon griped. "I thought you only talked when you wanted to get a cock in your mouth."

"What's wrong, princess? You afraid of a little competition?"

"You're barking up the wrong tree. I'm actually doing his brother," she snapped.

Teeth were bared and claws unsheathed as they squared off against each other. I felt the beginnings of a headache stir, so I signaled Dash to take care of them and headed upstairs for my gear. I needed to play a game to unwind because if I had to listen to any more of that, I would be tempted to shoot both of them between the eyes.

I came back downstairs after changing into only basketball shorts and sneakers. As soon as my foot connected with the carpet of the living room and all eyes shifted to me, I immediately regretted not wearing a shirt. Diana's eyes shamelessly trailed my body, and the way she licked her lips told me she was thinking of only one thing. Sheldon's snort and the sound of disgust interrupted her eye fucking when she turned her gaze to glare at Sheldon.

"I called Q," I directed to Dash, dismissing them.

"Dude, we can't play with only three players," he reminded me.

"Damn." I rubbed my forehead and hid my frown by aiming it at my feet. Right. How could I forget? My brother was lying in the hospital with his only remaining lung failing, and here I was ready to play basketball.

"I can call Buddy," Dash offered. I could hear the sympathy in his voice and could feel my anger grow, but rather than taking it out on my best friend, I turned on my heel for the door. "Fine. Whatever."

* * *

BUDDY FELL ON his ass for the third time in the ten minutes we had been playing. He sent me an uncharacteristic dirty look and swiftly jumped back on his feet and continued the play without missing a beat.

I knew they were all thinking the same. It was written all over their faces. I knew it too, so I guess it's why no one bothered to say anything.

I was falling apart.

For the last ten years, basketball had been my escape and punishing Monroe had been my drug. With Monroe gone, I felt as if there was nothing to keep be balanced, and I was too preoccupied for even the simplest of distractions.

I dribbled the ball, and as it bounced from hitting the pavement and made its way back into my hand, I was reminded of everything that waited to destroy me—and everyone I could hurt in the process.

Monroe.

John.

Keenan.

I took the shot...

I made the basket.

The play resumed, and the ball was in my opponent's hand and like always, I waited for an opening to get the ball back into my hands and steal another victory.

I watched my opponents, I studied their reactions, and I looked for a weakness and then took an opening. The ball was in my hands, and I was back in control.

Arthur.

Mitch.

My control of the ball faltered on my third dribble, but I quickly regained control, and just as I braced my feet to take the shot, I was blindsided.

My palms scraped the pavement as I slid across the concrete and gritted from the pain of the abrasions I knew I would find. The ball bounced away, and when I looked up, Buddy was standing over me with an apologetic expression.

"Sorry, man. I didn't mean to foul you like that." He held out his hand and waited for me to take it. I ignored it and jumped to my feet, much like he had except I felt my knees turn to jelly. His hand was still out, and a look of uncertainty was plastered on his face, so I took it in mine and shook it to show no hard feelings.

"It's not your fault. I should have been watching my back."

We each toweled off before making our way to the house. "Do you think they killed each other by now?" Dash joked. "It's been mighty quiet."

"Who are you talking about?" Quentin questioned as we entered the house.

"Some chick he's babysitting as a favor."

I made my way into the living room with Quentin and Dash following. Buddy had to go home and get ready for a date with a senior. I shook my head at the kid's charm and ability to pull girls in any age group.

"Where is she?" I asked Sheldon when I looked around and didn't see Diana. I was already fisting my car keys thinking she ran.

"She said something about using the shower to take a hoe bath."

"Isn't that a bird bath?"

"Not for her kind," she sneered.

I blew out a breath and then wondered again why Dash had brought her here. From the look in her eyes, I could tell she wanted to stir shit up. She was pissed, and I couldn't bring myself to care. I cared about Sheldon, but she was the least of my problems. For some reason, she thought she could get away with bossing everyone around. Including me.

"Stop being a royal dick, Dash spat"

"You're one to talk. Why do you think Willow avoids you?"

The twins began to bicker and hurling insults between them while Quentin and I looked on. It wasn't uncommon for them to fight. They rarely ever didn't argue. I assumed it was a twin thing.

Just as I was about to intervene, I heard Di's shriek of disbelief sound from behind me.

"Quentin?"

The twins stopped arguing immediately while Q and I whipped around to see her standing in the doorway. Her skin was as pale as a ghost. Not even when she told me about nearly being killed an hour ago had she looked so shaken.

My gaze bounced from Quentin to Diana before settling on Quentin's confused expression. He didn't seem to know her, but she knew him. She took in his confusion and curled her lip slowly. "What's the matter? Don't you recognize your childhood lover?"

"Diana?" Q took a step toward her, but Di quickly retreated. The tension in the room was stifling. My gaze shifted between the two as they stared at each other in anger, confusion, and wonder.

"I take it you two know each other?" Dash asked, stating the obvious while I mentally slapped myself for not making the connection sooner considering who Di's father was.

"Yeah, we know each other," Quentin nodded slowly. Anger was brewing in his eyes as they remained fixed on her.

"Mind sharing how?" Sheldon asked and crossed

her arms. She shot me an accusatory glance as if I had planned this.

"Keiran, what is she doing here?" Quentin asked without looking away from Di.

"Oh, he didn't tell you?" She grinned before I could respond. "He's my new babysitter. You know how Daddy can get into trouble sometimes because of his *business*."

"Jeez, is he still—"

"Don't do that. Don't pretend you care about what happens to me."

"Diana—"

"You *left*. You found happily ever after and left me to pick up the pieces you left behind. Don't worry. It's kept me warm at night in all the places it cut me the deepest."

The silence descending did nothing to help the tension in the room.

"I'll kill him," Quentin growled. That declaration was the first time he'd ever acknowledge his past. He'd gotten out before I did, but now I wasn't so sure his salvation was what it seemed.

Could Mario be dirtier than he seemed? His story of being kicked out of the bureau because of corrupt practices always had a few holes, but I was willing to overlook them until now. I told myself his business wasn't my concern, but that was before it jumped out at me in my living room and left me feeling like I'd just been caught with my pants around my ankles and my dick in my hand.

"No, you won't and don't pretend you care."

"And why the fuck not?"

"Because he's still Daddy."

"Are the Burkin bags and shiny, diamond bracelets worth it?"

Her eyes narrowed to angry slits. "You don't know what the hell you're talking about."

"Enlighten me, Diana. Because the last I checked, your father used you to make money. What am I missing?"

"Try the last ten years!" she growled and stormed out of the living room. Quentin started after her, but the hand I placed on his shoulder stopped him in his tracks. I ignored the hostile look he gave me, but after a moment, thought twice about it and took my hand down to rest at my side. Thankfully, he didn't make for the door again.

"We need to talk."

"Later."

"No," I snapped letting my anger show for the first time since she called his name in shock. "We talk now."

* * *

DASH LEFT WITH his sister, and I wasted no time with interrogating Q. We were sitting at the table in the kitchen with shot glasses filled with the hardest liquor I could find.

"What just happened in my living room?"

He took a shot and immediately poured another. "You know most of it."

"Then start with the part I don't know."

"First, tell me why you are still dealing with him, and why you didn't tell me?"

"Because he is the only way I can find Arthur, and I needed to keep everything as low key as possible."

Q released a hard breath and took another shot. I pulled the bottle away while giving him a pointed look. I wanted him relaxed, but I didn't want him drunk before I could get any answers.

"I thought you would have given up on that now that you're out."

"I couldn't even if I wanted to. I'm in too deep. He's going to be looking to collect on his payment."

"Do you really believe he pulled those kinds of strings to get you out on bail just to gain a worker? He can find someone like you on any street."

He spit the words out harshly, but I knew he didn't mean it as an insult. The fact of the matter was he was right. "I told him I would hand deliver his mole."

"You're double-crossing Mario?" His eyebrows raised in surprise as he studied me with doubt evident in his eyes.

"He was in on it. He wants to draw him out just as much as I do."

"Why didn't you stop all contact with him when he returned you to your uncle?"

"I didn't hear from or see him again for years. It wasn't until I went to juvie that I saw him again."

"You saw him?"

"Yeah. He came to visit me."

Q sat up straighter and ground his jaw. "He's been keeping an eye on you the whole time, hasn't he?"

"He's been watching the both of us," I clarified.

"Why didn't you tell me?"

"Do you really think you would have wanted to know? You've spent the last ten years avoiding your past."

His fist slammed down on the table before he ground out, "That doesn't give you the right to keep this from me."

"And Diana? What's the story between you two? You never told me you knew his daughter."

"You didn't even know she existed before."

"Exactly my point. You hid things, too." We could

have spent all night hurling accusations but we both knew it wouldn't get us anywhere. "What did you mean he used her to make money?"

"Your golden boy isn't clean. He's as dirty as they come," he spat.

"I know. He's greedy, but he isn't Arthur."

"Then obviously you don't know half of what you think you do."

"Enlighten me, Quentin," I snapped, using his words from earlier.

"Did Mario ever tell you why he broke his partnership with Arthur?"

"He said Arthur was becoming too suspicious, and his cover was in jeopardy when he started pressing the issue against child pornography."

Quentin's grim expression deepened as he shook his head and leaned forward. "That motherfucker wasn't against child porn. He broke it off because he wanted a bigger cut."

My mind raced from all the implications and before he could say more, I was already piecing together the rest.

I'd been played.

"Arthur was cashing in on the majority of the share because he was supplying the *fresh talent*. How do you think Arthur was so successful keeping his business undetected by the Feds? Mario was his eyes and ears, and for that, he believed it should have been a fifty-fifty partnership. When Arthur refused, Mario decided to break it off and start his own line of business while stealing from Arthur's *supply*."

"How do you know this?"

"Because I was his first recruit."

Son of a bitch.

"And Diana?"

"She was a convenience he made useful to get his business up and running."

"He used his own daughter?"

"To him, he didn't believe he was selling her. That motherfucker made us do sick shit to each other every day in front of a camera. We were just kids, man. We had no clue what we were doing. He coached us through it. Showed us what to do. When we complained too much, he beat us."

"And then what happened?" I asked though I already knew.

"You showed up."

"How did my appearance change things? I wasn't there long before he brought me to the States."

"Mario is sloppy as hell and isn't as nearly as careful as he thinks. I overheard a lot of his business dealings. I didn't understand much of it then, but I remember all of it. The bureau got word of him spending too much of his time outside of the United States jurisdiction. Arthur had business dealings in Canada, as you know, and within the States. They pulled him from the case because he had apparently failed to bring the bureau evidence that would allow them to convict or at least bring him in with a good chance of the charges sticking."

"He was found out."

"Big time. The bureau began investigating Mario. He lost his job, but the only reason they weren't able to convict was because he was never caught with anything illegal."

"Meaning us."

"Bingo. He brought us here to save his own ass. Being caught with us meant a conviction and time behind bars and becoming the bitch of a beefy inmate named MacDaddy."

"Where was Diana being kept? I never met her."

"With her mother, I assume. We were never left together long before and after sessions. He brought her in when he wanted to film and she always left after."

"Why would he bring Diana here knowing you lived in the same city? He had to know I would find out."

"He wouldn't think you'd care."

"Why do you say that?"

"You impressed a lot of people back then, Keiran. You were able to channel your emotions and throw away childhood possibilities and become what they needed of you."

"Are you trying to say they broke me?"

"Didn't they?"

"I wasn't afraid. I didn't show fear."

"But how much did you let them take from you?"

Quentin was actually older than I was by two years. Without medical records, we were able to lie about his age. Somehow, even then, we knew the significance of staying together. Q spent months in foster care while the agencies and local law enforcement attempted to track down his parents, but after nearly a year, no one stepped forward to claim him. He was eventually taken into the care of a couple. We'd never spoken about it before, but I knew he had possessed a small ounce of hope that he would find his parents. The parents who likely sold him to buy a hit or a beach house in Malibu. It just all depended on how much they thought he was worth.

"You were there, man. You did the same as I did. You made the same sacrifices."

"And when I was finally free, I was able to let go. Can you say the same?"

Letting go...

I kept hearing that phrase. It's like everyone got together to figure out how the hell they could get me to *let go*.

The last person to tell me to let go was Dash. I knew what to say to get him off my back, but this was Q. He knew what it was like and based on the story he had just revealed, he knew a hell of a lot more than I did. Mario had turned him and his daughter into child prostitutes. I swallowed down the bile and whatever feelings I had about the past. I dealt with it how it suited me, and all the Dr. Phil's of the world could go fuck themselves.

"You said it yourself, right? I was in too deep, so there's no salvation for me."

"You know that's not what I meant."

"It doesn't make it any less true. Now answer my question." When he raised his eyebrows in question, I asked, "Why do you think Mario trusted me with his daughter knowing you were here?"

"Anything Mario is into right now, he's thinking he could suck you into it. He's going to try because if someone like you isn't with him, then you're against him."

"I already know he knows I'm a threat."

"Then what are you doing dealing with him?"

"I'm selling my soul to the devil."

CHAPTER TWENTY

KEIRAN

QUENTIN LEFT TO pick up his foster sister from dance practice, leaving me alone with Diana. I found her in the bathroom primping for some unknown reason.

"Are you hungry?" I gruffly asked. My reluctance to be hospitable was apparent.

She turned from the mirror to face me. "Wow. For a second there I thought I would have to ask."

It was the first word she'd spoken since seeing Q again. Talk about a fucking blast from the past. Thinking about what Mario had done and all the lies he'd told and clever tricks he had pulled resulted in a lack of patience.

"I'll be in the kitchen. Hurry up."

I went back downstairs and prepared some steaks before throwing them in the oven. My uncle would be home soon, and I needed to prepare myself mentally for the confrontation that was sure to come.

Diana came downstairs ten minutes later just as my uncle walked through the door.

"I don't know what you boys have been doing around here, but shacking up with girls in my home is out of the question."

"My, my," Diana purred. "Now I see where you get your firm hand."

"Shut the fuck up, Diana." To John I said, "She's a guest. I'm doing a favor for a friend."

His eyes narrowed suspiciously, and for a second, I thought I was looking at my father. I wondered if he was faced with the same problem when he looked at me. Is that why he could never look me in the eye for long?

"What friend?"

"One of the guys from the team. Her parents kicked her out, and his parents don't have room in their house. As Captain—"

"You aren't on the basketball team anymore so are you referring to the same team that kicked you off?"

I ignored his blatant attempt to remind me that I had screwed up. At least in his eyes I had. I didn't care that Trevor and Anya were dead, and it was amazing anyone could expect me to be after they both set me up. It wasn't exactly a secret after Trevor attacked Monroe in the gym bathroom. "I told him she could stay here and she will."

I watched his jaw work. I was challenging him, and he knew it. Common sense told me to stop while I was ahead, but my anger toward him wasn't going away anytime soon.

"I want her gone."

"Fine. If she goes, then so do I. Have fun explaining to the authorities how you helped me become a fugitive."

"Are you threatening me?" He took a menacing step forward, but as usual, I held my ground.

"I'm simply reminding you that after all the strings

you pulled keeping me out of jail and in school, I'm sure it wouldn't be easy to prove your innocence. I mean... why wouldn't you help your nephew disappear? You did it before."

Out of the corner of my eye, I noticed Diana perk up at my admission. I needed to remember to censor what I said around her. She could very well be a mole he put in place to keep eyes on me, as he was known to do with Arthur. Mario and I were cut from the same cloth, which meant we didn't completely trust each other.

Trevor and Anya died while in Mario's care. Even though I *gifted* them to him, it was with the strict instruction not to kill them. Simply disappearing was cleaner than killing them. Killing them left a body to be found, which is how I landed in jail.

Her dad had yet to explain how Trevor and Anya were murdered, and though I haven't pushed the subject, it was always at the back of my mind. First, I had to take down Arthur and find Mitch all before my trial, which was scheduled to take place in less than two months. For that, I needed Mario, so making an enemy of him wasn't the smartest move.

"That has nothing to do with a teenaged girl living in my home without my consent. How do I know she didn't run away from home, and her parents aren't looking for her?"

"Um... actually, I'm twenty so legally, I'm an adult, Daddy O."

My patience was now completely gone.

Her throat was in my hand, and I was marching her backward out of the kitchen before John could respond. My firm hand around her neck was the only thing keeping her up and from tripping over her feet.

"Hey, hey, hey! I only like the rough stuff when I have nothing on," she giggled. It turned into a nervous broken sound after the look I gave her, warning her not to fuck with me.

She was quickly becoming a pain in my ass along with being an inconvenience. I didn't have time to babysit. However, after learning the things I had about Mario, maybe it was his plan.

Having his daughter in my care could have worked to my advantage, but now I wasn't so sure of his paternal feelings for his daughter. If I never met Dash's parents or even Monroe's aunt, there would be nothing to convince me that good parents existed.

"You know the way to the guest bedroom and, by the way, he's my uncle, not my father, so either you were stupid enough to come here without doing your homework or your father was just stupid enough to send you here period."

I shoved her toward the stairs and disappeared back inside the kitchen without waiting for a response.

"I didn't raise you to treat women like that," my uncle barked. He was standing by the door as if to come to her rescue. It was all I could do not to roll my eyes but then I caught on to the first part of his statement.

"Raise me? Is that what you call being gone three hundred and sixty-five days out of the year?"

"Regardless of how you feel about me, you will not treat women that way."

"Treat women like what?"

"We don't manhandle a woman the way I just saw you do."

"No, we threaten to take away their child." His lips thinned out in a hard line as he glared at me. Once again, I'd backed him into a corner. He had been gone for far too long after making too many mistakes to step in and be a parent now. "Look…" I released an aggravated breath, feeling myself giving in partially. "I won't bring trouble to your doorstep, and I can't toss her out, so you'll just have to trust me." I turned on my heel and left him to mull it over.

The hallway was clear so I assumed Diana did as I ordered. I followed after her to the guest bedroom. It was next to mine so if she ever tried to sneak out, I would hear her pass. I wasn't taking any chances.

The bedroom door was unlocked so I pushed my way in. She was centered in the middle of the bedroom, leaning back on her hands, wearing a playful expression. "It's about time you came. I'm ready now to test out those rough edges of yours and ruffle some bed feathers if you are."

"Just... stop. I need you to start talking. Why did your father send you here?"

"I told you—"

"I want the truth, not the rehearsed bullshit he told you to say. Q told me what happened between you two ten years ago. Is it true?"

"I don't see why Q felt the need to tell you any of that." Her eyes lowered with what might have actually been shame. She sat up and crossed her legs, letting her hands rest in her lap.

"He didn't go into detail." I had no clue why I wasted time reassuring her. I didn't care about her feelings. I cared about what was inside her head—her knowledge, her memories... her plans. The daughter of Mario had to have a plan. I just wondered who was meant to suffer. "Just tell me what I need to know. Make this easy on yourself now because I will get it out of you."

Her eyes narrowed as bitter resentment shone through. "If you knew me at all, you wouldn't waste your time on threatening me, but since you don't, I'll spell it out for you—I don't care about what you can or are willing to do to me. The life I've lived isn't one I will miss."

"Then maybe we can help each other."

"How?"

"Your father... how attached to him are you?"

* * *

I WAS TAKING a huge chance walking into this place, but after what I had learned last night, I was quickly running out of chances. I managed to turn every head when I walked in, and word would likely get out that I was here, but it was a risk worth taking.

Mario was dirtier than I'd thought, and he'd been playing me all along—right from the fucking beginning.

He toyed with my hate for the syndicate to use me as a pawn in order to take over Arthur's organization. His plan was to either kill me or recruit me once Arthur was out of the way.

He would never get a chance to do either.

I was going to beat him, my father, and Arthur at their own game. Sooner or later, someone would have to be the victor. I just had to ensure that it would be me.

"Mr. Masters, how are you?" The detective with the thick mustache who had arrested me weeks ago greeted me as he walked into the room. Another man, who I assumed was his partner, followed, and they each took a seat in front of me.

"Can we cut the formalities? I have school in an hour."

"Yes, that's right... For a high school boy, you sure have your hand in a lot of jars. What can we do for you today?"

"I have information you'll want to hear, but it comes with a price."

"Are you here to confess."

"Yes. I am."

The looks on their faces were priceless.

* * *

AFTER CAREFULLY ARRANGING all the pieces of the puzzle, phase one of my plan was in play. I pulled into the school parking lot with twenty minutes to spare. The coach including the entire team called a meeting this morning, and for some reason, I was expected to attend.

I'd already resigned myself to never playing on the team or any college team after. College scouts were no longer interested after my status as the only suspect in a double murder went national. There was even a petition to have me removed from the school, but it never generated more than a few signatures. The murders would always hang over my head like a dark cloud.

As I stepped from the car in the mostly empty parking lot, my gaze zeroed in on a familiar form entering the school.

What the hell is Fitzgerald doing in town? Better yet... Why is he at the fucking school?

He had no family here or any real friends other than Monroe, so if he was in town, then he was no doubt here to see her. Had she called him? If she had, then Monroe had bitten off more than she could chew. Fitzgerald was a no safe zone. I didn't know him, and I damn well didn't trust him.

I rounded the corner to find where the shit had disappeared to, and I was nearly knocked on my ass.

Fitzgerald was pinned against the lockers by Q as they devoured each other's lips. *Fitzgerald is into men?* I didn't even know Q was into men. I'll be damned if that didn't explain a lot including the day Q brought him to the jail.

I still didn't want him anywhere near Monroe. There was no give where she was involved. I realized I was being completely unreasonable and selfish, but I couldn't bring myself to care. I backpedaled around the corner and tried to erase the last thirty seconds out of my head. I wasn't homophobic or anything, but some shit I just didn't care to see.

If Jesse played for the other team, then that meant I could put Quentin on him, though it looked as if he might have been way ahead of me. I made a mental note to ask Q about his relationship with Jesse and why he had never mentioned it before. The last thing I needed was any more cards being dealt under the table along with my own.

CHAPTER TWENTY-ONE

LAKE

"Have you heard?" Willow asked as we sat down with our lunch trays at our normal table.

"Yes, unfortunately. It's all over school that Mrs. Needleman didn't wear a bra today and gave everyone a clear view of her nipple rings."

I had no clue if that's what Willow was talking about, but I prayed it didn't have anything to do with Keiran. After he used me and discarded me like yesterday's trash, I'd pretty much wished every bad thing in the book on him.

"Eww. Seriously, she's like sixty with nipple piercings. Gross. I just wonder why she wouldn't wear a bra especially since her shirt was transparent."

"Maybe they're new and she wanted to show them off," I guessed. I bit into my carrot and willed my eyes from straying to the other side of the room where Keiran sat with his usual horde of elite friends. I regretted deciding to eat in the cafeteria. My determination to not let Keiran affect me was hopeless.

"Anyway, that's not what I meant. The school and basketball coach let Keiran back on the team."

Apparently, God was busy today.

The carrot fell from my fingertips and landed in the tray as I stared at Willow. "You're kidding."

"Nope. Besides, Mrs. Needleman's nipple rings, it's all anyone's been talking about. Apparently, the school cares more about making it to the Championship this year than they care the guy is practically an axe murderer."

"Anyone ever tell you that you have a flare for being dramatic?"

"Pffft. Have you seen the way I dress? If that doesn't do it, then all is lost for humanity's brains."

"Why would they let him back on the team?"

She shrugged and bit into a chicken tender. "No one really expected him to be kicked off the team permanently. He's the school's golden boy. Not even a double murder could taint that."

"This is bullshit." I threw down my third carrot and stood up, pushing my chair back roughly and letting it scrape across the floor. Willow looked up at me and stopped mid chew.

"Where are you going?" she mumbled around a mouthful of chewed up chicken.

"I'm going to see what the hell is this school's problem." I moved for the door without waiting for her response. I knew she would only try to talk me out of it and tell me it wasn't a big deal. Nothing Keiran did seemed to be a big deal.

He must have sensed something was wrong because I felt his gaze following me. Against my will, I stopped at the door and looked over my shoulder to see him watching me. There was no way he could have known what I was up to, but his gaze challenged me anyway. His lips were set in a hard line. What did he have to be angry about? He'd gotten his way once again.

Time seemed to stand still during the battle of wills as we each silently fought for power. His head lowered predatorily, and his gaze darkened in a way that was meant to strike fear. Three months ago, it would have.

I let the side of my lip curl into a smirk that rivaled his own, blew a kiss and slammed through the doors.

The sound of the doors closing echoed behind me as I headed for Coach Lyons office. In the back of my mind, I wondered if my determination for answers was because of justice or my own personal vendetta. Either way, he should have never been let back on the team. I didn't give a damn what the law said. Not being proven guilty doesn't make you innocent.

I made it to the other side of the school where Coach Lyon's office was held. He was perched in his chair watching the tiny television and looking entirely too comfortable for someone who did a murderer favors. I knocked on the open door and stormed inside, not waiting for his acknowledgment or invitation. I closed the door behind me and stood in front of his desk.

He watched me calmly despite my having just invaded his space. "Coach Lyons, I need to talk to you."

"Young lady, I should throw you out of my office. That is not the way you conduct yourself toward a member of the staff."

Was he serious? Where was this guy's autocracy during the last four years I was bullied mercilessly by his star player?

"So if I was able to dribble a ball, you would be willing to overlook it?"

"I will not tolerate—"

"Why is Keiran Masters back on the basketball

team?" I demanded.

"I beg your pardon?"

"He is still being charged with the murder of two students. One of them played for your team. Did you forget that?"

"Of course, I haven't forgotten, Miss Monroe, but what I do with my team is none of your concern."

The man was a royal ass.

"The safety of the students should be your concern. You would sacrifice that for a championship?"

"He was allowed back into the school, which means he wasn't considered a threat. You have no business coming into my office and demanding answers from me, you little bitch. I don't answer to a child. Now get it out!" he bellowed. Spittle flew from his mouth and landed on his chin as his face turned beet red.

Just as I was about to respond, Keiran's deep voice sounded low from the door. "Monroe."

My gaze flew to his tall form darkening the doorway. He wore a blank mask, but even so, I could sense the angry vibes emanating from his presence.

I knew he likely heard every word I had said and knew what I had tried to do. I actually started to feel guilty until I noticed his gaze wasn't trained on me. He was staring down the coach who now sat back in his chair with a worried expression.

"Why did you follow me?" I asked accusingly.

"Wait for me outside."

"I'm busy here." I turned my head dismissively. I wanted nothing more than to get out of here, but I stubbornly wanted to do it on my own terms.

"Do you really want me to touch you right now?" He spoke the words softly, but the threat had an even worse effect than if he had screamed them at me. Why was he so calm? I had just tried to get him kicked off the team so why hadn't he lashed out?

"Fine." I gave him a look that said this wasn't over and attempted to move around him without touching, but his hand shot out and grabbed my arm just as I passed him.

"Don't go far," he ordered.

I looked down at his large hand on my arm and suppressed the shiver of anticipation I could feel building when I remembered all the things he'd done to me with his hand and all the places he had touched.

"I'm sure touching is a violation of your release. Be careful, Masters. One might think you were attempting to intimidate a witness."

He leaned close enough to whisper in my ear. "Any time you need me to intimidate you, baby, just say the word."

CHAPTER TWENTY-TWO

KEIRAN

I GENTLY PUSHED her out of the office, shutting and locking the door behind me. Coach Lyons still sat slumped in his chair with a wary expression.

"Can you believe her, kid? She wanted me to take you off the team."

"I heard."

"You heard... Well, uh... how much did you hear?"

"Enough."

He shifted in his chair nervously. "Listen, my temper got the best of me, but you should know I wouldn't remove you from the team. I didn't want you off in the first place, but it was out of my hands."

He offered me a shaky smile as if his pitiful promises meant something to me and all would be forgiven. As if I hadn't just heard him raise his voice at Monroe. As if he hadn't just called her a bitch and nearly spit in her face.

"Let me make this quick because I have a frustrating female who needs my attention. What I just heard makes me want to cut your tongue out and make you choke on it."

"Son, liste—"

"As I said... I heard enough. If you ever speak to her that way again, I'll make your wife a widow early."

I left him sputtering and red-faced in his office and went after my stubborn headache. I tracked her down just outside the cafeteria doors and quickened my steps to catch her. She knew I would come after her and as much as she pretended not to be afraid of me, she sought the safety of the cafeteria.

"Oh, no you don't," I said when I grabbed her arm and dragged her in the direction we'd just come from.

"Let go of me, asshole." I ignored her struggles and managed to pull her into an empty classroom without being caught. I was breaking every rule and taking too many chances even being near her, but fuck if she didn't make it hard to break old habits.

Once safely hidden away, I slammed her back against a nearby wall, pushed up against her, and hid my face in her neck. If I looked into her eyes right now, I could ruin us both right here and now. "You want to tell me what the fuck that was about?"

Her scent was making it hard to remember how we ended up here in the first place. All I could concentrate on was the fact I had her in my hands again. Two weeks cold turkey and I'd relapsed. It was about as much as I had expected.

She was fire and ice.

And she had me by the balls.

"I don't owe you an explanation. I'm only trying to right a wrong."

"Damn it, Monroe." I reluctantly lifted my head from her neck and abandoned her scent. "You aren't making this easy." How could I stay away from her if she were constantly doing things to pull me back in?

"Stop calling me Monroe. My name is Lake, and I wasn't aware I was supposed to make anything easy for you. Should I show you the same mercy you showed me?"

I grabbed her face with my hands and held her eyes. "I want you to realize what's at stake here if you keep pushing me."

"You never played fair before," she whispered.

Fuck.

I let her face go. Those twinkling blue-green eyes were pure torture to my dick. "I don't know what I want more—to kiss you or kill you."

"Why did Coach Lyons let you back on the team?" she asked, blatantly changing the subject.

"He didn't let me back on the team. He asked me to come back."

"He actually sought you out?" Her body rocked against mine in outrage.

"Yes."

"Why?"

"Why do you think?" I took a step back, needing to put space between us but not too much. She visibly relaxed as she watched me warily. I noticed her palms brace the wall at her side and every other second they would clench.

"You can't mean the championship is that important?"

"It is for a lot of people."

"Enough to overlook the fact that you're a murderer?"

"I didn't kill Trevor and Anya."

"Maybe you didn't light the match, but it doesn't make you any less responsible."

"And you?"

"What about me?"

"You continuously point fingers but conveniently forget that you are as much an accomplice."

"I didn't—"

I cut her off before she could make any more false claims of innocence. "*Maybe you didn't light the match* but you knew and you didn't say anything. Why?"

She stared up at me incredulously. "And give you another reason to threaten my aunt?"

"Is that your final answer?"

"It's the only answer."

"You were never a good liar. By the way... how does it feel to have your aunt back home safe and sound? How many lies have you had to tell so far? When she holds you and tells you she loves you, do you feel guilty? Or do you feel like a hero for all the *sacrifices* you made?"

"What I sacrificed, you can't even begin to understand or measure. You'd have to have a heart for that."

"I may not have a heart, but if I were you, I'd be afraid of what beats in its place."

I couldn't help myself. I had to get my hands on her again, so I did. I gripped her hips and pulled her into me.

"Try something like this again," I growled low and tightened my hold on her, "and one night I will crawl through your window and make you disappear. I won't need to kill your aunt. I won't need to hurt your best friend, and I won't need to use your buddy, Jesse. Do you think they would survive not seeing you again?"

"I'm over you threatening to kill me."

I couldn't resist stealing a kiss from her lips, and without pulling away, I whispered, "It wasn't a threat, and I have no intentions of ever killing you." I stole another kiss. "I'm much too selfish for that." I lifted my head to look her in the eye. "Stay out of my way, Monroe. I'm trying to protect you."

"From you?"

"And from them. But yeah... mostly me."

"And what if I just want to make you pay?"

"Then I'd say you were playing a very dangerous game."

CHAPTER TWENTY-THREE

LAKE

SCHOOL COULDN'T END soon enough. It didn't help that I had a test in all of my classes today, including gym class. The stress of the confrontation with Keiran earlier was weighing down on me as I walked into the precinct. I stormed up to both Detective Daniel and Wilson's desks with purpose.

"I have information."

The detectives looked up from their coffee seemingly startled as their faces furrowed with confusion. "Lake, what are you doing here? What information?"

"Information that will help you bring Keiran in. He cannot continue to walk free." Instead of looking grateful or relieved, the detectives shared a nervous glance. "What?"

"We aren't pursuing Keiran Masters any longer."

My stomach lurched before plummeting down to rest at my feet. "What do you mean? How could you not pursue him?"

"Masters also came to us this morning with valuable information."

"Well, apparently, he didn't turn himself in because I just saw him at school, so what could he have possibly told you that would make you drop the case against him?"

"It hasn't been entirely dropped. It's been temporarily suspended."

"Then wha—"

"I'm sorry, Lake, but we can't discuss it. It's high profile and if we blow this, it would mean not only our jobs but many lives, as well."

"After you convinced me to turn him in and testify, putting my own life at risk, you just decide to back out?"

"You don't understand what's at stake."

"Then make me understand! It's the least you could do, don't you think?"

The detectives did their silent communication thing I was starting to hate. "We have the chance to catch a much bigger fish. We have the chance to bring down the most notorious child slavery ring in history."

"And so now I'm just inconsequential?"

"Lake, we will continue to protect you. If Masters hadn't provided us with suitable proof Trevor and Anya's deaths were connected, then we wouldn't consider it. However, as of now, we don't believe he is a great threat to you or anyone else."

"You don't know him, Detective Daniels. He is calculating and manipulative. He's using you to get what he wants, and I am a part of that equation."

"We are on it, Lake. Trust us. If Masters tries anything, we will lock him up and throw away the key."

"And I am supposed to believe you? You don't know what he's done or what he's capable of."

"Lake... Keiran's freedom is based solely on the information he can provide us. If he does not deliver to us both Mario Fulton and Arthur Phalan, we will pursue the death penalty when he is tried.

The death penalty?

They would kill Keiran?

I didn't realize I was falling until Detective Wilson caught me.

* * *

AFTER DETECTIVE DANIEL'S had dropped the massive bomb in my lap, I went numb. The thought of Keiran dying hurt worse than finding out my parents were dead. As much hell as he'd brought to my life, it made sense. I didn't know them, but I knew him, and despite the hate I held for him, and the need to make him pay, I still loved him.

But this wasn't what love was supposed to be.

It wasn't how the rest of the world would see it.

They would see a young girl who had been so fearful of her childhood tormentor she, instead of reciprocating the hate, chose to love him instead.

I went to Willow's after I left the station. We spent the rest of the afternoon watching movies and doing homework. I wanted to avoid questions and most of all, Jackson. He'd been hanging around a lot and though my aunt warned me previously, it still made me uncomfortable. He was essentially a good guy, but I didn't like the way he was always watching me, reading and assessing me. He saw too much, and if he ever figured it out, he would tell my aunt.

When I finally pulled myself together enough to chance going home, I said goodbye to Willow, who couldn't manage more than a noncommittal glance.

With college right around the corner, Willow was working furiously to keep her grades up. Or at least that's what she said. Avoiding Dash may have had a little more to do with her constant need to stay distracted, though he seemed to avoid her just as much.

When I asked her what had happened between them after laser tag, she said me almost being killed was a reminder of what Dash had done, and she couldn't be with someone like that. She also made it a point to tell him someone like him wasn't worth breaking her mother's heart, which explained the stick up his ass.

Despite Dash's involvement, I couldn't help but feel responsible for keeping Willow from being with the only guy she'd ever shown such keen interest in.

I didn't hang around much longer after our homework was complete, but later, wished I had. All hell seemed to break loose soon after I came home, which was unfortunate because I wasn't prepared to handle anything else that required stimulation of the brain. I managed to hide it well, but I was still reeling from the effects of Keiran today. I was more upset that I could still feel anything for him.

So what did that tell me?

That I still hadn't learned anything from the past couple of months?

That Keiran was still very much in control?

I pulled into my driveway a few minutes later and saw my aunt was home, but when I walked inside, she was nowhere to be found. I figured she'd locked herself in whatever room inspired her today, and chose not to disturb her. Not even five minutes later, she decided to make her presence known.

"Lake, what is this?" My aunt demanded as she stormed into the kitchen where I was creaming my bagel. I was too distracted by thoughts of Keiran and forbidden moments in abandoned classrooms to eat anything more. She slapped a newspaper down in front of me, and the caption on the front sent my knife and bagel slathered in cream cheese, crashing to the floor.

"That's that boy, isn't it? Keiran Masters? He's from your school. He was here... Oh, God," she rushed out in one breath.

"Aunt Carissa, please... calm down. It's not what you think." Actually, it was exactly what she might have been thinking, but what else was I supposed to say?

"Why didn't you tell me about this?"

There are many reasons why I didn't tell her about Keiran being accused of murder. Fortunately, my aunt wasn't one to keep up with the news. She preferred fantasy to facts, and it was the main reason I was able to keep this a secret for this long. However, a gruesome murder of underage kids, one being an ex-police officer's son, was bound to come to light. I was just surprised she went this long without hearing about it.

"I didn't think you'd care," I lamely answered.

"Didn't think I—" She took a deep breath before her voice exploded in anger. "For crying out loud, he came over and had pancakes!"

"Aunt Carissa," I began but was cut off.

"Just tell me, Lake... are you in any danger?"

"Why would you ask that?" My face and voice remained impassive despite the pandemonium erupting inside my head.

"Because I really thought you were dating him. I can't say I'm comfortable with you seeing this boy if you are."

"No, I'm not seeing him. We were hardly even friends."

She searched my face for signs of dishonesty, and it was the one time I prayed my aunt didn't know me as well as she did. She seemed to give in to whatever answer she had found when she asked, "What happened

to those poor kids? How could anyone do such a thing?”

“Aunt Carissa, he was a suspect, but they let him go. I guess they found new evidence.”

She didn’t appear convinced by my explanation as she furiously scanned the paper before slamming it down to glare at me. “Why do I get the feeling you aren’t telling me everything?”

“What do you mean?” I asked as I fought to keep my gaze on her. If I looked away or let my voice change infinitesimally, my aunt would catch it. She was too observing.

“What is your involvement with this guy and don’t you dare lie to me. A hot guy doesn’t just show up and eat a person’s pancakes without having a reason.”

I struggled with an answer, but a story worth telling, much less believing, wouldn’t surface. *Damn the newspapers and damn Keiran Masters.*

“He, uh, asked me out once, and I said no. He showed up because he was pretty persistent about it, but that’s over now.”

She eyed me warily before peering down at the paper again, scanning it once more before shaking her head with a look of sadness etched across her features. “It’s so tragic. Lake, I want you to promise me you will be careful. I don’t know what I would do if something happened to you. After your mother died—” She paused mid-sentence and her eyes widened in horror. “Oh, Lake, honey. I’m sorry. I know this isn’t what you want to hear yet but—”

“Aunt Carissa, not now,” I urged but it sounded more like a desperate plea.

“Lake, I did this for you. I know you think you don’t want to hear it, but you need to. You’re already eighteen and will be graduating in just a few months. I couldn’t send you off into the world without knowing what happened to them. I'm sorry I lied to you."

"I know, Aunt Carissa. You don't need to apologize again. I just need time to figure this all out."

I couldn't tell her there was nothing to figure out or that instead, I couldn't bring myself to admit they were really dead. I couldn't even promise to try.

* * *

MY ROOM HELD a quality that wasn't there when I left this morning, and when my eyes landed on my brooding teenage tormentor leaning against the wall, I understood why.

"It occurred to me the little stunt you pulled today was not a one-time deal or a brief lapse in judgment."

Remembering his earlier threat, I quickly spun around to leave, but he was across the room with his hand over my mouth before I could cross the threshold. He pulled my arms back to rest at the small of my back. After I was restrained to his satisfaction, he quickly loosened his grip as if he were afraid of hurting me. I laughed despite my current position.

"So can you guess why?"

"I hardly think I need to be in this position or have you in my room in the middle of the night to play a fucking guessing game."

"Careful with those big words, little girl."

"Get over yourself, Keiran. We're the same age."

"That's where you have it wrong. I'm nothing like you."

I gritted my teeth to tamp down the onslaught of desire I couldn't shake but held on to the growing anger. "Say what you came to say and get out."

"What makes you think what I came to do involve words?"

"Because you seem to have a lot of them."

His deep chuckle vibrated all the way down my body. "Is that a challenge?"

"It's whatever you want it to be. I just want you gone."

His laughter ended, and I knew he was assessing me in the way he always did, gauging my sincerity. I felt my words and their meaning down to my soul, and still, I knew I didn't mean it. It frustrated me more than the sexual buildup he insisted on creating every time we were near.

I wanted to put him away forever. They wanted to kill him.

I was being pulled in two different directions—the need to hurt him and the need to protect him.

The sweet scent of his breath was intoxicating, and then I felt it—his lips near my ear.

He whispered, "And I just want inside you."

I felt the rush, the clench, and the goddamn fucking *need*.

Each encounter, no matter how close he got to me or how far he stayed away, made it harder and harder to keep my promise.

"Your scare tactics are getting old, Keiran. We won't be in high school forever." He pressed against me from behind but didn't make any further movements.

"If you think I'm trying to scare you, then my seduction skills need serious work. Besides, I don't need fear to control you anymore. My cock is pretty good at making you do what I want."

"And what will you do when I'm thousands of miles away and no longer vulnerable and available?"

"Who says I'll let you get that far?"

"And how do you plan to stop me?"

"In whatever way that works." He flipped me

around to face him. I had seen the intent in his eyes before I was falling backward, engulfed in the now stifling heat of my bedsheets.

"Keiran... no." The knife continued it's descent of my torso, slicing and ripping away my barriers. He wanted me exposed in every way. He needed me vulnerable. "Don't do this."

When he expertly ripped away the remnants of my shirt, ignoring my struggles, I screamed. A sound so unnatural and desperate it actually pierced my gut painfully and shook my body. He jerked upright to stare down at me in stormy surprise, but it was too late. The need for survival had already consumed me. My teeth sunk into the flesh of his right shoulder. I didn't stop biting. Even when I was assaulted with the metallic taste of his blood, I didn't stop.

I heard his curse and grunt of pain, but it only spurred me on. He could have easily dislodged me with a quick, merciless flick of his knife. The floodgates opened and released, turning my gaze murky.

Careful hands banded around my upper arms, lifting me away but keeping me close. "What the hell do you think you're doing?" he demanded, shaking me.

Was that a serious question? I shoved him away in disgust and if I weren't feeling so damn crazed, I would have laughed at his look of astonishment. "I won't let you make me a scared little girl again."

"Lake? Open the door! I heard you scream—should I call the police?"

Shit. I'd forgotten Aunt Carissa was home.

We watched each other for the longest time, both waiting to see what I would do. I held Keiran's gaze as I answered. "Uh... yes, I'm fine. I stubbed my toe and thought I broke it."

"Do you want me to look at it?"

"No, I'm fine. I'll be down in a moment to ice it."

Her retreating footsteps were the only sound between us as we stared at each other. "You need to leave," I ordered, rising from the bed once I was sure my aunt was out of hearing range. We now stood facing each other.

"Do you want those six weeks back? Do you want the isolation, the distance, the hard sex without an inkling of a connection? Do you want to feel like you have no way out? Do you want to feel forced and used? You might have come every time I touched you, but I know what it did to you, and if I pushed for a little more, you would have broken."

He grabbed me by my waist and yanked me to him without warning. "Give me the word, and I can make you feel like that again." He bent low to whisper against my lips, "Helpless..." He took my bottom lip between his teeth. "And thoroughly fucked."

My earlier resolve began to melt away with a whimper. "You are my scared little girl, Lake." I melted more at the sound of my name on his lips. Using my first name was a clear indicator I was affecting him at this moment—as much as he was affecting me. "And I am your big, bad wolf."

He kissed me for the second time today, and I let him.

In his arms, I didn't have the strength to fight him. I didn't have the strength to care that he was a monster carved from a past that was undoubtedly dark. I Just. Didn't. Care.

"Every time I get near you, I can't remember why I have to stay away," he groaned when he finally released my lips with a final nip.

That makes two of us.

"Are you staying away because you're mad at me or

because you think you are protecting me?"

"I am protecting you."

"Yeah. Almost being kidnapped was a clear indication of that." I rolled my eyes. Did I blame him for almost being kidnapped? No. I blamed the people who he came into this world blindly trusting to protect him.

"So what are you saying?"

"I don't know what I'm saying. When I woke up this morning, I hated you, and I wanted nothing more than to see you behind bars. I went to Detective Daniels and Detective Wilson offering to get evidence of *everything*."

I chanced a look up at his eyes, expecting anger but seeing only questions. "And?"

"And nothing. The first time I went, they turned me down saying it was too dangerous, and they couldn't risk me as a witness."

"And the other?"

I took a deep breath. "I went after school today." I waited for a reaction, but he only nodded and remained silent. "They told me they weren't pursuing you anymore."

"I made a very detailed confession today, but they are willing to overlook it."

"So long as you help them catch Mario and Arthur." His eyebrow shot up in surprise. "I kind of wrestled it out of them with guilt."

"Nice," he praised.

"Do you know they will pursue the death penalty if you don't bring them in?"

"Yes."

I ripped myself away from him and pushed him back. "Why are you so calm about it? They are going to *kill* you. You'll *die*. " I wanted Keiran to pay for many wrongs, but I didn't want him dead. I wouldn't be able to handle it. I didn't realize I was crying until he wiped away one of the many tears from my face.

"And that scares you?"

"Doesn't it scare you?"

He laughed. The fucker actually laughed. "I'm not afraid to die. I'm just unwilling."

"So what are we going to do?"

"We?" His smile was radiant, and his eyes twinkled as he stared down at me.

"You know what I meant."

"I love it when you pout."

"I'm not pouting."

"First, you are going to have to stop trying to set me up to go to jail."

"It's not a setup if you actually did it."

"I didn't kill them, Lake."

I tried not to smile at him saying my name and asked, "Well, then who did?"

"Mario."

"Mario?" It only just occurred to me that I never met the mysterious man who brought Keiran to Six Forks and helped him to seek revenge against me. "But I thought he was like a godfather or mentor to you."

"We were both a means to an end for each other. He just wasn't honest about his end. I thought we wanted the same thing, but he just wanted to make more money."

"He used you."

"Yes."

"Are you going to kill him?" A small part of me hoped he would say yes—then I realized Keiran might have actually succeeded in corrupting me.

"Bloodthirsty, aren't we?"

"You're one to talk."

"I won't kill him if I don't have to. There is a lot

more at stake."

"What?"

"The day Arthur tried to take you, he offered to help Keenan get a lung if I gave him Mario. He knew I was working with Mario to set him up."

"How can he get Keenan a lung?"

"He wouldn't say, but it's my brother—I have to believe it because I can't lose him." I didn't miss the vulnerability and sadness in his eyes when he spoke about Keenan. I knew he missed him. I did, too.

"You have to save your brother."

"I will."

"But how are you going turn Mario and Arthur in and keep your promise to Arthur?"

"I'm going to turn them in together, but not before I get that lung."

"Keiran—"

"I know it sounds complicated and probably won't work, but I'll die trying before I let my brother die."

"This isn't just about your need for revenge then?"

He picked me up and laid me on the bed again, laying me down before crawling in between my legs. My hair had unraveled from its bun and fallen in my face, so he brushed it back while staring into my eyes. "Not anymore."

I let him remove the remaining clothes on my body, and after he had removed his, he hooked my thigh in the crook of his elbow and lined his body with mine.

"Do you remember the night I first took you? It was right here, baby. Do you remember?"

"Yes."

"Did you want me?"

"I didn't have a choice."

"You always had a choice and you made it."

"I don't see how any of it matters now."

"Answer me."

"Yes."

He lowered his face to gaze at my breasts before meeting my eyes again while he sunk into me slowly. "And do you want me now?"

"Yes."

He spent the rest of the night swallowing my screams with his mouth while my unassuming aunt slept down the hall.

CHAPTER TWENTY-FOUR

KEIRAN

THE PERFECT WAY to end a school week was having Lake pinned against the side of her ride while trying to suck her face off. It had been a week since we called a truce, and since then, my hands had been glued to her body.

"Keiran," she moaned. It came out muffled because of my tongue halfway down her throat, but if there was anything I recognized it was the sound of my name coming from her beautiful- lips. She managed to wrestle her face away from me earning a hard look. "Don't look at me like that. You need to go to practice or you'll be late."

"They can start without me." I looked down at her attire and cursed the person who invented jeans for women. Then again, I didn't like other men looking at her bare legs either...

"You're the Captain."

"I know," I said and went for her neck, but when a worried look flashed across her eyes, I stopped. "What's up?"

"Is Dash okay with you taking the spot back?"

"Yeah... Why wouldn't he be?" She fidgeted against me, but when she ducked her head, I guessed why. "Dash doesn't care about all that, and frankly, neither do I. It's just a title, babe, and I trust him with my life."

"Okay."

"Now go before I teach you how to fuck in the backseat of a car."

"Keiran!" I rolled my eyes, lifted her, and placed her in her seat before buckling her in. When she continued to stare at me with a mixture of disbelief and curiosity, I took her keys from her hand and placed them in the ignition, starting the car. "Don't worry, babe. I'll still teach you—just not here." I quickly kissed her lips and slammed the door. I hung back to watch her drive off.

When the taillights of her car were no longer in sight, I turned to head for the gym. A steady buzzing sound filtered up from the inside of my jeans so I fished my phone out. An unknown number flashed across the screen and my entire body instantly went on alert. I might never understand why I answered.

"Hello, son."

Mitch.

"Why are you calling me?"

"I think we got off on the wrong foot."

"Is that what you call the intention to kill your son for money—the wrong foot?"

"This all could have been so different, son. It should never have come to this. Your mother dreams of love and a family that made pancakes together on a Sunday morning. I offered her money, status, and security, but it wasn't enough. Greedy bitch."

"Say you kill me, Mitch. Say you actually succeed." The sarcasm and disbelief in my words were hard to miss because we both knew he wouldn't succeed. Mitch was just greedy and desperate enough to try despite the odds. "What happens when the money's gone again? Will you gamble and drink it all away like you always do?"

"You don't know me, boy. You don't know what I'm capable of."

"You're right. I don't know you, but I know a shitbag when I see one. You all smell the same."

"Watch your mouth, boy."

"Hit a nerve, did I?" I chuckled into the phone hoping to raise his anger enough to do something fatally stupid like come out of hiding.

"They really did a number on you, didn't they?"

"I think it has been pretty obvious that. if you weren't twisted enough to sell your own son, my life would have been pretty much the same."

"Did you know that you almost died, son? I was forced to settle for a home birth because your mother was less than cooperative. I couldn't risk taking her to a hospital for obvious reasons. Despite the promise of wealth and status, your mother wanted to end things, but, of course, I couldn't let her escape with my meal ticket."

"Is there some point to your rambling?"

"Yes. By some stroke of misplaced luck, you came out in time, and the midwife I hired was able to unwrap the cord from your neck. If I had known what a waste you would be, I would have just let you die."

"At least you know what your first mistake was because, when I find you, I will kill you slowly and painfully. The last thing you do in your pathetic life will be to scream and beg for mercy."

"Those are some bold promises, son. They taught you well. I would have thought, by now, you would have forgotten about that part of your life and became... domesticated."

"How much did they give you?"

"Pardon me?"

"How much was I worth to you?"

"It wasn't a matter of how much you were worth to me, but how much I could get for you."

"How much?" I pushed through clenched teeth.

"I was paid ten grand for you. I wanted twenty, but they were a little less than compromising," he chuckled.

"I'm not buying."

"Oh?"

"As hard up as you claimed to have been for money, you sold me for ten measly grand?"

"Believe me, nothing about it was ideal to me, but I had no choice. I couldn't be caught with you. My brother isn't an idiot. He would have suspected me, but he also would have known if he took the chance and accused me without proof, he would be leading me to Sophia. He wasn't willing to put his precious son at risk. You, however, were dispensable."

"He's not John's son, you dumb fuck."

"Watch your mouth, boy. I am still your father."

"Yeah? Well, you're someone else's father, too. Care to take a guess?"

"What are you saying, boy? Spit it out." I smiled into the phone at the visual of my father's ruffled feathers and smooth demeanor cracking.

"It seems that when your men put my brother in the hospital after you ran like a coward, it was discovered that John and Sophia's blood wasn't a possible combination match."

A brief silence descended before he laughed into the phone.

"So the little bastard is mine. I might have

known…" I could imagine him stroking his chin as an evil leer spread like poison on his face. "All the better—more money for me."

"Why don't you come out of hiding so we can handle this man to man?"

"Man to man?"

"I'm not a little eight-year-old boy anymore, Mitch."

"No, you're not. You're all grown up, and you even got yourself a lovely piece. I can tell you really like her. A smart man would keep her close. Tell me, son, are you close to her now?"

Fuck. Lake.

"Stay away from her, old man, or you'll be wearing your balls around your neck at your funeral."

I'd already done a one-eighty and was in my car before I finished the threat. His humorless chuckle filtered through the line as I clutched the phone to near breaking. I listened for background noise to gauge where he might be but didn't hear anything past his slimy voice. I cranked my car and peeled out of the lot.

"We had a great conversation the last time we talked… She's a good listener."

"She's inconsequential. I'm sure you know where I am, so why don't you tell me where you are, and we can settle this once and for all."

"The only thing needed to settle is your death certificate so I can collect my paycheck."

"Then come fucking get it. What are you waiting for?"

"The opportune moment. I'm desperate, but I am not foolish. I like to think you got your brains from me," he chuckled as if we were old friends. I never before felt the pressing need to watch the life fade from a person's eyes.

"The only thing you gave me was a wasted existence."

I jammed my finger on the end button and sent out a quick text to Monroe all the while weaving in and out of the thickening five o'clock traffic: Where are you?

Just a couple more miles, and I would be able to calm my racing heart and still the pounding in my ears. My phone flashed less than a minute later with an incoming text: Shouldn't you be practicing?

As I turned onto her street, I replied with one word: Mitch.

Seconds later, I was in her driveway and exiting the car just as her front door flung open, and she exited with a bewildered look. I wasted no time bounding up onto her porch and whisking her back inside.

Monroe fired off endless questions filled with panic as I quickly checked the windows and doors of her house.

"Will you stop for one second and tell me what is going on?" She wore a crazy look on her face as she followed me into her aunt's bedroom. I didn't give a fuck about intruding on a stranger's privacy.

"Mitch called me about you."

I heard her suck in a breath before she asked, "When?"

"A few minutes ago. I think he was watching us." I exited her aunt's bedroom and took her hand in mine, leading her into her bedroom. I sat on the edge of her bed and pulled her down onto my lap. I couldn't explain the strong, unfamiliar emotion I was feeling, but all I knew was I needed to hold her close. She didn't object to my handling. Her gaze was fixed on my face, and I could tell she was overwhelmed. "Will your aunt be home soon?"

She blinked a few times, seeming to come out of

her trance and shrugged. "She's usually home by now, but she may be out with Jackson."

"Jackson?"

"The PI guy she hired to investigate my parent's disappearance. Remember?"

I'd forgotten all about her aunt's bogus book tour.

I shed my jacket and brought her down to sit on my lap. She looked panicked again as her eyes searched mine. "What?"

"My aunt saw the papers. She won't like you being here."

"I'm not about to leave you alone, baby." Her aunt would have to deal.

She shot up from my lap and fisted her hands on her hips. "This is getting out of hand. You need to go to the police about your father."

"What?" My fists clenched in my lap from the need to touch her and drag her back into my lap. The only thing keeping me sane was her.

"Your father is trying to kill you, your brother, and your uncle for inheritance money. Don't you think it's time you do something?"

"Mitch will be taken care of."

"So you are going to chance going to jail again?"

"I didn't realize you cared so much." I smirked up at her. The fury in her eyes danced and blazed brighter.

"You don't seem to care enough. What if he comes after me again?"

"I'm here, aren't I?" My voice lowered dangerously.

"Yes. You are here, and he's still out there."

"I'm doing what I can, Lake. At some point, it's going to have to be enough!"

I didn't mean to snap at her, and judging by the hurt look on her face, I knew I had fucked up.

"I think you should go."

I stood up, ready to apologize, but when I reached for her and she moved away with a cold look in her eyes, I felt my own anger flare.

"Fuck this," I spat.

I had noticed her flinch before I stormed out. I thought to wait outside so she wouldn't be left unprotected and would feel safe, knowing I was still here, but I wanted to punish her, so I got in my car and pulled out of the driveway to park down the street.

Just as I left the driveway, another car I recognized as her aunt pulled in. I watched as she passed, and when we made eye contact, I didn't miss the icy glare she shot my way.

* * *

SATURDAY MORNING PRACTICE required me to be up at six a.m.

I didn't need to drag myself out of bed because I stayed in my car the entire night staring up at her window. I knew the exact moment she went to bed, and it was all I could do not to climb through her bedroom window and make her forgive me.

I rubbed the sleep from my face and reached to turn the ignition when an unexpected knock sounded at my window. I tensed but relaxed infinitesimally when I saw who was standing outside my car.

I rolled down the window and took in the older, near replica of Lake. "Ms. Anderson?"

"I need to talk to you if you don't mind." I studied her carefully before climbing out of the car. I could tell by her body language that whatever it was wouldn't be good. I slid my hands into my front pockets and assumed a casual stance against my car door.

"How do you know Mario Fulton?"

I'm not sure how much time had passed with me standing frozen. Being who I am there wasn't much that surprised me, but hearing my former mentor's name come from her did the trick. When I said nothing, she pressed further.

"You have had numerous dealings with him over the past few weeks, none of which I'm sure were legal."

It felt like a slap in the face to realize I wasn't as careful as I thought. "And you know this how?"

"Let me just get to the point. I want you to stay away from my niece."

"And somehow your niece has something to do with Mario? What would that have to do with me?"

"I know you having dealings with him, and I know you were the one to murder those poor kids."

"Apparently, you don't know as much as you believe." I waited for the bait to take, and when it did, I drove on. "Those poor kids, as you like to describe them, were the worst kind of enemy for your niece."

"Worse than you?" she countered. A few months ago, she would have been right, but a lot had changed, including me. She seemed good at measuring people. I recognized the calculating shift of her eyes. She didn't carry the same naiveté her niece did. She seemed to find whatever answer she was looking for because she turned to go.

"Mrs. Anderson," I called.

She turned back and pinned me with an angry stare. "It's Ms."

"Well, isn't that a shame?" I flashed a sarcastic smile to which she didn't even flinch.

So much for family genes.

"How do *you* know Mario Fulton?"

For a moment, she looked like she would answer, but she only said, "Stay away from my niece, or I'll have you arrested." She walked away, and I was forced to simply watch her retreating form as she left me in suspense. I would have to do digging on my own.

Something else about Mario I could store for later. This war just kept getting better.

As for Monroe, I would stay away for now, but I had no intention of letting her go. She would have to be pried from my cold, lifeless fingers.

Chapter Twenty-Five

LAKE

FEBRUARY

THE GROCERY STORE was filled with the typical Sunday afternoon shoppers. Aunt Carissa was deeply involved in her next novel so that left me to take over the reigns, which included grocery shopping.

I hated grocery shopping.

Aunt Carissa would always get annoyed when I would come back with junk food and frozen dinners, which led to her having to do the shopping herself.

"Well, the good thing is we won't starve," she would comment. Hours later, additional groceries would magically appear without explanation.

Over the last two months, the relationship between us had been strained and becoming more so as time passed. The day Keiran stormed from our house, she confronted me about him and accused me of keeping secrets before forbidding me to see him. She never explained why and I never asked her to. She was right, of course. I did keep secrets.

The only part of our argument I fought internally was staying away from Keiran, but the feat proved easier than I thought. The decision was made for me Monday morning at school when Keiran breezed past me as if I didn't exist. Not a glance or even a flicker of acknowledgment. I might as well have been a ghost.

I told myself I didn't care and it would be the last time Keiran played me for his fool, but later that same day I had confronted him in the hallway before lunch:

"Am I invisible?"

His eyes flickered over me hungrily before dimming to a bored dull. "Can I help you?"

"You aren't still upset about Friday, are you?"

"Upset? No." He shrugged and pushed off from the wall he was leaning against. I expected him to invade my space as he was fond of doing, but he maintained his distance with a shit eating grin. "I just decided someone as ungrateful as you are isn't worth going to jail for."

Keiran was back to being the revered basketball star of Bainbridge High, and I was once again invisible and unimportant... at least to the masses. I clung to Willow and Sheldon for support, and they seemed to do the same.

Ten frozen dinners and many sugary sweets later, I was ready to check out when the voice of a stranger stopped me.

"Wow. You're prettier than I expected you to be."

I looked around curiously, not really expecting the comment to have been directed at me, but when I saw the owner of the voice look me over, I knew I was the intended audience.

"I'm sorry?" I studied the tall, dark-haired girl who looked around my age.

She flipped her well-glossed hair over her shoulder, rested her manicured hand on her hips, and asked, "So are you her?"

"I guess that depends on who 'her' is supposed to be."

A sly smile spread across her lips as she continued to watch me. "I can see why he likes you so much. You're just as warm as he is," she sarcastically answered.

"Well, it was nice meeting you." This girl reeked of trouble, and I had enough of it to last me ten lifetimes. Why was she so interested in who I was anyway? I've never even seen her before.

"Wait," she called out.

Despite my better judgment, I did just as she asked. Her heels clicked against the tile floor as she closed the distance between us. Who wore heels to a grocery store anyway? I almost laughed when I remembered thinking a similar thought about Anya and her habit of wearing stilettos for any occasion.

"Could you at least tell me your name?"

"I'd rather not so—"

"I'm Diana," she offered. "I'm a friend of Keiran."

A friend of Keiran? How could this girl, whom I've never met or seen before, be a friend of Keiran? She smiled slyly at what I was sure to be an astonished look.

"So at least we've established that you do know Keiran."

"How do you know Keiran?"

"He's a friend of my father. Apparently, they have history. Anyway, I'm here visiting. Maybe we should get together and hang out sometime."

I would rather chew my own arm off.

"Who is your father?" I found myself asking.

"Mario Fulton."

"Mario is your father?"

Her eyes narrowed at my question as if she had the right to be suspicious of me. "Do you know my father?"

"Not quite. His name came up few times."

"Interesting." She twirled her finger in her hair, feigning indifference. "About what?"

"This and that."

"So are you going to tell me your name?"

"Why do you want to know?"

"Because I hear you are a very special girl."

"Thanks. I'll keep that in mind."

"Don't you want to know why?"

"Sure," I answered impatiently. I had little interest in what she had to say. "Why?"

"Because it takes someone special to actually throw away cock as good as his." She grabbed her receipt from the self-checkout machine at the same time I did and flounced from the store. I followed behind her at a slow pace hoping she would be gone by the time I exited the store.

When I finally did, it was in time to see her hop in the familiar black muscle car. The engine roared to life before speeding away, taking my stomach and heart with it.

* * *

"THAT BITCH!" I watched Sheldon pace back and forth across the floor of her bedroom. Willow was curled around a pillow with me, rubbing my back. "Ugh. What a smarmy bitch," she continued. I'd just finished telling them about my encounter with Diana at the store. "I knew she was no good."

"Wait... You knew about her?"

A guilty flush spread over her skin as she sunk

down on the bed. "Yes. I didn't mean to keep it from you. It's just that I've been so wrapped up in everything that happened with Keenan, I—"

I touched her hand to stop her. "It's okay. I understand."

Sheldon had just begun to come out of her shell, and I think it had everything to do with Keenan being released from the hospital a month ago. He hadn't been back at school because of his lung. The patch on his lung was fragile at best, and the condition of his release required he stay in bed. I talked to him at least once a week, and according to him, anything was better than the hospital.

I wondered if Keiran still planned to go along with his idea to get Keenan a lung. It had been three months and nothing had happened. Finding out today that Keiran was still dealing with Mario, and even worse, babysitting his daughter, had me reeling.

"No, it's not okay," Sheldon's voice interrupted my thoughts. "That wouldn't be the way I would want to find out."

"How long has she been staying with him?"

"Three months?"

I felt my heart drop to my stomach, which twisted in pain. She was there when he was with me. Granted, we were only together for a week, but he laid claim to me long before.

"Yes, but I really don't think he has touched her."

"Why do you say that?"

"Other than the fact that he can't stand her?"

I nodded. "Well, I think her and Quentin have history."

"What? How?" This came from Willow, who had been silent until now.

Sheldon ran down the entire story of the day she

had met Diana, and by the time she had finished, I was as stumped as I was when I met her.

"Well, you know what they say—if you lay down with dogs, you are sure to wake up with fleas." I laughed at Sheldon's apparent dislike for the girl who was intent on making sure she wasn't liked. My laughter died when I thought of an idea.

"I think I know how to make myself feel better."

"You do?"

"How?" Willow questioned suspiciously.

"Ctenocephalides canis."

* * *

Rihanna's S&M blasted from the speakers as I made my way to school the next morning with my plan fully formulated. I bounced in the seat to the beat of the music.

All day, I rehashed my plan over and over, and when lunch finally came, I was bouncing with vindictive excitement. I skipped the cafeteria altogether and made my way to the tree where Collin sat with his usual abundance of books.

"Hey, Collin."

He looked startled as he looked up at me. "H—hi."

"I kind of have a favor to ask you."

"A favor?"

"Yes. I know we don't know each other well and this may be wrong of me to ask but I'm pretty desperate."

"What do you need?"

"Fleas."

"Fleas?" He pushed his glasses up his nose and peered up at me. "Why?"

"Revenge," I answered truthfully. He didn't react.

In fact, he barely looked bothered at all by my answer. Being picked on and ridiculed for the last four years probably stirred similar feelings a time or two.

"Well, it's winter so they will be pretty hard to get…"

"But I bet you know how, don't you?"

He reluctantly nodded and then took me by surprise when he asked, "What do I get in return?"

"What would you like?"

"Well… um." He blushed and ducked his head, which gave me a pretty good idea of what he was thinking.

"I'm not paying for fleas with sex."

His eyes widened when he looked back up. "No. Not sex. A kiss."

"A kiss?"

"Yes. I've never kissed a girl before."

I mulled it over and just as his face started to burn redder from embarrassment, I made my decision. "Sure. A kiss it is, but when and where I say. Deal?"

"Deal."

I sat down to eat lunch with him and to get to know him. If I was going to be his first kiss, then I felt it was the least I could do. In truth, I was honored. I could tell Collin was a good person and maybe with a little time we could actually be friends.

The rest of my classes, including fifth period, were a breeze because, instead of feeling nervous, on edge, and sexually frustrated, I calculated and planned. By the end of the day, I was practically rubbing my hands together.

Before showing up at Keiran's house, I called ahead to make sure he was at practice, and Diana was apparently being watched by Quentin. Surprisingly, Collin was able to supply me with the fleas right after school.

FEAR YOU

As it turns out, his basement was a museum for various bugs. Go figure. I haven't paid him his kiss yet, but I'd already warned him it would definitely be a public one. The larger the crowd, the better.

Keenan answered the door, shirtless and dressed only in sweats. He snatched the bag of burgers he made me bring him from my hands before retreating into the kitchen. I called out to tell him I was going to use the bathroom before disappearing up the stairs. He had no clue what I actually came here to do. I was here under the pretense of wanting to visit a friend. It's not that I didn't trust Keenan, but I couldn't risk the chance of him talking me out of it. Besides... who would willingly allow *fleas* in their house?

I snuck around upstairs, looking for the guest bedroom where Diana would likely be staying in. *If she isn't actually sleeping with Keiran.*

I pushed open the door directly next to Keiran's room and hit the jackpot. It was blatantly clear the room had been inhabited by a female and for a long time now. I fought back the flare of anger and shrugged off the bag on my shoulders. As tempted as I was to snoop, I didn't have much time before Keenan would get suspicious and come looking for me.

I removed the jars he instructed me to keep warm and carefully opened the first. The pillows were my first victim before I moved on to the sheets and then her clothes. Satisfied, I made my way to the bathroom and the shower where, just as I suspected, there was a feminine bottle of shampoo and conditioner. Opening the caps, I dumped a few fleas inside before screwing them back tight and hoping they would survive. I was down to my last jar, which I saved for the best part. I made my way back down the hall and pushed through Keiran's bedroom door. His room was exactly as it had been when I was last here during a much darker time. I remembered most how he humiliated me when he used my mouth for the first time.

It pushed me to do what I needed to.

I went through the same ritual I did with Diana's room before making my way back downstairs. Keenan was inhaling his last bite when I walked in the kitchen.

"Took you long enough," he remarked without looking up from collecting his trash.

"Well, you know how we girls like to primp."

He cut his eye at me and pursed his lips. "So it would seem."

He was suspicious but didn't press further. I shrugged and followed him out to the living room where we watched movies until it was no longer safe for me to be there without running into Keiran.

CHAPTER TWENTY-SIX

KEIRAN

AUGUST 17TH
DEAR DIARY,

I wouldn't dare speak the words aloud. Not even to Willow, and yet I'm having trouble admitting them to you even.

Today, I experienced the strangest feeling of my life. Fear has evolved into something much scarier.

Something much more potent and dangerous. One school year had ended and now another begins.

I missed him. How pathetic is that? To miss someone who hated me more than he cared to breathe.

But that wasn't it, was it? It was what I felt when I saw him again.

* * *

"WHAT THE HELL!"

It was the middle of the night when I was woken up. Screaming erupted soon after, and I immediately jumped up from the couch where I'd fallen asleep.

I scrubbed a hand down my face before trudging up the stairs to see what was causing all the ruckus. I definitely knew who, but the what was unknown.

All the lights upstairs were now on, and when I reached the landing, I saw my uncle and Keenan standing in the guest bedroom doorway.

"What's going on?"

"Well, you're little girlfriend is screaming down the house," Keenan snapped.

Coming home did nothing to ease our relationship. He refused to talk to me, but when he did, it was always a sarcastic retort. Wrong or not, I was growing tired of it. How many times could I apologize?

I pushed past them to enter the bedroom. Diana was standing in the middle of the room slapping at her skin. "What the hell is wrong with you?"

I was growing fed up with her. She had undoubtedly overstayed her welcome, but until I was able to bring Mario in, I had to deal with her.

Yesterday, when I saw her exit the store with Monroe and wearing a conspiratorial grin, I felt the urge to strangle her. I knew she said something to her when Monroe emerged from the store as pale as a ghost.

She spotted my car as soon she left the store, and though she couldn't see me through the dark tint, her glare was just as powerful. I couldn't get out of there fast enough.

Diana brought my attention back to her when she started running her hands furiously through her hair and running in place while shrieking and groaning. I rushed to her and grabbed at her hands and when I did, I noticed all the tiny jumping spots. Her entire body looked as if it was infested with them. Some of them jumped onto me, and I released her quickly nearly causing her to fall backward.

Why the hell was she covered in fleas?

"Why are you covered in fleas?" I asked, repeating my question out loud. This would have been funny if it weren't late and if I wasn't annoyed by her very existence.

"You tell me," she screamed. "It's your house!"

"Calm down," I ordered.

"No! This is gross. You don't even have pets!" She ran from the room to what I assumed was the bathroom.

I looked back at John and Keenan, who still watched on silently. I walked over to the bed whose sheets were crumpled. I could see even more fleas jumping about the sheets.

"Did you do this?" I asked Keenan. Diana was right. We didn't have pets, and with the amount of fleas present, I knew they had to have been planted.

"And why would I?"

I watched him before figuring he was telling the truth. Even though he didn't care for Diana any more than I did, he was on bed rest. If not him, then who?

Another shriek sounded from the bath and I took a deep breath before leaving the bedroom. I pushed open the bathroom door without knocking. If she were naked, then she would just have to deal. She had been trying to get into my bed non-stop for the past three months anyway.

"What is it now?"

The curtains were ripped back, and she nearly fell out of the shower in her haste. She held a bottle of shampoo in her hand where more fleas jumped about. There were even more on her face and hair. She was crying hysterically. I cursed and grabbed a towel to cover up her naked body.

"Keiran, what is going on? Why are there fleas in my house?" John asked, speaking for the first time.

"I don't know, but they had to be planted."

"Who did you have over here?"

"No one." I wracked my brain but continued to come up empty. Between school, basketball practice, and gathering as much evidence as possible, I had barely been home.

"Keenan?" John asked.

"No—" he started, and then stopped as a smile spread across his face. He shook his head and then burst out laughing. It came out strangled due to his condition, and while I wanted to order him to stop, I knew he wouldn't listen. Sometimes I think he wanted to die.

"Oh, this is rich. You really picked a winner."

"What the hell are you talking about?"

"Lake came to visit me today."

"She did what?"

"She came by. We watched movies, and she left, but when she got here, she said she had to use the bathroom, so she came up here."

I tamped down my jealousy over her visiting my brother to concentrate on the pressing issue at hand. "And she didn't use the guest bathroom downstairs why?"

"The shrieking bimbo covered in fleas might be my first guess."

"Son of a bitch..."

* * *

I HAD ONE thought when I arrived at school the next morning. A thorough inspection of the house revealed that the little bitch had not only infested Diana's room with fleas, but mine as well. We spent the entire night attempting to clean Diana and control the infestation until an exterminator could be called.

For whatever reason, Monroe liked to get to school ahead of everyone else. I never knew exactly why, but my guess would be to avoid me in the hallways. It worked to my advantage now.

The only hiccup would be if Willow were with her. I knew they carpooled together every day.

I scoured the entire place for her, starting with the library, but when I couldn't find her, I grew even more agitated.

If her car weren't outside, I would have given up, but I knew she was here. Luck was apparently on my side because, when I rounded the corner, I caught her coming out of the bathroom minus Willow.

By the time she spotted me, it was too late. I was on her. I dragged her to the nearest classroom, and she surprisingly followed without a fight.

When I turned to lock us inside, I caught the smirk on her face.

"You mind telling me what the hell you were doing in my house yesterday?"

"I was visiting a friend—not that it's any of your business."

"But you weren't just visiting a friend, were you?"

"Keiran, what are you getting at?"

"That little stunt you pulled is going to cost you."

"I have no interest in your mind games." She spun around quickly, her hair flying around her shoulders, and I caught a whiff of her intoxicating scent. It set me off.

I bent low and lifted her to my shoulder, ignoring her struggles as I carried her across the room to the teacher's desk. It was large enough and the perfect height for what I had in mind.

"Put me down!"

I did as she demanded but spun her around to bend her over the desk. The ruler sitting in a coffee mug near the edge of the desk caught my eye. I grabbed it and tested the strength of it against my palm. She tensed each time the ruler hit my skin.

"It's amazing, isn't it?" She tried to stand up, but I placed a firm hand on the back of her neck.

"Let me go you—ah!"

The ruler slapped against her jean clad ass, cutting off whatever she was about to hurl at me, and I wished more than anything I could see it redden.

"Lucky for you, I didn't sleep in my bed last night or else I would make this ten times worse for you."

"Go to hell and take your little slut bucket with you!"

I dropped the ruler next to her head and released her neck but planted myself behind her to keep her in place.

"What are you doing to me?" She didn't bother to answer sensing I didn't really need one. "I can't even punish you properly."

"Then let me go!"

"Tell me why you did what you did?"

"I don't owe you an explanation. "

"And why is that?"

"Because you don't get to ignore me for two months, flaunt your new girlfriend in my face, and then demand answers from me."

"What did she say to you?"

"Let me go or I'll start screaming."

"Scream. No one is here—better yet... why don't I give you a reason to scream? I know just the way to shut you up."

My hands traveled to the front of her pants and unbuttoned them slowly. I waited for a protest, but none came, so I ventured further. Her pants were lowered and my hands were in her panties, all before I could count to three.

She was already wet, but I couldn't resist teasing her with my fingers. I found the little nub and teased her there. Her legs shifted apart slightly, and I didn't miss the way her back arched, pushing her pussy into my hand. I decided to take it a little further and slipped a finger inside her.

Her little moan was all the encouragement I needed.

Another finger and she was moving against me, fucking my fingers.

I don't remember lowering my own jeans, but when I was forced to stop pleasuring her, she looked back at me with anger and lust in her eyes.

My hand dug into my wallet for a rubber while I held her gaze. I moved slowly giving her time to say no.

She didn't.

I grabbed her hair in my fist and yanked her head up to kiss her hard as fuck as I rammed into her from behind. She screamed against my lips and jumped up to her toes.

"Keiran—"

"Shut the fuck up. I gave you the chance to talk."

I forced her torso flat on the desk and leaned over her back. My hand held onto her hair as I shoved my cock into her mercilessly. I watched her beautiful features transform as the desk rocked under our movements.

I slid deeper and kissed the sweat droplets forming on her back.

Her eyes were closed, and her face drawn tight with

concentration as she tried not to let my will take over her as it always did when I was deep inside her.

I struggled with the same issue though I was better at hiding it than she was. The way her tight pussy owned me every single time...

CHAPTER TWENTY-SEVEN

LAKE

OH. MY. GOD.

It was the only thought I could process.

I knew he would find out that it was me who plant-ed the fleas, but I didn't expect him to react so... pas-sionately.

I needed him like I needed my next breath, but if I continued let Keiran have his way every time, he would ruin us both. I needed to take control. Somehow.

My opportunity came when he withdrew from my body unexpectedly. I looked back to see him sit in the chair before yanking me into his lap. "Ride me."

I was able to hide my surprise that he was placing me in control and did as he ordered. Keiran was many things, but submissive he wasn't. I knew just how to take control.

I lifted and sunk down on him, finding my rhythm until I was riding him the way I knew he liked. He taught me well during those six weeks, so I knew what I was about to do would send him over the edge.

He watched me carefully through half-lidded eyes, and as I quickened my pace, little by little, I clamped my inner muscles around his cock. By the time he realized what I was up to, it was too late. My pussy held him with a vice-like grip.

His hands banded around my hips to stop me, but he was already coming by the time he lifted me off his cock.

I forced his orgasm from him, taking control. His eyes darkened as he watched the triumph in my own.

"Get the fuck off of me."

His darkening gaze froze me over, and I hid the familiar shiver of fear by obliging him, but I couldn't let it rest there. I had a point to make.

"What's wrong?" I cocked my head to the side while I studied him. "Are you feeling used... or just thoroughly fucked? I've got to say it worked out for both of us..."

I made a show of looking down at the evidence of his release glistening on his muscled abs. When I let my gaze travel back up to his face, I smirked, mimicking the look he often gave me after he made me beg to come.

He shot up from the chair, and I quickly stepped back thinking he would make a grab for me, but he only bent down to rip his jeans back up his thighs.

His jaw clenched and unclenched, and I knew I had struck a nerve.

"It's funny how you are doing everything in your power to fight me, but every time I touch you, you spread your legs faster than a whore for a five dollar bill."

It was a good thing he was concentrating on buttoning his jeans correctly, or he would have seen me flinch before I was able to recover.

"If you could get your rocks off while hating me, then I figured I could give it a try. Two really can play that game."

"Do you want to know why I've ignored you?"

"I know why."

"It's not because of Diana," he said impatiently.

"Okay, then... Why?"

"The day we fought, I didn't leave you. I slept in my car outside your house, and the next morning, your aunt found me."

I knew this would be bad without hearing the rest of the story.

"She told you to stay away from me, didn't she?" When he nodded, I felt my knees weaken.

"What else did she say?"

"She asked me about Mario."

I don't know how long I stood there gaping at Keiran, but it must have been a while because he took my elbow and sat me in the chair we'd just finished having sex in.

"But how could she know Mario?"

He shrugged and said, "I asked, but she wouldn't say. I got the feeling it was personal."

"It's impossible. How could she possibly know him?"

"I don't know, but it isn't for a lack of trying. My only guess is the PI she hired has been doing some major digging. The news article you said she read maybe prompted her to keep tabs on me."

"She forbade me to see you," I confessed.

He didn't look surprised, but given what he had just told me, it wasn't expected.

Before he could respond, the sound of cars arriving pulled our attention away from each other.

"We need to talk later."

I stood up and crossed my arms over my chest. "I don't see what else we have to talk about. I want nothing to do with you."

"Tough," he growled. "You once again managed to suck me back into your web. Deal."

The first bell rang, and Keiran made his escape before I could muster up a big *fuck you*.

* * *

IT TOOK A moment for me to connect the day to the large amounts of heart shaped chocolates and flowers being exchanged throughout the day.

Valentine's Day.

It was also Keiran's nineteenth birthday.

For some reason, I felt guilty for not remembering, but it wasn't as if we were on good terms. I owed nothing to him.

After dropping Willow off, I went home with a sore body and a heavy heart.

So much for romance.

CHAPTER TWENTY-EIGHT

KEIRAN

IMMEDIATELY AFTER SCHOOL, I plotted and planned for the night. Once I had everything in place, I made my way over to her. There was a slim chance she would give me the time of day willingly, but I was prepared for that, too.

"What are you doing here?" she asked as soon as she opened the door with a bored expression. "I told you I didn't want to see you."

I fought the smile that tugged at my lips. The rapidly beating pulse in her neck and the way she squeezed her thighs together told me she was feeling anything but indifferent to my presence.

"I'm here for the scenery," I said, letting my eyes trail up and down her form. She wore those tiny pink shorts of hers with the stupid fucking teddy bears. I hated them because they made her long legs look so damn hot and those dancing teddy bears were mocking me. They got to be where I wanted to be... wrapped around her legs and digging deep.

"Why are you wearing a tie?"

The tie was Dash's idea, and I took his word for it being the charmer he is.

"Shut up. You coming with me or not?" *Why the fuck are you asking her?* My demon on my shoulder snapped and hissed at me. I was tempted to drag her out of her house and lock her away where no one would ever find us like the caveman she always accused me of being.

"Not." She moved to close the door, but I quickly kicked my foot out to stop it from shutting. "Move it or lose it," she growled.

So cute. Her growl was nothing compared to my roar, and she knew it, but I couldn't blame her for trying.

"Stop your shit, and go throw on a dress or whatever will give me easy access, and get your ass out here."

I bit the inside of my cheek when she unexpectedly stomped her foot down on mine and then kicked me in the shin. "Fuck!" I jumped back and tried my best not to cry like a bitch. "Monroe—" I started forward to grab her but was cut off by the hard barrier placed in front of me.

Did she just slam the door in my face?

Game on.

I typed out a quick text and made myself comfortable against the railing on her front porch. I didn't have to wait long. She flew out the same door she had slammed in my face moments ago and charged straight into my space.

Her chest heaved with her labored breaths as she murdered me with her eyes. "Where do you get off, Masters?" she growled.

Masters? Cute. So she wanted to be tough?

I pushed my chest into hers and moved her back

the few paces I needed to have her pinned against the door. "I haven't but I plan to."

"You come off any more like a pig and you might start to smell like one. Go—" My hand was around her throat before she could finish her statement. I quickly bit her lip, not caring about how rough I treated her. "Keiran..."

Her words trailed off when I tipped her head back to expose her neck to me. I spread hard nips all over her neck, being sure to leave a mark. "Keiran, stop," she moaned and pulled me closer.

"No," I growled against her neck. "I fucking missed you. I missed this. I missed tasting you."

"Why are you doing this to me?" she whined with lust in her voice.

"Open the door, baby. Let me in, or I swear I'm going to fuck you hard right here for all the neighbors to see."

"Oh, God."

The door opened quickly, and I had to anchor her to me to keep us from falling inside. I stole her lips in a kiss finally while I backed her through the door. I kicked the door shut and picked her up, carrying her through the hall and into the living room where I set her on her feet. It was as far as I needed to go for what I needed to do.

"I'm not supposed to be doing this. I'm not supposed to give in to you."

"You already have. Many times. What's one more?"

"My life," she whispered desperately while looking up at me.

"Not this time." I sealed my vow with a kiss that threatened to steal my soul and hers. Fuck. What was she doing to me? I wasn't supposed to care about hearts and minds and vows—much less admit I had either.

B.B. REID

"Why are you here, Keiran? Seriously." She pulled away from me to hug herself around her waist and fuck if I didn't feel jealous of her arms.

"It's Valentine's day."

"And? You don't care about that stuff. You have no reason to."

"But something tells me you do and every reason I have is standing right in front of me."

"So what? This is supposed to be your grand gesture?"

"If dinner and a fucking movie are what you call a grand gesture, then I guess so," I snapped. The more time she spent staring at me with a hard, distant look in her eyes, the more my confidence began to fade. The thought of her rejecting me irritated me—not that I could blame her if she did. This tug of war game between her and I had gone on for far too long.

"If this is your way of getting me into bed again, let me just warn you that you aren't heading in the right direction."

"Fuck." I ran my hands through my hair in frustration. "I'm not used to this. I don't know what the fuck I'm doing."

She walked up to me, wrapped her arms around my neck, and whispered, "You can start my asking me to dinner properly."

"Properly, huh? How would I do that?"

"You could say... 'Lake will you go out with me?'"

"But I already know you will."

Her arms left my neck before she turned around and headed for the stairs. "I'll see you around. You can let yourself out."

I felt the move before I could rethink and swept her up in my arms. "Don't test my fucking patience."

I bound up the stairs and headed straight for her

Page | **309**

bedroom where I dumped her on her bed.

I dropped my bag and quickly pulled out a long box. Her expression was fierce but still so damn cute as she shot daggers at me. I actually felt nervous when I extended it to her. She looked from it to me, but still didn't move to take it.

"Don't be a pain in my ass. Take the box. There is nothing in there that can hurt you."

"Are you asking me to trust you?"

I realized I had no right to ask it of her, but I didn't realize until recently just how much I needed it. "Yes."

Her eyes watched mine for signs of insincerity while I held her gaze openly. I saw the decision in her eyes a split second before she slowly took the box from my grasp. Her fingers peeled back the box while I watched on silently. The paper was discarded, and when she saw what was inside, she stilled.

"Shoes? You got me shoes?" I hid the smile that tugged at my lips from the sound of disbelief and the look of disappointment. I had no clue what she would have hoped was inside, but I did know one thing now... she wanted more.

"Do you like them?"

"Yes. They are beautiful, but why all the fussing and threatening for shoes?" The suede heels were nude in color with a white heel that was just the right height. The top of the shoes fastened into perfect bows.

"I want you to wear them for me on our date to-night."

"Back to that, are we?"

I took a deep breath and released it. "One way or another you are going on this date with me, so tell me what I need to do to make it okay with you?"

Her annoyed expression transformed into interest as she seemed to mull it over. When a sly grin appeared,

I felt the stirrings of dread. I always seemed to forget this wasn't the same girl I tortured mercilessly in the hallways of our school.

"Is this my glass slipper?"

"If I say yes, will you go out with me?"

"You could ask me—"

"I did—"

"On your knees."

The gleam in her eye told me she found it funny, but I knew she was serious. She wanted me to beg.

Like hell I would beg.

But I knew another way to make her agree.

I sunk to my knees without argument while holding her gaze. She wore a satisfied smirk that quickly disappeared when I gripped her around her hips and yanked her forward.

For once, she didn't talk. Her teeth sunk into her bottom lip as she stared down at me. Desire mingled with nervousness in her eyes, and I could tell she wanted what was about to happen. It's been way too fucking long.

"Keiran, wait—"

"No, baby. You wanted me to beg, right?" I pulled down her shorts. My hands were already ripping away her panties by the time they fell to her ankles. "Then let me beg."

I nearly salivated at the sight of her bare pussy. I couldn't wait another second and wasn't about to. I gripped her left leg behind her knee and settled it on my shoulder while holding her gaze. She gripped my shoulders with her small hands, and I relaxed when I realized she wasn't going to push me away.

My mouth descended early, and at the first swipe of my tongue, I felt her shiver and had to grip her tighter to keep her from falling. Her breathing was already heavy and deep, and as I continued to taste her, it became uneven. Her nails dug into my shoulders painfully, but it only spurred me to take more from her.

By the time she came, I was ready to skip the dinner reservations and eat her all night.

* * *

THE DRIVE WAS silent, and I had a hard time containing my drool. I managed to convince Lake to go to dinner after I made her come twice.

After I was done, she so very sweetly whispered over her labored breathing, "Happy Birthday" and then silently started to dress.

I found myself feeling happy it was my birthday for the first time ever. She was dressed in a pale pink and cream strapless dress that hugged her torso and flirted loosely around her legs.

The restaurant I took her to was one reluctantly recommended to me by Sheldon when I called her. It took a lot of convincing and bribing, but I managed to enlist her help setting up the night.

It might have been my birthday, but the night was for her. One way or another, I would win her over.

We arrived at the modern yet upscale restaurant, and then we were seated immediately. I could tell she had something on her mind and waited until after we placed our order to ask.

"What's wrong?"

"If I said nothing, would you believe me?"

"There's a slim to none chance."

"I'm not sure I want to do this with you. We've attempted to be friends in the past and it only ended badly, particularly for me."

"And that was our first mistake. We aren't meant to

be *friends*, Lake."

"I don't know if I can trust you enough to be more than enemies."

"What do I have to do?"

"Talk."

"Talk?" I repeated and then it dawned on me what she meant. Lake—"

"It's what I want. Take it or leave it."

I didn't think this was a conversation to have over dinner, but I knew she wouldn't back down. "What do you want to know?"

"I want to know what happened to you. Everything. You can start from the beginning if that helps."

"I don't know the beginning. Not the one that counts. I only know what John told me, which wasn't much."

"What was your first memory?"

"Starving. Learning what it meant and what it felt like."

"What was it like?"

"Painful. Never ending... Adaptable."

"Adaptable?" How could starving be adaptable?

"After a while, the hunger pains become little more than a nuisance. You learn how to push it to the back of your mind, or so I thought. I did any and everything they asked just for a little more table scraps."

"That is a horrible memory."

"It's just one of many and not all that bad compared to the rest."

"Tell me more," she urged.

"Why?" My voice sounded strained to my own ears.

"I want to know what could make an eight-year-old boy push a complete stranger off the monkey bars."

My fingers stabbed through my hair before pulling tightly. "Like what?"

"I want to know about Quentin. How did he end up here?"

"I thought he was dead. One day he just disappeared, and because I wasn't allowed to ask questions, I assumed the worse."

"So where was he?"

"Mario somehow smuggled him out before my father had me taken from the compound. I didn't know why at first."

"But now you do?"

"Yes, but it's not my story to tell." The hard look I gave her let her know not to push.

"So when you were returned to your family, he came with you?"

"Mario was pretty insistent on it. It made me wonder but he never talked about it, and I never asked. It's been years since I ever spoke about any of it with Q. I think he wanted to forget, and I was happy to oblige him."

"But not you... why didn't you want to forget?"

"Growing up as a slave isn't something that's easily forgettable. It was my life. The only one I knew and had. Would you be so quick to give it up?"

"You were afraid you wouldn't belong. You didn't want to get attached to a new life just to have it ripped away from you."

"You're starting to sound like a psychologist."

"You can't hide from me by being a dick Keiran. Not anymore." We stared at each other for the longest time, silently communicating what neither of us was willing to say out loud.

"This window of opportunity is closing fast." I was on edge. I didn't like exposure and Lake was skillful at splaying me open.

"I want to know more about Lily." She crossed her

arms and sat back with a hard stare.

"I told you about Lily."

"Was she your first kill?"

"No. I was damaged long before she came along. She gave me my name."

"Your name?"

I only nodded while I silently choked on her memory. "My mother named me Gabriel. Keiran was her brother's name. I was sold when I was an infant, so naturally, I didn't know my birth name. Not until I met my mother."

"That's heavy," she breathed out. "So who was your first kill?"

"Imagine a nameless, faceless person bound and laid out in front of you. Then someone places a knife, or whatever the implement of torture is for the day, in your hand and tells you every place to strike and when to kill. Now imagine you're only eight years old."

I blinked against the memories and shook my head. I fell into a trance as I relived my past.

"At eight years old, instead of learning to read I was learning to be a sadistic psychopath. It was practice, mental preparation for the future. I didn't know until I was older why they chose kids so young."

"Why?"

"They are easily corrupted. You can mold them however you want. They believe whatever you want them too. When I became of age, I would have been stronger and mentally capable of carrying out the jobs they needed." I rubbed his chin and said as an after-thought, "It's clever really."

She didn't hesitate to correct him. "It's sick, Keiran."

"That too."

"So, what then?"

"I was corrupted. I was so far gone that nothing about it bothered me anymore. That lasted until Lily showed up. I'd hear many things from the other kids about their life with their parents, but I never bothered to get close to any of them. I either shut them out or shut them up, but Lily...

She fought everyone including me. She never let me ignore her and then she made me want to protect her, so I did. She was changing me. I was beginning to hesitate when I would train and punish the other kids for table scraps, didn't seem like it was worth it anymore. It didn't make sense until Mario drove away, leaving me with my uncle.

"What made sense?"

"That if it weren't for Mario and my father's greed, I never would have made it. Even after she died."

"What do you mean?"

"I would have died, Lake. Lily was dead and no longer an influence, but she was already in my head. She was light and my conscious. I wouldn't have been able to train and eventually they would have killed me."

CHAPTER TWENTY-NINE

LAKE

WE FINISHED OUR dinner in stunned silence. He gave me a lot to process, but his past, as dark as it was, didn't make me want him any less.

"What are you going to do about Mario and Arthur? Why haven't you turned them in yet?"

"When Arthur made the deal with me, I convinced him that it would be safer to deliver him when school was over. If I brought him in sooner, it would raise his suspicions."

"So you have to pretend nothing is wrong?"

He nodded but didn't elaborate. "Do you want dessert?"

"I'm okay. Besides, it's your birthday," I smiled. He looked up in surprise. "We should get you cake."

"I'd rather have you for dessert."

His voice deepened, his eyes darkened, and I just knew if he could, he would take me right here.

Keiran paid for dinner, and we rode in silence back to Six Forks. It wasn't until he pulled up to my house and walked me to the door that he spoke.

"Thank you for being my first Valentine." He stole a kiss packed with emotion and desperation. I decided that sweet Keiran was so much more of a panty melter than brooding Keiran.

When he finally released me, I was about to say goodnight when the front door opened and Aunt Carissa stood in the doorway with Jackson.

I could tell by my aunt's expression that she wasn't happy, and considering what Keiran told me this morning, I knew exactly why. It only just occurred to me how much he truly risked by simply taking me to dinner tonight.

"Lake, we need to talk. Keiran, you need to go home."

Without a word, he turned to go, but not before daring another kiss from me. My aunt watched silently, and when he drove away, I walked inside with her and Jackson.

"Lake, I thought I made my feelings about him clear."

"Why didn't you tell me you approached him?"

"He is not the guy you think he is."

Telling her that I knew exactly who Keiran was would only serve to make this night worse.

"Your parents were two of the gentlest people. It's why I never understood why they picked the profession they did."

"What do you mean?"

At age seven, I'd never thought they could ever be anything other than my mom and dad. To me, it was enough. After they had disappeared, I didn't allow myself to think of them at all, much less how they earned a living.

"Angie and Thomas specialized in child abuse victims." My throat tightened hearing their names while she paused as if weighing her words.

"Were they social workers?"

"No, honey. They weren't social workers. They worked for the FBI. It was how they met."

Stunned.

Shocked.

Silent.

All three words were able to describe how I appeared on the outside, but none came close to doing the justice of the emotions wreaking havoc inside me.

The FBI? My parents?

"How could my parents have worked for the FBI?" The little I could remember of them was so ordinary. Day by day, our life amounted to the same routine set and rehearsed by my parents.

"Your mother always had dreams of someday making a difference, and so the day she announced she had been accepted into the Academy, I knew she had found her calling."

"What does this have to do with their disappearance?" Aunt Carissa got up to pour another cup of coffee, filling the gray and orange tomcat mug to capacity with the hot espresso liquid.

"The summer they left you here wasn't because of a vacation. It was a setup. They were going undercover to bring down a child slavery ring that managed to elude the federal government for quite some time."

I could already feel my heart pounding faster. This couldn't be the same. Fate wouldn't be that cruel.

"How do you know this? Aren't federal investigations super secret?"

A sad smile spread her lips. "Your mother was never good at keeping secrets. Besides... she wanted to prepare for the future."

"What happened to them?" It came out as more of a demand than a question.

My mind was already connecting the dots, but I needed to hear it. Never in a million years would I have thought Keiran and my past were connected.

"Oh, Lake. Are you certain you're ready to hear this? It doesn't have to be now."

I spoke around the painful lump lodged in my throat. "Yes, it does."

Finding out my parents were FBI agents was the final blow to the very fragile memories I held of them. The meager leftovers crumbled and shattered when I realized it was all a lie.

She looked at Jackson and a silent message passed between the two. If I didn't know before, I knew now something was going on between the two of them. Something more than an investigation.

When he nodded, seeming to give her the strength she needed, she started to speak.

"Mario Fulton is an ex-FBI agent who was let go on suspicion of corruption. He was assigned to investigate the disappearance of Liliana West. She was a little girl around your age at the time she was kidnapped."

Oh, no... Lily.

"Mario was a part of the same division as your parents. He knew them well."

"My parents were partners then?"

She shook her head and then wiped a tear away. "Your father was Mario's partner."

"What?" My breathing slowed to single harsh breaths.

"He was the one to raise suspicion against Mario after he uncovered evidence of a child slavery ring. But when that evidence started disappearing, and the organization became harder and harder to track, he began to suspect Mario."

"But why?"

"It was agreed between them that one of them would infiltrate and one of them would hang back as a backup just in case things went south. Mario volunteered to be the mole."

I nodded and then asked, "Where does my mother come into all of this?"

"When your father reported Mario, he was suspended until further evidence could be found that he was dirty. After that, he went rogue. When your father had enough to implicate him and find the man behind the child abductions, he offered to bring him in. Your mother didn't want to leave him at the mercy of another untrustworthy partner, so she went with him."

I was already crying, but I didn't feel my tears as my body numbed from every piece of the story that came together.

Mario was the one to kill my parents.

I just knew it.

"How did it happen?"

"I don't think—"

"Just tell me! Please." My voice trembled as my world spun on its axis.

My answer came swift and brutal. It was Jackson who spoke for the first time. "They were gunned down."

CHAPTER THIRTY

KEIRAN

I STOOD ABOVE them, still and silent, as I listened to her cries. I felt every tear she shed through my bleeding heart. I knew hearing about her parent's death would destroy her. She avoided it for too long.

After they went inside and I drove off, I parked down the street and double-timed back to her house. I climbed the tree that stood near her window and broke through the window. I dislodged the lock a few months ago when I was intent on using her for revenge.

I sat and waited for hours, clutching the banister while they attempted to console her, and in those hours, I plotted her revenge. Around midnight, she finally had enough and broke away from them while I quickly disappeared inside her bedroom to wait.

When she entered the dark bedroom, her eyes immediately found mine, and I could see the need in her eye. It was one that I was familiar with thought it was the first time I've witnessed it on her.

"Do it, Lake."

She took the invitation and was across the room in a flash. I encouraged each blow to my chest and slap to my face as she silently screamed through her agony.

"Take it."

She never let up. She never stopped seeking.

She needed an outlet. A way to release. I knew what it felt like to need to unleash your pain on someone. It would get pretty dangerous if it built up.

"Take what you need to get past the pain..."

I hit my chest indicating where she should strike, and she mimicked.

"...because I will not let you break. It would kill us both."

I bared myself. Let me become vulnerable for her. Only for her. Always for her. Her hits didn't affect me physically, but much deeper, it was fucking lethal. She killed me over and over.

"Why?" she wailed as her arms grew tired, and her screams fell to hoarse whispers. She fell against my chest and I could feel her tears soak through my thin shirt immediately.

"He won't live another day."

* * *

THE NEXT MORNING, I sat and watched her sleep while battling over what I wanted to do and what I had to do.

"Don't kill them."

It was the last thing she had said to me before she succumbed to sleep. It amazed me that, even after all she had gone through, she still managed to be so damn innocent.

I needed to move and I needed to move fast. Mario was still in the area, which meant Arthur was also close by, as well.

I've sat on this and pretended everything was normal for far too long. Since finding out Arthur had come to Six Forks, Mario had been laying low. We stopped meeting, and any phone calls placed were kept short, but on my end, they were tapped. I gave only enough to the police to keep them interested and without raising Mario's suspicions.

I knew Arthur would still have eyes on me, and with Keenan back in the hospital, I wasn't able to protect him. His condition had begun to worsen, and John immediately admitted him at the first sign of strain. The patch had run its course, and if he didn't get a lung soon, he would die.

Monroe began to stir, so I silently stood and crossed the room to her. I wanted to be gone before she awakened. She would try to stop me. Either she would succeed or I would end up hurting her again.

When I reached her bedside, I leaned as close as I could without touching her and whispered to her.

Her eyelids fluttered, but I was already gone by the time she opened them.

* * *

I CALLED UP Dash & Quentin and even dragged Diana from Keenan's room where she was temporarily holed up until she was convinced the fleas were gone. When I found out what she said to Lake the day I took her to the store, it took everything in me not to shoot her in the face. Lake never said a word about it, and I didn't ask. I just assumed she had become upset from seeing her climb in my ride.

After explaining to Diana I would rather lose my balls and grow a vagina than fuck her, she seemed to get it, and even appeared sorry. She apparently underestimated Lake. We both did.

As soon as this was over, I'd make it up to her if given the chance.

"Why am I here?" Diana questioned with her nose in the air. Quentin looked as if he'd tasted something foul.

I took a deep breath and released it slowly, feeling the vein in my forehand come to life. "You're here because you're not dead, and if you're not dead, then it means you serve a purpose."

"I told you everything."

"Do I look like I'm short of a brain?"

The day I brought Diana here, I interrogated her well into the night until I was satisfied I had drained her of every piece of information. After finding out not only was Mario an FBI agent, but the reason why Lake's parents were dead and Lily was never found, I realized I didn't know half of what I needed to know.

"I told you everything *I* knew. I stay in my dad's home, but I see him every couple of months. I don't know anything else."

"What did she tell you?" Quentin questioned.

"Hey, I'm sitting right here," she snapped. Quentin ignored her and waited for my answer.

"Money wasn't the only reason he broke the partnership with Arthur."

"What other reason was there?"

"He was sleeping with his wife. She got knocked up and threatened to tell Arthur when Mario wouldn't agree to make them exclusive."

I remember Esmerelda well. She was the closest thing I had to a mother when I was young, but she was no mother. It was her name that was on the license for the children's shelter. It was all a front to capture kids from off the streets, and even those who were kidnapped or sold. They would toss a few back to keep up the front while stowing away the unlucky ones.

"Damn." Dash shook his head. "What are we supposed to do with that?"

"I have an idea, but first…" I stalked over to the seat Diana sat in and watched her shrink lower and lower. "Is that all the information you have? Think carefully before you answer because if I find out you're lying, I will send you back to your father in pieces."

I clocked every breath she took and muscle she moved while I waited. "He had those kids killed."

"Is that right?" Quentin questioned. He didn't trust her and neither did I.

"Why?"

"I'm not sure. It had something to do with you disappearing a few weeks before. I guess he panicked. He didn't know if you were arrested and couldn't risk you ratting him out, so he killed them and dumped them."

"The police didn't connect the murders to me, and they wouldn't have. Lake told them of my involvement."

"Then shouldn't you be questioning her?"

"What else?" I pressed.

"I don't think he wanted to set you up. He wanted to dispose of any evidence just in case you talked."

The days I spent looking for my father led to Trevor and Anya's death, but even that night when I ran down Mario, he didn't confess. What else would he be hiding? His rash decision to kill them because of me only confirmed Mario didn't trust me any more than I trusted him.

"Why are you turning on your father?" Dash asked.

She scoffed, but when her eyes trailed to Quentin before she closed them as if in pain. "He's never been a father." Her voice shook with barely controlled anger and emotion. "He's my pimp."

Dash nodded as if he understood, and strangely, he likely did better than anyone else in this room. Not out of experience, but because he was always the voice of reason and understanding. He would always be the last to pass judgment, even with all the facts laid out in front of him.

"I have one last question. The same rules stand. Did your father send you here to keep an eye on me?" Diana had done nothing but try to fuck me since the very second I met her. She was relentless these past three months, and I wouldn't have suspected anything if I hadn't seen the turmoil in her eyes every time she came on to me. She was nothing more than a trained concubine, but it wasn't by choice.

"I told you why I'm here."

"I won't hurt you for telling me the truth, but I will hurt you for lying to me."

"And I am just supposed to believe you?"

"You don't have any other choice, Di." I purposely used her nickname to appear less threatening. I needed her on my side. She was the bridge between information I could use against her father, and if her father could plant his own daughter here, then it meant she was disposable to him.

Her small nod was the only answer I needed.

"So who do we take down first?" Dash asked.

"We take them together."

"How?"

"We get the detectives, Mario, and Arthur in the room together."

"Shouldn't we get the feds in on this?"

"It's too risky. We wouldn't know who to trust. Arthur and Mario both have agents, judges, and officers in their pockets."

"How do we know we can trust those two?"

I asked myself the same question repeatedly, but always came to the same answer. "Because Lake trusts them."

"And that's good enough for you?" Diana sneered.

"It's good enough for me," Quentin barked, cutting his eye at Diana.

"Me, too," Dash answered.

"Now that we are all on board here's what we're going to do."

* * *

AFTER EVERYONE WAS in position, I put the plan in motion by calling Mario. He'd moved out of the hotel a couple of months ago and kept his hideout a secret even from me so I would need to draw him out.

I dialed his number and rehearsed in my head while the phone rang.

"What's up, kid?"

"I need your help. It's bad."

The change in his tone was immediate. "What's going on?"

"My father showed up. It ended badly. How soon can you get here?"

"I can send someone."

"No. It needs to be you. I can't have anyone else knowing about this."

"How messy is it? I'll at least need to bring a clean-up crew. You know I can't move without my men."

"Fine. Just get here quickly."

"Where?"

I gave him the school's address and told him to meet me in the gym. A public place would be their better choice. It would make him think I was blindsided by my father, and I could avoid the suspicion that a secluded setting would bring.

Once the call disconnected, I dialed Arthur. This part of the plan would need to be executed perfectly. He would catch on to the smallest slip-up.

"Arthur."

"This is a surprise. May I ask the reason for your call?"

"Christmas is coming early this year. I have what you want. Meet me at the high school gymnasium. I'm sure you know where it is. We don't have much time, so you need to come now."

"Son, the last time I spoke to you about this, you were adamant about waiting until you graduated."

"I'm still unavailable, but Mario in a body bag is up for grabs."

"Why the sudden rush?"

"He slept with my woman. I'll even throw her in the mix, so you coming or not?"

I hung up the phone before he could respond or have the chance to question me further. Mario's history with sleeping with married women provided the perfect cover.

A man like Arthur was always suspicious, and it was suspicion that made me sure he would fall into my trap. If he thought he was being set up, he would want to deal with it. His status afforded him the confidence he couldn't be defeated.

I checked all the doors of the gym, ensuring there was only one way in or out. The last thing I needed was the wrong person walking in at the wrong time.

A quick text from Quentin and Dash let me know they were each in position, and it was clear for me to make the last call.

I waited for the line to connect.

"The school gymnasium. Now." Dressed in my basketball gear with my gun strapped to my thigh, I had about twenty minutes to work up a sweat, I grabbed the ball I had brought with me and played harder than I ever had before.

When the door behind me opened, I continued to play, seemingly unfazed by the intrusion. After all... I was only here to practice.

"Hey, kid. This is hardly the time for recreational fun. Where's the body?" I turned to face Mario, who stood confused with two men behind him.

"Is this all the men you brought?"

"I have one more waiting guard outside."

"Can I trust you?"

He let out a nervous chuckle and subtly looked around. "What's with the questions?"

"I need to know if I made a mistake trusting you." I knew he picked up on my meaning when he straightened and flexed his jaw muscles.

"Are you challenging me, kid?" The two men behind him went on alert.

"I'm asking a *friend* a question."

"Why the sudden doubt?"

"The last time I trusted you, two people ended up dead, and I was being blamed for it. You've yet to give me an answer."

His face reddened with anger. "He framed you, and the girl was a whore in the making, so does it really matter? You can trust me!"

"Like you trusted me?"

"What are you talking about?"

"You killed Trevor Reynolds and Anya Risdell because you were afraid I rolled on you when I disappeared after my brother was shot—so you killed them to frame me, isn't that right?"

"That's ridiculous!"

"Your daughter didn't seem to think so."

"The worthless bitch is only good for one thing and thinking isn't one of them." Anger flared to rage hearing him talk of his daughter that way. It confirmed everything I needed to know.

"I want you to leave Six Forks and never return. You can catch Arthur on your own." I turned to leave, putting the icing on the cake.

"Fine!" he roared at my back. "I killed them. You should be grateful. I did you a favor."

"Having me set up for murder was a favor?"

"You should blame that girl. She turned you in, didn't she? They never would have implicated you if it weren't for her. You should have killed her a long time ago!"

I remained silent, grappling with the need to kill him here and now. Keeping a cool head would keep her safe. It would end all of this.

"When? Long before she turned me in?"

"It would have saved a lot of time."

"I can see the fear in your eyes, Mario. Why do you want her dead?" I spent so much time learning what fear was to avoid it that I recognized it no matter how well it was hidden or covered.

Anger. Bravery. Indifference. None of them compared to the potency of fear.

"She's bad news."

"You don't even know her. You've never even met her."

"I know you let what's between her thighs make you forget who you are."

"If that's true, why is there fear in your eyes?"

"Don't flatter yourself, son. You're a teenager. I'm a man."

"So what about another man?"

"Are you threatening me?"

"If I were, would you kill me? Isn't that what happened to your partner?"

"What partner?"

"Thomas Monroe. The real reason you want his daughter dead."

The reason why I was given a second chance. I realized at some point while I held Monroe and wished upon wish I could take her pain away, that it was her parents who saved me. I had thanked them by hurting their daughter for ten years.

"Who told you about him?"

"It seems that Arthur isn't the only one after you."

"You little shit. After everything I've done for you?" He signaled to his men and they pointed their weapons. "I should have just killed you or let you die in the streets."

He watched me. Waiting for me to cower and beg. When I only offered him a smile, his eyes blazed with unrepressed rage. "Kill him."

"You haven't changed." The door to the gymnasium slammed shut as five men, including Arthur, walked in. Mario and his men swung around, but his guards were quickly gunned down by Arthur's men, leaving only Mario. One of the men shot Mario in the arm where he held the gun.

"Ahhhh!" Mario screamed. When he recognized who had intruded on our meeting, his face paled from more than just pain. "Arthur."

"Mario... it's been a long time."

"Big fucking mistake showing your face," he threatened even as he clutched his arm. Blood gushed from the wound.

"I believe I was invited." Arthur smiled and looked past Mario. "I have to say, Keiran, your work is a little sloppy, but with a little training, you'll be one of my best. Good job."

Mario looked back at me with accusation in his eyes. "You set me up!"

"You should thank me. I did you a favor." I threw his words from earlier back in his face with a smirk.

"Speaking of favors... you held up your end, so I'll hold up mine. Mario's blood type is O negative. Kill him and his lungs are yours. I have a surgeon waiting on standby as we speak.

Shit. This was not part of the plan. I was planning for at least one death today, but it couldn't be by my hands. If I refused, Arthur would become suspicious. I wracked my brain until I found the best excuse.

"We don't know if it's compatible. Keenan's body could reject the lungs."

"I don't give a shit about your brother. I only said I would get you a lung. Take it or leave it." There was no way in hell I was putting a piece of this scumbag inside my brother and using his lungs only for them to fail and kill him anyway.

Fuck pretending.

"I am not going to help kill my brother."

Arthur's expression became clouded as we stared each other down.

"Maybe with the proper motivation, you'll see things my way." He turned to one of his men and said, "Bring her in."

My heart fell to stomach. I knew without seeing who *her* was. She was unconscious and flung over the shoulder of the man who brought her in. When she was dropped carelessly on the gym floor and started to stir, I started forward but was held back by every gun pointing at me.

Mario's outrageous laughter was the only sound in

the building. "Did you think it was going to be that easy, kid?"

The butt of a gun slammed into the back of his skull knocking him unconscious as he continued to bleed out.

"I needed a little reassurance that this wasn't a set-up, but, after all, you did say I could have her." He peered down at Lake, a lustful grin spreading wide. "She will make an excellent addition to my stable."

I took one last look at Monroe whose eyes were open but had not found me.

"Do you remember what I told you, Arthur?" I watched the confidence fade from his eyes. "If you touched her again, I would kill you... even if I had to die with you." The gun I used to kill my mother was in my hand before any of them could react.

I would have to die today. I should have died a long time ago.

"No!" I heard her scream just as both gym doors burst open and a collection of "Freeze" and "Put your weapons down" echoed.

I knew what her intentions were the moment she jumped to her feet and ran over to me.

"Lake, no!" I screamed.

She threw up her arms around me as if to protect me, and I only had a split second to realize that one of Arthur's men still had his aim on her head.

I moved, but it was too late. The bullet hit.

"I'm sorry, baby," I whispered.

Her expression had turned from fear to shock before her body dropped to the floor.

* * *

MAY 27TH
DEAR DIARY,

> *They took him away today...*
> *Willow says I'm free.*
> *Freedom means possibilities of happiness.*
> *So why does freedom feel so empty?*
> *Is it wrong to miss him? Is it sick? Is it twisted?*
> *I think it's all of those things and more.*
> *It's painful.*

CHAPTER THIRTY-ONE

LAKE

"SEEING YOU LIKE this is hard. You don't look the same. You don't feel the same... and I have a feeling when you wake up, you won't be the same."

I touched the hand lying casually on the bedsheet.

"Is that true?"

The silence was louder than the shrillest scream.

"I only wished I could have saved you. I realize now there are more people who have hurt you than people you have hurt."

I laid my head in his lap, and for the first time, I didn't feel shame for my tears. It had been nearly twenty-four hours since Keiran took a bullet for me.

The fear I felt the last ten years was nothing compared to the utter desolation that brought me to my knees seconds before he fell. It didn't seem real until his blood soaked through his shirt. I'd attempted to stop it, but it only covered my fingers.

I didn't feel Dash's hands grab me, but when I felt the distance between me and my tormentor, my enemy, and my love, as it grew, I started to fight.

All I could think was that he needed me. How he would die if I didn't help. How I would die if he didn't survive.

Dash was forced to toss me over his shoulder to get me to safety. I hadn't realized it at the time, but when Keiran was shot, a gunfight had erupted around us. I didn't know who had died or who lived, including Keiran.

Outside, Willow and Sheldon had been waiting to take me away. As Willow drove us away, I stared at his blood on my hands. I remember wondering how long it would be before I stopped seeing it there. Was that how he saw himself? Was it why he was so tortured?

I fell asleep wondering about the eight-year-old boy who grew up in a nightmare.

* * *

"BUT, MAMA, WHY do you have to go? Can't only daddy go?"

"Oh, no! My little girl doesn't love me anymore!" He held his chest and dropped to his knee in front of me.

"Oh, Daddy, don't be silly. Of course, I love you."

"You like Mommy better than me?"

"Well..."

He looked as if he would cry, and I frowned when I thought I really hurt him. "Don't cry, Daddy. Mommy's a girl so I can play with her. Girl's aren't supposed to play with boys."

He laughed, kissed my cheek, and ruffled my hair, messing up the pigtails my mother had done that morning. "Just remember that, baby and Daddy will live a long time."

"Can't you both stay? Oh! I know! I can come with you." I picked up my book bag and started for the car.

Daddy laughed and scooped me up, sandwiching me between him and Mommy.

"Sweetheart, we would love to stay with you, but we have a very special trip, and it's no place for you."

"Is it bad?"

A look I didn't understand passed between them before they both looked toward the pretty house that belonged to my aunt. She was my mother's sister and really nice. I always wished for a little sister to play with, and every birthday, I wished even harder. Sometimes, they were too busy to play with me, and I got lonely.

"Come on, Lake. It's time for Mommy and Daddy to go." I hung tighter around my daddy's neck, not wanting them to leave.

"Daddy, don't leave," I cried. He desperately tried to wipe away my tears, but they fell fast and hard. This wasn't the first time they had left me, but this time felt different. It felt wrong.

My aunt had to pry me away from them, and when she finally held me, I buried my head in her shoulder and wailed.

Even through my cries, I could still hear my aunt whisper, "Be careful."

* * *

ONE OF MY favorite memories was the way my dad would rub my hair and sing me out of a nightmare when I was a child.

Sometimes, our memories were so vivid they would begin to look and feel real.

Somewhere far away a male voice whispered and

soothed, and I felt myself relax into sleep. I curled closer to the softness against my cheek and smiled from the comfort of him rubbing my hair. I missed this.

"How long has she been asleep?"

"I don't know. I woke up about an hour ago and she was here."

I frowned as the voices became clearer, and the familiarity was unlike how I remembered by father's voice, but then... it had been a long time.

So who was the other voice? It sounded familiar, too.

"Are you sure you want to do this, man?"

Quentin.

"I can't take the risk again. It was a mistake."

Keiran!

My head shot up from the bed when I finally recognized who the voice belonged to.

Keiran is awake.

"Keiran?" He was sitting up against the pillows watching me. A day's worth of stubble covered his lower face and his features looked worn.

I moved forward to hug him, but the cold look that grew in his eyes stopped me. "Is... is everything okay?"

"What are you doing here?"

"You—you were shot. I wanted to be here when you woke up."

"I'm awake. You can leave now."

I swallowed past the lump in my throat and asked the only question I could manage. "Why?"

"Because you don't belong here."

"But you're here because of me."

"Don't flatter yourself."

"I was there, Keiran. You saved me."

"No. You almost got me killed. I wouldn't have been shot if you weren't in the way."

My heart was grasping at straws as I tried to come to terms with what he was saying. I was smart enough to know it was all an attempt to protect me, but it didn't lessen the pain.

"Keiran, don't do this. I know you want to protect me, but this isn't the way."

"Protect you? I needed you out of the way. You suddenly decided to grow some self-respect and started talking to the cops. Lucky for me, you proved to be just like every... other... braindead female. All I had to do was show you a little attention, get you to spread your legs, and then you gave in."

"I wasn't the only one who gave in, Keiran. You aren't immune to me."

The door opened and John, Willow, Dash, Sheldon, and their parents all poured in.

"Maybe not, but I am bored with you. Gosh... even your parents couldn't get away soon enough. They practically committed suicide."

The final blow to my heart was exacting. I stumbled back while he continued to assault me with his icy stare. I looked for a break in his demeanor or a sign that this might be a ruse after all, but none came.

"You sorry son of a bitch!" Willow growled. She started forward, but Dash quickly grabbed her up in a desperate attempt to restrain her.

"You don't ever disappoint, do you?" Sheldon sneered with hatred spewing from her gaze.

He didn't flinch. Not even a flicker of acknowledgment or remorse.

When he lifted his chin and indicated for me to leave, I finally found my voice.

"I spent my whole life afraid of you. You were the monster under the bed and the devil who stole my soul."

Everyone was silent as all eyes remained on us.

They would all know. They would all see.

Don't think. Just feel.

"From the moment I met you, you did everything you could to hurt me. You pushed me, you ridiculed me, you isolated me. You used me to fight a ghost instead of fighting your demons like a coward."

I balled my fists at my side in anger.

I wanted to hurt him.

I wanted him to see what it felt like to be hurt by someone who counted.

"You're weak, Keiran. And now you're the one who is afraid."

Breathe.

"We have history. A tragic love story that should never have begun. But it did. And it started the summer I lost my parents, and then I found you instead. For ten years, I told myself they abandoned me. Deep down, I knew they were dead, but it all still felt the same. And I hated them for it."

Breathe.

"I guess that's something we have in common. We both learned how to hate before we knew how to love."

My eyes were glued to his although my vision had long since blurred as I allowed my tears to fall freely.

I can do this.

I repeated it to myself, but it became harder and harder to speak.

"You aren't the guy you think you are. You are so much worse. To make me fall in love with you and then run away—" I took another deep breath. "You wanted to destroy me, Keiran... Well, you have. You broke me just like they broke you."

I turned my back on him for the last time and took a deep breath.

FEAR YOU

"I heard you... before you left. I heard you, and now I see that you were right. You don't deserve to love me."

I walked out on the last person I would ever risk losing.

CHAPTER THIRTY-TWO

KEIRAN

"You're about as stupid as they come," John scolded as soon as the door closed. Willow and Sheldon had already run after Lake. The Chambers chose to wait outside but not before shooting me a disapproving look.

I sunk down in the bed to sulk. "I'm not in the mood. You guys should leave, too."

"Or what? You'll break our hearts, too?"

I rolled out of the hospital bed holding my chest. Luckily, the man who shot favored his aim to the right of my heart, but the steady throbbing came from my left and had nothing to do with the wound.

"What's wrong?" Dash asked. "Is it your wound?"

"It's all my wounds, man."

For once, the two of them decided to shut the fuck up. I sat on the edge of the bed, gripping the railing to keep from running after her.

When I woke up and saw her lying there sleeping peacefully, all I could bring myself to feel was relief that she wasn't hurt. She clung to me in her sleep as if she needed me. I was content to just sit and watch her sleep, but I needed to know she was safe.

I called Quentin, who had been waiting outside. As it turns out, he was the one to kill the man who shot me while Dash pulled Lake to safety, both risking their own lives and their freedom for her... and for me.

They had been there the entire time waiting in the sound room and recording every moment of the meeting. I hadn't gathered all the evidence I had wanted, but there was enough to put them both away for a long time.

The only hiccup was that Arthur was never meant to walk out of the gymnasium alive. He was too connected, and in a matter of days, he would be out of jail and free to come after us. Mario was supposed to kill Arthur and to be caught red-handed. The plan was doomed to fail from the start, but it was the only option. I was supposed to be the only one at risk. After planning everything out, I gave Quentin and Dash the strict instructions to keep filming. No matter what happened, I was not to be saved.

It all changed when Lake was brought in. My only mission became to save her. I wanted to be the very person I grew up hating. I wanted to be her hero.

A lot of fucking good that did me.

I managed to keep her from harm only to hurt her again, but after finding out from Quentin that Arthur was still alive, I was left with no choice. The further I stayed away from her, the safer she'd be. I would protect her from a distance.

Quentin tried to talk me out of it by pointing out that Lake was taken by Arthur when she had shown up at my house looking for me. Arthur had stopped by looking for a sign that I was setting him up. When she stumbled across them, he decided to take her as collateral instead. John had already been at the hospital with Keenan.

The decision to leave her alone wasn't easy. In a small space of time, I searched for another way to be with her and to keep her safe but came up short.

Who the fuck was I kidding anyway? Marriage, children, and Sunday morning pancakes weren't in the cards for me. Eventually, she would want more, and I would once again become the monster that tormented her in high school when I realized I was unable to give her what she needed.

She didn't need me.

She needed security and someone good.

I gave up on being good a long time ago.

"Are you sure you want to do this?" Dash asked, repeating the question Quentin had asked. I looked up realizing I'd forgotten they were in the room.

"I'm more than sure, and even if I wasn't, it's too late."

"What makes you so sure?"

"Because I know hate when I see it."

It was the only thing left in her eyes for me when she walked out.

* * *

THE DETECTIVES FINALLY showed up later that day to begin their interrogation. At the end of it, I wasn't being handcuffed to the bed, but I was warned they would keep in touch. Dash managed to get them the video of Mario confessing to killing Anya, Trevor, and Lake's parents, and then Arthur killing Mario's men. It all looked like a chance meeting that happened while taping my skills for basketball scouts, instead of intentionally setting anyone up to be murdered.

After the detectives had left, I worked up the courage to visit Keenan, but when I got to his room, I was surprised by the sight of Sheldon at his bedside.

Keenan was asleep, and from the way Sheldon held herself, I could tell she had no intention of waking him. I watched her silently cry over him for long moments before she finally noticed me.

"Dash said they had to give him medication for the pain."

I nodded my head and watched her fall apart. I envied her ability to cry. To openly shed her sorrow, her pain, her fears. I don't remember ever being able to cry. Not even for my brother, who was dying because of me.

"He's...d—dying."

"I know." My plan to secure a lung for Keenan had failed, and I would live with the guilt and failure long after he was gone.

"You know?" Her eyes turned cold as she glared at me. "Then why don't you do something?"

"I tried, Sheldon. I thought—"

"But you didn't think! You always did what you wanted to do because you were the big, bad, Keiran Masters. All he ever wanted was to love you, and you couldn't even show him just a little affection. His parents didn't care enough to just be there. And with you, he thought he had a chance, but you just wouldn't—" Her voice caught, and I could see her tremble from across the room as she hung her head. When she finally met my eyes again, they were full of hatred. "It should have been you."

CHAPTER THIRTY-THREE

LAKE

TWO WEEKS LATER
THE CHAMPIONSHIP

BECOMING A HIGH school dropout would have never seemed appealing to someone who never met Keiran Masters. More accurately—to someone who had never *slept* with Keiran Masters. Then to be foolish enough to fall in love with him. School and home were both unbearable. School for obvious reasons. After my aunt found out I had been kidnapped, *and* almost killed, she pretty much shut the door on trusting me.

After crying and holding me for hours, she grilled me endlessly.

Why was I there?
How did they know me?
How did I know them?

Jackson was there. He watched me lie about leaving my textbook in the gymnasium, and for a moment, I thought he would call me out. When I was finished, he didn't have to—my aunt didn't believe a word I said and that's when the yelling began.

I was grounded indefinitely and only allowed to go to school. I didn't offer up any typical teenage rejections because being forced to see Keiran in school was bad enough. I didn't want to run into him anywhere else.

The entire school and the whole town were still alive with talk of what had happened Saturday. This was the most excitement they had ever seen, and it all came from my dark prince.

The entire world was now privy to Arthur Phalan, who had been confirmed as the leader of one of the world's largest child slavery rings. After the gunfight, an officer lost his life as well as two of Arthur's men. The other two were facing serious charges, charges they weren't willing to do the time for. Federal agents were brought in, and in no time, they were singing.

The case against Keiran for the murder of Anya and Trevor was dropped. Keiran held up his end of the deal with the detectives and with a video confession of their murder, his possible involvement was considered in-consequential.

I was both relieved and devastated. Throughout the years, when Keiran became more and more sadistic, I always wondered what would have happened if I had gone to the police. Keiran getting off for a double mur-der charge quickly reaffirmed my belief that the police would have cared little for a young girl and her bully.

But then... I also had to admit that what Keiran did wasn't easy. He almost died to catch Mario and Arthur. Nothing about that is ever easy. Even when you're Kei-ran freaking Masters.

The doorbell sounded, breaking me out of the de-pressing orbit where my mind had been spinning. Shel-don and Willow had both opted to skip the game tonight. Sheldon couldn't bring herself to cheer and Willow avoided being in the same vicinity as Dash whenever she could.

Aunt Carissa was opening the door by the time I made it downstairs. "Hello, girls," she greeted as she closed the door and retreated back into the living room.

We escaped up to my room, and I turned to a movie channel.

"So I was able to get the juiciest burgers since everyone is at the game tonight."

"Do you think we'll win?" Willow asked.

"I'm sure we will." With someone who played as ruthless as Keiran did, I had no doubt but Keiran was still recovering from his gunshot wound so he wouldn't be playing.

"I'm not so sure," Sheldon answered slowly, and for a second, I thought I saw regret in her eyes.

"Why?"

She shrugged and looked lost in thought while she nibbled her burger instead of digging into it. "Dash said he doesn't seem into it anymore. I'm surprised they even considered letting him play. It's ridiculous. He rarely leaves the hospital except for school anyway."

"How is Keenan?"

She took a deep breath before answering. "The same. He's never awake for long anymore. They were talking about putting him in a coma soon to help with the pain."

"When?"

"In another week or so. The doctors are grasping for straws to keep him alive because they believe he has a good chance of getting a lung. He's young, healthy, and he's reaching a critical stage."

"He's holding on, Sheldon. He'll make it. He has, too."

* * *

Victory had been ours. We took the championship thanks to Dash and Buddy because, as it turns out, Keiran didn't play.

In the middle of French, I felt the pressing need to pee so I excused myself for the bathroom, forgetting my cardinal rule of never going to the bathroom alone.

I didn't remember until I was in the deserted hallway and my anxiety kicked in. I considered going back in until I told myself I was being stupid.

The closest bathroom was right around the corner, but when I made it, there was an Out of Order sign hanging. I should have taken it as a sign, but my bladder was not to be ignored. The next closest bathroom would be the one in the gym, and at that moment, I knew fate was against me.

With a swift kick in the ass, I made my way to the gym. By the time I arrived, I could barely walk and realized I would have to go through the gym floor to make it to the bathroom in time. When I opened the gym door and peered inside, I let out a breath of relief that no one, mainly Keiran was inside. Maybe fate wasn't so cruel after all. Besides, Keiran had class this period anyway.

When I entered the bathroom, I made a point to pass the stall Trevor had attacked me in and made quick work of relieving my bladder. Satisfied, I hurried out of the bathroom and collided with a wall. I bounced straight through the door and landed on the tile floor of the bathroom. My legs kept the door from closing, and when I looked up, I saw startling gray eyes staring back at me.

I quickly stood up, not liking the way he towered

over me, but even on my feet, he still made me feel small... and helpless.

The door swung closed, and I waited a beat, hoping he would be gone when I opened it. I didn't get the chance. The door burst open, and he swaggered in, but the look on his face was anything but casual.

"What are you doing in here?"

"I'm sorry. I thought this was a *free* country."

He scrubbed his hand down his face. "Tell me."

"Well, for obvious reasons... I had to pee."

"And you couldn't use the bathroom closer to your class?"

I crossed my arms over my chest and leaned back against the wall. To him, I may have appeared casual, but I was anything but. I needed to keep my legs from giving out. I was right back at square one. We hadn't been this close since he woke up in the hospital and humiliated me for the last time.

I looked at his chest and thought about the wound that was still very much fresh. I wasn't even sure he should be in school. I was more than relieved the rumors weren't true and Keiran hadn't played while wounded.

"It was out of order. Anything else you would like to know?"

"Stop pushing me, Monroe."

"Big surprise—I'm Monroe again, and I'm not pushing you. You are the one cornering me in the bathroom. Why are *you* out class, anyway?"

"I keep my promises."

"What the hell does that even mean? What does it have to do with me?"

"Watch your mouth."

I dropped my casual stance and stood up straight. "Or what?"

His arm shot in between my legs and lifted me up the wall bringing me to his level.

I could feel his arm pressing against my center as my legs straggled his arm and could do nothing but wrap my legs around him to keep from falling. He leaned in and whispered,

"Or I'll shut you up." A crooked smile appeared on his daring face. "Or at least I'll keep you from talking."

"Put me down," I ordered. When he didn't move, I tried another tactic. "You'll open your stitches."

I could see a sweat forming on his forehead and knew he had to be in pain, but he was intent on proving a point.

Well, so was I.

"Are you afraid, *Lake?*

"Why would I be afraid of you? I've learned all your tricks, and I'm no longer impressed."

"But I think you are. Scratch that..." He ran his teeth down my neck. "I know you are."

"There's nothing left between us to make me afraid." He lifted his lips from my neck so I could see the storm brewing within the depths of his eyes.

"You're afraid you'll want it, and you're afraid you'll miss it."

"You're wrong."

"Am I?"

"I'm not afraid of that," I pressed. "I'm afraid you'll walk away again. And you will. It's what cowards do. But you want to know what I do know?"

He dropped my legs and stepped back, but it was too late. I wouldn't back down.

No mercy.

He taught me that.

"I know you were afraid of me, too."

The room disappeared into a black abyss much like

my mood.

"For ten years, you controlled me, hated me, tortured me."

I clocked every misstep, hitch, and falter as I advanced on his retreat.

Oh, how the tables have turned.

I learned something in what might have been our darkest hour...

"But I was the one who actually held all the power."

My fearless predator...

"And you knew."

Was nothing more...

"So what scared you more?"

Than a wounded...

"That you weren't truly in control?"

Cornered...

"Or that you had no clue of what I could mean to you?"

Animal.

"You can hide behind your anger and use your past as a shield, but you can never pretend I didn't know you. You opened the door enough for me to see. I know you, Keiran, but do you really know me?"

Confliction.

That's what I saw in his eyes. It reminded me of something important Keenan once told me:

"I'm afraid for him because every day, he has to fight the person he is to be the person he wants to be."

"What happens if he loses?"

"People get hurt."

"What makes you think I want to know you? I may not hate you, but you're still nothing to me. Don't make the mistake of thinking otherwise."

"I've made so many mistakes where you are concerned, Keiran. What's one more?"

I forced myself to walk away with my head held high.

He wouldn't get another piece of me.

* * *

THERE WAS NO better feeling than finally standing up to your childhood bully. When I walked back to my classroom, I was on cloud nine and had chosen to ignore the pull that demanded I turn back.

I should have turned back. I should have gone in any direction other than the one I took.

Instead of taking the shortcut through the gym, I unknowingly took the long way through the hall where no one ever goes because everyone with common sense would have cut through the gym unless there was a class.

Not me.

I could never make the smart decisions.

Waiting for me had been Trevor's father and former police officer.

I didn't have time to scream, run, or fight. A cloth had been placed over my face, and the next thing I remembered... was nothing.

Now, here I was, scared and alone in the hard, unforgiving grip of Mr. Reynolds.

After Trevor had assaulted me in a public bathroom, Mr. Reynolds lost his job thanks to his son spilling the beans of his involvement. The only good that came out of being nearly beaten and raped was finally being able to clear my name and essentially, Keiran's name.

"I told my son to leave you alone, but he didn't listen and look where it's gotten him," he spat. "Cunts like you are always causing trouble."

"Mr. Reynolds, please," I begged for the hundredth time or maybe it was the thousandth. "You don't have to do this."

"Shut up, girl." His hand brutally slapped my cheek, causing me to fall backward. *At least, I'm out of his hold.* The smell of his rancid breath alone made me want to puke. "You beg when I tell you to."

"Cecilia! You can come in now. She's almost ready to perform."

Heels clicked against the wooden floor, and then the door opened to reveal a blonde woman in a dark blue, expensive pantsuit. My blood felt as if it had been drained from my veins when I recognized her instantly.

"Mrs. Risdell?"

"Hello, dear. I'm sorry it's come to this, but I simply cannot let Keiran Masters go unpunished for what he did to my daughter."

"Mrs. Risdell, please listen to me. Keiran did not kill your daughter. This is all a misunderstanding."

"Do not dare lie to us to protect him. It will only make things worse for you."

She set down the bag she held and pulled out a camera. When she turned it on and pointed it at me, I asked, "What are you planning to do?"

Mr. Reynold's hand dropped his belt and began unbuckling it. Mrs. Risdell stepped forward with the camera. "You, my dear, are going to put on a show for your little boyfriend, and then we are going to do to you what he did to our children."

The leers that appeared on their faces made me shudder in revulsion. "And what will you do when I'm dead? Where do you think you will go? There is nowhere you can run and no one who will be able to help you."

"Don't kid yourself, little girl. This is the one time

he will lose."

"Enough talking," Mr. Reynolds snapped. I was tossed on the bed, and when he immediately followed behind me, I kicked out. He effectively dodged my flailing feet until he managed to capture them in a tight grip. "Stop fighting or I'll dislocate every bone in your body, starting with that pretty face of yours."

He sat on my chest and grabbed my wrist, squeezing them between his large hands, and for a moment, I was afraid he would make good on his threat. My chest burned from my fleeing air supply as I was helplessly pinned to the bed under his weight. Handcuffs appeared, and he quickly used them to bind my hands. Panic surged, making my heart race, and my breathing fluctuated dangerously. The heat scorched every inch of my skin before my body turned ice cold, flitting from one extreme to the next.

"Paul?"

"What?"

He lifted from my chest and quickly gagged me before scooting down to the foot of the bed where my feet lay. My ankles and feet were spread apart roughly.

"What's wrong with her? I think she's seizing." Alarm was evident in Mrs. Risdell's voice as violent trembles wracked my body.

"What do you care? The little bitch is going to die anyway."

"And what are you going to do? Fuck a corpse? We need her to suffer first."

Her sick reasoning seemed to get through to Mr. Reynolds because he paused from tying my feet to the bed to study me with his beady, blue eyes.

"There's nothing wrong with her. She's faking it, and yeah... I'll fuck a corpse if I have to." His smile widened as he stared at me.

Oh, God. I closed my eyes and pictured myself anywhere else but here. I didn't know how long I had been out, but I knew someone had to know by now that I was missing. Willow would know.

Keiran would know.

CHAPTER THIRTY-FOUR

KEIRAN

THERE WERE ONLY so many times you could hurt some-one before they decided to fight back.

For ten years, I waited for the moment when Lake would finally fight.

There were many days I would become frustrated to the point of violence, but instead of hurting her, I would start a fight. I would fight, and then I would seek her out only when I was sure I wouldn't physically hurt her.

I knew that now.

No matter how much I threatened to kill her, deep down I didn't want to hurt her.

But the hatred... that was real.

I hated her with everything I had because it was the only emotion I had to give. I realized, even then, I was giving her everything.

She was the bane of my existence, and at the very same, the reason I cared to exist.

I wanted her like the rest of the world. Like me.

Her innocence.

Her bravery.

Her selflessness.

I wanted it all gone.

She. Just. Wouldn't. Fucking. Break.

I left the bathroom only when I knew she was gone. I wouldn't stop to consider that maybe she was right. I am a coward.

Before heading back to my class, I took a detour to her class. I peeked inside the window of the door—when I didn't see her, my first reaction was anger.

I immediately began to tear the school apart looking for her, hoping she had gone to hide, but when I couldn't find her, anger transformed into panic.

I retraced my steps and burst into her classroom, startling the teacher, who immediately began to scold me in rapid French.

"Where is she?"

Willow shot up from her seat, tears immediately forming. She must have sensed something was wrong, too. "She went to the bathroom, but she didn't come back. What happened?"

"Mr. Masters!" the teacher yelled in outrage.

"How long did she need to be gone for you to fucking notice?"

I walked over to her desk and grabbed up her bag. I quickly searched through it but didn't find her cell phone, which meant she at least had it on her.

As I stormed out with Willow on my heels, I dialed the detectives.

"Is he out?" I demanded as soon as Detective Wilson answered.

"Excuse me?"

"Arthur. Is he fucking out?"

"No. He's not out. What is this about?"

"Lake is gone."

"Gone? What do you mean gone?"

"She's fucking missing, dipshit!"

I ran down the last time I had seen her, and when he assured me they were on it, I hung up. I wasn't about to wait. I would paint this fucking town red if I have to until I found her.

* * *

I PULLED SHELDON, Dash, and Quentin out of class, ignoring the shit I got for it. None of them had seen Lake. It had only been a small amount of time since I had last seen her, but I was grasping at straws. By the time I was done grilling everyone she knew, the entire school was aware of her missing, which also meant her aunt would be called soon.

"You have a real track record for making friends. First, it was Trevor, Mario, and then Arthur... "Who else could there be?" Sheldon asked.

Trevor.

No. Trevor was dead.

But his father wasn't.

"Fuck!"

I was running for the parking lot with Dash and Quentin hot on my heels.

"Keiran! What the fuck, man? What is it?"

"Officer Reynolds. It has to be him. He's got her."

"Shit!" They both cursed.

I was spinning tires out of the school parking lot in a matter of seconds. I had only one idea of where to look, and I prayed he would be stupid enough to take her there.

Less than ten minutes and I was pulling into his neighborhood. I parked two houses down and cut the engine.

"Should I call the cops?" Dash asked.

"No." I pulled out my gun from under the seat. "He's mine." I stepped out of my ride, ready to go to war if need be when Quentin stopped me with a hand on my arm.

"Wait."

"What?" I growled. Every second I hesitated, Lake could have been suffering.

"When we get in there, we don't know what we will find."

He was warning me.

"I know."

"So what's the plan? There might not be just him. What do we do?"

I didn't have to think about it. If he had her, he made a grave mistake.

"Kill them all."

I didn't wait for their approval before I pulled away, making my way silently and quickly to the house. If I had to, I would do this alone.

I made quick work of the lock while listening for signs of life on the other side. It was quiet, which only made my desperation increase. When the lock popped, I opened the door slowly and looked around. Quentin and Dash spread out, and we checked every room upstairs and down with no sign of her.

My fist dented the wall when I realized I had wasted valuable time looking in the wrong place.

"Keiran?" Dash called out. "You might want to come look at this."

The sound of his voice came from the back door where he was peering out the window.

"What is it?" I snapped. I wasn't willing to waste any more time.

"Do you recall Trevor's father having a shed?"

I took a look and was out the door, sprinting in the next second. All reason had left, and all I could think about was getting her back. Whatever it took.

The shed was large enough to be a miniature house, which meant it was large enough to fit more than two people inside. I forced myself to slow down and assess the situation carefully. Lake was in there. My instincts told me she was. If I alerted him to my presence, he would kill her.

A low sound caught my attention, and we immediately stopped to listen. There were two voices speaking.

"I can't wait to try you out, little girl. Thanks to your boyfriend sticking his nose where it didn't belong, I haven't had any ass in almost two years."

"Paul, just get on with it. This isn't for pleasure."

My blood boiled when I recognized the voices coming from the other side.

Officer Reynolds and Mrs. Risdell.

Neither one of them would make it out of this alive.

"Shut up or you'll be next," he threatened.

"Could you please just get her undressed?"

It was all I needed to hear.

I shot the lock off the door and kicked it in, taking everyone in the room by surprise.

Mrs. Risdell began screaming, and Reynolds scrambled off the bed where he had been on top of Lake. As soon as he righted himself, he reached for his gun, but I'd already crossed the room and had the muzzle pressing against his head.

"Move an inch and you die." Of course, it was a lie. He was going to die anyway, but give a man in a similar situation an illusion that he will live, and he will be more cooperative.

"Keiran," Dash whispered near my ear. "Help her. I

got him."

I looked up and first saw that Quentin had Mrs. Risdell's face down on the ground with his boot on her back. She was still screaming, so I signaled him to shut her up before handing the gun to Dash and turning to Lake. She was watching me with wide eyes that glistened with tears.

I undid her gag, and when I touched her handcuffs, I turned back to Reynolds. "Where is the key?"

"I'm not going to tell you, boy."

"Fine." I took the gun back from my Dash, aimed, and then shot out his kneecap. Bone crunched and blood splattered as he howled in what I was sure was agonizing pain.

Dash held him while I searched him for the key instead of asking him again. With the key in hand, I freed Lake and quickly checked her over before gathering her in my arms. Her silence scared me most of all.

With the gun back in Dash's hands, I carried her out of the shed and away from the last two people who would ever get the chance to harm her.

"Talk to me, Lake. Please." I sunk down to the ground with her in my lap. "What did he do to you?"

If I hadn't been holding her face between my hands, I would have missed the small shake of her head. "You came," she whispered low as if afraid if she spoke any louder, I would disappear.

"You scared me, baby." I was content to sit there, holding her, but Reynolds screams only grew louder, so I sat her on the ground and handed her my cell phone. "Call for help."

It was the only instruction I gave her before disappearing inside. My gloves were burning a hole in my back pocket, so I pulled them on but not before shaking them tauntingly at Mrs. Risdell. "Remember these?"

It had the desired effect. Her eyes widened, and she began sobbing and babbling incoherently. I pulled them on slowly and motioned to Dash and Quentin.

"Get them on their knees. I want them apart."

Fortunately, for them, this would be quick and mostly painless. I didn't have much time before the cops would show. That first gunshot would have alerted the neighbors. Reynolds grunted when Dash forced him onto his shattered kneecap.

"You can't do this," Reynolds screamed. "I'm a police officer."

"Was," Dash growled. "You *were* a police officer. Today, you're just a dead fucker."

Usually, Dash was the voice of reason, but what almost happened to Lake had left even the most reasonable person I knew feeling murderous. It only proved that these two needed to die.

"This is all your fault! You made my wife leave me!"

"No. You made your wife want to leave when you and your son chose to use her as a personal punching bag. I just showed her the door." I still don't know why Trevor's mother chose me to help her.

Maybe it was out of desperation to tell someone, but I only told her she had two options—to kill them or leave.

She chose the latter.

"So who wants to die first?"

The gun was already pressed against Reynolds skull by the time I finished asking the question. Killing them was a no-brainer. I only wished I had the time to do it slow.

My finger pulled the trigger back, but just before I could feel the metallic click, the shed door flung open.

"Keiran!" Lake ran inside with a horrified expression. "Don't do this!"

Shit.

"Wait outside," I ordered without sparing her a glance. I could feel her gaze trained on me, judging.

"The police are coming. I could hear the sirens."

"Then there is still time." I stood back further and took aim.

"Don't do this. This is an execution."

"Kind of the point."

"You told me that you once wanted to be good. You have that chance right now, Keiran. You never truly were what they tried to make you until now—if you do this."

"Why do you want them alive after what they were going to do to you?"

"I want them dead as much as you, but not if it's going to take you away."

"She's right, Keiran." Dash's reluctant voice made me look up. In my peripheral, I could see Quentin nod in agreement. "This is your chance, bro. Take it."

I looked down at Reynolds kneeling before me and at Mrs. Risdell hovering in the corner.

On the outside, I was steel and ice, but inside, I battled with the chance at redemption and the need to kill.

When I was a slave, I was forced to kill people who never wronged me. Here I had the chance to actually kill with reason.

I felt like it was owed to me.

To punish those who wronged me.

To protect the ones I loved.

I needed to do it. Isn't that why I was placed in these circumstances?

"Keiran..."

I heard her call, but I only shook my head in denial.

"You're not a slave."

I'm not a slave.

"Or a killer."

Not a killer.

"You're not a monster," my mother's ethereal voice whispered.

CHAPTER THIRTY-FIVE

KEIRAN

ELEVEN YEARS AGO
THE PLAYGROUND

"NOW CAN YOU teach me how to dribble between my legs like you?"

"You're still not dribbling right. I told you to use your fingertips more. You're still using your palms."

"It's too hard," Keenan whined. Anger flared up inside me as I eyed the tears trailing down his face.

"What did I say about crying like a baby?"

He stopped crying immediately and looked up at me with frightened eyes. "You said you'll hurt me."

I puffed out a breath from my chest into the summer air and took the ball from him. I started to dribble figure eights from front to back between my legs in a slow motion so he could see. I chose not to talk him through it because I didn't trust what would really come out of my mouth. I refused to apologize for what I had said because I meant it. I just sometimes wished

I hadn't meant it. I didn't want to hurt him.

He watched in amazement as I did tricks with the ball. I didn't have any special training or techniques taught to me. I just did what felt natural when I had the ball in my hand.

After dodging Keenan's attempt to steal the ball from me like I told him, I positioned my body to make a three-pointer, but the sound of a child's wail inter-rupted my concentration. I turned to eye two other boys my age pushing and shoving a smaller kid around. Before I could rethink it, I felt my feet carry me swiftly over until I was running. I didn't stop once I was on them. I hit the closest with my fist as hard as I could and then planted my foot in the other's gut, bringing them both down simultaneously.

"I don't want to talk about this," I said before they could talk. "Pick up and get lost."

The collective gasps of shock when I cursed fell deaf on my ears. I wasn't like the other kids, and I wouldn't pretend to be. When they scrambled, I turned on my heel without sparing the little boy a glance, and trudged back to my cousin who was watching him with his mouth open.

"Hey, wait! Wait, please!" I heard behind me but didn't stop. I picked the discarded ball up from the ground on the way, not realizing I had dropped it when I ran over. Just as I stood upright, small sneak-ered feet came into my vision, and I met the glossy eyes and a toothy grin of a little boy with light brown, curly hair. "Hi," he breathed.

I ignored his greeting and made a basket but caught the fallen look on his face before he covered it up with another smile. "Can you teach me how to do that?"

"Go away, kid."

"But you're a kid, too," he pouted.

"He's not a kid," Keenan spoke up. I guess he was good for something after all.

"Well, what grade are you in?" he demanded. I eyed him in his blue overalls and dirt-smudged face and tried not to laugh as he attempted to stand up to me.

"What's your name, kid?" I asked rather than answer his question.

"Buddy."

"Buddy? What kind of name is that?"

He shrugged his little shoulders. "I don't know." He hopped from one foot to the other as a frown wrinkled his forehead. "It's what my mommy and daddy and sister call me. But they call me Chance too, so I guess you can call me that if you like."

I could tell by the look on his face he didn't like the name. "I'll call you Buddy," I offered, making his face light up.

"Yeah, me, too. I guess it's better than Chance," Keenan added.

"So can I play with you guys?"

"Why?"

"I want to learn how to shoot like that."

"You're too small," Keenan griped.

"Am not."

"Are too. You won't be able to make the ball reach the basket."

"I'm not too small. I can reach anything. Like... um... like the monkey bars. I bet I can get on top."

"No way. Prove it."

He looked at me with hopeful eyes, but I made sure to give nothing away as I stared back at him. "Do you want me to do it?"

"Do you want to do it?" I countered. He must have

taken it as a challenge because he puffed up his small chest and ran over to the monkey bars. When he reached the ladder, he chanced a look up before turning back with nervous eyes, but again, I didn't offer him an out. I wouldn't take pity on him, and he must have sensed it because he turned back and began to climb. It took him a little longer because his legs were shorter than the kids it was meant for, but he eventually made it up to the top.

"See? I did it!" he yelled and flashed a toothy grin.

"You have to get all the way on top!" Keenan ordered. I quickly shot him a look that shut him up and moved closer to the bars. There was no way the kid would survive if he fell.

Buddy shot Keenan an impressive glare before slowly crawling his way on top of the monkey bars. His shaking and panic didn't start until he looked down. I could see the trembles form in his arms even from down here.

"You can come down now."

"I—I can't. It's too high."

"Just move slowly like you did when you climbed up."

"I can't. I'm scared. Please help me." Buddy was full out crying now as his sobs shook his body, and his hands formed a death grip on the bars.

"Quit shaking or you're going to fall! I'm coming to get you," Keenan yelled.

"No. Let him get down. He can do it."

"But what if he falls? He'll be hurt, and we'll get in trouble."

"We didn't make him do it. He wanted to prove a point and be stupid, so let him prove his point. He can't be afraid forever."

"But Keiran—"

"I said no. If he falls so be it."

"Buddy!" A frantic voice called from a few feet away. I watched two girls run up to the monkey bars from the main playground. The girl who called out Buddy's name wasn't much bigger than he was. Her wild, curly, red hair was a rat's nest on top of her head. I didn't know much else about her though because my mind became transfixed by the person she dragged behind her.

It was her.

The girl outside the burger shack.

There she was again, looking perfect and... innocent.

An unfamiliar feeling similar to an electric shock started at my fingertips and worked its way up to my brain. Why was she still here? It had only been two days since I first saw her at Pies, Shakes, & Things, but her still being here made me... afraid?

No.

I haven't felt fear in two years, and I wasn't about to start now because of some girl I haven't even met. She had to go.

My eyes never once left her, though she didn't seem to notice me at all. More kids started to gather around the monkey bars as Buddy's cries grew louder until he was nearly screaming. No one moved to help him. Most of them had witnessed what I did to the other two boys, so they assumed I either would help him, or I knew better than to interfere. I'd all but forgotten about him when she appeared. Her appearance was perfectly polished, complete with rosy cheeks and bright blue eyes.

She nudged the wild looking girl and said something to her. Whatever her response was seemed to annoy her because she released a heavy breath and *took a step forward.*

Was she?

I wasn't about to let her get up there.

What if she hurt herself?

Why did I care?

By the time she touched the ladder, ready to start her climb, my old self from six months ago was in place. I wanted to make her hurt.

"Stop."

I would forever remember the moment her eyes met mine. A sea of green and a sky of blue. I tracked every subtle movement her body made—the way her hair blew when the wind picked up, the single bead of sweat on her brow, the way her lips parted as if she were dying of thirst, how her fingers clutched at the bars, and her chest heaved up and down as she watched me watch her.

Buddy started to cry harder and said something about going home. Whatever it was caused the girl to break our connection and start to climb the bars again. I was on the other side before I realized my feet had even moved. My hand closed around her foot, stopping her from taking another step.

"No," I said again. What was the stupid girl trying to do?

"Look, I don't know who you are or what your deal is, but he needs help, and he is going to get it from me. Got it?"

She was halfway up the ladder before I could think of what to say. She left me feeling stumped, and I didn't like it one bit. I didn't waste any time grabbing the bar and following after her. She was disobedient, and disobedience had to be punished.

It was very easy for me to sneak up on her because she was so focused on Buddy. He must have seen some-

thing in my eyes because his widened in fear, and before he or she could react, I'd pushed her off.

I regretted it immediately after it happened, but it was too late. All I could do was watch her hit the ground with a sickening crunch.

She was still.

Too still and for a moment...

I thought I had killed her.

CHAPTER THIRTY-SIX

LAKE

I don't know what drove me here, but somehow, I had ended up at the playground. For some reason, I felt the need to be here. This was the place it all began. It was where I first laid eyes on my tormentor. He gave me a lot of memories to hold on to for the rest of my life. Most of them were bad, but it was all I had. The good memories were the ones I would cherish. An involuntary shiver ran through me when I remembered the hard way he took me, and the way he controlled my body and my desires. I would miss that. I would miss him.

"I am so stupid," I grumbled and kicked at the sand beneath my feet.

"Then I have to be the dumbest shit in the world."

I closed my eyes and kept my head down. *It wasn't real. He isn't here.*

"Look at me, baby."

A small sound escaped me when I realized he really was there. "Why are you here?"

"The same reason you are... I think I came to find you. Were you thinking about me just now?"

"Why does it matter?"

"It matters," he merely stated.

"But why?" Because my head was down, I didn't see him come closer until it was too late. He lifted my chin with his finger, but I kept my eyes tightly closed.

Instead of deterring him, he pressed tender kisses, first on my eyelids, and then all over my face. "Because it means I have a chance."

"A chance for what?"

"To make you stay."

I felt his hands on both sides of my face. "Why are you doing this?"

"Open your eyes."

"Tell me why—"

"Not until you look at me."

Nope. No way. My knees weakened from the feel of his hands.

"Please," he whispered against my lips before his connected with mine in a tender kiss. His arms wrapped around my waist and pulled me closer. The way he handled me made me feel fragile as if I would break at any moment. *I probably would.*

I finally opened my eyes when he delivered a final peck to my lips and rested his forehead against mine. When I looked into his eyes, they were no longer stormy. They held hope.

"I love you."

I shook my head, causing our foreheads to rub together. He gripped me tighter as if sensing my need to escape. "I might have even loved you that day in the pharmacy. You were so beautiful... and so scared. For the first time since I met you, I didn't want you to be afraid of me."

"Could have fooled me."

"My biggest regret in life was making you cry, and if I have to spend the rest of it making sure you never have another bad day, then I will die a happy man."

"I thought you didn't have regrets."

"Only the ones I can't change."

"What about Mitch? And Lily? Will I have to spend the rest of mine convincing you I'm not her ghost?"

"I want to show you something." He dropped his arms from my waist and pulled his shirt over his head. I gave him a crazy look. It was fifty degrees, maybe colder outside, and he was standing before me without a shirt.

"Keiran, what are you doing? This is hardly the time to think about sex."

"No, that comes later."

"Cocky, much?"

"Hopeful." I softened at his words and the look in his eyes. "Remember when I told you I confess my sins the only way I know how? That's why I had the tattoo made.

"I can't believe I'm seeing this for the first time. It's beautiful," I finally said after I stared at his back in awe.

Even after the times we had sex, I realized I never actually saw his back. One of us would always run.

I ran my fingers down his back where the tattoo lay. The dark petals sharply contrasted against his skin. Some of the petals were broken in different ways and some looked mended. The mended petals showed a drop of moisture that touched precisely the broken parts. The raindrops were bright blue with a tinge of green reminding me of my own eyes. One particular petal stood out amongst the rest. The tip of the petal hung loosely from the rest barely hanging on and above it was a falling raindrop. The way it fell was peculiar... almost like a shooting star.

"It was for her?"

"No... It was for nothing."

"Do you really believe that?"

"Yes."

"Then why a lily? Out of any flower or dumb tattoo teenage boys are inclined to get, why something that obviously means something to you? What does it all mean? The broken petals? The raindrop?"

He laughed and shook his head. "It was Keenan's idea. I told him to make a lily. He—"

"He thought you were healing."

"What?" Keiran's head snapped around.

"That's what the raindrops are for. They are the healing balm. Most of the petals are mended, but some are still very much broken."

Silence descended between us as I continued to admire his back, and he continued to stare at the wall ahead. His back was tense and stiffened even more as I continued to touch him. "It's beautiful, Keiran. Do you think it might be true?"

"What might be true?'

"That maybe, just maybe, you could be healing?"

"Well, then I would be forced to admit something is wrong with me." The teasing lilt in his voice involuntarily made me smile.

"It's good that I know you're joking, or I might be worried."

He turned suddenly to face me and gripped me around my waist, bringing me close. "Why are you fighting for this?"

"Why are you fighting this at all?"

"Because I've killed people, Lake. I've killed, and I'm willing to kill without much provocation. Do you really believe someone like me could ever be good? I can never be a boyfriend, or a husband, or even a father."

I ignored the pang in my heart at his rejection of a future. "You aren't as doomed as you might think, you know."

"I'm not redeemable either."

"Then why didn't you pull the trigger, and why did you want to protect me?"

"Because if I had to protect anyone, it would be you."

"Are you saying I'm a default?"

"I'm saying that you matter. Regardless of how much I don't want you to."

"You really know how to make a girl feel special," I quipped.

"I'm not a sunshine and roses kind of guy. I'll probably never be able to lay you down on a bed of roses and make love to you."

I slipped my arms around his neck. "Maybe I don't want roses." I bit his bottom lip, which instantly led to a kiss that threatened to consume us both. "Maybe I prefer your thorns."

"One day you will."

Don't fight this, baby. "One day isn't today," I countered.

"Are you willing to take that chance?"

Yes. "Maybe."

"I'm not worth it."

"For a guy who oozes sex appeal, you have zero self-esteem."

"I really wish a lack of self-esteem was the problem. It'd be much simpler then."

"Simpler how?"

"It would make everything possible."

"Why did you hate her so much?" No matter how I felt, I was still afraid that one day he would wake up and realize that he would never believe I wasn't Lily.

He buried his face in my neck and breathed in.

"Because she did what I didn't have the strength to do. She didn't let them take her soul. That's what made her strong... That's what made you strong."

He thought I was strong?

"In the hospital, you said I broke you, but it's not true. I can't break you, baby. I never could. When she died, I thought I died with her, and when I saw you for the first time, I thought she sent you as a reminder of all the evil I'd done. But the day you told me that you loved me, I realized she didn't send you to punish me. She sent you to keep me alive."

"Do you really believe that?"

He didn't answer, but his hand reached into his pocket and pulled out a folded piece of paper. "I want you to read this."

I hesitantly took the paper from his hand and unfolded the careful squares. The paper was worn and discolored from time, but when I saw the first words, I knew it was from his mother. I couldn't read it quick enough:

Gabriel,
My sweet boy.
I lost you. I didn't protect you.
I lost you because I didn't protect you.

I can only hope, wherever you are now, you are safe, and you are loved. Loved better than I ever loved you. If this letter ever finds you, I hope you can one day understand what I did was the hardest thing I've ever had to do. I would die a thousand deaths if I could just do it over again—if only there had been a way for me to have protected you both.

A mother should never have to choose.

A mother never should choose.

John... your uncle... He wanted so much to bring you home. He loved you, too. I'm also to blame for what I forced him to do for the sake of your brother. It destroyed him as much as it destroyed me. I know deep down we will never be the same. Our love is lost with you and our souls are forever damaged.

I only hope one day, someone will be able to love you unconditionally. I hope someone will one day give you forever.

I didn't realize I was crying until one of my tears blotted the paper.

"I don't know what to say."

"Say yes."

"Yes?"

"You are my forever, Lake... will you give me forever?"

CHAPTER THIRTY-SEVEN

LAKE

TWO MONTHS LATER

"ARE YOU MINE?"

"Keiran!"

"Answer me, Lake."

"I fucking love the way you say my name."

"Tell me now or so help me, I'm going to fuck it out of you."

"I think you already are," I teased.

He thrust into me hard and kissed me even harder. "Damn it, girl. What are you doing to me?"

His hand came up to clutch my left my breast as he began a hard rhythm that lifted me on my toes with each forceful thrust. My moans turned to squeals and then screams as my body welcomed the familiar pounding. He made me suck his finger to muffle my screams while another finger pinched my nipple.

I flooded his cock from the slight pain. God, even after all this time I still loved the fucking pain.

FEAR YOU

The sound of the desk rocking mirrored the tandem of my wildly beating heart.

I loved every minute of it.

"Keiran, please—" My head fell back, and I let out a long, guttural moan when his hips moved in a deep grind. He pulled almost all the way out of me and slammed back inside. I gasped.

"You sure?"

"Stop, Keiran. They'll hear."

"I don't give a fuck. What did I promise you earlier?"

"You're a sick fucker," I gritted, working myself on him. I needed to come, but he was acting his usual asshole self.

"And you're a mouthy little bitch. Give me what I want."

"No." He dug his cock deeper and harder into me. "Keiran!"

"Give. Me. What. I. Want!"

I screamed uncontrollably and gave in. "Please let me come... I love you."

"Again."

"I love you. Shit!" He hit a spot deep inside me that finally sent me over the edge.

"Mouth," he gritted. "Who do you belong to?"

"Just fuck me!" I was beyond frustrated from the pent up need.

"Who!" he demanded.

"I'm yours!" I screamed. I bit down on his shoulder as my orgasm rocked my body, and I shook uncontrollably against him.

He suddenly pulled out and ripped the condom off. I felt hot splashes hit the fabric of my dress. The aftermath of our mutual orgasm was as intense as the sex. It took a few moments for our breathing to even out, but he watched me with a cocky grin on his face.

"Why did you do that? Now I'll have to go home!"

"You shouldn't be wearing this dress. It's too short."

"You don't think you're being controlling?"

"Yes."

"I see."

"Are you upset?" He lifted his head and looked down at me.

"I don't know how I feel." I truly didn't. Even after being officially together for the last two months, to have him openly admit he wanted to control me was still hard to take in. Would it make me weak if I let him?

"I am not going to abuse you. That's not what I want. I want to make you happy, but I also need to keep you safe. When I said there wasn't a greater threat out there to you than me, I lied, or at least I thought it was true at the time."

Before I could respond, he lifted me by my arms and set me on my feet next to the teacher's desk.

"Besides... it was either this or break his face in. Why did you kiss him?"

"I told you, it was part of the deal for the fleas."

I'd forgotten all about my promise to Collin until I saw him sitting in the cafeteria instead of outside in the rain. When our eyes collided I saw the hurt and embarrassment and couldn't feel lower. I knew word would get back to Keiran who thankfully had a meeting with Coach Lyons but a promise was a promise. Unfortunately, that meeting must have been a quick one because he walked in just as my lips were pressed again Collin's and so our little rendezvous began. He had already been pissed about the dress so to see me kissing another guy no matter the reason blew a certain fuse that left me sore between my thighs.

"Turn around and bend over. I've been craving the taste of your pussy all day."

I did as he said, and when his hands lifted my dress once again, my heart began to race with anticipation.

He clutched my hips and pulled me into his groin causing my back to arch. "Fuck, your ass is hot." He slapped it again. "Perfect."

I knew when he moved away when I could no longer feel his still hard cock nestled in my butt. He hooked his hand around my thigh and lifted it to hang off the desk. I heard him growl a second before his tongue touched me. The sensation of him licking and sucking me became too much, and as I came into his mouth, I reached behind me and grabbed onto his hair. I was sure my fingers were digging into his scalp, but he didn't seem to mind as he moaned and continued to lick me with his tongue. His lips placed delicate kisses on my now sensitive pussy before standing up. I looked behind me just as he was slipping on another condom.

"Like this, baby," he said turning me to face him. He lifted me up on the desk. "I want to see you come this time." He slipped inside me slowly. I loved it when he took me hard and fast, but I loved it when he was slow and sweet just as much. He took my lips with his as he began to move inside me. I wrapped my legs tighter around his thrusting hips and whimpered into his mouth every time he thrust deep, hitting that sensitive spot inside me.

"You feel so good," I moaned.

"You feel even better," he groaned before he bit the top of my breast.

* * *

KEIRAN AND I managed to sneak from school so I could

shower and change. He was giving me the silent treatment, so I used the time to think over the last two months.

A lot had happened since Keiran and I became official. Most of it had been great as Keiran and I got to know each other on a different playing field. We were no longer the tormentor and the tormented. We were no longer enemies.

The hardest time was one day when I came home from school and I had been calling Keiran ever since he hadn't shown up for fifth period. For the entire day, he had been acting strange, but surprisingly more affectionate, as if it would be the last time we were together. I walked through the door after school in time to see Aunt Carissa knee Keiran in the balls. He fell to his knees and groaned in pain, but thankfully, didn't retaliate. After everything, it would kill me to let him go.

I rushed forward but didn't know who actually needed help. I just prayed Keiran didn't try to hurt my aunt.

As it turned out, Keiran told her everything starting with the day he pushed me at the playground. The only part he was smart enough to keep secret was the six weeks he blackmailed me into being his sexual slave. I had no doubt she would have done more than knee him if he had.

It took a lot of work and groveling on both of our parts, but we were both finally able to earn our way back into her good graces. The hardest part of it all was living with her disappointment and hurt.

Jackson had also stuck around after Mario was arrested. They eventually confirmed what my gut was telling me. Aunt Carissa had fallen in love. I was sad I had missed the romance but was too happy for them to let it bother me for long. I was just glad she had finally found someone.

Mario and Arthur's trial was set to begin in two weeks, and the detectives were sure that they would be convicted... as long as Keiran, Quentin, and Diana all testified to more than just what happened at the gym. They would have to testify to everything.

Diana was still around. She was actually the cause of our first argument as a couple. I found out she was still staying with Keiran even after her father was arrested. According to him, she helped bring him down and was no longer trying to seduce him, but it was the principle.

So what did he do?

He convinced my aunt she was practically an orphan and had nowhere to go.

And what did my aunt do?

She moved her in.

It was hard at first when she found out Diana was Mario's daughter, but when she shared her story, it warmed my aunt up to her. I had to admit, it warmed me up to her, too.

Sheldon still couldn't stand her.

Diana and I weren't exactly BFFs, but we got along. She was actually part of the reason for today's classroom session. Keiran had been working overtime kissing my aunt's ass. He had refused to touch me again until I was out of her house. She took me shopping and suggested a red, low-cut dress that flirted around the edge of decency. My reluctance was the reason she was adamant I wear it and shamefully, it worked like a charm. Not only did everyone in the school, girls and guys, drool, but Keiran about lost it when he saw me.

I made him break his oath and now he was all grumpy.

We pulled up to my house and Keiran cut the engine before coming around to open my door. He was testing his ability to be a gentleman, and I have to say, I loved it just as much as his rough edges.

"Make it quick," he ordered. "You have a test next period."

See? Rough edges.

"You know we wouldn't be here if you weren't so stubborn. If you hadn't stopped touching me, I wouldn't have had to resort to drastic measures."

"I'm not in the mood, Monroe."

I chewed on my bottom lip to keep from saying something sarcastic. I hated when he called me Monroe and he knew it. I could see the smirk forming on his lips.

I fisted his dark gray shirt in my hands and stepped closer until my lips rested right under his. He moved forward to kiss me, but I dodged his lips and smiled sweetly.

"You know... you get to see me in a dress again to-night. Are you prepared to stake your claim and per-form your boyfriend duties?"

"Or we can just skip it, and I can perform my duties all night—no interruptions."

I smiled and let him kiss me before pushing him back and catching him by surprise. "You'd like that, wouldn't you. Maybe I'll make *you* wait."

"Monroe..."

"Don't forget your suit after school, Masters!" I skipped into the house to change my clothes leaving him standing in the driveway with a hard dick.

* * *

PROM NIGHT. EVERY girl thought about the day of her prom. It was the second best night next to her wedding night.

I was the exception to little girl dreams because I always had the intention of skipping this night. I expected nothing good to come out of it. Not if Keiran was there.

So why was I standing here—showered, shaved, primped, and ready? Well, almost ready. I looked over at the beautiful, turquoise dress hanging on the back of Sheldon's door.

The white bodice of the dress was strapless with a heart shaped neckline that would push up my breasts. The turquoise faux pearls decorated the top in a mass of swirls and trails. The bodice tapered at the waist and led into the princess skirt that reminded me of a tutu. It stopped just above my knees and twirled when I moved.

I could still remember the way Keiran's eyes darkened when I emerged from the dressing room to model for him. I thought I'd succeeded in making him speechless—until he'd said, *I need you now.*

I'm glad we both loved the dress because after we'd christened the dress in the dressing room, we had no choice but to buy it. After the mind-blowing, sneaky, dressing room sex, we spent almost an hour arguing at the cash register. The first argument was who was going to pay. He won that argument, but when the sales associate announced the total price, it sparked the second argument.

We ended up leaving without the dress after I promised to tear it to shreds with a kitchen knife if he bought it.

I felt my body heat as I remembered him taking me home immediately after and punishing me one screaming orgasm at a time. He never let up until my aunt came back. The next day, I came home to find the dress laid out on my bed and a note lying next to it:

I spent the last eleven years making your life hell. I'm ready to spend the rest of mine making it up to you. Spoiling you is just the start. Will you let me?

And as usual, I caved. The dress really was beautiful despite the ridiculous price. I was even more curious to see how Keiran planned to make up for the last eleven years.

Sheldon and Willow walked in, breaking me out of my thoughts. They were dressed in gowns that Willow made herself. Willow's strapless dark purple dress was short and similar to mine except hers had a black lace bodice. Sheldon wore a long, flowing black dress that had a strapless silver studded bodice.

They decided to go as each other's date.

"What time is Keiran picking you up?" Willow asked.

"In about twenty minutes." I hurried to finish dressing and took a final look in the mirror as the sound of more than one male voice came from downstairs.

Sheldon and Willow hurried out ahead of me when Dash yelled up the stairs. Despite all the tension, we decided to go as somewhat of a group. I really thought Willow and Dash would have worked through their differences by now, but she still allowed her mom to keep them apart. I realized Dash hadn't quite given up on them when he asked me a month ago if Willow was going to prom. Turns out, he had asked her, but when she turned him down, he told her he was done chasing her. Willow didn't stop crying for nearly two weeks and barely ate. It wasn't until Sheldon magnanimously asked her for her hand to the dance, as she put it, that she finally came around.

I slipped on my heels, took a deep breath, and made my way downstairs.

The first thing I noticed was Keiran waiting by the

stairs dressed in a black suit and shirt that had to have been tailored by God for him. He wasn't looking my way, so it allowed me to drink in the sight of him in a suit. He definitely made black look good.

I descended the stairs. When I managed to make it next to him without him noticing, I knew something was wrong. If I weren't busy drooling before, I would have seen the hard set of his jaw. I looked in the direction of where his attention was fixed and took in the scene unfolding.

Sheldon stood pale and frozen to the left side of the stairs as she stared at the tall figure occupying the doorway.

"Keenan... How—how are you?"

He wore sunglasses that shielded his eyes, but I could see his lips pressed in a hard line and his jaw working. The room was silent as everyone's attention zeroed in on the tension that now overtook the atmosphere.

"I'm not dying anymore if that's your real question."

The hostility in his voice couldn't be mistaken, and if he was anything like his brother, there was sure to be rage simmering beneath his shades.

"I'm glad you're okay. We—"

"Cut the sympathetic bullshit. You didn't care enough to bring your selfish ass to the hospital. There is no need to feign concern now."

And just like that, he was gone again, leaving us all to stare after him in shocked silence.

John had been notified the next day after Keiran had decided to let go of his past and to not kill Officer Reynolds and Mrs. Risdell that a set of lungs was available for Keenan.

Talk about a sign...

He had the transplant immediately. He was then released from the hospital after a month long stay to recover. Everyone was extremely happy except him. The doctor assured us he was going through the normal emotions an organ transplant would typically go through. Fear. Anxiety. Stress.

He wasn't out of the woods yet because, at any moment, his body could decide to reject the lungs or he could suffer from infection. So he was constantly in and out of the hospital for blood tests and X-rays.

And tonight, we were all together getting ready for prom without him. It had to hurt.

He still wasn't speaking to Keiran so the tension and distance between them only grew each day. It made Keiran's hunt for Mitch an obsession. After the phone call Keiran received six months ago, Mitch had gone silent, but Keiran never gave up his search. Sometimes, he would slip back into that dark place, and I did everything in my power to bring him back. I was prepared to do whatever it took to help him. No one, least of all me, expected him to change overnight though I think he wished he could.

"Lake?" I was so lost in my thoughts, I hadn't realized when Keiran had taken my hand in his and everyone had walked out.

"Oh, uh... Huh?"

"Are you okay?"

"Yes, but do you want to go see about your brother?"

He looked backed at the door where Keenan had disappeared for a long moment before he shook his head slowly. "Pushing him would be a mistake."

"What if he never—"

"Shh, baby. You look beautiful tonight. I don't want you crying."

"What makes you think I'm going to cry," I accused even as I heard the tremble in my voice.

He offered me a crooked smile and squeezed my hand. "Because you're always crying... and you snore."

I laughed and hit his chest, and he feigned pain until I realized he might not have been faking it. "Sorry! Did I hit it?"

"Yeah, but don't worry. I can take the pain," he whispered seductively.

"Don't get too excited. I want a dance out of you first."

He groaned, and for the first time, Keiran pouted. It would be really interesting to see Keiran dance. "One dance and then I get to have you."

"Sure. So can I see it now?"

He released my hand and held my gaze as he slowly unbuttoned his shirt. Covering the remnants of how I almost lost him was a tattoo mimicking my handwriting that read 'Forever, Lake.'

Now I knew why he mysteriously had me write the words on a sheet of paper a few weeks ago.

"I couldn't take seeing the look in your eyes every time you looked here. It's not a memory I want you to carry. When you look at me, I want you to see forever. I want you to remember our promise to each other."

"It's beautiful. Did Keenan do this?"

He shook his head, and then kissed me, but I think it was more to distract me.

"What are we going to do? Mitch is still out there, and Arthur could get out at any moment."

It was a wonder he hadn't already, but there were so many fingers pointing and evidence uncovered, including dozens of children found in Canada in a compound like Keiran had described who were finally set free. Arrests of police officers, judges, and nearly all of

Arthur's workers were also made.

"I have something to show you." He pulled out a sheet of paper, and for a moment, I experienced déjà vu. Was it another letter from his mother?

CHAPTER THIRTY-EIGHT

KEIRAN

SHE TOOK THE paper from my hand, but I sensed her hesitation. She turned it over and slowly began to read it. I could see the confusion in her eyes and the way her body tensed. I received the letter today and must have read it over a hundred times. The words were burned into my memory:

> *Youngblood,*
> *Every warrior knows how to fight, but a smart warrior knows when to survive. If you are reading this letter, then I can only assume you are the latter.*
> *I have one question to ask you and that question is simple.*
> *Do you believe in fate?*
> *My daughter came to visit me yesterday. I have you to thank for that. You protected mine without anything in return, so I only felt the need to return the favor. You never know what can come from trusting someone with your secrets...*

Two nights ago, I met a powerful man named Arthur. He offered me a great deal in return for protection.

I accepted, but with the price of a secret. A secret much like yours.

He's no longer a problem.

-Rufus

"I don't understand. Who is Rufus?"

"He's an old inmate I met the last time I was in jail. Two years ago, he came looking for his daughter, who was being beaten by her husband, but she couldn't get out. He confronted her husband, but they got into a bad fight. Unfortunately for him, the husband was a cop and he was an ex-con with a criminal record."

"The woman... She was Trevor's mom, wasn't she? And he's her father?"

I nodded my head but said nothing.

"Is Arthur really dead?"

I nodded again.

"Did you know Rufus before?"

"No. It was some fucked up coincidence. I don't even know what made me help her. I just did."

"Maybe it was your own mother's past. You said your father abused her."

"I didn't know it at the time I helped Trevor's mom, though."

"Well, then you know what that means, don't you?"

"What?"

She leaned close to me and wrapped my arms around her. "It means you're a hero."

I swallowed hard against the onslaught of emotion, but mostly for the small ounce of insecurity that I couldn't be what she needed. "Is a hero what you want?"

She shook her head. "You were born out of greed and you were raised out of greed. You lived your entire life being who someone wanted you to be. Who do you want to be?"

"I want to be yours, but are you sure you can live with a broken love like ours?"

"I think it's been proven I can take whatever you throw at me. Love is much more powerful than fear."

I couldn't deny what we had was born out of darkness, but instead of pulling her into my dark world, she led me to a light I wasn't sure I even deserved.

I may not be a monster, but I am still anything but a hero.

"I love you, Keiran."

Still... *forever* was a long time for change.

The End

DEAR READER . . .

I HOPE I gave you what you were looking for—Keiran, "The Dark Lord," as Willow spitefully dubbed him, with all his unredeemable qualities managed to find his happily-ever-after with the only person who was brave enough to venture into the dark and pull him out.

Bringing them together was no easy feat, but if they could do it, I know there is hope for Keenan & Sheldon...

ACKNOWLEDGMENTS

WRITING FEAR YOU was a lot different from when I wrote *Fear Me*. With my debut novel, I didn't have the support of my family, readers, or bloggers because I kept my dream a secret for as long as I could for fear of failure.

This time around, I had a huge support system. *Fear Me's* success was a wonder, and I have many people to thank for it. Because of you all, there is heavy anticipation for *Fear You* and I love it.

Family and Deven—as always, thank you for the support and putting up with my lack of time. Your patience has not gone unnoticed.

Pussycat Promotions, you guys put me on the map, and I owe a lot of my reader base to you ladies. Thank you, Kimie, Sharee, Kimmy, and Stephanie.

Robin, you were wonderful. You were always available and ready to help, and I'll never forget it.

To ALL of the Twisted Sisters, you rock! I love everyone's craziness and openness. Di, you were my inspiration for Diana though I'm not sure people will love you too much. However, your constant request for me to kill you offered me many laughs. Thank you!

Josi (J.L.) Beck, you blew in like a storm and like the dork you are. Thank you for listening to my many rants and your support. You graciously offered to advertise *Fear You* in your book and that means a lot to me. We are becoming great friends, and I hope it stays that way!

FEAR YOU

Jordan Silver you rock for many reasons with your unique, special ways! Thank you for welcoming me to your readers.

Rogena, I am so excited we are working together to edit *Fear You*. I can't wait to see it all come together.

BEBE's STREET MASTERS! My newfound and wonderful street team. Ladies, you are wonderful. That's all I can say. We are a family of weirdos, and I love each and every one of you. Thank you for all the hard work.

Lisa, Angel, Tracey, Lydia, Vickie, Jamie, Ria, Sammy, etc. The list goes on for miles. You guys are awesome readers, and I thank you! If you have been an avid audience, then you know who you are!

Amanda, thank you for two awesome covers! I can't stop staring!

ALSO BY B.B. REID

Broken Love Series

Fear Me

Fear You

Fear Us

Breaking Love

Fearless

The Stolen Duet

The Bandit

CONTACT THE AUTHOR

Join **Bebe's Reiders** on Facebook!

Twitter: _BBREID

Instagram: _BBREID

www.bbreid.com

ABOUT B.B. REID

B.B., ALSO KNOWN as Bebe, found her passion for romance when she read her first romance novel by Susan Johnson at a young age. She would sneak into her mother's closet for books and even sometimes the attic. It soon became a hobby, and later an addiction. When she finally decided to pick up a metaphorical pen and start writing, she found a new way to embrace her passion.

She favors a romance that isn't always easy on the eyes or heart, and loves to see characters grow—characters who are seemingly doomed from the start but find love anyway.

Fear Me, her debut novel, is the first of many.